ISBN 978-0-265-20666-9
PIBN 10211435

OR

# BIRTHS, DEATHS, & MARRIAGES.

## By
## Theodore Hook.

J. Lawse                                    W Greatbach

*"One instant and all would have been over,*
*a faint sound caught his ear; it was the*
*waking cry of his infant boy."*

LONDON
RICHARD BENTLEY,
NEW BURLINGTON STREET
CUMMING, DUBLIN   BELL & BRADFUTE, EDINBURGH
1842

# ALL IN THE WRONG;

OR,

# IRTHS, DEATHS, AND MARRIAGES.

BY

## THEODORE HOOK, ESQ.

AUTHOR OF
"SAYINGS AND DOINGS," "MAXWELL," "THE PARSON'S
DAUGHTER," &c.

LONDON:

ICHARD BENTLEY, NEW BURLINGTON STREET.

BELL AND BRADFUTE, EDINBURGH;
J. CUMMING, DUBLIN.

1842.

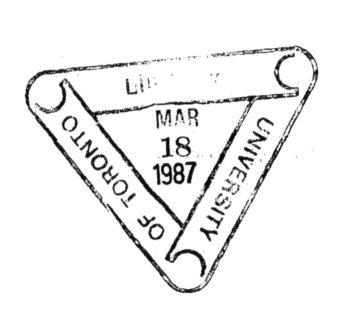

# ALL IN THE WRONG;

## OR,

## BIRTHS, DEATHS, AND MARRIAGES.

---

## CHAPTER I.

"You are a very wise gentleman! — and a very fine gentleman! — at least in your own conceit: nevertheless, 'Pride will have a fall,' and you and your daughter will live to repent what you are doing. However, it is no affair of mine: I don't care, it won't hurt *me*."

So said Mr. Jacob Batley to his brother John, during one of many discussions in which they were in the habit of indulging, touching their worldly pursuits. Jacob was a merchant who had made a fortune and retired. John, a younger son, had entered life in a Government-office, had held place under a feverish administration, and had for some time represented one of those select but judicious constituencies to which the nation is indebted for its knowledge of the powers of such men as Pitt and Fox, Burke, Sheridan, Brougham, Romilly, and indeed of all men of genius and ability, against whom the doors of the House of Commons would have been closed if their discriminating patrons had not chanced to have a private key of them in their pockets.

The different courses which the brothers had pursued had naturally produced a striking difference in their habits and manners, their modes of thinking and of acting. Jacob, who had stuck to the shop till it grew into a warehouse and he himself from a trader to a merchant, was one of those men who are coiled, as it were, within themselves, and, like that little animal called the *Oniscus Armadillo*, roll themselves up out of harm's way the moment anything like danger approaches.

B

John, on the contrary, was polished, politic, and plausible : he could promise with fluency, and refuse with elegance. He had flirted, and loved, and married a beauty, who had left him a widower with one daughter. All he had to live upon was the pension which his services had secured him ; nor had he, in more profitable times, done anything in the way of what Jacob called " laying by something for a rainy day," so that his beautiful child, besides her face, figure, and accomplishments, had nothing in the way of fortune except that which her uncle at his death might bequeath her.

Hence the frequent invitations of Jacob to John's house ; hence the submission with which John heard the lectures of his wealthy relation, feeling at the same time for all his worldly maxims the most sovereign contempt.

Jacob was perfectly aware of the inducements which actuated John in his proceedings, and chuckled at his own perception, and perhaps at the anticipation of the disappointment of his brother's expectations.

" I tell you, Jack," continued Jacob, " you are wrong : — it is nothing to *me;* but it's nonsense filling the girl's head with notions of high connexions and titles, and such trumpery — your carriages and your horses, and your dinners — psha ! — you can't afford it ; and you *know* you can't afford it."

" My dear brother," said John, who seldom ventured to call his impracticable relation by his Christian name, " I really do nothing more than is expected of a man holding a certain place in society."

" Expected by whom ? " said Jacob.

" The world," replied John.

" The world ! " said Jacob — " umph ! You mean the two or three hundred families that live up in this part of the town, not one of whom would care if you and your daughter were in Newgate. The world ! — what would the world do for your child if you were to die in debt, as you will ? You are insolvent now, and you know it. All these trumpery things about your rooms wouldn't fetch five-and-twenty per cent. of their prime cost whenever you break-up or die."

" Nay, but " ——

" ' Nay, but,' " said Jacob — " that's it : you won't hear reason.  Have you insured your life ?"

" Why, there's a difficulty," said John ——

" To be sure," interrupted Jacob : " you have ruined your constitution by dissipation, and your life's not worth a farthing."

" But, my dear brother," said John, " it would be impossible to bring Helen forward if I did not indulge a little in the gaieties of the world."

" There goes ' the world' again," said Jacob : " I'm sick of the word."

" When my girl is established," said John, " I shall, of course, alter the whole establishment, and live quietly."

" But how is she to *be* established ?" said Jacob.  " She has no money ; and where are you to find the man who will take her without a dump ?  She might marry one man I know of, and he right well to do.  To be sure, he is rather old, blinking a little as to his eyes, and a bit gone in his mind, — but that's just it.  The alderman, I do think " ——

" The alderman !" said John, casting a withering look at his brother — " Helen marry an alderman !"

" Yes, and jump to get him," said Jacob.  " What better do you propose ? "

" Why," said John, looking carefully round the room, and closing one of the doors which stood half-open, " she has two lovers at this moment — both capital matches. You see them here constantly, — one, Lord Ellesmere, and the other, Colonel Mortimer.  The genuineness of her character, and the openness of her disposition, render the concealment of her feelings a serious effort ; and, as I leave her uncontrolled in the exercise of her judgment in such matters, it is not difficult to pronounce that Mortimer is her favourite."

" Colonel Mortimer," said Jacob, " is the man, I think, who ran away with somebody's wife — plays a good deal, runs horses, sails yachts, and all that sort of thing, eh ?"

" It is the same Colonel Mortimer," said John, " who did these things ; but so changed, that not a vestige of his

former character remains.   He married the lady, who, in
fact, ran away with *him*: they lived happily together, in
the most domestic manner, and he nearly died of an illness
brought on by the loss of her."

"Very fine — very fine indeed!" said Jacob: "that's
*your* version of the history, is it?   He runs away with his
friend's wife; they live domestically — that is, because 'the
world' won't visit her; she dies — perhaps of a broken
heart, — and he is near going off the same way from remorse: mayn't that be true?   It's all nothing to me;
nothing will ever break *my* heart; and I never mean to
run away with anybody's wife: only, if *I* had a daughter,
I would sooner cut her legs off than let her marry such a
man."

"I assure you," said John, "that I have spoken upon
this very subject to one or two women of the world" ———

"'The world!' — there you go again."

"Well, but what I mean is, women who really understand the ways of society, and they all agree in the eligi-
bility of the match; and since you doubt the possibility of
Helen, without a fortune, marrying a rich man, I may as
well say at once that Mortimer has at least ten thousand
a-year unincumbered."

"That's it," said Jacob — "there it is.   Now I see;
you sell your daughter for her share of ten thousand a-
year."

"Nay, but if Helen is attached to him — if the affection be mutual, surely the ten thousand pounds per annum
are not objections."

"Not if the man were what a girl ought to love," said
Jacob.   "Now, Alderman Haddock *is* a man" ———

"My dear brother," said John, "if you are not joking,
do not talk of such a thing."

"A quiet, comfortable establishment, — everything her
own way," said Jacob: "a capital house in Bedford
Square, with a nice garden behind, and a beautiful villa
close by Hornsey Wood."

"Your picture is tempting, I admit," said John;
"but I fear the pursuits of such a life would not be congenial."

" Congenial, — pah ! " said Jacob : " I've done. *I* can't marry a rake, and have my heart broken : of course, it's nothing to *me ;* only, if I could have got the girl out of harm's way, and settled her snug and comfortable, it would have been a good job. However, that's over ; let her marry the colonel. I know no ill of him ; he never cheated me out of *my* money — never shall : not to be had. I have no daughter — that's another good thing : however, I'll tell Haddock he has no chance."

" What ! did he ever think he had ? "

" Think ! " said Jacob, " what should an alderman who has passed the chair, think ? — why, exactly as I do — that she would not have hesitated a moment. However, it's nothing to me : *I* can't marry an alderman, so I don't care ; only " ——

Now, the truth is, that the younger of the two middle-aged Messrs. Batley would infinitely rather have seen his daughter starve than marry this Alderman Haddock ; and of this the elder of the Messrs. Batley was perfectly aware : and another truth is, that Helen herself participated most cordially in her father's feelings. Jacob, however, felt it his duty to himself to express his opinion and make his suggestions, inasmuch as the manner in which the one was treated and the others were received would justify him in doing as he pleased with the fortune which he had acquired by his industry.

Her uncle Jacob was no great favourite of Helen's. His uncouth manners ill-agreed with her notions of society ; and his appearance in the domestic circle, when it happened to be enlivened by any of her more worldly acquaintances, was extremely disagreeable. Nor did the efforts of her well-bred father entirely succeed in concealing this feeling from Jacob himself : it was therefore doubly important to him, if possible, to secure a *parti* for the young lady, whose fortune might enable him to remove her from the chance of becoming dependent upon his worthy brother. Every day convinced him more and more of the importance of such an arrangement, inasmuch as every day threw some new light upon his daughter's disinclination towards her uncle, from whom, it should be observed, not a syllable in the way of promise, or even hint at the probable disposition of his wealth, had ever dropped.

The period, then, had arrived when the lovely Miss Batley found at her feet two pretenders to her hand — and heart. Lord Ellesmere was dull, heavy, and, if he had not been a lord, would probably have been reckoned stupid. He had, however, as all dull, heavy lords have, his admirers, his puffers, and his toadies; but, whatever they might say of his morals, it went but a very little way to counteract the movements of the gay and gallant Colonel Mortimer. It is true, the title and coronet were in one scale, and nothing but a commoner's fortune in the other; still the fortune was considerable, and thus it was that Helen lived in a state of perpetual agitation, expecting every day to be called upon to decide between their comparative attractions.

Batley was a Whig — Lord Ellesmere a violent Tory. The colonel sympathised in politics with Batley, and this was an additional claim; besides which, his agreeable manners and conversational qualities rendered him particularly acceptable as a son-in-law. In short, Batley had more than implied to Helen which way his prepossession lay; and even if he had not, the warmth with which he uniformly received her untitled suitor must have convinced her that *he* was the husband elect, as far as the future father-in-law was concerned.

And now for Helen herself: — she was beautiful, highly accomplished, and naturally gifted. Constantly associated with her father since her mother's death, her mind had naturally received its impressions from *him:* her views of " the world," as her uncle Jacob would sneeringly have said, were in perfect accordance with *his;* and the result of this similarity of feeling was, the acquirement of a tone of thought and conversation which, to strangers who did not know the excellence of her heart, gave her an air of what might be colloquially called " off-handishness." But be_ low the surface lay the precious metal of which her character was really formed. She was kind, generous, liberal, and good, in the fullest sense of all these words; but her playfulness and gaiety, captivating as they were, not unfrequently met with the reproof of some, while they dazzled the eyes of many, even to a blindness to the mild radiance of her innate virtues.

Helen had, before she was eighteen, been flattered, praised, and almost beatified. Odes had been written on her eyes, and sonnets addressed to her eyebrows: ponderons lines " To Helen Dancing," and elaborated extempores " On Hearing Helen Sing," had graced the Annuals. Helen had been painted by Lawrence, drawn by Chalon, enamelled after Lawrence by Bone, engraved after Chalon by Finden, mezzotinted by Cousins, and lithographed by Lane. Dances had been dedicated to her, and collections of poems inscribed to her: in short, all that could have well been done to turn the head of a young lady had been tried, — yet Helen remained unspoiled.

It was quite clear to " the world," about the period at which Jacob and John maintained the conversation with which this volume begins, that the suspense in which they, as well as the two parties more intimately concerned, were kept must speedily be terminated. For once " the world" was right : the initiative was taken by the young lady some three nights afterwards at an assembly, where Lord Ellesmere became so " very particular" to Helen, that she was compelled to convince him, in the most unequivocal manner, of the hopelessness of his case, — a determination on her part formally ratified the next morning by her fond parent, who thus saw the last obstacle to his wishes with regard to Mortimer removed. It is not often that a father rejoices in the rejection of a lord by a " gentle belle" who happens to be his daughter ; personal esteem, however, and the belief that Helen's happiness would be more unequivocally secured by her union with his lordship's rival, were the bases upon which his satisfaction was founded : and when the disconsolate baron drove from the door for the last time, Mr. John Batley kissed Helen's flushed cheek in a manner indicative of his entire concurrence in the line of conduct she had adopted.

Strange to say, on the day in which this eventful rejection took place, Colonel Mortimer did not call in Grosvenor Street. Helen waited, and lingered. The horses

were at the door,—her father ready to accompany her: —
she declined riding, insinuating something about an apparent indelicacy in showing herself so immediately after
having broken a heart. Dressing-time came:—no Mortimer! Dinner-time:—no Mortimer! What could have
happened? Surely she could not have deceived herself into
a false belief of his affection for her: surely papa (a man
of the world) could not have so miscalculated as not to
have assured himself of the seriousness of his intentions.
Had his absence any thing to do with Lord Ellesmere's
rejection, or with her conduct the preceding evening?
That Lord Ellesmere was rejected, seemed to be the only
certainty in the midst of all these speculations—that was,
of course, irrevocable—but if Mortimer should really intend
nothing? Helen began to think that she had been hasty.
Lord Ellesmere was not so very stupid—nor so very violent
a politician; and, at all events, he *was* a Peer, and his wife
would be a Peeress:—and Helen was out of spirits, and
even went the full length of crying for vexation.

. Mr. John Batley most assuredly did not cry, — but Mr.
John Batley was particularly uneasy: still, Colonel Mortimer never could have gone so far in his attentions as he
had, unless —— And yet,— to be sure, there might still
remain a dash of the *roué* in his character. He had the
reputation of being a lady-killer, — and it certainly looked
odd : — it might have happened that he had heard of what
had occurred in the family, and had thought proper to retire as soon as he found the field his own. In short, it was
altogether unaccountable, and by no means agreeable. No
man was more likely to feel deeply the frustration of his
designs in such a matter than Batley: the mortification of
being deceived by appearances would of itself be a deadly
pang; to have been outmanœuvred by the colonel would
naturally lie heavy on his heart; and such were the iras-
cible feelings by which he was agitated, that the night
closed upon him with a determination on his part to demand
an explanation of conduct which seemed so entirely irrecon-
cileable with honour and the ways of "the world."

Poor Helen's thoughts were differently directed. Her
affection for Mortimer was warm and sincere ; the extra-

ordinary evidence of his neglect, so suddenly inflicted, agitated her dreadfully ; and the womanly mortification, which in the day had been excited by wounded pride, was transformed before the next morning into an agonising conviction that she had lost the only man she had ever loved.

After a restless, wretched night, came on another day, — but not Mortimer ; and neither Helen nor her father (both equally anxious on the subject) ventured to propose to the other any measure calculated to relieve their suspense : even Batley himself, having slept off his chivalrous resolution of the preceding evening, began to consider the absurdity of making an appeal to Mortimer on a subject with regard to which he had made no kind of declaration ; and Helen, whose heart beat rapidly during the ceremonial of breakfast, would have suffered it to break before she would consent to take any step which could be supposed by " the world " to arise from a wish to recall her truant lover.

The suspense, however, which was so irksome, was speedily converted into a certainty, something worse. The arrival of that invaluable record of all " worldly" proceedings, " The Morning Post," settled the question. In its fashionable columns appeared the following paragraph, the perusal of which, in spite of all efforts at repression, drove Mr. Batley into an agony of rage, and threw Miss Helen into a fit of hysterics :—

" Colonel Mortimer left London yesterday for Brighton, on his way to Dieppe, whence he proceeds on a tour through the Continent."

This of itself would have been sufficient to produce even more serious effects, but, as the French say, " *Malheur ne vient jamais seul ;* " and just as Jack had soothed his daughter into a state of consciousness, and resolved to reread the " extremely disagreeable" announcement previously to discussing it, his eyes, missing their aim at the particular passage, just glanced upon another about half an inch lower down in the column :—

" It is confidently reported that Lord Ellesmere is immediately to be created an Earl."

This was beyond endurance. The first impression upon Batley's mind was, that the circumstance could not be acci-

dental — that some malicious demon had placed the two
articles in juxta-position, and perhaps invented both.    Ay,
— if *that* were true : — the drowning man caught at the
straw — but it saved him not ; — the recorded facts were
incontrovertible.

"Did you see *this*, Helen?" said Batley.

"See it! — yes," said Helen, believing that her excited
parent alluded to the defection of the colonel.

"The idea of making *him* an earl!" said Batley—"what
will they do next?"

"What! — who an earl?" said Helen.

"Your discarded friend Ellesmere," was the reply, and
"The Morning Post" was handed to Helen, in order that
she might satisfy herself ; her tear-dimmed eyes, however,
rested instinctively upon the one loved word : with Isabel
she could have said—

> "Walk forth, my loved and gentle Mortimer,
> And let these longing eyes enjoy their feast."

But, alas! *her* "loved and gentle Mortimer" was now beyond recall ; and when she came to read the announcement
of his rival's approaching elevation, she felt no pang like
that her father had endured, at the loss of rank sustained
by her rejection of his lordship : had he been a prince, and
the competitor for her heart with Mortimer, *his* fate and
*her* decision would have been the same.

"It seems, Helen, that something strange has happened,"
said Batley : — "have you and Mortimer quarrelled?"

"On the contrary," said Helen, who talked fluently in
his praise ; "I never saw him in better spirits or temper
than on Wednesday morning, when he was here."

"Did you see him at Lady Saddington's?"

"No," replied Helen : "he said he should be there, and
perhaps was ; but, you know, I came away early, and he
is generally late."

"Yes," said Batley.    "I begin to wish that you had
not been quite so decisive : Ellesmere is a man not to be
rejected — and —— but we certainly were not aware of
this."

"My dearest father," said Helen, "let what may be the
result, I never shall — never can repent the course I have

adopted. You have taught me to speak frankly upon all topics affecting my happiness, and I have no disguises from you. I never could have altered the sentiments I entertain for Lord Ellesmere, and I am sure it would have been unkind, as well as indelicate, to have permitted him to continue in doubt upon the subject, after what occurred at that party."

" I find no fault, Helen," said Batley ; " I have always desired you to think for yourself: still it appears to me, that, however sincere you may have been in the expression of your feelings towards the man who is indifferent to you, you have been less candid with regard to *him* who, if I know anything of ' the world,' occupies a very different place in your estimation."

" Equally sincere, believe me, my dear father," said Helen. " I never disguised — in fact, there was no reason why I should disguise — the pleasure I derived from the society of Colonel Mortimer. From all you had said, I concluded that you had no objection to his visits, and therefore, so far from affecting an indifference which I did not feel, I have treated him in a manner perfectly consistent with the opinion I entertained of him."

" And now, tell me, Helen," said Batley, — " in your conversations has he ever alluded — seriously, I mean — to the probable result of your acquaintance ? — has he led you to believe that that result would be a proposal similar to that of Lord Ellesmere ? — or " ——

" Why, my dear father," said Helen, " Mortimer's manner, and conversation, and accomplishments, are all so exceedingly unlike those of Lord Ellesmere, that it is impossible for me to establish a comparison between them. Mortimer, as far as I am concerned, has never practised what ' the world,' I believe, calls making love. He is extremely agreeable — delightful ! — and I tell you honestly, I never saw anybody I liked so much ; — and I —— in fact, my dear father, you have seen the progress of our intimacy, — and I — admit the " ——

And here Helen, who had endeavoured with all her energy to keep up this description of her feelings with every possible gaiety, and had to a certain extent succeeded, fell into a second hysteric, the symptoms of which rendered it necessary to ring for her maid, with whose assistance she was removed to her room.

When Batley had assured himself of his daughter's convalescence, and that rest and quiet only were essential to her restoration, he proceeded to his library, to think over what had happened. The marriage of his daughter to Mortimer was the great object of his ambition, and he had for some time so perfectly satisfied himself that things were going on as well as possible, that the sudden shock occasioned by the departure of the lover, as he had considered him, was not at all alleviated by Helen's description of the nature of his attentions, and he began to apprehend that the tender feeling in the *affair* was confined to Helen. That would, and did, naturally account for her rejection of Lord Ellesmere : — might it not equally account for the disappearance of Mortimer ? Might he not, seeing the marked attentions which the noble lord was paying, with an evident, and, probably, avowed object in view, consider himself, having no such intentions, bound in honour to withdraw ?

Batley began to fear that for once his knowledge of " the world" had failed him, and that he ought earlier to have brought Mortimer to some definite point. Now, it seemed impracticable : he had no plea for asking him a single question touching the matter, — except, indeed, that the quitting London without mentioning his intention, or calling to take leave of the family, might justify his writing him a friendly letter of inquiry into the reason of his abruptness, in which Helen should only be mentioned incidentally. This seemed a bright thought, and the *diplomate* resolved to act upon it immediately ; and, in order to begin his operations scientifically, he proceeded forthwith, after hearing a favourable account of his daughter's progress towards recovery, to call at the hotel whence Colonel Mortimer had taken his departure the preceding day.

The reader will please to recollect that he has been introduced to the diplomatic Mr. Batley under peculiar circumstances ; that he has been domesticated with him in the first instance ; and that, as the proverb says " No man is a hero to his valet-de-chambre," so no man *is* as he is in " the world," while engaged in family affairs with his own connexions and relations. Once out of his own house — afloat in the full tide of London-life, — Batley was a different creature ; and those of his acquaintance whom he chanced to meet on his way to Mortimer's hotel, every one of whom would have been too happy to take his arm and enjoy his conversation, could by no possibility form an idea of the real state of his mind, while he, with smiles upon his countenance, and an air of gaiety, was positively distracted at the idea of losing such a prize as a husband for his daughter, who, by one of those singular coinci-deuces that rarely occur in " the world," was equally agree-able to father and child.

Arrived at the hotel, Jack made his inquiries after the colonel, as if he expected to find him at home.

" The colonel left town yesterday, sir," was the answer.

" That's odd," said Batley. " What time ? "

" About half-past one, sir," said the waiter.

" Leave any letters or messages, or —— ? "

" None, sir," said the waiter.

" Gone to Brighton ? " said Jack.

" Yes, sir," replied the man ; " gone to Brighton first, and then to France."

" When do you expect him back ? "

" I don't think, sir, the colonel will be back for some time," said the waiter.

" His servants all gone ? " asked Batley.

" No, sir, his groom and the boy are not gone yet ; they stay with the saddle-horses."

" Ah ! — where are they — here ? "

" At the stables, I fancy, sir," said the man.

" Umph ! " said Batley, pausing for a moment to con-sider what advantage was derivable from inquiries in that quarter, — for Jack was of that school which has for an axiom, the justification of the means by the attainment of the object ; — " Ha — well — then I'll write. Does not go immediately to France ? "

" I think not, sir," said the waiter, " for a day or two."

" Oh ! " said Jack — " thank you — thank you ! " — and away he went, leaving the waiter deeply impressed with the

extreme politeness of his behaviour. And whither went⁻
he? — to the stables! — from the inmates of which he felt
a hope that he might derive the most authentic informátion
on the subject nearest his heart.

Thither he repaired; and, amidst the washing of carriages, the clatter of pail-handles, and the auxiliary hiss-
ings of sundry harness-cleaners, the anxious parent ascertained that Colonel Mortimer had ordered that his horses
should be sent down to his country residence, Sadgrove
House, in Worcestershire; that the carriage-horses were
already gone, and that the saddle-horses were to follow the
next day.

Hence did the diplomatist discover that Mortimer's
absence was not likely to be a temporary one, and that, for
once, the newspapers were correct in their statement, —
the reason probably being that the colonel's own man had
furnished it, — leaving "the world" to wonder what could
so suddenly have caused the occultation of so bright a
planet in the hemisphere of fashion. The conclusion dis-
coverable from this intelligence was of the most disagreeable kind; but it nevertheless strengthened, and before he
reached home confirmed him in, his determination of not
losing a friend so estimable as the colonel, without one
effort either to regain him or ascertain the cause of his
defection. Accordingly, the *diplomate* sat himself down,
and wrote him the following letter : —

"Grosvenor Street.

"My dear Mortimer,

 ' I had a dream, which was not all a dream;
 The bright sun was extinguish'd, and the stars
 Did wander, darkling, in the eternal space,
 Rayless and pathless.'

"'The world' is in 'amazement lost!' — all London
is wondering whither you are gone, and why. We are, in
fact, in a total eclipse : some folks surmise that you have
not gone alone : for myself, I cannot comprehend the
matter, or its suddenness. Surely, if some fancy had
struck you on the minute, you would not have gone without
saying 'farewell' to us. *We* cannot have offended you,
even if any one else has done so; and I cannot suffer you
to go farther than you have already gone, without endea-

vouring to catch some little account of your plans for the future, and of the cause — that is, if you are not resolved to mystify the metropolis altogether.

" To me the news of your departure seemed incredible. One reason for my incredulity was, the account of its appearing somewhat authoritatively in the newspapers; and the other was, our not having received the least intimation of it from yourself, which, as Helen and I were vain enough to think ourselves something like favourites with you, has given us both a great deal of uneasiness.

" Pray write, even if it be but five lines, to let us hear what you propose doing, and whither, in fact, you are going. I admit that I am extremely anxious, because I honestly confess that I feel deeply interested in your proceedings ; and trust that your strange departure is not in any way connected with the disagreements among the trustees of your Welsh property, about which you were good enough to consult me. In fact, we miss you, and want exceedingly to know why. Even poor little Fan seems to inquire after you as earnestly as Italian greyhound can ; and Helen declares that something must have affronted you. For our parts, neither I nor Helen, nor even the affectionate Italian, are conscious of having done so, and therefore those of the trio who think and recollect are most anxious to know the real cause of your disappearance. If there should be any thing in which my humble services can be made available, do not hesitate to let me know, and I will put myself at your disposal immediately.

" Helen desires her best remembrances, and adds her request to mine, that you should write by return of post, to give a true and faithful account of yourself. Pray do, and believe me, dear Mortimer,

" Yours, faithfully and sincerely,<br>" J. Batley.

" P. S. — I see ministers are going to create Ellesmere an earl : — what will they do next ? He is no longer a visitor here ; so that, not having seen him in the course of the day, I am not certain whether the rumour is correct."

This letter, having been first submitted to Helen, who.

saw nothing remarkable, or indelicate, in its contents, and
who especially admired, if she did not actually originate,
the postscript, was despatched to Brighton, which place in
due course it reached the following morning.   The effect
produced by it remains to be seen.

---

## CHAPTER II.

HELEN BATLEY, whose career is likely to occupy a considerable portion of the reader's attention, was singularly
situated in society.    From circumstances, connected in
some degree with her father's wifeless condition, she possessed few female friends of her own age.   She had been
confided to the care of *chaperons*, who were either un-
married elderlies, or widows without families; and her
father's house, ungraced by the presence of a mistress,
seemed to serve rather as a temporary retreat from "the
world" than a home, under the roof of which might be
associated companions of her own sex likely to become the
recipients of the communication of her thoughts and feelings.

Neither were those to whom her volatile and restless
father entrusted her exactly the sort of persons to whom
such a trust could advantageously be delegated ; and certainly, of the whole *coterie*, the one least likely to do her
good was the one whose society she most preferred.   This,
perhaps, was natural, inasmuch as she was never troubled
by her favourite maternal friend with any thing in the
shape of advice, except as to the colour of a riband, or the
texture of a dress.   Lady Bembridge was a woman of
"the world," as uncle Jacob would have said, who lived
but for such pleasures as it could still afford to a widow of
sixty.   A good jointure without children, an excellent
house, and a turn for ostentatious hospitality, combined to
procure for her a constant round of gaiety, in running
which, her great object was to be popular.   She was
always a flatterer, and never dealt in personalities : always
spoke hypothetically, and generally hypocritically.   To be

everything to everybody was her object, and therefore it is not to be imagined that she would hazard the favourable opinion of Helen by intruding anything in the shape of corrective observation upon her. Advice, like medicine, is never palatable ; and Lady Bembridge was like the fashionable physician, who first ascertains what his patient would like before he prescribes, and then prudently directs the unconscious sufferer to do the very thing he wishes to do : a course of proceeding rendered more beneficial to the invalid by convincing him that his own views of his complaint, of course always favourable, are in strict accordance with those of Sir Gregory Galen, or Sir Peter Paracelsus, as the case may be.

On the morning of Batley's visit to Mortimer's stables, Lady Bembridge, much as usual, called on Helen, in order to " make arrangements " for the day. In a moment she saw that Helen had been crying : she knew that Mortimer was gone, — therefore did her ladyship affect not to perceive the tear-marks, or to own her knowledge of the colonel's departure.

" It seems to me, Helen dear," said her ladyship, " as if this evening would be a very good opportunity for the play. We have no engagement ; and if a comfortable box were to be let, probably it might be agreeable."

" My dear Lady Bembridge," said Helen, " I could not go to the play if you were to give me the world !"

" I am sure," said Lady Bembridge, " I am not going to ask why ; but I *did* think, that when young ladies avow themselves admirers of certain authors, there could be no great objection to their seeing their best works well acted."

" Plays are all very well ; they interfere, however, with everything else : and — I don't know — the men who act comedy are so vulgar ; and, as for tragedy, one has enough of *that* in real life, without going to a theatre."

" I am sure, my dear Helen," said Lady Bembridge, " I am the last person in the world, as you know, to inquire how much of tragedy mingles in the occurrences of *your* life ; but I should really think, dear, if anything unpleasant were to occur to any young friend of mine,

placed in ' the world' as you are, it must be — I know,
Helen, you will pardon me, love! — it must be her own
fault."

" Oh! my dear Lady Bembridge," said Helen, " indeed
it is not so! No: what has happened is *not* my fault.
Dear Lady Bembridge, I will tell you all: I am unhappy
— and without having done any one thing in the world
justly to make me so. Mortimer is gone to France —
gone on a tour!"

" You do not really mean that!" said Lady Bembridge,
with an expression which would have done credit to a
professional actress.

" True, — quite true! — Isn't it strange!"

" Why, my love," said Lady Bembridge, " one cannot,
you know, form an opinion hastily upon an individual
case: but—now, dearest, you will see what I mean — if a
very lovely girl, of about your age, — in fact, just such a
girl as yourself, — encourages, — at least, when I say encourages, I mean, suffers the attentions of two men, — one
a nobleman distinguished in society, and the other a commoner equally celebrated in ' the world,' without coming
to a decision, is it not possible that patience may wear out?
and — I don't mean to say ——"

" No, no, — I know you don't, dear!" said Helen,
who, when she became animated, so called the dowager;
" but I did no such thing. You know every turn of my
mind; you know that I did decide about Lord Ellesmere;
else, my dear Lady Bembridge, why did I implore you to
come away from Lady Saddington's?"

" My dearest!" said her ladyship, taking Helen's hand
between her's, " I didn't know anything about it. Sometimes girls have headaches, or are tired; and when I am
*chaperon*, I never ask why they wish me to stay late or
come away early. When one sees an avowed lover, such
as Lord Ellesmere has been of yours, making one of the
retiring party, it is impossible to know."

" What could I do?" said Helen: " he *would* offer me
one arm, and you the other: I could not make a scene.
But I told you, my dear Lady Bembridge ——"

" No, Helen, dear," said Lady Bembridge, " you told

me nothing. A young lady who tells me that she has been very much flurried, and in a state of agitation so peculiar that she wishes to go home, only tells me that something particularly interesting to her has occurred, and I am left to conjecture of what particular sentiment the agitation has been indicative. I never knew, till this moment, the real truth of the story : — so, then, Ellesmere is discarded."

" Yes," said Helen — " but then Mortimer is gone ! — and oh ! my dear Lady Bembridge, if I have lost him by my own want of decision, — my own missishness rather, in · liking to have lovers in order to teaze them and please my-self, I never can have a moment's happiness !"

" My dear Helen, you must not talk in this way : I am quite sure you have nothing to reproach yourself with. To be sure, a man like Mortimer, taken even with all his im-perfections on his head, is not to be found every day ; and when a young lady feels conscious that she has secured the heart of such a man, not to speak of his fortune, which, I am sure, is the last thing such a girl as you would think about, he ought not to risk her own happiness and his by apparent indecision : but this does not apply to your case, dear !"

" I cannot help thinking it does," said Helen, " nor can I help reproaching myself with a thousand little coquettish tricks of which I ought to have been ashamed. You know, my dear Lady Bembridge, this must have been the case, or how could Lord Ellesmere have, to the very last, fancied himself the favourite ? "

" You must not agitate yourself," said Lady Bembridge. " Rely upon it, if a man like Colonel Mortimer were really attached to a young lady, and had withdrawn only because he thought a rival preferred, he would, on ascertaining that that rival was dismissed, instantly return, and kneel to re-ceive his fetters again : he couldn't help himself."

" Not," said Helen, " if he had discovered that the young lady had been playing a double game ? — And that *I* should be that young lady, whose leading faults in ' the world' have hitherto been sincerity and frankness ! I never was reproached with anything very wrong, except speaking my mind too freely ; and yet — yet — here I have *not* been sincere."

" You see this matter in a wrong point of view," said
Lady Bembridge. " Follow my advice ; come and take a
drive. Let us engage the box, and go to the play. A young
lady, whose admirer has suddenly left town on a tour, ought
not to permit ' the world' to suppose that she is affected by it."

" But I am affected by it," said Helen, and the tears
ran down her cheeks ; " and I cannot conceal my sorrow,
even if I wished it ! "

Lady Bembridge looked at her young friend with a half-
serious, half-comic worldly look, and pressing her hand,
said archly, as dowagers sometimes will say things —

> " ' The boy thus, when his sparrow's flown,
>     The bird in silence eyes ;
>   But soon as out of sight 'tis gone,
>     Whines, whimpers, sobs, and cries.' "

" Lady Bembridge ! " said Helen, starting from her
chair, " you know I cannot bear to be laughed at ! " and
in the next instant she was out of the room, leaving the
*chaperon* as much surprised at the rapidity of the young
lady's movements, as at the ill success of her extremely
ill-timed attempt at pleasantry.

Helen, however, was seriously wounded by what had
occurred, and upon a mind like hers, the combination of
feelings — some perhaps not quite so amiable as others
— which the circumstance had excited, operated violently.
She had lost the lover of her choice, and she had discarded
his rival, whose peerage was at her feet ; and, as has been
already observed, beyond and over and above the one deep
grief which the former of these circumstances created, was the
worldly regret that she should have thrown away the advantages of the match with Lord Ellesmere for the sake of the
man who had evidently abandoned her. All this worry
and excitement produced an accession of fever ; and after
Lady Bembridge, who followed her to her room, had obtained pardon for her endeavour to laugh off her sorrows
and remorse, she took her leave, promising to send her own
favourite physician to visit her, observing as she went, " that
however incompetent the doctors might be to ' minister to
a mind diseased,' still they were of great service in check-
ing bodily illness."

Helen, for the first time, rejoiced at her ladyship's departure. The silence which succeeded to the voluble hypotheses of her "worldly" companion was of itself soothing, and the poor victim to her own indecision uninterruptedly indulged in an ecstasy of tears.

It was during this time that another scene in the domestic drama was being enacted in Mr. John Batley's library, where brother Jacob, having heard the history of Mortimer's flight and Ellesmere's rejection, made at least a twentieth effort to induce Jack to listen to Alderman Haddock's proposals for the deserted Dido.

"Psha, Jack!" said Jacob, "I told you so:—cat in a tripe-shop;—Jack-ass between two bundles of hay:—didn't know where to choose. No difference to *me;* thank God! I have no daughter. I care for nobody: but you'll see the end on't, that's all I say,—and a pretty kettle of fish you'll make of it!"

It was during such discussions as these, that Jack, the brilliant and polished, had to exercise the most rigid control over his temper, and submit with apparent patience to the *dicta* of the uneducated Crœsus from whom he hoped to derive eventual independence.

"My dear brother," said Batley, jun., "you are altogether misinformed. Colonel Magnus, Mortimer's particular friend, told me this very morning that he doubted the fact of Mortimer's intended absence, and hinted to me — this is *entre nous* ——"

"Of course, whatever that means."

"Means, Jacob," said John, "why, that it goes no farther. He hinted to me that he rather thought Mortimer had an affair upon his hands, and had given out the history of his tour to mystify inquirers."

"An affair!" said Jacob — "Oh! that means, I suppose, another duel — not that it necessarily follows. An affair of honour! — an affair of gallantry! Ah! — well, you are safe with *me;* I shan't say a syllable. I don't care if Mortimer is killed half a dozen times over;—why should I? *I'm* not going to fight, and haven't insured *his* life; it cannot make any difference to me."

" No," said Jack, " but it would make a serious difference to Helen."

" Why," said Jacob, " I don't see that. She has contrived to catch two fools already, — why shouldn't she do the same thing again ?"

" My dear brother," said Jack, " you speak of female affections as if they were as easily transferred as so much stock."

" Stock, John !" said Jacob — " no, no : you don't catch me comparing the fly-away fancies of a giddy girl with the four per cents, or the three-and-a-half reduced."

" But the sentiment !" said John.

" Sentiment, my eye !" said Jacob ; " I don't understand what it means : I never knew what it was to be in love — never shall, now. I admit that I once took a fancy to a widow at Wapping, in regard of sundry ships, Class A, lying in the London Docks, of which she was mistress ; but I found it wasn't all clear and above board, — and that she had a nephew, and there was a will to be disputed ; so I left the widow and the craft : — but as for sentiment, — Lord bless your heart ! she was old enough to be my grandmother, and so big that one of her own puncheons would have made her a tight pair of stays."

" That's it, you have never felt the passion, and therefore cannot appreciate its power."

" I suppose I haven't !" said Jacob : " no matter ; I shall never want for anybody to love as long as I live — always sure, too, of a return — I love myself. As I say, of all the houses in the street give me Number One — that's my maxim."

" You *say* so," said John.

" Never say what I don't mean," replied Jacob ; — " and another thing I never do : — never try to jump higher than my legs will carry me — d'ye mark me, Jack ? There isn't a man, woman, or child to whom I owe tenpence : I never drink my port till it's paid for : — no running in debt, — as you do, Jack : — however, as I've said a hundred times, it's nothing to me."

" Only, as a brother," said Jack, " you might perhaps take some interest."

"Not I, I never take any interest—except for my money:
— and as for a brother, —why, we are all brothers, if you
come to that: — and hang me if I know one of the family
who would stoop to pick up a pin to save *my* life ; — I'm
sure I wouldn't, to save one of theirs."

" But, surely," said Jack, " Helen deserves some of
your affection : she is truly attached to *you*, and " ——

" Fudge, Jack !" said Jacob, rattling all the shillings
in his breeches-pocket — " attached to *me !* — no, I'm not
after *her* fashion — I don't live in ' the world ' — hey ?
She may be attached to me as Peter Post-Obit in the play
is attached to *his* friends, in the hopes of what she may
catch at my death : — but it won't do ; I'm not to be
had ! No, — if she were a staid, sensible sort of body,
and would marry Haddock, I should say something to her :
— but, no — the alderman, like myself, is not a man of
' the world ' — not that I care three dumps for *him*, if you
come to that."

" Why," said Jack, " Helen's habits and manners are
different from those of the alderman ; and an accomplished
girl ——"

" Accomplished fiddle-stick ! " said the merchant. —
" What are accomplishments ? You over-educate your
girls — make them dance like figure-girls, — what d'ye
call 'em there, — all up and down the sides of the stage at
the playhouse, with a fringe to their stays which they call
petticoats ? — make them play and sing till their hearts
ache : — and what for ? — to catch husbands : that's it, —
isn't it ? —And more fools they to be trapped."

' " I don't see that," said Jack. " Accomplishments, in
which amateurs now excel the professors of twenty years
since, are ——"

" Accomplishments," said the merchant, " stuff ! What
are the accomplishments ? — all very fine as baits — but
once let the accomplished girl be married — see, then, what
happens. The husband is gained ; a family is coming ;
and she thinks just as much of twanging her harp, rattling
her piano-forte, or colly-wobbling with her voice, as she
does of flying : it's all pretence.—If Helen married Haddock ——"

" My dear Jacob, ———"

" And, my dear Jack," said Jacob, " if you come to
*that*. — I say, even if she married this Mortimer — which,
in course, she won't now, — she would never sing or play
afterwards ; nor would he ask her. Everything is very
fine till you have got it. A singing wife is like a piping
bullfinch ; great fun for your friends, — deuced tiresome
to yourself. Now, as I am all for myself, and nothing for
my friends, I only speak as I think."

" My dear brother," said Jack, " upon one point I
really wish to undeceive you, because in your blunt, off-
hand way of speaking, you may unintentionally do Helen
and me a very serious piece of mischief, by representing
the marriage between her and Mortimer as off. Colonel
Magnus his particular friend ———"

" Psha !" said Jacob, " Colonel Magnus !" — that's
another man of ' the world ;' a Brag in good society ; a
fellow I saw through the first day I met him : — not but
he is clever, for he never brags straightforward, — all his
infernal conceit comes out as if by chance, and he leaves
you to draw your own conclusions ; all his boasting is by
implication : but he's an empty-pated fellow, and as con-
ceited as a man-milliner, and not very unlike one."

" Magnus like a man-milliner !" exclaimed Jack, " why,
my dear brother, he is absolutely the pattern-man of the
day."

" Yes," said Jacob, " that will do ! a ' pattern-man !'
— just so — so is a man-milliner ; — and the bosom friend
of Mr. Mortimer ! — I understand. I feel what comes of
friendships ; I never had a friend in my life, thank God !
I don't care a farthing about it ; but, mark me, *that* Colonel Magnus is most likely to be the man to persuade
Mortimer to have nothing to do with Helen."

" On the contrary, he is loud in her praise."

" Loud in her praise !" repeated the brother ; " and do
you give any man in this world credit for what he says ?
— psha ! The world is full of cheats ; — it's a great
huge cheat, itself ; — it is that makes me stand aloof :
every body who makes professions — lies ; no man, let him
talk as he may, cares one straw for anything but self, —

that I know. But I'm even with them: I'm like the dusty chap that lived on the river Dee; ' I care for nobody,'— not ' *if* nobody cares for me,' as the miller says, but because I know nobody *does* care for me: — so much the better — who wants them ?' "

It is true that Mr. Jacob Batley had a somewhat forcible manner of expressing his extremely unamiable feelings and principles; but he was a shrewd observer of things, and the estimate he had formed of the merits of Colonel Magnus was not very far from being correct. The colonel had been long the intimate friend of Mortimer : they had been in the same battalion of Guards, — had lived constantly together. Magnus was the *confidant* of Mortimer in that affair to which reference has already been made; his adviser in council, and had been his friend in the field: to Magnus, therefore, every incident connected with Mortimer was familiar, and Mortimer would in vain have attempted concealment with *him* : —moreover, he certainly *did* think that Mortimer might do better than marry the beautiful yet flighty Helen; and perhaps fancied that the blissful retirement to his place in Worcestershire, of which he spoke in raptures, might, more than was agreeable, separate him from a companion in whose society he delighted, and whose hospitality was particularly agreeable to him.

As to the particular feeling to which Jacob alluded, Jacob was right. Magnus had but a small fortune, but he had a fine place in the country, in which he could not afford to live ; still he was a man of station, and (to a certain degree) of property, however much it might be encumbered. The general tone of his conversation was such as never to betray him into falsehood, but to leave his hearers, as Jacob said, to infer that he was really something to be looked up to. This style of language, combined with a fine person, Antinous-like features, pallid cheeks, an immoveable steadiness and almost scornfulness of countenance, gave him a kind of swaggering importance in general society, in which he mightily rejoiced. How far his influence over Mortimer, superadded to his knowledge of foregone indiscretions, contributed to the events hereafter to be detailed, is not at

present to be ascertained; suffice it to say, that Colonel
Mortimer seldom acted in any important case, without having first asked the advice of Colonel Magnus.

It was in the natural order of things that nothing like
congeniality should exist between the two colonels and such
a person as Mr. Jacob Batley. The old citizen was by far
too quick and discerning not to discover the precise place
which he held in their estimation, and this knowledge gave
increased force to his natural feelings of misanthropy, or
rather self-love, — for, in fact, he did not so much hate
others as love himself.

" Well," said the worthy citizen, " I wish you well out
of it. You are in what I call a mess — but you won't take
advice, and I can't afford time to waste it upon you if you
would : — no, — go your own way, it's nothing to me : I
don't care whether she marries either, both, or neither. I
know I have got a deuced good dinner to eat at Haddock's
at six, and a capital bottle of port to drink after it, and a
snatch of supper if I want it, and a glass of punch beyond
*that;* and a comfortable bed to go to afterwards, — that's
enough for me. I have put myself out of harm's way —
sunk enough in annuities to keep me safe for the rest of *my*
life ; blow high, blow low, all's one to Jacob :—wherefore,
good morning ! I shall look in to-morrow or next day. I
suppose I shall hear how you get on — not that that's what
I come for, only I like an object when I want a walk, and
so I come to inquire — ha, ha ! Good bye t'ye, Jack."

" Strange, unaccountable creature !" muttered Jack, as
he rang the bell. " Is it the possession of wealth that steels
the heart against mankind, or is it the knowledge, gained
by that possession, of the rapacity of the world, which puts
the rich man on his guard against its impositions ? I, if I
ever had a guinea in the world that I could call my own,
was never easy till it was gone ; and often have I shared it
with a poorer friend, or even given it all away to some deserving object, — and here is this brother of mine, rolling
in riches, a perfect callosity. Well, I would not change
with him."

This being a soliloquy, Jack's effusion, so favourable to
himself, will pass uncensured on the score of boasting : he

said little more than the truth, although the callosity, as he called it, of Jacob, as far as he himself was concerned, was in some degree attributable to frequent applications for assistance, which Jacob sometimes responded to favourably, because he was afraid his own name might be implicated in any exposure of Jack's embarrassments : so, even in any exception to his general rule, it will be found that self was still the ruling principle.

In the state of mind into which Mr. John Batley had worked himself during the last six and thirty hours, the sound of an approaching visitor was dreadfully exciting; and just as Jacob had quitted him, his nervous system was violently acted upon by the announcement of no less a personage than Magnus himself.

" My dear colonel," said Jack, " I am too glad to see you."

" Why," said the colonel, " I have called rather to ask your advice, than to bring any intelligence of our friend, from whom, however, I expect to hear every hour. The fact is, that I have heard you express a wish to be again in parliament: — now I think I have an opportunity of, — I won't say, returning you, — not actually that, — but of putting things so favourably *en train*, that little doubt can be entertained of success."

" Why," said Jack, his eyes brightening at the prospect of again sitting in the Wittenagemote, " I admit that I should be disposed to enter into any negociation that way tending, not from personal vanity, but because I think — of course what I say is confidential — that I *might* be of use : — I *have been* behind the curtain, and might perhaps turn the experience I have gained to some account in picking holes in the coats of — eh ! — you understand."

" Perfectly," said the colonel: " I will state the fact. A large proportion of the electors of Mudbury, the town in the neighbourhood of which a good deal of my Wiltshire property lies, have been long anxious to show any little attention to me in their power. About a week ago, some sixty or seventy of them came over to my place, — a thing quite unexpected on my part, — in twenty or thirty carriages ; and my man, who announced that they were arrived,

was the first person who told me anything at all about it.
I immediately said, ' Hawkins,'— my man's name is Hawkins,— I said, 'sixty or seventy of them, — oh ! —show
them into one of the small drawing-rooms, and have luncheon,
or something of the kind, put down in the large dining-
room.' I thought that was not a bad precaution : that
class of people have a high regard for their personal comforts, and as it is said that Englishmen can finish nothing
satisfactorily without a dinner, so I have observed, that they
can begin nothing at all comfortably without a luncheon."

" I see you are quite alive to the little imperfections of
our noble countrymen."

" *Au fait,*" said Magnus ; " else why have I lived so
long amongst them, contrary to my taste and inclination ?
*N'importe*, these fellows came, and I found that they were
a deputation from a vast proportion of the electors of Mudbury, pressing me to come forward. Now, the fact is, my
dear Batley, you know I have a certain position to maintain, and as far as any of the necessary labours, as I call
them, of one's station are concerned, I am ready. As high
sheriff, why, of course, with a certain degree of influence
and property, and all that, in a county — it's a duty to —
to — uphold the office properly, which is, in fact, unavoid-
able : but the House of Commons, the heat, and the smell,
and the late hours which one must keep, and the odd sort
of hats the people wear — in fact, to me — I declare I
could not, in justice, undertake the thing ; — I love my ease
too much."

" Ah !" said Jack, smilingly and bowingly, " there it *is :*
that is precisely the reason why things are going to ruin."

" No, Jack," said Magnus, " a vote's a vote, and I could
give no more ; — so, feeling that I was very much obliged
to my dirty-faced friends, I gave them a sort of impromptu
*déjeûnér*, and made them a speech. They begged me to
express myself before the main body of their party at the
town hall. I immediately ordered my carriage — I happened luckily to have some of my own horses down at the
time—put four to, —outriders and that sort of thing,—and
went over to Mudbury. Of course, my coming was a thing
looked at, and to be talked of ; and I think the affair went

off remarkably well. I repeated my declaration of ill health, and all that ; and then I was solicited to name a friend :— there is the fact. The thing struck me as likely to be agreeable to you, and — so ——— "

" 'Gad," said Batley, " you are extremely kind. I really am infinitely obliged."

" I thought, perhaps, it might be agreeable," said the colonel ; " I therefore told several of my Wiltshire tenants — for, in other counties where I have property, my influence is more decided — that, of course, moving in society as I did, I must know a considerable number of eligible persons to bring forward, and that I would consult some of those people best qualified to judge with regard to my choice ; but, just as I was stepping into my travelling carriage, it struck me that you, perhaps, were the best person in the world for the purpose ; I desired Wilkinson, my *homme d'affaires*, who is quite in my confidence, and who gets through a world of business in the shortest possible time, not to write to the Marquess of Pimlico till I had seen you. In fact, I thought it would please you, and I knew it would please Mortimer."

The last observation puzzled Batley a good deal. It seemed clear, that if Mortimer had decidedly broken off all connexion with his family, his being either in or out of the House of Commons must be a matter of indifference to him ; still he liked the notion, and looked upon Magnus as a man very little inferior, in fact, to what he was in his own opinion. There was still a point to be discussed, the settlement of which was yet wanting to confirm the exalted opinion which Jack had formed of his friend. What that was may be easily guessed : Was the return to be made free of expense ? — or was it expected by the magnificent colonel that Jack was to secure the favourable opinions of the independent electors by any outlay of his own ?

Little did Jack, with all his knowledge of the world, think that the magnificent colonel's only reason for not sitting, himself, for that respectable town, was the impossibility of getting elected upon personal influence alone, and the equally disagreeable impossibility of raising a sufficient sum for the purpose, without some dreadful sacrifices.

" With regard to the expense," said the colonel, " it
will be a mere flea-bite — three thousand pounds will be
the outside ; so that you may be quite sure that my disinclination does not arise from that cause ; and, in fact,
having a good deal of East India stock, and West Indian
property,—all that sort of thing,—I ought to be in the
House to look after my varied interests, independently of
the stake I have in the country itself,—but—I cannot
endure it. so, you see, my dear Batley, the offer of seces-
sion in your favour is, in point of fact, no compliment?"

" Why," said Jack, his face considerably elongated,
" I — I — that is — I — think — that no difficulty can
arise upon that point." (Hereupon his sanguine imagination darted rapidly towards his brother's coffers.) " I
think that I can manage that——"

" Manage!" said Magnus — "of course. 'Gad, the
idea of not managing three thousand pounds, I suppose,
never entered the head of mortal man. I merely mentioned the sum, because, upon my life ! the thing's dog-
cheap. In fact, these matters have become much more
reasonable since we carried the Reform Bill."

" True," said Jack,— " anything better calculated for
the advancement of bribery I never recollect, although I did
vote for it."

" Excepting always the ballot," said Magnus. " Now,
of course, with the number of tenants I have in different
parts of the kingdom, it would be dangerous openly to
tamper with them ; but if the ballot could be established,
and for which, if you accept my offer, of course, you will
do me the kindness to vote, the system is infinitely easier,
— plainer, and utterly beyond the reach of detection.
*Par example*, if I say to any one of the three or four
hundred of the people I have in Wiltshire, ' I will give
you ten pounds for your vote, or I will abate ten pounds
of your rent '—the case is flagrant ;—Thessiger, or any
of the leading Conservative parliamentary lawyers (and,
*entre nous*, Jack, the legal talent is all Tory), — these
fellows would knock us over ; but with the ballot, where
nobody knows anybody, and a bet does not consequently
invalidate a vote, I say to Hawkins, or Jenkins, or Watson,

or Jackson, as the case may be, ' Are you going to ballot ? '
— ' Yes,' says Taylor, or Jenkins, or Watson ; ' I am.' —
Well, don't you see ? —with the vast spread of influence
I have, I say — ' I tell you what, Watson,' or Tomkins, or
as the case may be, ' I'll bet you ten pounds the Tory candidate comes in.' — ' Done !' says Watson, or Tomkins —
and away he goes, and does his *possible* to keep the Tory
out."

" A good notion," said Jack, " and I believe generally
understood by our party ; however, with respect to our immediate negociation, will you give me till to-morrow to
think it over ? "

" To be sure," interrupted Magnus, " the thing is an
affair of not the slightest importance to *me*. I make you
the offer, because, knowing your principles, I do not in
the slightest degree compromise my own ; and the fact is,
that having a good deal of interest in other places, our
dear friend Spoony — you know whom I mean — has been
good enough to offer me a baronetcy, if, — don't you see ?
— not that I wish for it, or indeed would accept it, — it is
now too common a reward, — so, *entre nous,* take your time,
and let me know at your leisure, whether my proposition
is agreeable."

Batley bowed an acquiescence, and cast " a longing
lingering look behind," on his brother and his fortune ;
but, knowing how very thick the coat of that pine-apple-like
relation was, almost despaired of being able to avail himself
of the not too liberal offer of his friend.

" Well, my dear Batley," said Magnus, " I have now
opened my budget, — I think you ought to be in parliament, — as I say, you don't care for the smell and the
heat and all that : — to a man accustomed to perfect ease
and well-ventilated rooms, it is quite another thing : —my
greatest care, by Jove ! in all my houses, is about the ven-
tilation ; and, I declare to you, I find a vast difficulty, —
my rooms are so large — small rooms, by the way, are
worse, — so hot in summer, and so cold in winter, — that,
upon my life, half my time is passed with those architect
people and builders, — who, in point of fact, know nothing
about the matter, — in trying too keep myself at a proper

temperature. Don't put yourself out of the way about the offer; I dare say we shall either see or hear from Mortimer to morrow, and then we can talk it over."

And so ended this dialogue, which, as I have already observed, completely mystified Jack Batley, who, though prepared for the mortification of being obliged to decline the seat, inasmuch as he shrewdly suspected that Jacob would have seen him lodged in one of the new-fangled parish bastiles before he would give or lend him the *quantum sufficit* for the seat, was, nevertheless, elevated to a great extent by the continued attentions of such a man as Colonel Magnus, considering above all that he was the intimate friend of the much-desired Colonel Mortimer.

---

## CHAPTER III.

THE ambition of Mr. John Batley having been fired by the offer of the colonel, he began to consider the mere probable means of raising the sum required to conciliate the affections of his future free and independent constituents; and having revolved the matter in every shape and way, he at last came to the resolution of applying to Jacob, having worked himself into the belief, that upon such an occasion his heart might be moved and his purse-strings opened. An invitation to dinner was the preliminary step, John having invariably found that his amiable relation was much more accessible after a hearty meal well washed down with generous wine, than at any other period.

These fits of amiability were not peculiar to Jacob Batley; it is upon record that a certain curmudgeonly money-lender would never turn a favourable ear to his thoughtless customers, until he was more than half-tipsy. One of his most constant *clients* used to declare, that, when he first knew him, two glasses of port wine produced the desired effect; but that from the long habit of borrowing by the one, and of drinking by the other, before the witty spendthrift had concluded the connexion, two bottles at least were necessary to bring him to the lending state.

Jacob, a cunning trader, was perfectly conscious of the character of Jack's invitations, and looked for a financial application of some sort, as a sequel to the bidding, as naturally as he expected to hear thunder after a flash of lightning; nevertheless, he uniformly went, and, kind as he might appear, comparatively, towards the close of the evening, it was not once in twenty times the object of his solicitous host was realised; and when it was, it was because the refusal would have brought discredit upon his own name.

Other matters, however, arose in the course of the day, which were of deep interest to Jack. More important was the return of Mortimer, than his own return for Mudbury. Return, however, he did; and the first house he went to after his arrival, was that of John Batley.

There is no doubt but that this event was considered by Jack, as indeed it proved to be, the deciding move of Helen's life; and it was with unaffected warmth he welcomed the accomplished gentleman to his house.

" What did you think had become of me ? " said Mortimer, with an archness which implied that he perfectly well knew, from the cautious style of the letter he had received, his real opinion of his abrupt departure.

" Why," said Batley, " to tell you the truth, I was apprehensive that some fighting business had called you so suddenly away, and I began to get nervous and fidgety."

" No," said Mortimer, " my fighting days are over; all I now look forward to is quiet, and retirement. I am sick, dead sick of the world, of its heartlessness, its unprofitableness; and if I can find a really true, ingenuous creature, who will confide her destinies to me, and second my resolutions to become a good man, I am prepared to surrender my freedom.

The lyre of Calliope's son never sounded more melodiously in Pluto's ear than did these words on that of John Batley, Esq. Here was no equivocation as to the actual disposition of the gallant gay Lothario; and, although he affected still to be searching for such a partner

in life as he depicted, still he would not have continued
" harping upon my daughter," as Jack thought, unless she
was in fact the object of his affection.

" I should think," said Mr. Batley, " that there is no
young lady of common intelligence who would not be too
happy to strengthen you in such admirable resolutions."

" Faith ! I don't know," said the colonel. " If I were
poor, and found favour in the eyes of a woman who would
make sacrifices for me, and share my pittance whatever it
might be, I should feel a confidence in her affection ; but
the worst of it is, I have been so perfectly a man of ' the
world,' have seen so much evil, have done so much wrong
myself, that I cannot conquer my doubts and apprehensions, nor make myself believe that I *can* be loved for myself alone."

" This is a diffidence which——"

" No, no," interrupted Mortimer, " it has nothing to do
with diffidence ; it is mistrust. And since we *are* upon
the subject, let me be candid at once—is Helen at home ? "

" Yes," said Batley.

" Now, Batley," said the colonel, " we are both men of
the world, — you are no more blind than I am, — you
know what I feel towards your daughter, — yes, you
do."

" I admit," said Batley, " that I think she is honoured
by your favourable opinion."

" I have watched her," said Mortimer, " carefully. Her
mind is pure — her manners frank and attractive ; but —
I will be candid with you — she was the sole cause of my
abrupt departure from town ; nor should I have returned
for months, had it not been for one line in your letter which
announced the cessation of Ellesmere's visits here."

Batley, with a civil inclination of his head, listened, con-
gratulating himself inwardly upon the success of his diplomacy.

" That line brought me back," said the colonel, " because
it not only imparted a welcome fact, but proved that you
knew I considered Ellesmere a rival, and used the intelligence as a hint that the coast was clear."

Batley remained listening, but not quite so well satisfied

with the dexterity upon which he piqued himself, and feeling even foolish at the detection of his real purpose.

" I will be frank with you, my dear friend," continued Mortimer ; " and if Helen smiles, and you sanction it, she shall be the guardian angel of my future destinies. Think, Batley, on what small matters great things turn : her rejection of Ellesmere one day delayed, would have separated us for ever."

" My dear Mortimer," said Batley, " whatever Helen decides upon I sanction ; she is my only child, — the dearest object of my existence. The rejection of poor dear good-natured Ellesmere was her own act, unadvised by me ; if it had its origin in any tender feeling towards another, I know nothing about it."

" Well, then," said Mortimer, " I have your permission to make the attempt."

" Most assuredly," answered the happy father ; " and my best wishes for your success."

It was not unamusing to see these two masters in the art of *finesse* playing each other off, each fancying that he was out-manœuvring the other. Mortimer's propositions of reform and retirement were as much sneered at by Batley, as Batley's affected ignorance of Mortimer's feelings, and his desire that the match should take place, were pooh-pooh'd by Mortimer ; nor were Mortimer's views of the subject rendered less striking by the knowledge which he had gained upon his return to the hotel, touching the ardent anxiety expressed by Batley, with regard to his destination, when he paid not only the house, but the stables, his visit of inquiry.

But a different scene was about to be enacted in the boudour, where Helen and her friend Lady Bembridge were seated, the third person of the party being a certain Captain Stopper, against whom Mortimer entertained the most unconquerable antipathy, and for whom Helen felt not much greater admiration. Helen, however, whose eyes had been red with tears, and whose heart had been aching ever since Mortimer's departure, no sooner heard of his return (which event had been communicated by the captain) than her sorrow converted itself into anger, and when Mortimer entered the boudoir, she received him with a studied coldness which threw her father into a fit of agony.

In a *piquant* little book of rare merit, ycleped " *Maxims and Hints for an Angler*,"— speaking of a trout, the author says, " Never mind what they of the old school say about ' playing him till he is tired ;' much valuable time and many a good fish may be lost by this antiquated proceeding : — put him in your basket as soon as you can."

This advice, as regards fishing, coming from an experienced pen, seemed to anxious Jack perfectly applicable to the affairs of humanity ; and Miss Helen's disposition for playing with *her* fish after having hooked him was particularly annoying to him.

Mortimer felt the alteration in her manner quite as much as she intended he should, and at the moment when her bosom palpitated with delight at his return, she turned from him, after having permitted him to shake her hand, in order to ask Captain Stopper which of the new Murillo's he admired most, — the captain being of that particular order of persons who are not able to distinguish the difference between a sign-board and a Sir Joshua.

" I thought you were out of town, Colonel Mortimer," said Helen, after having received a convenient " I don't know which I like best," from Captain Stopper, touching the pictures.

" I *have* been, as you might have guessed by my not having presented myself at *your* door," said Mortimer.

" Well, my dear Helen," said Lady Bembridge, who saw in a moment that a crisis was at hand, and felt, by the restrained tone of Helen's conversation, and the restlessness of her father's manner, that she was *de trop*, " I'll run away. If a person have a great many commissions to exe_ cute for country cousins, and wishes to get through her shopping, the best way is to begin early."

" Good morning !" said Helen,—" not that I see any reason for your hurry. Perhaps I shall see you again by_ and-by."

" It is not impossible," said Lady Bembridge, still bust_ ling to get away, and not only to get away herself, but to disturb Captain Stopper, who appeared perfectly satisfied to remain where he was, having been highly pleased by the peculiar kindness of Helen's manner upon this special occasion. This, however, was too much for Batley's patience, who felt as if he were on the edge of a precipice, and resolved, even at the risk of apparent rudeness, to get rid of the gallant soldier.

" Have you five minutes to spare ?" said Jack.

" Five hours," replied Stopper, " if I can be of use to *you.*"

" Then, come and look at a young horse," said Jack, " that I bought yesterday : I should like your opinion."

" Why," said Stopper, " giving an opinion of a horse after a man has bought him is like advising a friend in the choice of a wife after he is married."

" Come then," said Jack, " never mind, — I sha'n't be offended if you abuse him."

. " Shall you be at Lady. Sandown's to-night ?" said Stopper to Helen.

" Are *you* going ?" said Helen with apparent interest.

" Yes," said Stopper.

" Are you quite sure you mean to go ?"

" Positive."

" Come !" said Jack.

" I see I must consent to be the judge," said Stopper, who was actually dragged from the paradise of Miss Helen's sanctum. " Adieu ! — good morning, Mortimer !"

And so they went their way, Jack having no horse to show, but satisfied that having got his plague out of the house, he could *finesse* some excuse for not visiting the stables.

" Well, colonel," said Ellen, as soon as they were alone, " you are an extremely polite person. I see you one evening at dinner — you are full of news, and anecdotes of everybody — except yourself, as it seems, — for the next morning off you go, without one word of preparation, and leave all your friends to wonder and surmise. I believe you do this sort of thing to make yourself interesting."

" Why, Miss Batley," said Mortimer, " if I could have fancied that my staying in London or going to the country could in any degree have excited *your* interest, I should

certainly have made a point of announcing my departure;
but it so happened, that when I sat next you at dinner I
had not formed the intention of leaving town; and when I
did form it, what I saw at Lady Saddington's did not tend
to make me think that anything I might do could be of importance to *you*."

" What you saw !" said Helen —" what, were my actions watched ?"

" They were, Helen," said Mortimer, "and were the
cause of my sudden flight."

" Colonel Mortimer !" said Helen ——

" Yes, Helen, — yes !" sighed Mortimer.  " I went
late; the crowd was, as you know, immense, and I was lost
in the general confusion; but my eye rested where my
heart was, and I saw that the envied place in the room was
filled by Lord Ellesmere.   I saw his earnestness of manner
— his entire devotion to you.   I saw you and Lady Bembridge leave the room before supper, and Ellesmere your
companion.   He did not return, and I felt the pang of
knowing that his society was preferred by you to the gaiety
of the scene, — or even to the certainty of meeting me."

" But, Colonel Mortimer," said Helen, " how — why —
or for what reason should you feel displeased with me for
leaving a hot room when I was tired, or for accepting the
arm of an intimate friend of my father's ?"

" Helen," said Mortimer, "the time is past for dissimulation.   You know why I felt as I did: you know my
thoughts as well as I know them myself.   You know, Helen, that I love you, fondly, tenderly, sincerely !   Could I
endure the sight of you flying from the place where you
were sure I should come, with a man whose attachment to
you is notorious ?"

" Oh, Colonel Mortimer !" said Helen, " do not charge
me with dissimulation !   Forgive me: think no more of
that evening: it is past—over for ever !"

" I know, dear Helen !" said Mortimer, fondly pressing
her unresisting hand: " had not that been certain, I should
have returned to Italy, and have tried, by a recurrence to
the mad pursuits of my earlier life, to dissipate the recollection of the happy hours I had passed with you; but,

thanks to Providence! that mystery is solved, and you —
yes, you, dearest Helen — will form the happiness, the
pride of my future existence!"

Helen spoke not, but big tears rolled down her flushed
cheek, and she trembled like a leaf.

"Calm yourself, beloved girl," said Mortimer: "speak
not — I feel that I am blessed. Do not, for worlds, break
the charm which is over me; — I am neither rejected nor
despised!"

The look which Helen gave, confirmed his happiness;
and before Batley returned from not looking at his horse,
Colonel Mortimer and his future wife had calmed themselves into something like rationality; and when he arrived,
his eyes were blessed with beholding the man whom of all
others he desired for his son-in-law, sitting *tête-à-tête* with
his darling Helen.

"Give me joy, Batley! — she consents!"

"I do give you joy," said Jack, "and I give her joy
too. Come here, Helen: — here she is, my friend; take
her, and assure yourself that you possess a treasure."

This appeared to "the world," as well as it did to
Mr. Batley, a brilliant match: and most brilliant, because
it blended true love with wealth and station. Helen herself felt at once relieved of a weight of anxiety, arising out
of the circumstances of her father's life. No longer was
that cautious conduct which he was so perpetually incul-
cating required. There was now no mystery; she loved
Mortimer, and had owned it; she might now speak of him
as she thought, and listen to his praises, without either
deteriorating them, or denying his merits: and yet it was
a step of unusual importance.

Mortimer was her senior by nearly twenty years. His
wild career had been run either before she was born, or
while she was yet an infant: with the particulars of his
moral offences she was unacquainted: she heard him
generally set down as a *roué;* she had read in the peerage
the record of his leading crime, but she attentively watched
his conduct and listened to his conversation, without seeing
or hearing anything confirmatory of what she considered
the malicious hints thrown out. He was, however, him-

self sensitively alive to any allusion to his youthful follies, and particularly so in *her* presence. This sensitiveness rendered the society of Mr. Jacob Batley (who was certain every moment to make some remark that way tending) excessively disagreeable to him; and unfortunately, as has just been stated, the said Jacob had been invited to dine with the family that very day, — a circumstance which would assuredly not have taken place, had Jack known that Mortimer would have dined with them also; or had he been aware of the character in which he was to appear for the first time in the family circle, and of the conse- quent probability of getting *him* to furnish means for the attainment of the much-desired seat in parliament, without troubling his brother on that interesting topic. As it was, and having constantly before his eyes the hope of eventually possessing the said brother's wealth, and the consequent fear of offending him, he thought the best thing he could do would be, to ask Colonel Magnus to join the party, and desire Helen to get Lady Bembridge also, on her return from shopping, to stay and dine *sans façon*, hoping by this means to prevent any dialogue between Jacob and Mor- timer, and, by rendering the conversation general, hinder- ing the former from what he called "giving Master Mortimer a touch-up as to morality."

All these arrangements were satisfactorily completed; Mortimer was separated at dinner from Jacob by Lady Bembridge and Colonel Magnus; and between Jack's volubility on one hand, and the whispering converation carried on by Helen and her lover on the other, any col- lision between that "hero of many a tale" and his future connexion was prevented. But just as Helen and Lady Bembridge were on the point of leaving the dinner-room, the worthy citizen, leaning forward so as completely to command Mortimer's attention, said, *apropos* to nothing —

" Pray, colonel, how long have you been a widower?"

The question seemed to paralyze every one; no reply being made, he continued —

" I don't ask for mere curlosity; — in course it's notping to me; — but my friend Haddock and I were talking over your affairs, and we differed as to your age; and he said ——"

. "My dear Mr. Batley," exclaimed Lady Bembridge, rising, "the moment ages become the subject of conversation, ladies run away."

This dexterous movement was instantly taken advantage of by Helen, who also made a step towards the door.

"Perhaps," said Mortimer, who turned deadly pale with anger and confusion, "perhaps, as mine appears to be the particular age about to be discussed, you will permit me to partake your flight;" saying which, and having received a gracious look from Helen, the offended Mortimer left the room in company with the retreating beauties.

"What! is he gone with the women?" said Jacob.

"'Gad!" said Magnus, "you did not expect him to stay?"

"My dear brother," said Jack, "how could you think of asking him such a question, and so abruptly, — and before Helen?"

"Question!" said Jacob: "Why, I asked him the question, because I wanted to know. As for abruptness, I don't know what you mean. I don't care who asks *me* a question, — nothing worries me."

"No, but," said Colonel Magnus, "there are so many recollections connected with his former marriage, that his feelings ——"

"Feelings!" said Jacob contemptuously, "psha! what are feelings? — the woman's dead, crying won't bring her back: and if it could, I suppose, as he's dangling after Helen, he wouldn't wish it could. I never lost a wife, — took good dare I wouldn't — never had one — too much trouble to look after."

"But, my dear brother," said Jack, "you are not aware, for I have had no opportunity of telling you, that Colonel Mortimer has proposed to Helen, and been accepted."

"Whew," whistled Jacob, "then *she*'s settled; — that accounts for his starting and staring when I asked about his widowhood. I don't care, — that's one good thing: if he is angry, he must get pleased again."

"Yes, only," said Jack, hesitatingly, "there *are* points in a man's life, to which it is not always agreeable to refer; and ——"

"Whose fault's that?" said Jacob: "the man's own;
he shouldn't have done anything to have been ashamed of;
— as for *me*, I never pity anybody; — *I* have never done
anything I care for talking about — that's *my* comfort."

"Truly it may be so," said Magnus, "but Mortimer's
case is a singular one: his youth at the time — he was, in
fact, entrapped by an artful woman considerably his senior
— in truth, a thousand circumstances of extenuation distinguish that affair from many others of a similar nature."

"I dare say they do," said Jacob, "but fact's fact: he
ran away with her, old as she was.  And as for trapping,
— I should like to see the woman that could trap *me*: —
no, colonel, no; what's right's right, what's wrong's wrong,
and wrong never comes right: that's my maxim, — no
swerve — straight path.  I never make allowances; nobody
ever would make allowances for me; that's all I know."

"I trust," said Jack, "that the results of his marriage
with Helen may agreeably disappoint you."

"*Me!*" said Jacob, — "disappoint me! — not a bit of
it.  It's all the same, as far as I am concerned: I sha'n't
trouble my head one way or the other.  I have my
opinion, but that I shall keep to myself."

"Well," said Magnus, wishing to divert the conversation, and addressing himself to Jack, "have you thought
over what I said on the subject of the borough?"

This subject was nearly as ticklish as the other.  Jack
had had no opportunity of broaching the business to his
brother, and sat upon thorns during the opening of the
topic.

"No," said he, "no: — that is to say, I have thought
it over, but I have had no opportunity — of — that is ——."

"Oh!" said Magnus, giving a significant nod, "I
understand.  My reason for asking is, that I find time
presses.  With regard to my own tenants and immediate
dependents, of course, the thing is safe, generally speaking; but when one has three or four hundred fancies to
consult, why, even if they *are* one's tenants, it is difficult
to ensure unanimity.  As for myself, as I said, I wouldn't
walk across my drawing-room to be returned: — my drawing-room! — 'gad, no, — seven-and-thirty feet is a positive

journey : — but I mean, that I wouldn't stretch out my hand to secure their ' sweet voices.' "

" What!" said Jacob, " are you talking of elections ? — Umph ! A man, what I call up to the mark, might do a deal for himself and others in the House just now. I know a point to be gained merely by being noticed ; — a regular blot to be hit, by which any calf's-head, served up with brains and tongue, would get both profit and popularity."

" Then," said Jack, " my dear brother, the opportunity offers : three thousand pounds will do the job, and the colonel will secure the return."

" Positively," said Magnus, — " as safe as if the first letter were franked."

" Indeed," said Jack, " I was going to speak to you about it, as the colonel knows."

" To *me !* " said Jacob ; — " why to *me ?* "

" Why," said Jack, " knowing the kindness you have always shown me, I thought, perhaps, you might be induced to afford me the opportunity of again sitting, and that ——"

" Psha, Jack !" said Jacob ; — " what a notion ! What in the world should you be in Parliament for ? — you are nothing of a debater. You have got your pension, and what you would say would go but for little : you might talk against time, — do the duty of a division bell : — stuff ! "

" Well," said Jack, " I certainly do not mean to press my talents or claims upon you, but it would be a great objcet with me to avail myself of my friend's offer."

" All I can say," said the Colonel, " is, that it is as snug as Sarum senior used to be ——"

" Umph !" said Jacob.

" Think of that," said Jack, elated by the considering mood into which Jacob had fallen.

" It might, to be sure," said Jacob, " be a good, thing, looking at it in one way."

" All I can say," said Jack, " is, that if you are disposed to assist me upon this occasion, it shall be the last time I ever will mention the word money to you ; and I

am sure you, my dear Magnus, will forgive me for talking
of private matters in this manner before you, at the same
time that you may serve as a witness to my declaration." —

"Three thousand pounds!" said Jacob; — "two years
of the session over."

"Yes," said Magnus; "but, understand me, — I am
prepared to guarantee ———"

"Stop, colonel, stop!" said Jacob; "this bargaining
may get us into scrapes. I take care of Number One.
Jack is my brother; but if I talk upon this matter, and if
I go further into it, we must be alone: nothing like caution. Nobody would pity me if I was clapped-up in
Newgate under the Speaker's warrant — bah! — well,
thank God! nobody will ever try to make *me* wear such a
wig as he does — no. Three thousand pounds isn't much :
— but is it all certain?"

"All plain-sailing," said Magnus. " You know, amongst
the people with whom I live, of course, a man is obliged
to be cautious, as you say, and sure of his card. I might,
perhaps, throw my influence into another scale, but I
prefer independence. Connected as I am with so many
interests, and with such a variety of duties to perform, I
wish to maintain a personal neutrality; and therefore, certainly, not wishing to make such an offer to anybody poli-
tically opposed to my party, I prefer delegating my vote to
somebody who, taking the same views as myself, can afford
from the various engagements of society — and, I may
add, health and constitution — sufficient for an adequate
exercise of his duties."

"Three thousand pounds," again repeated Jacob.

"It is not so very large a sum!" said Jack; "and under
the guarantee, as to the period of sitting ———".

"No," said Jacob, "no."

"I see," said his delighted brother, — "I see that you
like the notion. Need I say, how grateful I shall be?"

"Grateful!" said Jacob; — "what d'ye mean by grateful? —you will be grateful when you get the money —
for a week perhaps; and then, once in the seat — psha!
—there's no such thing as gratitude in the world. Nobody ever was grateful to *me;* — I suppose I never did

anything to make anybody grateful. I'm sure I never was grateful to anybody ; I don't want to be grateful. I work my way ; what I get, I earn : I don't know what gratitude means."

" But," said the colonel, " in this case, a fraternal feeling ——"

" Fraternal fiddlestick !" said Jacob. " What difference does it make to me whether Jack is *your* brother or *mine* ? — we are all brothers. Why, if I had indulged in fraternal feeling, I should have been in jail before now ; his anxiety about this very affair arises out of the question between a seat in the Commons or in the King's Bench."

" My dear Jacob !" said Jack.

" Ha, ha, ha !" said the colonel.

" Laugh, my lads !" said the merchant : — " many a true word is spoken in jest. No, — if the seat is certain for three thousand pounds, with a guarantee, the thing isn't dear."

" Why," said Magnus, " you speak of it as a regular bargain ; — now, that is by no means the case. My people are all perfectly independent, only there are certain contingencies which ——"

" Well," interrupted Jacob, " I am ready to listen to all the conditions, but not with a third person present : that's flat. I trust nobody, I will not get myself into a scrape."

" My dear Jacob," said Jack, " you are kindest of the kind ; your prudence is perfectly praiseworthy. The invalidation of the whole thing, and personal difficulty to yourself, might result from the possibility of my being called upon hereafter as evidence to the transaction."

" That's what I say, Jack," said Jacob, finishing his bumper of port, and knocking the foot of the glass upon the table.

" Well, then," said Jack, giving the colonel a signal with one of his eyes, " I will leave you two to talk the affair over. I tell you *my* feeling on the business — I know *that* of the colonel ; and whatever sacrifice you may make, in spite of your views of gratitude, I ——"

" There," interrupted Jacob, " no speeches. I never believe a word a man says when he tries to flatter ; it's all humbug!—no man means what he says. You go and look after the arrangements up-stairs; Colonel Magnus and I will discuss the other concern."

" Thank you, my dear brother!" said Jack. " Here, Magnus," (delivering the bell-rope into his custody,) " ring for wine when you want it, and make yourselves comfortable."

This delegation to the colonel was upon the principle already noticed, of mollifying the merchant by a progressive exhibition, as the doctors call it, of red port; and Jack, satisfied that between the ebriety of the dandy, and the inebriety of his respectable relative, he should in less than an hour be the member elect for Mudbury, proceeded to join his daughter and her distinguished intended.

" Well," said Jacob, as soon as his brother was out of the room, drawing his chair close to the Colonel, " now we are alone — 'gad, I think, as I said, that a good deal is to be done in the next session by a practical man. As to our colonies, and the slave emancipation, and that — I deal rather largely in that line, and know a thing or two."

" Ay," said the colonel, " you mean the apprenticing question ?"

" Yes," said Jacob — " that, you know, is all stuff — nonsense! As I say, a black is a black; and, as Lord Brougham writes, till you can make the black man white, why, you can't give him a white man's feelings — that's my view. Well, they want to emancipate these blacks — talk of humanity — what does that mean ? — why, don't you see,— call the slave ' slave,' or call him ' 'prentice,' he'll still be black; and, as Brougham says, (I always stick to him,) ' if he isn't whipped he won't work.' Well, now, they want to set these fellows free — good ; — we say no ; but if they will, why, we ask twenty millions of money — a goodish lump out of a poor country — not to change the nature of the cretur — not to make him white — not to turn his wool into hair — not to stop flogging him, — but to call him a ' 'prentice,' and not to flog him unless his flogging is permitted by a justice, who is to be paid for seeing how the flogging is done. Now, my idea is, that although this thing mayn't be carried for four or five years, still a man with a notion of what's what, — might make a hit in the House, and ——"

" —— Benefit the cause of philanthropy."

" Philanthropy ! fiddlestick ! not a bit of it ; — do good to himself."

" Very probably," said the colonel ; " but, my dear sir, do you think that Mr. Batley has considered the subject sufficiently — quite out of his line — to secure that advantage to himself or the cause ? "

" Mr. Batley, said Jacob, filling his glass, " is up to every bit of it — has all the Aldermanbury secrets at his command, and can show up the whole system, ay, to the very bottom."

" I had no idea that he——"

" He !" said Jacob, looking intently at the colonel, " who d'ye mean by *he* ?   I never talk of he's or she's,— I am speaking of myself."

" Oh !" said Magnus, " but I understood that our worthy host was to be the person to represent Mudbury, under our patronage."

" Patronage !" said Jacob, " I never patronise anybody, nor anything — why should I ?   Who ever patronised me ? Nonsense !   You tell us of an opening at the House of Commons : of what use would Jack be ? — none.   All he says is gabble gabble gabble — stuff ! — very fine in diplomacy, — bows, and smiles, and all that, — but no weight in parliament.   All his cherry-clappery rattle, with a pension in his pouch, will go no way there, compared with what I may think fit to say upon subjects with which I am perfectly conversant, having a hundred and fifty thousand pounds in my pocket into the bargain."

" You, sir ! " said the colonel.

" I, sir ! " said Jacob ; " I speak for myself — whom else should I speak for ?   You tell me, as I have just said, that there is a seat in the House of Commons which you can command : well, I should like to sit in the House of Commons, — especially for a borough which returns only one — have it all to myself — no partnership, no colleague, no bother — I, all alone.   Well, you offer it to Jack ; of

what use can it be to *him* ? and if it is, what do I care ?
he never would put himself out of his way for *me*. We
are alone — I know the world — he wants me to give him
three thousand pounds to put him into parliament ; I
want to be in parliament myself : now, if that can be done,
I'll make the three thousand, four ; and — pass the wine,
colonel — that will cover all contingencies."

Colonel Magnus stared with astonishment at his companion.  He was prepared to admit all his failings and all
his selfishness, still the present exhibition far exceeded his
most sanguine anticipations.  But this selfishness, hateful
as it appeared even to Magnus, came qualified through that
" golden mean," which gives, like the less valuable tint of
jealousy, a colour to every thing it falls upon : — the words
" make the three thousand, four, to cover all contingencies," rang in the ears of the colonel so loudly, as to drive
out everything that had preceded them ; and all he said
at the moment was —

" Then you would like to sit, yourself ? "

" To be sure," said Jacob, " who else ?  Why, there are
half a dozen whipper-snappering shopkeepers in parliament
— paupers — beggars, — who flourish about, and frank, and
look fine, and do jobs.  Why should'nt I, who care for no
man — with a business better than the Bank itself, — why
shouldn't I sit there too ?  If you choose, therefore, I'm
your man, and four thousand the sum ; — only, no bother
— no contest — no rotten eggs and poll-cats — understand
that.  Reform has done wonders — makes the thing easy
when it *is* 'snug.  I stand no nonsense.  If I thought my
little finger was to be jammed against a post, I wouldn't
stir."

" Rely upon it, there will be no opposition :- I only wish
Mudbury sent two members instead of one, so certain is
my interest."

" If it did," said Jacob, " I wouldn't have it.  I hate
community of interests : — never had a partner — never
had a wife — and hang me if I believe I ever had a
friend."

" Then," said Magnus, who with equal magnanimity
threw over his dear friend Jack in consideration of the

additional thousand pounds, " I am to consider what you propose final as to this."

" Done and done," said Jacob ; " that I believe is what you say at Newmarket; it is what we say when we bet hats in the city; and whenever and wherever to-morrow you like to settle definitively, I'm your man, and the stumpy down, upon the prescribed conditions."

" I will call on you at your counting-house," said the colonel.

" Do," said Jacob, " that's business-like ; — but how are you to find out Lillypot Lane ? "

" Leave me alone," said the colonel: " I know London pretty well : — so, now, shall we go to the ladies ? "

" *You* may, colonel," said Jacob, " but not I. I think I am rather in disgrace with your friend Mortimer. I suppose the wound will heal — no matter whether it does or not: — however, I shan't try to-night. Give me another glass of port, and I will toddle homewards, and, if I am not too late, perhaps get one glass of hot punch and a cigar at ' The Horn.' "

" The what ? " said Magnus.

" ' The Horn,' in Doctors' Commons."

" A most ominous sign for that particular neighbourhood," said Magnus.

" And a capital place for a chop and a bottle of blackstrap," said Jacob. " You fine gentlemen don't know half the good places in this world."

" Well," said Magnus, " if you are really going, I think I shall retire also. I have no carriage here, and, if you have no objection, I will walk with you. I am going to Crocky's for my whist, — sober and sedate."

" Ah ! " said Jacob, " as it's dark, you don't mind taking my arm — eh ! Never mind, colonel, the member for Mudbury may be better worthy notice ; — not that I mind ; —let every tub stand on its own bottom ; and, you mark *me*, if I sit in *that* house till I grow to the benches, I'll never pair off: no community for me. Come along."

And thus did these two worthy gentlemen quit the house : the affectionate solicitude of his brother (for himself) being almost equalled by the colonel's philosophical

E

abandonment, for the sake of one additional thousand, of his dear friend and Amphitryon.

*Ainsi va le monde,* as Jacob would have said if he had spoken French.

---

## CHAPTER IV.

Iᴛ was perhaps fortunate for the tranquillity of the Batley family, that uncle Jacob had effected his retreat from Gros- venor Street without exhibiting his comely person in the drawing-room. Certain it was that the colonel was bitterly offended by the question he had put at the dinner-table ; indeed, he had taken an opportunity, soon after Mr. John Batley joined the ladies, of drawing him aside, and com- plaining of his brother's want of feeling.

" The circumstances," said Mortimer, " connected with that marriage, and the death of my poor Amelia, are of a nature not to be alluded to without wringing my heart to its very core.   Heaven knows that, if repentance and self- reproach can atone for vice and folly, my sufferings must have gone far to wash out the stain that fell upon my earlier life.   A reference to it drives me almost mad ; and when made in a tone such as that adopted by your brother, the feeling is still stronger.   Do, pray, put him on his guard, and explain to him that the occurrences of my youth- ful days are interdicted subjects in my presence."

" It is wonderful," said Batley, " how impracticable he is.   He has no intention to offend, but he has no feeling by which he can appreciate the feelings of other people, and I fear he is now too old to mend."

" Only save me from the recurrence of such a thing," said Mortimer ; " and, above all, beg him not to notice what occurred to-night in the way of apology, if he should express any wish that way ; let it be forgotten."

" I'll manage him, rely upon it," said Batley.

" Batley," said the colonel, after having looked at him earnestly for half a minute ; " do you think — do you know — whether Helen is acquainted with that affair ? "

Batley knew that she was to a certain extent, as indeed it seemed impossible she should not be, inasmuch as her curiosity (interest is perhaps a better word) naturally had led her to inquire who Mortimer's former wife was ; and, moreover, she, like many other young ladies, was not unfrequently in the habit of consulting that important book of fate " The Peerage ;" and there, as we have already heard, she *had* seen recorded the divorce of Lady Hillingdon, and her subsequent marriage to Mortimer : but Batley, who wished to prove Helen infinitely more innocent and ignorant touching that affair than Helen really was, expressed considerable doubt whether she knew anything at all about it.

A smile which curled upon Mortimer's lip sufficiently expressed his incredulity upon that point, as he said with impressive earnestness, " She ought to know the history — she ought not to marry such a man as I *have* been without a knowledge of his early faults."

This puzzled Batley : it seemed as if Mortimer himself felt that a girl of delicacy of mind and purity of heart might feel a repugnance in uniting herself with such a man. If this should be started, and if Helen should be frightened into refusing to complete her engagement upon that ground, everything would be lost, the match broken off, and Helen, in all probability, doomed to a continued state of single unblessedness.

Batley was beaten by his own ingenuity ; and all that Mortimer could extract from him was, a sort of equivocal stammering of, " Why, I — really I — upon my word, I," in which he dealt for about a minute — time sufficient to assure the colonel that Helen did know the whole history, and did not see in it any ground for objection.

" Come," said Mortimer, " Helen *does* know the story — I hope she does — my heart will then be at rest : tell her it myself I cannot ; but if she is already informed of it, there ends one of my great difficulties, — for, Batley, bad as I may have been, I could not now find it in my heart to mislead such a girl as your daughter, even upon the most trifling point."

" Why then," said the sensitive parent, " I will ho-

nestly tell you that I believe she does know the leading
facts of the case; indeed, you may rely upon it, the very .
cause of this conversation, my tough-skinned brother,
would take care she should not die uninformed of them."

" Heaven defend me from *him!* " said Mortimer,
" though he *is* your brother. It seems quite extraordinary
that Nature can form men of such opposite characters and
temperaments as we see every day. Mr. Jacob Batley
would discuss for an hour, without flinching, a subject the
slightest allusion to which would throw me into agonies."

" A rough diamond," said John.

" Which, as far as I am concerned," said Mortimer,
" requires cutting."

" I don't mean to press him upon you, I assure you;
but there is good in him."

" Of that I have no doubt," said the colonel; " and
it seems but reasonable there should be, for, as far as my
experience goes, very little comes out of him. No: I know
you are too much a man of the world to be offended
about it; but I must beg, — at least when Helen is present, — that he may not be of our parties. You have no
idea of the misery in which I live during his presence:
I feel like a fellow on the tight-rope expecting every
minute a rude push from the clown which is to topple him
over."

" I assure you," said Batley, who would willingly have
sacrificed fifty vulgar brothers, if he had had them, on the
shrine of the elegant colonel whom he worshipped, " it
shall not occur again. Indeed, to be candid with you," —
and when Batley *was* candid, his ingenuousness was quite
overwhelming, — " he would not have dined here to-day if
I had anticipated the pleasure of your company, nor if I
had not had a point to carry very near my heart."

" And what may that be? " said Mortimer.

Now came the moment. Mortimer had made the ex-
pulsion of Jacob a sort of condition in the treaty of alliance
between them: Jacob's assistance to further the parliamentary scheme was therefore not to be gained by any more
of that hospitable conduct which his brother was in the
habit of observing towards him whenever he happened to

require his aid ; and, consequently, Mr. Batley, jun.
thought he might most seasonably sound his intended son-
in-law as to *his* disposition with regard to the three
thousand pounds required for the seat. If, thought Jack,
he hates my brother so much as to exile him from my
house, he must be aware that I cannot expect him to assist me in the enterprise against the worthy people of Mudbury ; and, as money is no object with *him*, he will not
hesitate to secure himself against the intrusion of a person
whom he so much dislikes by an outlay of this sort, which,
while it guarantees peace to himself, gives him the additional gratification of serving *me*.

" Why," said Batley, having screwed his ' courage to
the sticking-place,' " the fact is, I am anxious to be in
parliament again ; — and — perhaps you are aware our
friend Magnus has the power of meeting my wishes."

· " I know," said Mortimer, " that Magnus, who is, as
the phrase goes, ' hard-up,' is hawking about a Wiltshire
borough, which he believes he can command, but I do
*not :* besides, you don't mean to pay for coming in, I
presume ? "

" Why," said Batley, " I did think of it. Since the
Reform Bill has passed, I see no other chance except
standing a contest in one of the large boroughs, which I
am not up to ; as for counties, they are out of the question : and so I naturally directed my views towards my
brother. Now as I know by experience that nothing but
the soothing system is likely to succeed with him, I had
begun a series of invitations to win him over ; and, in
fact, the one which he accepted to-day has had some effect,
for I got him to talk upon the subject with the colonel, and
left them discussing it when I came up-stairs."

" I think," said Mortimer, " you could lay out your
money more wisely ; or, more wisely still, not lay it out
at all. All I can say is, if a seat in parliament were an
object with me, by the process you propose to adopt, I
should give it up in despair. — Come, let us join the
ladies."

This *cut-short* did not quite please Batley, who found
that, however liberal or noble a man's sentiments may be,

the moment the word money is mentioned, he sinks to the common level of humanity. Jack congratulated himself that he had not gone the length of asking Mortimer's assistance, which, it was clear, he would not have afforded; and he fell back upon Jacob as his only hope.

Mortimer left his future father-in-law somewhat abruptly, and returned to the front drawing-room, where Helen and Lady Bembridge were still *tête-à-tête ;* but his manner was subdued, the smile which had played so agreeably on his mouth had vanished, and a cloud seemed to hang on his brow. He had decided, — and the beaming, blushing Helen was his own : — but, could he see her without a recollection of the past ? — could he forget those passages of his life of the details of which he devoutly hoped she was ignorant ? No : — let the man of the world be ever so hardened — let him fancy himself callous to the appeals of feeling or conscience — his courage fails him when his looks rest upon confiding innocence like Helen's. He was wretched in the midst of happiness, and gazed upon his treasure, as her father justly called her, with a feeling of doubt and distrust. " When she knows me, she will despise me," said to himself this wealthy, worldly man : his love for her, devoted as it was, was devoid of that singleness of heart so essential to earthly happiness. The besetting evil of his life was mistrust, not only in himself, but others. He had himself triumphed over the confidence of a fond husband — he had been wooed and won by a fair creature, strange to say, not unlike Helen personally ; and as he sat, abstracted and away from her, gazing on her bright eyes, her snow-white forehead, and her jetty curls, — instead of contemplating the bright vision with delight, a deep-fetched sigh from his inmost heart was mingled with the thought that such had once been his loved — his lost Amelia !

The associations which lead men to certain actions are unaccountable, their effects extraordinary, and sometimes absurd. In this case most certain is it, that the sympathy which first attracted Mortimer to Helen *was* her resemblance to the unhappy Lady Hillingdon, his former wife. And yet, if the likeness could have led to any conclusion, it might have reminded him of her misconduct and miser-able fate. And so in point of fact it did. Whilst he sat that very evening, contemplating her beauty,—he pictured to himself the perils of her future life; married to a man much older than herself, and consequently more exposed to the arts of flatterers, who, like the Mortimer of other days, would no doubt be found in her train, pursuing the course which he had followed, even before she was born.

" No," said Mortimer to himself, " she must live great part of the year at Sadgrove; there, her influence will be truly beneficial to me; there, in a quiet retreat from the giddy world, she will exert a genial influence over our neighbourhood; benevolence and charity will be the lead-ing attributes of her character; and there, she will eter-nally bind my affections, draw me from this idle town, make me happy here, and," added he, with a sigh of mis-trust, " hereafter."

All this, reasonable as it might be, was not what was to be expected from an ardent lover. Nor *was* Mortimer ardent, however devoted he might be. Helen saw that he was not at ease,—not happy as she would have wished to see him; and of course, as perfectly unacquainted with what had recently passed between him and her father, as with that which was passing in his mind at the moment; she quitted Lady Bembridge, and, throwing down some absurd sort of work upon which she fancied she was em-ploying herself, crossed the room, and, seating herself be-side him, said—

" Dear Francis, what *is* the matter?—you look ill,—you look melancholy,—nay, you look cross; frowns do not become you."

Mortimer smiled, and took her hand. It was the first time she had called him Francis; it was the first time she had ventured to discuss the character of his countenance, or give an opinion as to what became it, or what did not. The smile was one of doubtful import,—the pressure of the hand was tremulous.

" I will smile, Helen, if you wish it."

" Not if you are not in a smiling humour," said Helen;

" I hate anything that is not natural, — as my thoughts are, so are my looks, — my face is, I am sure, the index of my mind, — I couldn't smile if I were not pleased. And yet I have seen women in parties look as lively as I do now, while their hearts were breaking."

" Why really," said Lady Bembridge, " if a woman have any grief rankling in her bosom, it is a difficult task to gild the countenance with a mirthful expression."

" And what," said Mortimer, " made you think the hearts of those laughing ladies were breaking, Helen?"

" Oh !" said Helen, " because I knew their little private histories, and have seen all through their conduct ; — nay, I have heard a husband in a crowded room speak as rudely, and nearly as loudly, to his wife, as he would have done with the same disposition if they had been alone, — and I have seen the patient beauty, pale with fear at the violence of her lord and master, her cheek pale as a lily, and her lips blanched with fear, force an expression into her countenance, not only placid, but gay, when spoken to by another unconscious person at the same moment. I have wondered as I watched, and loved her for hiding from the world the harshness of the man whose ill-humour she would not betray."

" Well then," said Mortimer, half whisperingly, " if we ever *do* quarrel in public, you will, I hope, emulate the example you extol."

" Quarrel !" said Helen, gazing on his fine countenance, " what *should* we quarrel about ?"

" I am sure I don't know," said Mortimer ; " I am only providing against the most unpleasant contingencies."

" No," said Helen, " let us go into the country, — let us leave this noisy town, — I am getting heartily tired of it : — *I am*, Francis," — this last asseveration was caused by a sort of incredulous shake of Francis's head,—" all I ask is peace and quiet, and the society of those I love."

" I think," said Mortimer, " you will like Sadgrove, — it is a nice place. It wants the addition of a few more rooms, which we will give it, Helen. The Severn runs its silvery stream at the foot of the knoll on which the house stands ; and I assure you, though not very extensive, the park is as prettily thrown about, and as richly wooded, as the best landscape gardener in the world could desire."

" I am sure I shall like it," said Helen : — " *you* like it ?"

" Yes, I used to delight in it."

" When were you there last, Francis ? "

" Last l" said Mortimer,—and his countenance resumed the expression which the conversation of the last few minutes had in a measure dispelled, — " last ! — I haven't been there much lately, — I — that is — not for four or five years."

" It is a delightful neighbourhood."

" A remarkably fine country."

" Ay !" said Helen, " but I mean a delightful neighbourhood. I have a cousin living not twenty miles from Sadgrove, and he says nothing can be more sociable."

Mortimer made no answer. When *he* lived at Sadgrove with Amelia, Sadgrove was a desert. This fact never occurred to him when he looked forward to the solitude of Sadgrove as a delightful passage of his future life, in which, like another Adam, he might enjoy his paradise with one sole companion : — the expression " delightful neighbourhood" brought to his sensitive mind an entirely new picture of his former retirement. Neighbourhood, — what did it mean ? When he lived there, the gates of Sadgrove Park rusted on their hinges, and the grass grew on the sills of the lodges ; it was then indeed a retirement, and he still looked to it as one ; nor till this moment had he anticipated any difficulty in reconciling a young creature, who possessed a desire for the pleasures of the country and the enjoyments of rural life, to a seclusion which is the lot of those who, by the gratification of some unholy passion, purchase a perpetuity of solitude, even in the midst of the multitude.

Helen's abstract notion of a country life (having been on visits with her parent to various country houses) was, the transference of London into the country. A greater ease, and more perfect sociability, rendered her happier when away from the trammels of town society ; but, of the enjoyments to which Mortimer looked forward, — the quiet stroll by moonlight ; the *tête-à-tête* in which the husband

was to read while the wife was to draw; or the morning
during which the husband was to shoot and the wife to do
what she could to amuse herself; the visits to cottages;
the inquiries after sick old women; the superintendence of
infant schools, and "all such," she had no idea. The
windows of a drawing-room looking over the Vale of Llan-
gollen or the rails of Grosvenor Square, were still the windows of a drawing-room; and a boudoir well muslined up,
whether it were blinded from the glare of Park Lane, or
sheltered from the bright sun beaming on the wide sea, was
still a boudoir; and, therefore, Helen's idea of a charming
country was, where she might do exactly as she did in
London, only in a purer atmosphere, for a certain part of
the year: and it was for this reason that she was glad to
get away from a routine of society of which towards the
end of the season she grew tired, to that which, as she felt,
she might in her new capacity choose for herself.

Old Flint, in "The Maid of Bath," when endeavouring
to win the consent of Miss Linnett to their marriage, asks
the young lady if she is fond of the country, "because I
think it is the most prettiest place for your true lovers to
live in — something so rural. For my part, I can't see
what pleasure pretty misses can take in galloping to plays
and to balls, and such expensive vagaries; there is ten times
more pastime in fetching walks in the fields and plucking
the daisies. All pastime and jollity there! for what with
minding the dairy, dunning the tenants, preserving and
pickling, nursing the children, scolding the servants, mend-
ing and making, roasting, boiling, and baking, you will be
merry and happy as the days they are long."

Now, although most assuredly no two animals of the same
species could be so different in genus as Flint and the elegant Colonel Mortimer, the inducements which the graceful
roué was holding out to Helen, as to Sadgrove, were, with
all her professed love of rurality, not much more congenial
with her taste than those which Foote's admirable miser
suggested to the celebrated maid of Bath.

Mortimer's thoughts had been driven into a new channel,
and in a moment a new prospect opened to his view. This
vaunted retirement of Sadgrove — what would it be? —

in fact, no retirement at all. Sadgrove was no fitting theatre whereupon to enact the drama of his reformed life : within a few miles of Worcester, one of the gayest cities in the empire ; in the midst of thickly-studded country houses, with Malvern at hand, and a thousand rural gaieties sur-rounding, his system of seclusion was little likely to be car-ried into effect.

" What then ? " thought he. " Helen has gone the round of London society for three or four seasons ; if she still retain her taste for the amusements incidental to a country life, why should she not enjoy them ? To *me* the very difference of our position at Sadgrove to that in which I was placed during my last residence there, will so far alter the character of the place, that the recollections which I so much dread will perhaps not haunt me. Helen is right ; we *will* be gay, — we will receive and entertain ; and whenever we get tired of visitors and wish to fall back upon our own resources, we can." These anticipations, first inspired by Helen's artless observation, cheered him, and his face resumed that expression the absence of which Helen had lamented to perceive.

It is not necessary, in the present stage of Mortimer's association with Helen, to detail the various conversations in which they indulged with regard to their future plans. Mortimer soon ascertained the extent of her admiration of the country ; and upon the principle which suggested itself on the first evening upon which she had expressed her opi-nions, he resolved to make Sadgrove, in spite of its lugu-brions name, everything that was cheerful.

The time " progressed," as our Trans-Atlantic friends have it. The marriage of Mortimer and Miss Batley was the talk of the world ; and paragraphs anticipatory of the splendour of the *trousseau,* and other matters connected with so distinguished a union, filled the newspapers. Batley himself seemed to " ride on a whirlwind," and if he did not " direct the storm," anybody, to have seen him, sparkling and chattering in the highest spirits, would have imagined that he himself was on the eve of marrying an heiress.

Meanwhile Jacob, excluded by command of Mortimer,

and therefore decidedly affronted, pulled up haughtily, and declared that he never would set foot in Jack's house as long as he lived : and it unfortunately having occurred that his volatile brother was obliged to give him the hint to ah-stain, the very morning after his *tête-à-tête* with Colonel Magnus, Jacob, lest his return for Mudbury should be of use to that gentleman, wrote to cry " off," merely because Jack, in pressing upon him his own anxiety to sit, happened to repeat Mortimer's statement with regard to the colonel's affairs.    Hence, in order not to relieve the embarrassments of any man who was a friend of Mortimer's, arose the re-linquishment of his personal object ; and hence, of course, resulted his refusal to advance one farthing to aid the views of poor Jack.

It must be evident that the younger Batley, powerfully acted upon by Mortimer's expressed desire, that the bear should not come to his steak in Grosvenor Street, had sealed his own fate, and that of Helen's, as far as regarded the worthy of Lillypot Lane, by making him understand how desirable for the present his absence was.    It is true that Jack softened down the harshness of the suggestion, by throwing out hints as to the love of retirement so much de-sired by two persons on the eve of marriage, and the em-barrassment which they felt in the presence of strangers, the various matters they had to consult about, and con-cluded his " warn off," by assuring him that the exclusion was not personal to him, but that there would be no visitors admitted until the wedding took place.

" You are quite right, sir," said Jacob ;—" a brother is seldom considered a stranger, — but no matter, — the day will come, — when you, and the fine young lady whom you have taught to despise me, because you want her to marry a rake without principle, may be down on your mar-rowbones at my feet : — wait till that day comes, and then you will hear me say, ' When you were gay and great, as you thought, you drove me from your door — it's my turn now :' and, mark you, *brother*, don't call me hard-hearted if I do ; for if the thing happens, do it I will."    And so went Jacob his way, his brother not quite unmoved at the last appeal : — nay, Jack, although neither awed nor acted upon by Jacob's threat in case of a contingency which he was confident never could occur, felt a pang at what had happened, and an anxiety to appease him : " but it would be of no use," said Jack, " it might only irritate him the more ; it were best to let him take his course."

It might have been better not, — but *that* time will show.

Now it was that Jack's anxiety to secure Mudbury raged with double ardour. — Mortimer could not be applied to ; the repulse he had met with settled that question ; and any recurrence to the subject would probably alarm the nice feelings of his proposed son-in-law. Was there no other channel ? The vacancy would be declared in ten days, and that was but a limited period in which to make arrangements : for, as Jacob had truly said, " John Batley had been in the money market before," and the advantageous marriage of his daughter seemed to him not unlikely to add to his facilities in again applying to his friends, who had, for considerations equivalent thereunto, previously afforded him that aid his nearest relation had denied.

About this period in our history, the happy day was fixed for the nuptials : every preparation was making to render Sadgrove worthy the presence of its future mistress : the settlements were drawn ; and the fair Helen, with eight hundred pounds per annum as pin-money, and a jointure of two thousand five hundred a year, was accordingly congratulated by her elderly female friends, and proportionably envied by her young ones. Mortimer's kindness and attention were of the tenderest character : the prospect of his future happiness had driven away the gloomy reminiscences which, until his heart had been again engaged, had distracted his mind. He was an altered man ; the thought that he was loved, really and sincerely loved, raised him in his own estimation ; and if happiness be attained in this lower world, Mortimer may be said to have been, at the present juncture, happy.

The state of nervousness in which Batley existed during this trying period cannot be described ; his life was, as has already been stated, one continual flurry : but little was either he, or Magnus, prepared for the course which brother Jacob thought proper to pursue. Suffice it to say, that within six days of the declaration of the vacancy at Mudbury, Colonel Magnus informed Jack that his impracticable brother had gone down to the borough, *and was canvassing for himself.* The name of the rich Batley worked wonders ; and it became pretty evident to Magnus, by the letters which he received, that Jacob's straightforward principle of buying the votes for himself, instead of trusting to the gallant officer's agency, was likely to take Mudbury out of his delicate hands.

The instant diplomatic John had, in all the confidence of fraternal affection, permitted Jacob to understand that Magnus was in the first instance to buy, while in the second he was to sell, Jacob said to himself, — if that be the position of affairs, it is quite clear — tenants of the colonel's or not — I may as well outbid him in the market at first hand, as give him a premium for his agency. The colonel wrote strong letters of remonstrance to his dear friends at Mudbury, and declared his intention of bringing down a gentleman of weight, consequence, and notoriety, to contest the borough against any other candidate. But the independent reformers knew their man : they knew that the colonel's influence was what they called " moony," produced only by reflected light ; that, in fact, whatever his nominal extent of property in the neighbourhood might be, he had no solid claims upon them ; and therefore, with long leases in their possession, they prudently resolved, in order to support the purity of election, to rebel against what might be supposed an undue influence, and pocket the cash of Jacob Batley, of whom they had never before heard, in order to evince that independence, which is at once a characteristic of the party to which they adhered, and so illustrative of that glorious march of intellect in which the British empire rejoices.

## CHAPTER V.

IT becomes necessary, for the better understanding of our history, that the reader should now be introduced to a personage, of whom as yet no mention has been made, but whose character and conduct may perhaps deserve more of his commendation than the attributes of certain others of the family party would be likely to command.

Mrs. Farnham was the sister of Colonel Mortimer; she had married young, and for love, but neither imprudently nor without the approbation of her parents. Her husband was sufficiently wealthy to afford her all the comforts, without any of the glare, of society, by which so many young and lively women are fascinated, but which had no charms for Emily Mortimer. Her career as a wife was a happy one; but, in less than six years after her union with Mr. Farnham, she became a widow, and had never since returned to England. In the society of an early attached female friend, who, like herself, had lost an affectionate husband, she seemed resolved to pass the remainder of her days on the Continent; and although childless, the two daughters of her companion had so much engaged her affections, that they appeared to constitute one family of love.

When Mortimer's affair with Lady Hillingdon became matter of notoriety, his sister was absent from England; and, after the death of her husband, and that of the unfortunate partner of her brother's criminality, Mortimer paid his sister a visit. Then it was he earnestly entreated her to come to England with her friend and her children, and make Sadgrove a home, not only for herself and them, but for him: but Emily strenuously refused. She, though nearly and dearly connected with him, could not bring herself to make those allowances for his conduct which his more worldly friends were ready to concede; and his stay at Florence was not rendered sufficiently agreeable to induce him to protract it. He quitted her only to seek, in scenes less beneficial to his mind and morals, an oblivion which he sought in vain; and, when he returned to Eng-

land, worn out with hoping for tranquillity, his eyes fell
upon the beautiful Helen, and, as we have seen, he devoted
himself to the attainment of happiness by a union with
youth and innocence.

It was now his great object to induce his sister to come
to England, to grace this second marriage with her countenance; and he accordingly renewed his entreaties that
she would quit Naples (whither she had removed), and
greet his lovely Helen as a sister.

" My dear Francis," wrote Mrs. Farnham in answer,
" forgive me for adhering to my determination to remain
here until my excellent friend thinks it necessary to take
her daughters finally to England. . The climate agrees
with me—I delight in the brightness of an Italian sky—
you know how warmly I enter into all matters of art and
*virtù*, and how ample the resources here are for the gratification of a taste which I could no where else so well cultivate.

" If I could imagine that my presence would increase
the chance of your future happiness, or give pleasure to
your bride, I would gladly make any sacrifice to do as you
wish; but, really and truly, I have grown so unworldly,
and know so little of English manners of the present day,
that I think my society would rather *gêne* you than be
agreeable; and as to my remaining with you permanently,
I am convinced, by experience acquired from looking at
the domestic circles of others, that there must be no divided
power in a family, and that the intervention of a mother,
or a sister, in the dominion which ought to belong to the
wife as mistress of her house, is invariably destructive of
domestic happiness. Your picture of the future is delightful; —God send the reality may be equally so! It has
been for years the wish of my heart to see you reclaimed
from-irregularities, which have been induced rather by a
readiness to give in to the indiscretions of others than by
any disposition of your own. The opportunity seems now
to present itself, and I fervently hope you will avail yourself of it, and become all I ever wished you to be.

" Ten years' difference in our ages, Francis, permits me
to write gravely; and upon one point I write most earnestly.

If Miss Batley be the person you represent her, leave her none of your earlier failings to find out, — be candid and honest with her in painting the indiscretions of your youth. So may you expect candour from *her*. Trust a woman by halves, and you make her doubtful, suspicious, restless, and jealous; tell her all, and she becomes your friend, your confidential friend, whose faith no temptation will break.

" If you should bend your steps hither, I shall be delighted to greet you, and to prove to your wife how cordially I rejoice in calling her sister. Do not, therefore, imagine that my disinclination to do all you wish, arises from any cause but a dislike to returning to England at present. You are fond of Italy — why not come? You will move here as stars of the first magnitude; and we can make up a little agreeable society which will delight your Helen. Present my warmest congratulations and good wishes to her, and press my invitation with all your wonted eloquence."

More, much more, did Mrs. Farnham write to her brother, which he read with his usual distrust. " No, no," said he to himself, " she has no objection to come to England. The objection she has to being present at my marriage arises from her sensitive delicacy, and the recollection of how I was situated when I last knelt before that altar. Her motives are evident to me through the thin veil with which she tries to cover them. She foresees unhappiness in my marriage — at least, she doubts when she speaks of my future comfort, and hopes that my prospects may not be illusory. I am not good enough to be honoured with her countenance — well! — I could have wished it otherwise — but no matter — so be it."

Mortimer, conscious how obnoxious his character was to censure from those who knew his history, was seriously annoyed by Mrs. Farnham's letter; and such, with all his experience of the world, was his sensitiveness, that he was unable to rally for hours, from any sudden shock to his feelings. He had made up his mind to having his sister present at his marriage; he had spoken of her coming to Helen with something like certainty, and had delayed the ceremony expressly for the purpose. He fancied that her

F

refusal, couched even as it was in the kindest terms, would lower him in the esteem of his future wife.

This disappointment to his hopes preyed upon him so much as to produce a serious illness,—not unfrequently the result of those dreadful struggles which it required to stem the violence of his temper ; and when, after the lapse of five or six days, he was restored to the society of his betrothed, there hung about him a gloom which even Helen herself thought inappropriate to the event so near at hand.

While this was passing, Mr. Jacob Batley was labouring in his agreeable task, not only of frustrating his brother's hopes as to Mudbury, but in that of undermining the interest of the gallant colonel himself. Sharp, shrewd, and active, he had no sooner renounced all connection with Colonel Magnus, whose name, like that of his friend, had been not unfrequently in the money market, than he proceeded to the London banking-house in correspondence with the Mudbury bank ; and, being on terms of intimacy with one of the partners, commenced a series of inquiries touching the real value of the colonel's influence, and what sort of people he might have to deal with. The result of which conversation was, a resolution to proceed direct to the scene of action, first sending down what is termed a good electioneering attorney, as his agent, to examine the ground ; and, in order to make a favourable impression in advance, he paid a considerable sum into the London house on account of their provincial clients, without giving any reason for so doing : well convinced that the tacit lodgement of a thousand pounds more than he had proposed to " stump," as he called it, to the colonel, would make a sensation in the place — where it was sure to be spoken of — not calculated to damage his interests when he announced himself, as a free and independent candidate come to rescue them from tyranny, oppression, and slavery.

To further this design, the lawyer whom he had engaged was one whose activity and sharpness were proverbial in the particular line of business for which Jacob had retained him ; and, as in love, horse-dealing, and electioneering, it is held that " all is fair," Mr. Brimmer Brassey, of Barnard's Inn, was considered one of the most desirable acquisitions for a candidate in a contest that could be made.

Mr. John Batley's efforts to procure the means of introduction to the " free and independent " vassals of Colonel Magnus were by no means successful, and the day drew near when it was absolutely necessary for him to give a definite answer to the *soi-disant* patron. The reply, however, became infinitely less important to the colonel, when his agent at Mudbury wrote him word that a gentleman of the name of Brassey was actively canvassing for a candidate to be proposed whenever the vacancy should be declared, whose "appliances and means" were such as already to have prejudiced a decided majority of the electors in favour of the " great unknown."

However disagreeable this intelligence was to the colonel, it was by no means a surprise ; the fact being, that the influence which he proposed to sell he must first have bought ; his personal weight in the borough ensuring him, under the provisions of the Reform Bill, nothing more than a priority of purchase. The sound straightforward sense of Jacob Batley hit this point in a moment, and before he had walked half-way down Davies Street with the colonel, on the night of the bargain, his sharp business-like mind had worked itself through the sophistry of Magnus, and by the time he reached " The Horn," he had come to the conclusion that the Mudburyites were a disposable herd, and that he might as well buy the flock himself as employ a salesman. To it he went, delighted, to beat his brother, who had sacrificed his fraternal affection to his zeal for his daughter's interests, and to jockey the colonel, who was the friend of the man upon whose suggestion his brother had so acted.

Brimmer Brassey was a stirring person, and likely to make himself and his principal popular amongst the Radicals. He was always over-smartly dressed ; his countenance was florid, edged with much black whisker ; he wore his hat — a silk hat — on one side of his head ; a coloured handkerchief round his neck ; a chain, questionable as to metal, by way of guard to an equivocal watch, over a velvet waistcoat. He was well able to drink punch;

weak or strong, hot or cold, as the case might be, at any
time, and in any quantity ; smoked cigars if desired, and
went the whole length of pipes if necessary ; was upon intimate terms with several of the actors of the minor
theatres ; sang songs which were not in print ; told anecdotes which astonished the natives ; had a friend who
benevolently lent money to anybody, upon the least imaginable security ; and in fact was the most accommodating
person in his peculiar line of the profession to which he
did not do too much honour.   At Mudbury, he was all in
all ; the way he talked — the way he sang — the way he
dressed — the way he drank — and the way he paid —
were the theme of universal admiration ; and, if the mere
representative of the coming candidate did all this, what
would the candidate himself do when he became the representative of them all ?

When Magnus read his agent's account of this unexpected invasion of an enemy, and the evident defection of
his friends, he was, as may be imagined, a little " put
out."   Who the stranger was, he had not yet discovered ;
but he was not long in obtaining information ; and the
reader may pretty well ascertain, not only the feelings of
the still dangling John Batley, who could not leave nibbling
at the bait, though he felt he had not strength to bite, but
of the colonel himself, when he found that John's brother,
having taken advantage of a knowledge of the *carte du pays*
extracted from, rather than afforded by him, had, having
well-paved his way, been announced as a candidate whenever the vacancy was declared.

Magnus would have made it a personal matter with anybody else, and have called out the man ; but, besides not
wishing to have any such affair with such a person, he felt
assured that the opening letter of a correspondence, that way
tending, would have been legally and technically replied to
by Mr. Brimmer Brassey, whose name had become painfully
familiar to his ears through the communications of his now
desponding emissaries at Mudbury.

To describe our volatile friend John Batley's feelings,
when he heard the name of the probably successful candidate, would be difficult.   Not only was he agitated and ex-

cited by finding Jacob thus pointedly opposed to him, but
because he felt assured, that this decided declaration of hos-
tilities was occasioned by his having, at Mortimer's desire,
" shut his doors" upon him. All the hopes of his life were
exploded; and, in the present practical manifestation, he
beheld the annihilation of the expectancy upon the ulterior
realization of which he had been for the last twelve years
living. Still Helen was settled — the great care of his life
was off his shoulders; and, come what might, he should
never want for anything so long as the pension list lasted.

During the progress of the contract between Helen and
her wayward lover, she felt gradually less enthusiasm, and
even less hope of perfect happiness with the man of her
choice. Now that the doubts and difficulties incidental to
a lover had subsided into a certainty of securing the object
of his affections, it seemed to her as if he already treated
her with a sort of authoritative superiority which, with her
animated disposition, she was by no means likely to be satisfied with. There was no deference in his manner towards her; while it was but too evident that he expected
an agreement on her part in all his suggestions, and, in
fact, something like implicit obedience to his dictations.
Since his recovery, he seemed to have become watchful of
her looks, and even of her smiles; and betrayed a restlessness, which she had never before observed, if she lingered for
a moment behind in conversation with even the old chaperons to whom she had been so long entrusted. Nay, when
Captain Stopper, with whom the reader may recollect Helen
thought fit to act a little scene the day Mortimer returned,
presuming, naturally enough, upon her good-nature on that
occasion, and the interest she appeared to take in his proceedings for the evening, spoke to her at the door of Howell
and James's, Mortimer hastily withdrew her from the tête-
à-tête, and exclaiming in no sweet tone, " Come, Helen, we
are keeping other people from getting up!" handed her,
not too gently, into the carriage; having done which, he
walked away, without too kindly taking his leave, till dinner-time.

" Dear Lady Bembridge," said Helen, " what is the
matter with Francis? — surely something must have hap-

pened to put him out of temper. Perhaps his late indisposition has left some little irritability in his constitution.
Did you see how cross he looked?"

" There are things," said Lady Bembridge, "which are
never seen or felt except by the person who is particularly
interested in the conduct of the other person of two. It is
impossible to form an opinion of the conduct of any existing being without being previously aware of his motives :—
if indeed a young lady engaged to one man does think fit
to bestow an encouraging smile upon another ———"

" What other, Lady Bembridge?"

" My dearest, I meant no personal allusion to anybody,"
said her ladyship; " I only meant generally, that as love
cannot exist without a due proportion of jealousy, anything
like marked civility to a remarkably good-looking captain
in the guards might perhaps induce the intended husband
of the young lady, being, as it should happen, by a few
years the senior of the captain, to ruffle the serenity of a
temper not too serene at the best of times."

" Am I to understand," said Helen, " that my speaking
to that silliest of all simpletons, Captain Stopper, is to put
Colonel Mortimer out of humour?"

" Dear Helen," said Lady Bembridge, "who mentioned
those names? I was merely supposing a case by way of
accounting for a strange *brusquerie* which might somehow
be conjured up."

Helen felt herself colour, and rejoiced that the rapid pace
at which she and her companion were driven hindered her
chaperon from fixing her penetrating eyes upon her countenance, the flush of which, she was conscious, was followed
by a shudder which she could not control. A world of
thoughts rushed into her mind. It seemed that Mortimer
felt it no longer necessary to gild over the weaknesses of his
character, and that even before marriage he began to display a restlessness not very dissimilar from jealousy. Helen gave her head a toss unconsciously, and said something
to herself which it was quite as well nobody heard : — had
the words reached Mortimer's ears, the chances are that
their marriage would never have taken place.

Helen was, as Mortimer told her father he knew she was,

noble-minded, generous-hearted, and good: no one who could have read her heart, and reviewed her most secret thoughts, would have questioned it for a moment: but she was high-spirited, and when conscious that she was right, fully prepared to act upon that consciousness, and treat with indignation the slightest suspicion cast upon her truth. As she herself has said, her great fault was her candour,— her want of caution in the use of words: what she thought she spoke: so that however much she might have prejudiced some against her, by such a course of conduct, nobody could charge her with dissimulation. That she accused herself of a want of decision in the case of Lord Ellesmere, and attributed to herself a mode of proceeding not altogether reconcilable with the principles upon which she had always acted, merely proved how quick she was to perceive her own failings, and how ready to acknowledge them when discovered. The truth is, Helen might be led, but was not to be driven: trust her, and she was fidelity itself; suspect her, and pride predominated over every other feeling.

On the day in question, the dinner in Grosvenor Street was not what dinners there generally were. Mortimer continued gloomy, Helen reserved, Batley out of spirits about Mudbury, Lady Bembridge was out of sorts about nothing; and, notwithstanding all this, the wedding was fixed for the following Friday.

---

## CHAPTER VI.

"THAT connection of yours," said Magnus to Mortimer, "has played the deuce with me at Mudbury: I am completely blown up."

"Connection of mine!" said Mortimer; "do me the kindness to permit the fact that he is the uncle of my future wife, and bears her present name, to die and be lost in oblivion."

"Frank," said Magnus, "he has contrived to make good his footing where I felt myself quite secure; and,

as I am at this time advised, has reduced his return to a
certainty."

" Did you not," said Mortimer, " reckon somewhat too
securely upon your influence ? "

" Influence !" said the colonel — " you know the fact
— you know how I stood : I had the electors in hand,
but I could not come to their terms *impromptu.* It was
completely out of my calculation that this fellow should
work into my labyrinth by the clue I gave him myself, and
supersede me on my own ground."

" Never mind," said Mortimer : " let him get into the
House of Commons, or any other, save mine ; and the mortification of being foiled at Mudbury will be outbalanced by
reading his absurdities in parliament, if his impudence
should ever be adequate to the making a speech."

" As for Mudbury," said Magnus, " of course to me,
having so small a part of my property in its neighbourhood,
I care nothing about losing it ; in fact, it is hardly worth
the trouble of keeping ; but having actually come to an
understanding with the ' free and independent electors ' for
fifteen pounds a head, (the reform price of the Bucking-
hamshire borough I told you of,) and upon which tariff I
had grounded the bargain, it is deucedly hard, after the
fellow's having promised four thousand, which would just
have put about twelve hundred pounds clear into my pocket,
to find him not only trading on his own bottom, but spoil-
ing the market by giving the ' great unwashed ' twice as
much as they had consented to take from *me.* However,
we will get up a petition if he *is* returned, and if we can
prove a case or two against him, let him look out."

" Ah ! Magnus," said Mortimer, " would I could interest myself in such matters ! I almost regret that I hadn't
turned politician, and endeavoured to employ my mind in
some engrossing pursuit, that might have kept from my
memory thoughts of other days."

" Frank," said the colonel, " your mind *should* be stored
with thoughts of other days, — not of days that are gone,
but of those bright days that are to come. As for memory,
take a sponge — out with all the records. Look forward,
man !—you are about to marry one of the loveliest girls

in London, and are, consequently, an object of universal envy."

" Envy !" said Mortimer, " do they envy me the possession of Helen ? Ay, ay, there it is : — that envy will change its character. Helen — well, well — the die is cast, and we must hope for the best. I wish now — but it is too late — that we had arranged not to go to Sadgrove immediately after our marriage."

" 'Gad, I don't see why, Frank," said Magnus : " what can be more lovely, more verdant, or more gay ? I should say it was of all places the best adapted for a honey-moon."

" True," said Mortimer, " it is gay and bright and green. All the charms of Nature combine to make it delightful — but — Amelia lived there — died there ! I dread visiting it with Helen for the first time since her death."

" Come, come," said Magnus, " you must get over this ; recollect I am acquainted with all the facts of that case. Your false delicacy — for so I must call it — is much on a par with the sensibility of a sentimental lady, who, having lived with her husband what they call a cat-and-dog life; when she becomes a widow, and the worthy gentleman is six feet under ground, begins to weep and wail and look back upon her past existence as something exquisitely delightful, and talks with enthusiastic veneration of the man whom, when alive, she quarrelled with every day, laughed at, ridiculed, and even " ———

" Stop, stop, the cases are not parallel."

" They *are* so far parallel, Frank," said Magnus, " that no man on earth could have behaved better or more honourably, more generously, than you did in that unfortunate affair of your comparative youth. It is true Lady Hillingdon died at Sadgrove, but everybody must die somewhere, and " ———

" My dear friend," said Mortimer, again interrupting him, " I cannot, intimate as we have been for so many years, inspire you with one particle of my feeling upon such subjects. It is all useless to say why, or why not, I am affected by returning to Sadgrove ; the sentiment is, I dare say, undefinable : — so it is — so let it be : but, problematical as the whole history is, I am miserable in my happiness."

Magnus, who (for often do friendships subsist between men, apparently, from opposition of temper and character) could not in the slightest degree assimilate with Mortimer on certain points — he who, with his iron nerves and immovable countenance, went straightforward through whatever he undertook with a resolution not to be daunted by circumstances, and a firmness which no minor considera tion could shake, was perfectly at a loss to comprehend why the recollection of Lady Hillingdon, so intimately associated with Sadgrove, should, now that she was dead, at all interfere with the enjoyment of new pleasures and new pursuits there, the *locale* being quite as agreeable as it was during her lifetime, and affording, by the change of circumstances, every prospect of increased cheerfulness.

"My dear fellow," continued Magnus, "if your principle were to be acted upon, there is not an heir in the empire who would rejoice in the death of his parent. The whole of our nobility are only tenants for life ; and if this repugnance to occupy the castles of their departed predecessors were to affect their minds, we should have all the mansions in the empire shut up or converted into workhouses or county hospitals. The highest dignities of the nation, like the foggy sovereignty of the city of London, are all transferable. My lord mayor Sniggs on the ninth of November steps into the state coach, out of which my lord mayor Figgs stepped on the eighth, and finds himself bowed to by all the same people, — sword-bearer, mace-bearer, train-bearer, lacqueys and all, — who, four and twenty hours before kotooed to the then lord mayor ; — the reign there is certainly short, but certain. In loftier circles the same things happen, and the same unconscious coach and horses, driven by the same coachman, and swarmed upon by hanging clusters of the same gilded footmen, draw through the thronged streets to-day amidst the shouts of the people, the monarch who succee s to him that "died but yesterday," and who in one week finds imself precisely in the place of the one "just gone before," inhabiting the same rooms, attended by the same servants, eating off the same plate, drinking the well-stored wine from the same cellar, dispensing honours which erst flowed from other hands, and receiving the adulation which so shortly previous had greeted other ears. If recollections like yours were to interfere with this——"

"Ay, ay," interrupted Mortimer, "all that is different; succeeding to the estates of one's ancestors is another affair; custom makes that nothing; no more than a man's sitting in his church under his father's monument, and over his grave, with the conviction that, when the time comes, his bones are to moulder beneath the crimson cushion on which he slumbers out the sermon. Sadgrove is different. It was to Sadgrove Amelia first came to me. Solitary as was our after-life, she was the star that brightened its gloom. Charles," said Mortimer, with a tremulous agitation which startled his friend, "she lies buried there,—how can I bear to visit it with Helen?—poor girl!—with such feelings, ought I to marry her?"

"This is a burst of passion," said Magnus, "for which I confess I was not prepared, Frank. If your feelings are so strong upon this point, I should certainly not go to Sadgrove;—why not go down to *my* place—stay *there*,—I will put everything *en train* this very day."

"No," said Mortimer, "thanks, thanks! but no, I *must* live in my own house sooner or later, and I will make the plunge at once—gaiety shall be my resource,—my plan of retirement must be relinquished, and I will endeavour to destroy the recollections I dread, by making Sadgrove as unlike what it was in other days as possible."

Those who read this evidence of the unsettled state of Mortimer's mind, the recollections with which it was teeming, the mingled repentance of past faults with lingering regrets for the sharer of them, the doubts by which he was agitated, and the fears by which he was assailed, cannot shut their eyes to the difficulties of Helen's position — difficulties of which she herself was unconscious. To those who could have known the truth, it must have been evident that her career as a wife would be little else than a struggle between certain unhappiness and the uncertain experiment of reclaiming a man of the world, not only from its present attractions but from the memory of the past.

That Batley was altogether blind to the difficulties of the case is not to be believed. Batley had been much in the habit of associating with Mortimer when Mortimer was younger, and Batley was not older than Mortimer was at the time of his offer to Helen. Their intercourse had been that of men of the same time of life. Frank Mortimer at seven and twenty, and Jack Batley at seven and thirty, were, in common acceptation, contemporaries; and in their association, long before any idea existed, on the part of either, that a nearer tie would bind them, Jack had seen enough of the character of his friend, to have questioned, had such a thought come into his head, his qualifications as a domestic husband.

It was after the period of Jack's greatest intimacy with him, that the affair with Lady Hillingdon occurred; a circumstance not particularly well caculated to increase an admiration for his morals, although, in fact, the view which Magnus took of the case was that generally received. During the life of Lady Hillingdon Mortimer was out of the world; on her death he launched into excesses on the Continent, until, palled with various devices to which he had recourse in order to dissipate his grief, he returned home thirsting for ease and retirement, and the comforts of a quiet life; his approach to which rekindled the memory of those which he had enjoyed before, and created for him, in the confusion of his feelings, something nearly bordering upon misery in the midst of his happiness.

And in *this* mood he was to lead the beautiful Helen to the altar on the following Friday.

As to the change in his determination with regard to his " manner of life " in Worcestershire, it is but fair to state, that he was first induced to think doubtingly of the seclusive system by the manner in which Helen had received the *programme* of their proceedings in the country. His announcement of the alteration of his plans was received by the young lady in a very different way. When he talked of fêtes and parties, her bright eyes sparkled, and she felt gayer than she had for some time, not more on account of the prospect opened, than because Mortimer himself seemed gayer than he had recently been.

The anticipation, too, of mixing with an entirely new community — of being herself a brilliant novelty to fresh admirers — was exciting, and, to use her own phrase, " charming."

" That *will* be delightful," said Helen, with all her native frankness ; " tired to death of the same faces, night after night worried with the same nonsense, talked by 'the same people, it will be ' charming' to get into a new sphere ; and even if the change be not for the better, it will be a change, and that *is* something."

" The change," said Mortimer, " will not be so marked as you seem to expect. Several of our neighbours are friends of yours : it is true that there are some eight or ten families who seldom come to London, but to those I am afraid you will not be disposed to devote your attention."

' " Well, then, dear Francis," said Helen, " they will serve us to laugh at, at any rate."

" Why, not exactly that. They are people of rank and consideration ; looked up to and loved by their tenants and dependants ; and, although their names do not figure frequently in those oracles of fashion, the ' Morning Post,' or the ' Court Journal,' they do not think so little of themselves as you seem disposed to think of them."

" Oh !" said Helen, " if they are stiff, starchy people, that will soon wear off. Do these ' natives' come much to Sadgrove ? "

" When invited," said Mortimer, looking rather confused, " by so kind a hostess, they will, no doubt, be too happy to accept the invitation."

To this little complimentary speech Mortimer added, in an under tone, something which he muttered for the purpose of mystifying the end of his answer, and getting rid of the subject ; Sadgrove, during his residence there, not having been a place to which, what Miss Helen Batley was pleased to call " stiff, starchy people," were particularly likely to go. To the infliction of such questions and remarks, the " gallant gay Lothario" felt he must make up his mind, and the only consolation which he permitted himself, under the circumstances, was, that they were proofs either of Helen's innocence of the ways of the world, or ignorance of the worst points of his particular case.

"Oh, rely upon it," said Helen, "I will do the honours entirely to your satisfaction; and, as for popularity, you will see that we shall be the most popular people in the county."

"It depends entirely on yourself, Helen," said Mortimer; "they are not in the habit of often seeing such a person as you. All you have to guard against is a disposition to ridicule peculiarities which, to a mind like yours, offer, I admit, some strong temptations. However, I shall not point out their oddities, but leave you to discover them, trusting to your caution after you have enlightened yourself."

Whether Mortimer would have given Helen a catalogue *raisonné* of his country neighbours or not, it is impossible to say; for their conversation was interrupted by the arrival of Mr. John Batley with the intelligence that the member for Mudbury was that day gazetted for the foreign appointment which vacated his seat, and that a new writ had been moved for; and this information he gave Mortimer still in the hopes of something like encouragement, even at the eleventh hour, to start, and make an effort, upon Magnus's interest.

The colonel had left town for his place near this independent borough, and, *faute de mieux*, resolved upon opposing Jacob Batley, himself; not with any hope of defeating him, but for the special purpose of running him to all the possible expense which a contest might involve. But when he reached the scene of action, no Mr. Jacob Batley was there; he had quitted the field; nevertheless, the canvassings of the gallant colonel were by no means successful; even they of the deputation who

> "Swarming like loaches,
> Had made their approaches
> In ten hackney-coaches,"

to solicit him to represent them, bowed coldly, and kept aloof in a manner sufficiently marked to convince the colonel that his fate was sealed. As soon as the writ was sent down to the sheriff, the walls were covered with placards announcing to the independent electors that a candidate of truly constitutional principles would offer himself on the day of nomination, and entreating them to make no promises.

These placards were imported from London by Mr. Brimmer Brassey himself, who arrived at "The Royal Oak" late in the evening, and forthwith summoned his friend the native attorney, and the select few who were aware of the proceedings, in order to organize the attack. Colonel Magnus announced his intention of coming forward without fail; and the inhabitants of the pure and patriotic borough were in raptures at the thought of the contest.

The Blues, however, secret as were their machinations, could not baffle the activity of the colonel's agent. It was clear that the majority was safe, bought at so much per head; but it was also clear that Jacob Batley was not the man to represent the borough. Who the candidate would be, was still a mystery; and all that could be extracted from Mr. Brimmer Brassey, when questioned, either in joke or earnest, was—"You'll see—I say nothing—you'll find I'm right—rank, character, and money,—that's the thing, gentlemen;—next Tuesday will enlighten you all— till then—I don't let the cat out of the bag:"—a bit of smartness, on the part of Mr. Brassey, which entailed upon the respectable individual who actually did come forward, the *sobriquet* of "Tommy," which he never lost; it being applied to him by the wags of the place, as a suitable appellation for Mr. Brassey's cat which was not to be let out of the bag till the nomination.

The day of nomination *did* come, but with it no Mr. Jacob Batley. The Town Hall was thronged. Colonel Magnus made his appearance, and was loudly cheered, a circumstance which did not produce the slightest perceptible change in the expression of his fine countenance. Conscious that his friends had been bought, and certain of defeat, these manifestations of approbation sounded most discordantly; but, if he had been torn with burning pincers' or subjected to any other of the pious inflictions of the Holy Inquisition, not a muscle would have moved.

The business of the day having been opened, a call for the candidates was raised, and Magnus stepped forward and addressed the throng in a short speech, which was loudly cheered at its conclusion: whereupon Mr. Stambury of Ballsmere proposed, and Dr. Bulch of the High Street seconded, Colonel Magnus "as a fit and proper person to represent the independent borough of Mudbury."

When the equivocal noises which this announcement excited had in some degree subsided, Mr. Hogthorpe of Cackley rose and addressed the electors. Every period of his address was received with enthusiasm; every pause was filled up with cheering; and a tremendous shout of ecstasy rang through the Hall when, in conclusion, the honourable gentleman proposed Sir Christopher Hickathrift, Baronet, of Tipperton Lodge, as a candidate for their suffrages. This proposition being seconded, Sir Christopher, who had been sitting by the side of Mr. Brassey, rose up, and was, as the reader, after what he has heard, may naturally expect, saluted not only with loud cries of " Tom, Tom !" —" Puss, Puss !" and such like familiarities, but with some abominable imitations of the different noises in which cats in general delight, under the varied circumstances of their manifold lives.

Sir Christopher bore this persecution from the yet faithful friends of his opponent with infinite good humour, although, as he confessed himself perfectly ignorant of the cause of the vocal performance with which he found himself greeted, he abbreviated his scarcely audible address; and when, after he had finished, and the names of the candidates were proposed to the assembly, the show of hands was declared to be immensely in his favour.

Now came the colonel's turn to be magnanimous: up he rose, and stated to the meeting, that his object in presenting himself to them, as a candidate for their suffrages, was, to preserve the borough from being mis-represented by an individual whose name had been very freely mentioned as intending to offer himself to their notice that day. To avert that, which he could not but consider a calamity to the borough, he was ready to make every personal sacrifice. He need not disguise from gentlemen, so many of whom were aware of the fact, that neither his health nor pursuits were of a nature to render a seat in parliament desirable. It was on their account, and with a deep regard for their interests, which he never could cease to feel, that he had come forward; and he would have persevered to the last vote on the register in fighting their battle.— (Cheers.) As it was, the case was different—(cheers and mewings):—a most honourable and respectable gentleman of their own county had been proposed to them, — (more cheering and more mewing,)—and feeling that their interests could not be placed in better hands, he begged leave most respectfully to decline any opposition to the honourable baronet's return, and to withdraw from the contest, — begging, in retiring, to return his heartfelt acknowledgments to those gentlemen who had done him the honour to support him on the occasion.

After this came chaos, and after chaos, the chairing of Sir Christopher Hickathrift, a ceremony rendered the more interesting by being performed during one of the heaviest storms that had been known for fifty years.

It is right that the reader should be informed how it came to pass that this triumph was decreed to lawyer Brassey's cat instead of Jacob Batley, although it is probable he guesseth at it already. Sir Christopher had long been looking wistfully at the seat, but a want of resolution on his part had left it out of his reach. The promptitude and liberality, as it was called, of Jacob, startled the waverers, and when Sir Christopher's man of business in Mudbury ascertained from Mr. Brimmer Brassey the real state of the case as far as his influence went, he next proceeded to find out whether the man who possessed that new and pure influence was particularly anxious to sit for the borough himself. Jacob certainly did wish to sit, but that was not his main object; it was to defeat others that he was labouring; and as the electors could by no possibility entertain any personal regard for Jacob, and as Jacob felt no regard for anybody on the face of the earth, a hint conveyed from Sir Christopher's attorney through Brassey, that he might put four or five hundred pounds into his pocket by transferring his newly-bought friends to him, had its effect. Sir Christopher's lawyer and Brassey settled the arrangement, and Jacob, instead of being carried about the streets, and made to give a splendid entertainment at "The Royal Oak," in addition to all other charges and expenses thereunto incidental, gladly pocketed somewhere about four hundred and seventy pounds by the bargain, and on the day of the election dined alone at his favourite tavern, " The Horn," and finished his bottle of port previous to the imbibition of his accustomed glass of hot punch, chuckling with satisfaction at having defeated Mr. Mortimer's particular friend at a rate so extremely advantageous to himself.

On the Friday following this return, Grosvenor Street was enlivened by the appearance of various carriages about the residence of John Batley, Esq., whence Francis Mortimer was to lead the blushing Helen to the altar in the church of St. George's Hanover Square. The proceedings upon such occasions, being always very similar, have been too often described to need explanation here :— the same tears, the same lace-veils, the same *déjeunér*, the same dressing for church and undressing for the journey, the same congratulations, the same elegant travelling carriage,— all, all over again for the ten thousandth time. On this important day, Mortimer received from the hands of his father-in-law the treasure which he had, amidst a thousand conflicting feelings, won, and from which was to be derived his future stock of earthly happiness. Some of his prevailing doubts and recollections flitted across his mind as he knelt before the clergyman, nor was the last occasion upon which he had plighted his faith to one who had broken her's, absent from his memory.

However, married he was, and the party at breakfast was gay and numerous : Mr. Jacob Batley was of course not of it, at the which John Batley was much vexed, and Helen, who, repulsive as were her uncle's manners, could not forget their relationship, was greatly pained; but his exclusion was a condition of Mortimer's, and excluded he was. Magnus was, of course, a guest, and performed his part with becoming dignity : he spoke but little, but what he did say was emphatic and solemn.

When *the* travelling carriage was driven up to the door, Mortimer beckoned Magnus to the back drawing-room.

" Well," said be, " you haven't inquired where we are going; and as you only arrived last night, perhaps you won't guess."

- " Going ! I conclude to Sadgrove." · · ·

" No," said Mortimer, " I found it would not do: I couldn't bear it. We are going to Paris for a month or six weeks."

" Then," said Magnus, " I know how that will end: you will go on to Naples, or wherever your sister is, and not return for months."

" On the contrary," said Mortimer: " I am not in such good-humour with my sister, for refusing to come to *me*, as to think of going to *her*. If she had done as I entreated her, and come over to this country with her friend and her family, she would have changed the whole character of Sadgrove; she and those whom she loves would have made a little domestic circle of our own, and with her character she would have made an admirable companion for Helen, who, strange to say, is not quite spoiled by the world's adulation, but who still requires a woman of strong mind and correct views to regulate her conduct. My sister Jane is that woman:—but no—she recoils from me—she despises me; of that she has succeeded in making me conscious: further I do not intrude upon her. In Paris we may get rid of all but present thoughts: there is much good English society there, and there we may with propriety emerge from the ridiculous solitude to which custom dooms a newly-married couple in England. We shall make it out there till shooting begins, when Sadgrove will be bearable; for the promise of plenty of birds will bring down plenty of friends, and we shall then, I trust, go on admirably."

Magnus, who, as usual, heard unmoved all the details of his dear friend's intended proceedings, satisfied himself that the ceremony which had just taken place was not to be considered as unquestionably productive of happiness to the parties concerned. The necessity of creating an artificial gaiety which Mortimer evidently found, the importance of stifling old recollections, — in short, the struggle which he was making merely to try an experiment upon his own character and disposition, seemed to the immovable colonel an affair replete with hazard; for it was clear that, added to the grief which still preyed upon him, and the mistrust

which he had of himself, he had certain misgivings with
regard to Helen, and the desire that somebody dear to him
should be near her to direct her, was no trifling evidence
of the state of his apprehensions.

" You have nothing to do," said Mortimer, " come over
to us at Paris ; we shall probably make some excursions
during our stay —let us make a little party. — What do you
say ? "

" I can say nothing," said Magnus, " for I am a creature
of circumstances. I have a good deal of money locked up
in those infernal Spanish bonds, and I do not like to leave
them, for, with the game the brokers are playing in conjunction with the foreign news-writers, not to speak of the
despatches written at Falmouth and forwarded to town by
the Spanish packets, a man may be ruined before he knows
where he is. But write to me — let me hear from you ;
and, upon my honour, if business permits, I will run over
with the greatest possible pleasure."

Even in this last request Magnus saw another instance
of Mortimer's anxiety not to be left, as lovers ordinarily
wish to be, altogether alone with his bride, and of a restlessness which augured ill for the future. He, however,
pressed Mortimer's hand warmly, and permitted his features to assume an expression of congratulation ; but it relapsed into its former rigidity, when Mortimer, on leaving
him, said, " Charles, you have been with me once before
upon an occasion like this."

Magnus playfully pushed him forward towards the
drawing-room, where the bridal party were waiting his return to witness the departure of the happy couple. That
Helen looked beautiful nobody could deny ; that she looked
happy is another affair. The change of character effected
by the ceremony so recently performed, the entire alteration
of duties produced by that sacred rite, the vast futurity
opening to her view, so different from the days that were
past ; the entire surrender of herself to an authority which
the day before she did not acknowledge, and the abandonment of that exclusive obedience which previously she implicitly yielded to her father ; the whole combination of
circumstances, the balance between perfect happiness and

something less than happiness, the apprehension, the doubt, the dread, the joy, the sorrow, — for they all mingle in the heart of a bride at the moment when she hears the carriage-door close upon herself and her husband, and finds herself, for the first time, confided to the protection and the love of an alien to her blood, — Helen deeply and intensely felt; and the pang which rent her heart as she received her fond father's parting kiss — the last of those kisses of devoted affection which were hers while she had none other to look to or love but him — was one of the bitterest she had ever endured. It seemed like the tearing asunder of a thousand tender ties, the abandonment of home, and all its associations. She was gently forced from his embrace by the imperturbable colonel, who led her to the door, while she sobbed bitterly.

Mortimer was scarcely less affected; indeed the whole party seemed to sympathise so deeply, that a much more melancholy scene was enacted than a man of the world would, in these times, expect to see at a funeral. Magnus alone remained calm, firm, and placid, and having deposited his charge in one corner of the travelling-chariot, and Mortimer having taken possession of the other, and pulled down the blind to avoid the gaze of the gaping crowd, the word was given to the postillions, and Mr. and Mrs. Mortimer were on their way to Dover at the rate of twelve miles an hour.

Batley made his excuses for retiring to his room, and shortly after three o'clock the house was deserted, and looked duller than it had appeared during the whole time it had been Batley's.

## CHAPTER VII.

FEW were the days that elapsed after Helen's wedding before Mr. John Batley presented himself at Jacob's counting-house in Lillypot Lane; but vain were his attempts to obtain admission upon his first application. The request to see him. on the part of his brother, was pressed upon him by a confidential clerk : " Well," groaned Jacob, " if it must be so, it must.    I may, for all I know, commit an act of bankruptcy by denying myself, considering I never dine here : let him in then — not that *I* want to see him ; and I don't suppose I should if he did not want something of *me.*"

" My dear Jacob," said Batley, as he entered the counting-house in a sort of theatrical pace, his lips smirking and his eyes twinkling, " I am delighted to "——

" That'll do, sir !" interrupted Jacob.    " I know : the quality folks are gone, and now Jacob is suddenly becoming very delightful.    If you have anything to say on business, be short ; I have little time to lose upon talk."

" I merely came to say, my dear brother," said Jack, that now I have cleared my house of the only man that ever objected to your society, I shall be too happy to see you again under my roof.    What say you to to-day — only four of us — at a quarter past seven ?"

" Psha !" said Jacob.    " You know what Mr. Pitt said to the Duchess of Gordon when she asked him one day to come and dine with her at nine.—'Very sorry he could'nt, for he was engaged to *sup* with the Bishop of Lincoln at eight.' — Quarter past seven ! — no : by that time *I* shall have dined, and had my port, my punch, and perhaps my pipe, — ay, even before you think of sitting down.    Why, d'ye suppose when I go to your fine banquets in Grosvenor Street that I haven't dined before I come ?    What do the women do ? — I have caught them at it when I was let into your house : — they eat like aldermen at luncheon : don't care a button for an old fogey like me — no : — before *me*, at it they go; cutlet after cutlet ; a little bit of this, and a little bit of that ; and — eh ! — psha ! — heavy luncheons make delicate dinners.    I'm up to *that !*    No, Jack, — if I am not good enough for your company, I am better left out altogether."

" Nay," said Jack, " but you should do *me* justice : I am always delighted, as you know, to see you : and whether you dine before you come, and make *my* dinner, like Mr. Pitt's, a supper, I care not.    You must know, Jacob," —

looking at him with a marked expression of affection, " you must know that to *me* you are always welcome. Colonel Mortimer is peculiarly circumstanced; he is nervous, — sensitive, — and ———"

" Yes," said Jacob; " that is to say, he has done a heap of things of which he is ashamed. He is all over irritability, and plain speaking won't do: it never does with that sort of man : — and yet, the sort of man who cannot hear truth without wincing, is the man you have chosen for a son-in-law ! I could tell you something more about *him* and *his,* but it is nothing to me, — I don't want to get into any worry; I know what I know, — and what I know, Master Johnny, I keep to myself."

" Still, you will come and dine with me."

" I won't now, and that's flat," said Jacob. " You fancy your invitations are favours; they are worries. Why should I, living in Lillypot Lane, take the trouble to dress myself up with silk stockings and pumps, as they call them, to go pottering up to Grosvenor Street, to eat, or or rather look at, for I never eat, a parcel of what you call entries or entrays, or something — meat made nasty ; dishes with poor honest turkeys smothered with dabs of pudding, and suffocated with chestnuts and cray-fish, which never were meant to be near them ; salmon pelted with capers; or fowls bedeviled with lumps of nastiness — truffles you call them — lumps of fungus that dogs rout out of the ground under trees with their noses, and all that; tongues varnished like pictures; and a paw-about mess that you call pitchamele, and the rest of it ? No, no : I am glad to see you, because I like you as well as I like anybody else ; but all the green and yellow smashery that you fancy fine, and get the gout by eating, I look upon with sovereign contempt. Give me a plain, wholesome dinner at four, and no luncheon ; — as to your fine feeds, keep them."

" Well, if you like plain cookery ———"

" If I" exclaimed Jacob — " why, what cookery did you like when you were young ? — you didn't care much about it *then*. Rely upon it, the best sauce is a good appetite ; but you have spoiled yours. I would bet you a

guinea that I would make you eat more, if you would dine
with me at ' The Horn,' at five say, — I'll give you an
hour, five, — than you have eaten for a year, barring lun‑
cheon — provided that you pay your share.  I never give
dinners at a tavern, and I never dine at home. — You see,
Jack: — every tub on its own bottom."

" I should be very glad," said Batley, " to dine with
you anywhere, and on any terms ; but to-day I have a few
friends to dine with *me*."

" Friends, have you?" said Jacob: "small party, I
take it.  What was the man's name that lived in the tub,
and walked about with a lantern to look for a man ?  If
you lived in a tub, you might walk your legs off before you
found a friend ; but as you occupy a house, and keep a
table that you can't afford, the smooth-faced hypocrites
come at your call, and do you the honour to eat your
victuals and drink your wine, and then go away and laugh
at you.  I suppose that tom-foolery is nearly now at an
end: having married Helen, I conclude you will get rid of
your house."

" Why," said Batley, junior, " that would look strange.
The world would wonder——"

" There you go again," exclaimed Jacob.  " The world !
— why——"

" But I have another object in view."

" Oh !" said Jacob in a tone expressive of the utmost
indifference : " and what may *that* be — more wild geese,
or more wild oats ?"

" Neither," said John, " but the fact is——"

" Ah !" said Jacob, " that is what you  generally begin
with before you bring out a bouncer.  I know ' facts ' are
not always truths : but go on, because I have  business of
consequence to do, and——"

" I will be brief," said Batley.  " The fact is, brother,
that when a man has been used to a home and  female so‑
ciety, he feels a loss when deprived of it which nobody
dissimilarly situated can appreciate.  I lived happily with
my poor dear wife, and at her death Helen was sufficiently
grown up to be a companion, and to rally round me female
friends.  She is now gone.  I anticipate nothing but

wretchedness in the life I am destined to lead, and, having long foreseen this, have for some time resolved upon marrying again.

" Marry again !" said Jacob, — "well, that *is* something to talk about. I never married once."

" And therefore are insensible to the delights of a home cheered by the presence of an amiable woman," said Jack.

" Psha !" replied Jacob. " You have contrived to do remarkably well for a long time without 'the presence of an amiable woman :' what's the use of beginning again now ? "

" Pardon me !" said John — " not exactly ; while, as I have said, Helen was with me, I felt that I *had* a home, where her presence ensured that society in which, I admit, I rejoice ; now she is gone, it will be a blank."

" Yet you were never easy till she went."

" Can't you conceive it possible, brother," said John, " that a father may sacrifice his own comforts for the advantage of his child ? "

" I can't enter into that," said Jacob, " I never had a child. However, if you choose to marry, you will marry, I suppose, to please yourself ; and as I have nothing to do with it, I don't want to hear anything about it. Mr. Grub, bring the letters ; I can't waste *my* time."

" And you won't come ? " said John, insinuatingly.

" Psha ! no," replied Jacob, shaking his head ; and John took his leave, not at all pleased with the tone of his brother's observations on his marriage, yet still hoping that time would soften all asperities, and that when he did die, if his death should precede his own, he should find in his will a proof of the affection which he had never discovered while alive.

That John Batley should feel disposed to marry again does not seem so extraordinary. John had married young, —was a young father, — and, as he truly said, the relative ages of himself and Helen had, in some degree, alleviated the grief which he felt for the loss of her mother, by placing her in the position of mistress of his house, at a somewhat premature age, perhaps, — but there she was, — and, as he vainly endeavoured to impress upon Jacob's mind, *there* was female society ; and John liked female society ; he had been a sort of male coquette all his life, and loved dangling at fifty-four as much as he did-when he was less than half that age ; and it is astonishing (perhaps not, because the case is so common) that a habit of that sort does not wear off with time, as might be expected. The man of fifty-four flirts, and is not ill received ; but he does not appreciate the mode of his reception ; he does not feel himself much older than he was five-and-twenty years before ; he scarcely sees an alteration in his own person ; all that he wonders at is, the extraordinary flippancy and forwardness of boys of five-and-twenty, forgetting that when he was of their age he considered an old fellow of fifty-four a " regular nuisance."

Wonderful, however, have been the changes within the last half century : the march and influence of age have been neutralised to an extent which our grandfathers could not have believed. Fifty years ago, the idea of a man of sixty in a black neckcloth, with curls and trousers, and a fancy waistcoat, with amethyst studs in his shirt-bosom, dancing quadrilles, never would have entered into the head of a human being. The dress might have been as gay, or gayer, but it would have been made up of pomatum and powder and a bag or a club, with shorts, and shoes and buckles. At one period, the pig-tail, which superseded the club-knob, which had previously succeeded to the bag, would have been indispensable ; nay, there are at this moment half a score matured gentlemen, who thirty years since sported tails, knobs, and pigs, with powder and pomatum, aforesaid, walking the assemblies of London in picturesque-coloured wigs, fancy waistcoats, and symmetrically cut pantaloons.

The question was, what sort of woman Batley would marry? and the question again resolved itself into another, what sort of woman would marry Batley ? To those who knew him best it would have appeared probable that he would have sought for noble blood ; but when a man of Batley's standing takes that line, he must not expect to have it young. Lady Angela and Lady Seraphina are, no doubt, to be gotten hold of; but they must be poor and elderly; and it remained with Batley to decide whether to flourish amidst " the sublime and beautiful ". in Burke's Peerage, with a sort of negative reception in the family of the lady, were of sufficient importance to outweigh the attractions of a younger bride of less pretension. What he did in this momentous affair time will show.

Finding all efforts to interest his brother in his projects useless, he left him to the enjoyment of money-getting, which seemed the absorbing passion of his life, and resumed a career of gaiety, by which he hoped to dispel the gloom of his home, and bring himself into notice in his new character of a disposable widower.

Days and weeks wore on, and the honey-moon of Mortimer and his Helen was over, and yet no symptoms appeared of their return to Sadgrove. Helen, tired of Paris, and the praise which was lavished on her, sought for change ; but, whenever she touched upon home, Mortimer interposed some very good reasons why they had better wait a little ; and this so often as to protract their stay for nearly seven weeks, during which period Mortimer received several letters from his sister, to which he duly returned answers ; but Helen observed that he never made the slightest reference to their contents. She thought he seemed more gloomy than usual after receiving one of them — for he had relapsed into gloom very soon after his marriage ; and although she did not like to make any inquiries, she still felt uneasy at perceiving what she considered a want of confidence in her.

This feeling induced her to write a letter to her father, from which the reader may infer that the harmony of their union was not so sweet as might have been expected.

    " DEAR FATHER,          Paris.

" YOUR kind letter was most welcome, and I will take care of the commissions you speak of, although a little puzzled as to the person or persons for whom the gaieties are designed. I speak sincerely to you when I tell you .that I am tired to death of this Paris, — one lives so con-

stantly abroad, so constantly before the world. I don't
know how the French themselves feel, but I do think
there is nothing like home in Paris, — and Paris is
France.

" I am a good deal vexed by Mortimer's manner. I do
not know why, but he seems to have something constantly
weighing upon his mind. He is as kind as any human
being can be, and I enjoy his society beyond description,
but I do think something worries him constantly. I would
give the world to go to Sadgrove, as he originally proposed ;
but whenever I mention it, he always interposes some
objection, which I suppose is good, but which does not
always appear sufficient. He has been writing a great deal
to his sister, and seems much to wish me to be known to her ;
but, from all I can gather, she declines the *honour ;* why,
I cannot exactly imagine. Colonel Magnus, as you know,
has been staying with us for the last ten days, and, somehow, I begin to dislike him more than ever. He and
Francis talk about matters of which I am wholly ignorant,
and they laugh and look grave by turns ; and I believe
the procrastination of our return is somehow connected
with Mrs. Farnham's answer to Francis's last letter.
I wish I were at home with all my heart. I do not, because I must not, mean my own dear home with *you*, but
I mean Sadgrove, which is *my* home now.

" You cannot think, dear pappy, how strange it seems
to be treated with a sort of formality and restraint by one
whom one loves. You always told me, when you came
home, all that you had heard and seen. You expressed
your wishes, imparted your thoughts, and all without
reserve or constraint ; but Francis does not treat me so.
If anybody speaks to me civilly, — I mean any of these gay
Parisian dandies, to whom one must in good breeding be
commonly civil, — he looks grave and almost angry ; and
when I, seeing that, (for, as you know, I can see as quickly
as my neighbours,) entreat him to take me to his favourite
place in Worcestershire, he knits his brows, and even —
don't be shocked, pappy — swears, and then begins to talk
of his sister, and her disinclination to visit it. Whatever
the cause of this may be, I am certain Colonel Magnus

knows. I know he is a great favourite of yours. I never could like him, and I must own my feelings have not assumed a more favourable character since he has joined us here.

" During our excursion to Tours, Francis visited some old friends of his, a Count and Countess St. Alme ; they returned with us here, and we have seen a good deal of them since. She is an Englishwoman, but not exactly to my taste, — handsome, and somewhat apt to do what you have sometimes scolded, — at least, as much as you were in the habit of scolding me, for doing,—I mean saying off hand things. I certainly do not pretend to equal her in that sort of talent, or in knowledge of the world ; whether I am grown fastidious, or whether, being married, I have become graver, I do not exactly know, but I cannot quite like her ; she seems, however, a great favourite with Francis. She has one son, of whom she appears dotingly fond, and I do not wonder, for he is a remarkably engaging boy.

" I wish, dear pappy, you would write to Francis and urge his return ; I am sure we should be happier, — at least, I should. Francis has bought me some beautiful china, and trinkets that will dazzle you ; but what are trinkets if the heart is not at ease ?

" Colonel Magnus brings accounts of your being particularly gay, and says that your dinners are quite the rage. I am glad to hear this ; for though, dutiful as I am, I did not flatter myself that the loss of my society would be fatal to your happiness, still, we are such creatures of habit, that even so dull a companion as I may be missed. I even miss the flirting and barking of poor dear little Fan, and should jump for joy to hear her welcome me to Grosvenor Street.—I hope she is well.

" I have written to-day to Lady Bembridge, but I have only heard from her once since we have been here. I wrote also to poor dear uncle Jacob, but not a word of answer. I wanted, if possible, to soothe his angry feelings towards Francis—as for Francis's feelings towards him, I fear they are beyond my healing. I have tried once or twice to introduce the subject, but have been stopped on the

instant.    I believe if there is anybody uncle Jacob cares'
for, it is myself, though I have never experienced any
farther mark of his affection than the negative one of not
being spoken to quite so roughly as everybody else.

  " Thank you very much for your kind letter of the 8th,
and for the little bit of news it contained.    I was telling
Francis some of the gossip, but he did not seem to like it;
and, when I was setting forth the extraordinary indiscretion
of poor Mrs. Z., he took me up rather parentally, I thought,
and said, ' Helen, we all have our failings,—let us be sure
we are more perfect ourselves than our neighbours, before
we remark upon them,'—so I held my tongue like a good
girl, determined to avoid being snubbed.    Write, however,
like a dear good pappy as you are, and be assured I shall
be most grateful for anything you can tell me;   for,  next
to being with those whom I have so long loved, my greatest
pleasure is hearing from them ;  and so adieu, dear pappy,
and believe me truly and sincerely
                    " Your affectionate child,
                            " HELEN  MORTIMER."


  Batley read this letter with mingled yet opposite feelings.
The  affection of the daughter delighted him ;  but he was
not quite satisfied with the tone which she assumed in the
character of the wife.    It was evident that the reserve of
Mortimer had generated something like distrust on the part
of Helen ;  and it even appeared to Batley, from the absence
of any reference to his name as joining in remembrances
to his father-in-law, as if he had been in no degree a party
to her writing.    It was clear, too, that Helen was not so
happy as she had expected to be ;  and it was equally clear
to Batley that he remembered some story of an old attachment of  Mortimer, older than that of Lady Hillingdon,
and of a subsequent marriage of the lady to a foreigner ;
and, if he had not himself been in full pursuit of his present matrimonial object, he would have taken steps to
ascertain the precise facts of this nearly forgotten historiette ;
as it was,  he had scarcely time to look over his daughter's
letter, though its perusal left upon his mind a sort of nervousness which qualified the whole of his day's occupation,

and of the real cause of which he was himself scarcely conscious.

At this period of our history, in which some new mys-
tifications begin to arise, it may not be amiss to let the
reader glance over a letter, one of a series which Mortimer
received at the period to which Helen referred in her's to
her father. It may be considered "vastly ungenteel" to
expose a lady's correspondence; but, considering that the
recipient of the letters was her brother, and that we shall
get more satisfactorily at facts than we could by any other
means, we must waive ceremony, and put upon record one
of the missives with which the exemplary Mrs. Farnham
favoured, or rather troubled, Colonel Mortimer. An extract, however, will suffice.

"I cannot," says this exemplary lady, "bring myself
yet to believe what I am positively told is true. Francis,
my brother, my beloved erring brother, you already anticipate what I am going to say; let me be right in my
anticipations of your answer. I hear that you and your
young wife are living upon terms of intimacy with the
Count and Countess St. Alme. I am sure this must be
calumny, it can *not* be true — no, dear Francis, until you
admit the fact, I will not believe it. Recollect I am old
enough to remember all the anxieties of our poor father;
recollect that you, the idol of both your parents, were the
constant object of their care, the constant theme of their
conversation to me. Recollect how much you confided in
your only sister: let me not believe the history they tell
me : — the Countess St. Alme the associate of your young
wife ! — no, Francis, no, — they libel you.

"Your repeated invitations to England, I tell you, are
useless; I have already given you my reasons. But do
not yourself delay returning to your proper home : — take
there your innocent bride, — be good, — be happy : — let
me entreat, implore you, do this; and this I earnestly
urge upon you, convinced that all I hear of this countess
is groundless. If it should be true ! — but, no, it cannot be:
— if it should, let me, with all the power I may have over
you, press your instant removal from Paris. Surely, what
you have already suffered, — the torture that you have

endured, — the misery you have experienced, — must of
themselves act as incentives to such a step : — if not,
Francis, let a sister's prayers, — prayers breathed to heaven
by one who, through a life now past its zenith, never has
wilfully or willingly offended the sacred Power to which
she appeals, — move your heart and fix your resolution.
Go, my brother ! — do not expose yourself, and the young
creature whom you have taught to love you, to trials which
may, in their results, destroy her happiness, and for ever
ruin your still redeemable character.'

From this we gain an insight into matters of which poor
Helen was evidently ignorant ; yet she had seen enough in
the boldness of the countess, and the subserviency of the
count, to feel a decided distaste to the society of the favourite associates of her husband.

Mortimer's answer admitted the fact of a renewal of his
acquaintance with the countess, but denied either the im-
propriety or indelicacy of it. The Count and Countess St.
Alme were a most amiable couple, universally esteemed,
and generally visited, — and why should they not be ?
The countess was an English lady of birth and station,
and had married an elderly gentleman of the name of
Blocksford, who, some eighteen years before, had died, and
left her with one son, which son was, as Helen had stated,
his mother's idol, and naturally so, for, as she says in her
letter, he was " a remarkably engaging boy."

After leading an irreproachable life as a widow for four
years, she married the Count St. Alme, a smallish French
gentleman with a particularly long red-tipped nose and
thin legs, by whom she had in the first year of her marriage a daughter. The child, born somewhat prematurely,
died, and since that period the countess had had no increase
to her family.

That, as Helen saw, the countess talked, and laughed,
and even flirted, nobody denied, — and what the harm ?

     " Where virtue is, these are most virtuous."

Although Helen herself, young as she was, had already
suffered a little, for a gaiety of manner, of which she
admits herself in her letter to be conscious ; still people
only said, " What a lively creature !"—" What an odd

creature !"—"What extraordinary things she *does* say !"
—-for upon a principle not unfrequently recognised, that a
free tongue is the safety-valve for exuberant spirits,
voluble volatile ladies of this school generally escape the
graver imputations which those who, as Horace Walpole
says,

" Know the country well,"

are apt to cast upon the quieter and more calculating of
their own sex.

Something, however, it was too clear, *had* occurred in
Mortimer's youthful days, which rendered the renewal of
his intimacy with the Countess St. Alme objectionable in
the eyes of Mrs. Farnham ; and the circumstance coming
to her knowledge just as she had admitted to her friend and
associate at Naples that her heart was beginning to melt,
and that she really thought she might be induced to visit
Sadgrove, put an end to all further hopes upon that particular point.

We have already seen the difficulty which Mortimer felt
in revisiting the former scene of his equivocal happiness
and certain misery. It must be clear,—at least if Mrs.
Farnham be supposed to know the truth,— as regarded the
count and his lady, that the attraction, which even Helen
saw the latter possessed for her husband, acted still more
powerfully as a repellent from Sadgrove ; but perhaps even
the reader is not prepared to hear, that failing in his sister,
and greatly disturbed by her lecture, the St. Almes were
invited to supply her place, and to form three of the family
circle at his paternal home.

" I have been endeavouring to persuade the count and
countess," said Mortimer, with a carelessness of manner
well calculated to disguise the deep interest he took in
Helen's reply, " to go over and pass a month or six weeks
with us at Sadgrove."

" Then you are really going to England, Francis," said
Helen, exactly as he anticipated.

" Of course, love," said Mortimer : " where should a man
live but in his own house ? "

" No," said Helen, —" there we agree ; only by pro-

H

longing your stay here, you give no proof of your disposition to go."

"I hoped," said Mortimer, "that my sister would have
come to us and gone with us, but she throws me over;
and I really think—you know, dear Helen, a country-
house, quite alone, is not delightful."

Is it not extraordinary that Sadgrove, and the solitude
imposed upon him during his residence there by circumstances, were so strongly fixed in his mind, that he could
not imagine the possibility of rallying round him and his
charming wife all that he chose of society? He dreaded
the recollection of what it had been; and in order to
render himself secure from a repetition of what had happened there, endeavoured to secure, by way of enliveners,
two persons who, if what Mrs. Farnham implied was true,
would not have objected to make it agreeable even under
the former *regime*.

"Not quite alone," said Helen. "But why should we
be alone?—there are crowds who would be happy to come
to us."

"I see, you dislike the St. Almes."

"Not I, indeed, dear Francis," said Helen,—(which,
having glanced over her confidential letters, we happen to
know was not entirely truth,)—"I think he is rather dull
and prosy,—and odd,—and queer; but _____"

"And the countess?" said Mortimer—"is she too
lively?—are her *bon-mots* too frequent?—does she
startle you by her repartees? I should think not, Helen;
for having yourself been, like Britannia in Thomson's
song—

'The dread and envy of them all,'—

I mean of all the beaux, belles, and blues of London, you
must understand the play of such artillery, and know
that the brightest wit is not incompatible with the purest
heart."

Helen paused and felt herself colouring: her pure heart
*did* beat:—Mortimer had shot his bolt beyond the mark.
Who had insinuated that the heart of the countess was not
pure? Who had complained of the gaiety of her conversa_

tion ? Why did Mortimer recur to the conduct of his wife, by which he had been captivated?

"I am sure," said Helen,

"With a smile that was half a tear,"

"anybody, dear Francis, that you like, I like."

"No, Helen," said Mortimer, "I do not require any such implicit obedience; I never could myself afford it. You love your uncle — I hate him ; and, much as I love *you*, never could bring myself to endure him. What I meant, dear girl, was, to consult you whether it would be agreeable to you to have the St. Almes with us for a few weeks."

"Oh ! quite agreeable," said Helen,—"quite ;"—and was near bursting into tears.

"Well then," said Mortimer, "I will ask them,—or you shall,— it will look better : and, to tell you the truth, I think, — and indeed that was one of my motives for speaking to you about it,— I think the countess fancies you do *not* like her ; so an invitation this evening, in one of your most winning ways, will convince her to the contrary, and we will start for England in two or three days."

Poor Helen was now completely trapped. She saw by Mortimer's manner that he had made up his mind that these odious people should accompany them to England, and remain on a visit with them. She felt such an awe,— not of Francis, but of the countess,— that she dared not venture to remonstrate, though she was aware that, for a time at least, it would be fatal to her own comfort: — besides, taking it upon other grounds, the admission made by Mortimer, that the enjoyment of his young wife's society, without other adjuncts, would not ensure his happiness, was by no means either gratifying or consolatory.

Nobody can duly appreciate the state of Helen's feelings during the interval between the conversation with her husband and dinner-time. Her whole mind was occupied with the duty she was forced to perform, when she and the countess should be left alone ; for Mortimer and Magnus had drilled the count into the social but extremely

ungallant English custom of "sitting and sipping" a little
wine, after the ladies had retired.  At dinner she was pale
and flushed by turns : she reflected upon all the plans she
had suggested for the employment of her time at Sadgrove ;
and perhaps (for as to any sinister motives on the part of
Mortimer, even if there had been any just cause to doubt
him, she never suspected them) — perhaps she did not feel
pleased with the idea of taking possession of her sovereignty associated with a lady, whose maturer age gave a
greater confidence in her intercourse with the world, and
who began to treat her rather as a promising young woman,
than as she had been treated "for a season or two," as one
of the first class of London beauties.

The task was to be performed, and so entirely did Mortimer rely upon Helen's obedience to his wishes, that he
communicated to the count, shortly after the ladies went,
the fact that Mrs. Mortimer was most anxious that he and
the countess should accompany them to England.   Lucky,
therefore, was it, — or unlucky, as the case may be, — that
Helen did as she was bid ; and dressing her fine face in
smiles, made her request to her vivacious visitor, who,
however pleased she might be with the invitation, did certainly not appear so much surprised as a lady might naturally be expected to be at an impromptu of that sort.  The
countess said, — That she should be delighted, if the count
would agree to it, there could be no doubt ; and it would
above all be such a charming opportunity for Francis
Blocksford to see a little English society.  "Oh, you are
so good, Mrs. Mortimer !"

The count had not been in the saloon five minutes
before the announcement was made to him, — his permission asked, and granted ; and so much having been achieved,
Helen resolved to settle herself into a course of beginning
to like the countess.  But Helen, who was as quicksighted
as her neighbours, felt a sort of check when her eye
glanced over the persons of Mortimer and Colonel Magnus,
who were standing in a window sipping their coffee, and
evidently talking over the arrangement ; and she saw upon
both their countenances an expression which conveyed to
her mind that in some way, or for some reason which she

could not exactly define, they were enjoying the triumph Mortimer had obtained over her feeelings, and that in the features of the colonel there was depicted an exultation at having made the suggestion himself.

As time will develope the effects of these proceedings, it is scarcely necessary to say more than that orders were forthwith despatched to have Sadgrove prepared for the reception of its master; that invitations were forwarded to several friends to join the circle; and that every sort of gaiety that could be devised for the purpose of welcoming the party should be displayed: in fact, all the doubts which previously served to cloud the mind of Mortimer seemed to have vanished, and in less than ten days the Mortimers, Magnus, the St. Almes, Master Francis Blocksford, and all were on their way to the

" Fairest isle ! — all isles excelling."

---

## CHAPTER VIII.

THE arrival of Mortimer and his bride at Sadgrove was celebrated by a kind of *fête*, prepared, to be sure, under his own directions, and paid for out of his own pocket; but it had, or was intended to have, the effect of a spontaneous ebullition of popular feeling, with which Helen was to be gratified and flattered, — flattered as far as her share of the attention went, — and gratified by seeing how much her husband was esteemed by his tenants and neighbours: — and there were sheep roasted, and barrels of ale broached; and there were music and dancing, and flowers and fireworks, and every available display of rural festivity.

The poor neighbours did, in truth, rejoice; not, perhaps, that Mortimer had returned, — for he had lived, during his former residence there, in a manner not likely to render him so popular as he wished to fancy he actually was, but because the shutting up of the " great house " of a small place is always a misfortune to the humbler neighbours;

one of whom was heard to say upon the present occasion,
" It does my heart good to see the great kitchen-chimney
smoke again ! "

These external manifestations of gaiety might perhaps
have been somewhat consolatory to Mortimer ; but it must
be confessed, that after four or five days had elapsed, and
he did not find the drive from the lodges to the house
ploughed up by carriage-wheels, he began to feel the restless anxiety which universally characterises a man of doubtful reputation.   The clergyman of the parish had called
without his wife and daughters, and the attorney had tit-
tuped up on his cob ; but the Muffledups of Wigsbury, the
Bigstuffems of Dogsford, the Cattletons of Lapsworth, the
Stiffgigs of Snapsworth, and the Peepsburys of Littleworth,
came not ; and these people, although to be found no
where but in their native county and in " Burke's History
of the Commoners," *were* something : in fact, they combined in themselves the principal landed interest of that
part of the country, and were, moreover, the " stiff, starchy"
people of whom Helen had such a constitutional horror.
Bores they would unquestionably have been had they
come, but to Mortimer their not coming was more painful than their society.   Deeply imbued with the primitive
simplicity of their rural ancestors, they did not consider
the gaiety and innocence of Helen adequate to the purifi-
cation of the atmosphere of Sadgrove, nor think the liber-
tinism of Mortimer sufficiently qualified by the change in
his condition.

This was a serious blow to Mortimer.   For the Muffledups, the Stiffgigs, the Peepsburys, and all the rest of their
tribe, he entertained the most sovereign contempt ; but
therefore did he the more deeply feel the disinclination
they evinced to his acquaintance — not for himself, but
because the manifestation might produce an effect upon
Helen likely to degrade him in her estimation.

This marked inattention, to call it by no more positive
name, could not long escape the notice of Helen ; but short
as had been the period during which she had been Mortimer's
wife, there was something in his look and manner which, to
a being all quickness and perception, checked her from

making any inquiries into the cause of the absence of the promised visitors.

Mortimer absented himself from church on the first Sunday after their arrival at Sadgrove: there might have been more reasons than one for this omission of duty. The associations of circumstances connected with the dead might have kept him aloof from a trial which would probably have proved too strong for even his firmness; while the circumstances of his non-association with the living might have induced him not to provoke any exhibition of a positive refusal of intercourse. Helen regretted his absence; but when she and the Countess St. Alme returned, she remarked to her husband that he was not singular in his determination of not going, for that there was scarcely any body in the church except the humbler parishioners — two of the *non-juring* families having pews therein.

"Magnus," said Mortimer to his *Fidus Achates*, "I am by no means pleased with my reception in the home of my ancestors; something tells me that I am not welcomed as I ought to be here."

"My dear fellow," said Magnus, "rely upon it, it is the reputation of your lovely wife that keeps these timid rustics away — they are afraid of her: her sarcastic turn is known, and as you have yourself told me of your fears that she might scare a whole herd of them by one observation, so they, depend upon what I say, are terrified lest she should annihilate them: — nobody likes to be laughed at."

"Nay," said Mortimer, "but, after all, they are not so decidedly obnoxious to ridicule as that: they are certainly not of the world, worldly, — in the acceptation of that word as implying fashionable, or gay, or easy, — they are only correctly dull and respectable: — no; the truth is, that they are of my sister's school, and poor Helen will suffer for my transgressions."

"She seems to have overcome the disinclination to the Countess St. Alme which you suspected her to have felt in the outset."

"So I perceive," said Mortimer; "and I begin to be as desirous that their intimacy should stop where it is as I before was that it should exist. The countess is one of my earliest acquaintances ; and though I solemnly assure you that my sister's suspicions about any closer connection are groundless, I own that I was glad to meet her again, and was pleased with her society at Paris ; but I am not quite sure that I ought to have acted upon the impulse of a moment, and have made her an inmate here, especially at starting: the daylight rouge, — to say nothing of the arched brows not altogether Nature's own, — are not calculated to melt the ice of Helen's ' stiff, starchy ' people ; and, if I had reflected, I should have anticipated the disadvantages of such an association. However, it is done ; and the course now to pursue is, to render the circumstances less remarkable by filling the house with London friends ; amongst a crowd of tigers, my vivacious hyæna will not shine out so remarkably."

The reader will perceive by this, that the suspicions of Mrs. Farnham with regard to the countess were groundless as far as her brother was concerned : and if the reader will sift every suspected *liaison* of a similar nature, he will find that ten out of twelve of all such histories are equally groundless.　Under the circumstances, the prudence of Mortimer's conduct in inviting her to Sadgrove was exceedingly questionable : but it is as well to set him right with regard to conduct which, had his sister's views been correct, would have assumed a deeper colouring than that of a mere want of consideration.

In pursuance, however, of his new determination, invitations were sent off to the most agreeable of Mortimer's friends ; and Lady Bembridge and Mrs. Delaville, and one or two more very proper ladies, were bidden, by way of " ballast " to the gayer portion of the party.　Jack Batley was of course amongst the chosen, and every preparation was made to gratify the sporting propensities of the men in the morning, and secure the gayer and more graceful amusements for the ladies in the evening.

There seemed to Mortimer but one of two courses to pursue.　The neighbours certainly " fought shy " of him, therefore his only line was to withdraw within his own circle, and to exclude all those who did not seem to wish to be included, while he contrived to make Sadgrove celebrated for the gaiety and agreeableness of its parties, the varied character of its amusements, and so pique the "puritans" into a regret that they had been so fastidious.

Helen certainly was not so much enchanted with her rural position as she had anticipated; her natural disposition for sly satire found no materials to work upon, nor did her mind exhibit any congeniality with those pursuits which Mortimer had hoped might render her an object of esteem and veneration with the poorer neighbours. The oddness of manner, the strangeness of accent, the mispronunciation of words, or their misapplication to any subject under discussion, into which any of the poor people might be betrayed, were beyond her power of resistance, and she laughed outright, much to the discomfiture of the rustics. In fact, hers was a London mind; and all her fancy for the country, mixed up as it was with marriage, was little else than an anxiety for change of place and station, blest with the society of the man of her heart.

The clergyman of Sadgrove, a most exemplary man, was amongst those who had paid a visit to the "hall." But, with all his piety and all his zeal for doing good, he was no beauty, and this fact destroyed all his merits in Helen's eyes. It must be confessed that he was what the people call an "object;" and so much did this operate to his disadvantage with Mrs. Mortimer, that she could not trust herself to discuss with him sundry matters relative to Sunday schools and infant schools, and other establishments, in the maintenance of which he was particularly active, lest the extraordinary cast of his countenance and the peculiar tone of his voice should betray her into some inadvertent breach of decorum.

Mortimer, however, considered it important to be extremely benevolent, and to be seen frequently going about the village with the reverend doctor, to consult him as to the best mode of providing for both the spiritual and temporal wants of his parishioners, and, by a moderate sacrifice of time and money, acquire a good name in his neighbourhood, or, at all events, to do his *possible* to get rid of a bad one.

It ought not, however, to be concealed that this life of

effort and self-reproach was one of anything but happiness to Mortimer; every word uttered by his friend the countess, which had reference to " other days," grated upon his ears; and his repentance for having brought her into such immediate contact with his young wife increased hourly.

Francis Blocksford, the lady's son, remained only a short time at Sadgrove. His object being to see England previous to entering at Oxford, of which university he was destined to become an ornament, he proceeded, after a brief sojourn, to London, where his uncle was residing, to whose care he was consigned. Ridiculous as it may appear, Mortimer felt pleased at his departure. He was a graceful, handsome fellow, and, though not more than seventeen, a French education had given him the air of the " world," and Helen liked him, and his high spirits made them all laugh, and his good humour made them enjoy his conversation; but the affection and admiration of Mortimer were not altogether unqualified by a restlessness which, if he had not been ashamed, he might almost have fancied jealousy.

He was gone, however, leaving his " dear Mrs. Mortimer" two of his drawings — for as an artist, *inter alia*, he excelled; — and they were framed and hung up in her boudoir. One was a view of Sadgrove; the other a view of the Château de St. Alme, near Blois, the seat of his most amiable father-in-law, which the Mortimers had visited during their excursion.

Upon what little things great things turn. These drawings, and their hanging up, were not much in themselves, but ——

Well! the answers to the numerous invitations to shooting and all other sports were received, and all in the affirmative: the house would be thronged, and gaiety would reign universally, the spirit to invigorate and enliven the hall being, as the wine merchants say of Madeira, all " London particular;" and Mortimer rejoiced while he felt not only that the dulness of Sadgrove but the particular intimacy of his wife and the Countess St. Alme would be broken in upon.

. One answer which was received to these biddings we ought to give, inasmuch as it may serve to let the reader into another portion of our story, for which, however, he has in some degree been prepared. Ecce!

" DEAREST HELEN, " Grosvenor Street,
Oct. 18——.

" Nothing in this world can give me greater pleasure than accepting your and Mortimer's invitation to Sadgrove. Tell him, I like flint guns still; I may be wrong, but I tried caps and they brought on a degree of deafness: the sharp snap produces this. I will, however, not inflict upon him a poker, which, as you know but little of the country, I may be permitted to tell you such gentlemen as your husband call a single-barrelled gun.

" But now, Helen; — this *entre nous* — our confidences have lasted long, and have never been broken; — what do you think? — I want you to ask two other persons besides myself—inseparable from me now — Lady Melanie Thurston and her daughter — you remember them every where. Lady Melanie posted upon every sofa in the world with a sort of tiara on her brow, looking like the figure-head of His Majesty's ship ' Fury,' — enough to make one sick, — pray, ask her, — she longs to go to you, — she lives at 136. Harley Street: — her daughter is nice — very nice — make Mortimer pleased with *her*. The old lady has a sort of western circuit of friends, and it would suit her very well; and I really do not see why we might not all go down together: — manage this.

" I was delighted, after your letter from Paris, to find that you were so soon coming home, and I hope you find Sadgrove all you wished. I remember the Countess St. Alme as Mrs. Blocksford; she was extremely handsome, and was a daughter of an East India director, whose name I forget — rather satirical — and so on; but if I don't mistake my Helen, she is a match for her.

" I am vexed to hear that you don't think Mortimer well: as to his spirits, they fluctuate with the weather; naturally so, the more mercurial they are. As for what you say about shutting out the neighbours, let Mortimer do as he likes.

" I met poor Ellesmere the day before yesterday. ' I really believe you did him a mortal injury by refusing him: he seems an excellent person, and has been very much distinguished by a vote of thanks from some great county meeting for something wonderful that he has done. He is certainly not a liberal in politics, but I believe he spends five or six thousand a year in doing good. I hope Magnus is agreeable, as I hear he is all in all with Mortimer: the affair at Mudbury has damaged him considerably in his importance, and, as I am told, stops a great deal of the swagger of his conversation;—he was certainly overreached there.

" As to uncle Jacob, he is unapproachable: not one bit will he advance towards reconciliation; and I fear that all my expectations of an improvement in my affairs at his death, which, according to the law of nature, however much I may lament the event, will probably take place before mine, will vanish. However, dear child, you are put beyond any difficulty of worldly circumstances—lucky for you. All I speculate upon is, what Jacob *will* do with his wealth. To give it to anybody seems contrary to his principle, and to leave it to any national establishment equally at variance with his love of self. One thing is clear—neither you nor I, nor Mortimer above all, have the slightest chance.

" Now then, Helen, do not forget Lady Melanie Thurston and her daughter. The infliction of a mother-in-law upon a lady who is herself a wife is not much:— and so the secret is out. You may tell it to Mortimer, and the world will know it before long:— and so recollect I cannot go to you without my friends.

" The inquiries after you by the few people in London are really kind; but, of course, we are but few at this time of the year. There are, I believe, about four or five hundred thousand nobodies jostling one another in the city every day, doing what they call ' business;' — brother Jacob amongst the number. But in *these* parts humanity is extremely scarce. Adieu! dear Helen: best regards to Mortimer, and believe me

" Affectionately yours,

" J. BATLEY."

"As I suspected," said Helen to herself — "my dear pappy is going to marry again. Well, *my* consolation is, that he did not favour me with a commander-in-chief while *I* was under his roof. Now we shall see what his choice *is*. Thank Heaven! my chaperon, Lady Bembridge, is not the apple-getting goddess; for, my poor pappy, I am sure, would have been bored to death."

To Mortimer the contents of this letter were imparted, so far as concerned the special invitation, but the letter itself was not thrown down frankly for his uncontrolled perusal: — such was the restraint which thus early had been established — only by manner — over the young wife's conduct.

"Ask them?" said Mortimer — "to be sure, my dear Helen. You know Lady Melanie and her daughter — let your father be pleased, and he pleases me: — besides, Miss Thurston plays the harp — the only fault of which excellence is, her never knowing when to leave off. However, as music is always a charming excuse for general conversation, she will make it lively: — have them, by all means."

Everything promised gaiety, and Mortimer himself was gay, which was everything to Helen. The presence of Magnus, she felt, was a sort of weight upon her: he engrossed a good deal of her husband's society, and the solemn pomposity of his manner, and a sort of command he evidently had over his host, acted as, what is generally understood in the world to be, a wet blanket. This, and a certain degree of assumption on the part of the Countess St. Alme, kept Helen in a kind of fever, although as Magnus, who was a great ally of the countess, said, she had not only begun to bear with her, if not to like her, but was really amused by her vivacity — all of which, be it recollected (and it is never too early to date a feeling destined to rankle), Mortimer attributed rather to her being the mother of the stripling Blocksford, than the friend of his earlier days.

The mind is mysteriously framed; and as no two countenances (which are the indices of minds) are alike, so no two minds exactly resemble each other. Mortimer, the

once followed and worshipped idol of his day, and, being
at forty-five or thereaway, a bridegroom, handsome beyond
dispute in person, his manly beauty mellowed by time with
tints which gave even better effects to his classical features,
shrank with suspicion from the bright beaming countenance
of a handsome young man his own godson! Ay, there it
was!—the affection which he could not fail to feel for the
son of the favourite friend of his youth, was "sullied
o'er" with a jealousy of the personal attractions of that
very individual, and in his mind the seed was sown. He
heard Blocksford talk of his own contemporaries as "old
fellows of five-and-forty"—and "old chaps of fifty"—
and this before his vivacious Helen, whose eyes, inno-
cently enough, were fixed upon the ingenuous countenance
of the young Frank, while he was unconsciously planting
daggers in the heart of the more matured Mortimer.
Ridiculous as this littleness may appear, it was registered
in the heart of the master of Sadgrove, and lay smouldering under the anxieties which swelled it, ready to burst
into a flame upon the slightest provocation.

This incubus was removed—but even *then*, Mortimer
seemed restored only to a negative degree of complacency.
Magnus and he roamed about with gloom upon their
countenances, and St. Alme in vain endeavoured to mingle
in their morning strolls, before the time arrived for shooting. There was something altogether uncomfortable in
the *ménage;* and what seemed to render it most uncomfortable of all was, as we have already seen, Mortimer's
growing dislike of the perpetual association of his wife and
the countess.

"I don't think," said the countess to Helen upon one
of these occasions, "that Mortimer seems as happy as he
ought to be ——"

The calling him Mortimer did not quite please Helen.

—"With *you*, my dear Helen."

That was not entirely agreeable.

—"He ought to be the happiest of men—his fortune
adequate to every luxury of the world, and this place one
of the nicest in the kingdom — and with a wife ——"

"Oh! countess," said Helen.

" I am sincere, my dear Mrs. Mortimer, — I cannot imagine anything wanting to make this place a perfect paradise."

" It *is* lovely," said Helen ; " and I am so glad beyond all other things that we are not worried by the visits of the people about the county ; they would bore me to death : and then their visits would be to be returned ; and then we should have to have them here at dinner, and then have to go ten or fifteen miles through dark nights and bad roads to dine with *them*. I thought, before I was married, I should like to have them, for the sake of laughing at them ; but I am better pleased as it is, especially as Francis is anxious to shut them out."

The countess looked, and wondered whether Helen were, in truth, unconscious of the real state of the case, half-inclined to enlighten her : however, she thought better ; and resolved to let her remain in a state of blissful ignorance, in which she could not but wonder she had been left so long.

A few days brought down the guests, and very soon all Sadgrove was filled with *les braves convives*, Lord William this, Sir Harry that, Colonel one thing, and Captain t'other thing, besides the Dowagers and the Misters, and the Honourable Mistresses, and the Lady Marys, and the guns and the valets, and the maids and the men. Such a gathering never had been seen there, since the death of the late respected Algernon Mortimer, Esq., who slumbered in the family vault in the adjoining church, whose sporting performances were carried on in an extremely different manner, and whose domestic arrangements were wholly at variance with the present proceedings of his most amiable heir, now keeping " wassail " in the hall of his ancestors.

And then to see how the neighbours turned up their eyes and lifted up their hands at the madcap pranks which the goodly company played. The boys of the village were delighted with the skill and agility of the dandies, and the girls, especially the pretty ones, amazed at their condescension. The ladies made friends of all the cottagers, and pets innumerable were found amongst the neighbouring children. Everything was gaiety and benevolence, good-humour and hilarity, and nothing could be more charming than such gay doings at the mansion. But in the midst of all this there were eyes watching, and minds full of thought; and however gay and thoughtless the guests might be, the master of Sadgrove was still ill at ease.

"Mortimer," said the Countess St. Alme as Francis was driving her in a phaeton to see some coursing, "I am sure of one thing, and you ought to be ashamed of yourself."

The abruptness of her manner startled her companion, who almost hated her for being the mother of his namesake.

"And why?" said Mortimer.

"You are jealous of your young wife," replied the vivacious lady, — "groundlessly jealous — but jealous you are; and besides the ungenerous character of such a feeling, consider its consequences."

"Jealous!" said Mortimer — "ridiculous! And who is the cause?" — and he trembled for her answer; so thoroughly did he despise himself for harbouring a feeling he could not overcome, yet dared not avow.

"Oh! nobody in particular," said the countess, "your Helen will never give you cause for *that* sort of jealousy: but you are jealous of the whole world — of every man that comes near her. I know every turn of your mind; you watch her when she speaks — when she looks. If she is talking to the most indifferent person in the room, you seem to haunt the spot where they are seated; if she stroll out of sight, even with my poor dear little ugly old husband, out you go and follow them: — now this is all wrong, Mortimer. If anything in the world can spoil a fine ingenuous character, such conduct as yours is sure to do it. Conscious of no ill intention, a young woman of high spirit and candid disposition cannot fail to feel affronted by implied suspicion, implied too in a manner evident to everybody with whom she happens to come in contact."

"You mistake me, countess," said Mortimer. "I admit that I feel a strong anxiety about Helen in society, but not jealousy. She has a habit of saying things which cut and wound, and this half unintentionally : in fact, she does not know how to restrain herself — what she thinks she speaks ; and now that she is mine — I — in short, I am afraid of her committing herself."

" No, Mortimer," said the countess, " 'lay not that flattering unction to your soul.' Her frankness and ingenuousness were, as you have told me, what won you : it is *not* a fear that they should offend, but a dread lest they might please too much, that agitates and keeps you hovering near her ; — take my advice, — we have known each other long enough to give me that privilege, — do not let her fancy herself suspected. Poor Mr. Blocksford was addicted to something like the course you are now pursuing, — it never answers, Mortimer."

The conclusion to which the countess came, after citing her own case as one in point, was, to say the least of it, whimsical ; and Mortimer could not resist observing that, since the countess argued from experience, he would endeavour to check a habit of which she accused him, but of the existence of which he did not admit himself to be conscious.

To a man distrustful of himself, rather than of his young and fascinating wife, nothing is so annoying as even the most frivolous allusions to the most trifling circumstances made by the early friends of the lady, they being persons who, for all the husband knows, might have been in other days *aspirants* for her hand.

" Do you remember," said Lord William, "my dear Mrs. Mortimer, that joke one evening at Lady Summerville's, about you and the pine-apple and the bouquet ? "

" Oh, perfectly," replied Mrs. Mortimer, " and you on your knees like Romeo in the garden."

" And the Ascot day," cried Sir Harry, " when three hearts were broken at one blow."

" I never shall forget that," answered Mrs. Mortimer, laughing exceedingly ; "and to see poor Lord Robert after the *éclaircissement.*"

"That was altogether a most agreeable excursion, Helen," said Mrs. Petherton — " I wonder you ever gave up blue ribands after those verses — don't you remember ? "

" Oh ! perfectly," replied Mrs. Mortimer, " I assure you
I have got them perfectly safe — for, to say truth, they
were very pretty."

" Is poor Tom dead, Mrs. Mortimer ? " pathetically asks
Sir Harry.

" Oh dear, no ! " replies Mrs. Mortimer, " he is in Italy,
and married."

Now all these references to long by-gone nothings kept
Mortimer upon the rack ; the ease and gaiety with which
Helen, who of course knew (which he did not) the real
character of the incidents of which her friends were speaking, appeared to him misplaced levity, and evidence of a
frivolity which pained him ; then the scene between his
rival Ellesmere at Lady Saddington's, and Batley's letter
of recall after he had taken his departure for the Continent,
recurred to his mind ; and then, gazing with a mingled
feeling of delight and doubt upon his laughing wife, he
muttered to himself Lord Townley's question in the play,
" Why did I marry ? "

The arrival of Helen's father and the Thurstons seemed a
favourable epoch at which Mortimer should begin the cor-
rection of this scrutinising habit ; inasmuch as if, though
Helen were unconscious, it were sufficiently evident to attract
the notice of others, Batley would observe it.    He therefore determined, for the next week at least, to banish all
solicitude, and enjoy if possible the gaiety with which he
had surrounded himself.

Batley, luckily, was in particularly high spirits, and
seemed to be in the highest degree of favour with his
ladies ; and when Mr. John chose to make the agreeable,
nobody could better succeed : — as he was now avowedly
on his promotion, there could be little doubt of the activity
of his exertions.

" Do you think her pretty, Helen ? " said Jack to his
daughter, speaking of Miss Thurston.

" Ye-es ; " said Helen, " pretty, but *gauche ;* she seems
always straining after effect ; — her harp is agreeable, but
there is no feeling — none of that soul-fraught energy
which gives music and everything else its real value to *me*."

" Come, come, Helen," said Batley, " recollect in her,

you see your future *belle mère,* and I must insist upon your duty."

" Rely upon me," said Helen. " And when is it to be, pappy?"

" Why the matter has not gone that length yet," said the matured lover ; " I should say a few days now would settle it."

" But you are accepted, I presume," said Helen, with a kind of mock dignity.

" Oh !" said Jack, " that part of the story is all understood. I have put the case hypothetically, and Laura and her mother are, as the people say, ' quite agreeable.' I think that our domestication here for the next week will afford the most favourable opportunity imaginable of concluding the negotiations, and it would be particularly agreeable to me to receive the hand of so amiable a person under the roof of her who has been so many years my companion and my delight ; — *entre nous,* Helen, — not that I am worldly, — the young lady has forty thousand pounds, besides the reversion of mamma's jointure when she dies."

" Why, you will be the envy of all the fortune-hunters in London !" said Helen.

" Lady Bembridge is in her airs about it," said Batley, " she fancied herself the object of my solicitude ; but, as I say, Helen, a man is so much younger for his years than a woman. Mortimer and you, for instance, are admirably suited ; — I, — to be sure, there *is* a difference between Mortimer's age and mine, and I have what is erroneously called the advantage, but still Laura is older than *you,* and so that brings the matter all right."

" I wish," said Helen, " I could see Mortimer more lively : as I wrote to you, he seems to have something preying on his mind which affects him more particularly here."

" Shall I tell you, Helen?" said Jack: " I have always made your confidence with an implicit reliance on your natural good sense, and, in what I am going to say, I only afford an additional proof of my estimation of your character. You must not notice, nor care for, and especially not let him see that you care for, the gloom about which you

speak ; it is connected with circumstances of other days:—
tell me,—has he been to church yet ? ”

" No !” said Helen, opening her bright black eyes with
an expression of wonder at the question so unexpected, yet
so pertinent, " no ! but what of that ?—he has had a cold ;
besides, he went last week to Welsford church,—and——”

" Hush, hush, my Helen ! ” said Batley, " never mind
what other church he visits : I speak only of *this*.   You
know, for I told you before you married him, all the circumstances of his unfortunate affair with Lady Hillingdon? ”

" Ah ! ” said Helen, and those fine eyes were raised to
heaven with an expression of painful regret, " I thought of
that, but——”

" Do not agitate yourself, my child,” said Batley, " nor
fancy that any recollection of Lady Hillingdon is to interfere with your happiness ; all will be well in time ; but I
know (for Magnus has told me) the dread that Mortimer
has of first visiting the church here, — under the family
pew lies buried the woman who sacrificed everything for
him.   In the human mind some one single circumstance of
a long life stands registered deeply and firmly, from which
the heart revolts as soon as it recurs.   All the wrongs Mortimer did, all the sacrifices he made, all the punishment
he has undergone, all the sorrows he has felt, are coneen-
tred in that one spot.   If he could muster resolution once
to revisit that tomb, the spell would be broken, and by degrees he would even derive consolation from his visits.”

" But, father,” said Helen, " when you tell me this, do
you expect *me* to derive consolation from the intelligence,
or that my anxiety about Mortimer is likely to be decreased
by knowing that his grief arises from the loss of one to
whom I am the unworthy successor ? ”

" No, Helen, no !” said Batley, " you mistake the point.
The struggle now going on in his mind is not between regret for his former wife and affection for you ; the conflict
is merely with regard to what, in common parlance, is
called ' breaking the ice.’   Time will do this ; but, as I tell
you, I know his feelings upon this point, and also the dread
he has of making a scene before the congregation which

might result from an effort to master these feelings prematurely."

It must be confessed that Helen, after this conversation, was by no means more assured of the transient nature of Mortimer's grief than before it took place. In fact, she was conscious of an absence of that entirety of affection which, with her characteristic enthusiasm, she had anticipated in marrying the man of her heart; and, though her father might have arrived at a time of life when worldly considerations are supposed to influence what the Morning Post would call the "votaries of Hymen," she felt rather sorry than pleased that her vernal parent had given her so sad a clue to the abstraction of her husband.

Batley, however, rallied her into a smiling humour, and left her to dress, with an injunction not to take the slightest notice of Mortimer's melancholy or its cause; and, added he, as he whisked himself out of his daughter's boudoir, " Don't make a particular *confidante* of the Countess St. Alme."

This last hint, coupled with the tone of the countess's *innuendoes* as to Mortimer, sent Helen to her dressing-room with feelings which ought not to fill the bosom of a noble-minded girl less than three months married.

## CHAPTER IX.

THE conversation which Helen had held with her animated parent was by no means calculated to tranquillise her mind. As far as expounding to her the cause of Mortimer's gloom, it was, however, to a certain extent, satisfactory; for though a knowledge of the strength of his feelings for another might not be particularly gratifying, still it relieved her from all apprehension that *she* was herself the cause of his melancholy.

Her father's caution about the countess troubled her: she had, to please and gratify Francis, forced herself to like her ; she had become familiarised with the *brusquerie* of her

manner, and if she had not made her a *confidante*, she felt
no dislike to her society. Once or twice, when speaking of
Mortimer, Helen thought she perceived a desire on *her* part
to refer more particularly to the history of his early life
than was either necessary or agreeable, and an expression
of wonder why he should permit the recollection of the
past to mar the brightness of the present.

" *My* course," said Helen, " is clear : doing no wrong,
what have I to apprehend ? This sadness of Mortimer's
will wear off : I will neither question him about it, nor
appear conscious of its existence, but endeavour, by making
everything around us as cheerful as possible, to rescue him
from its influence."

This wise determination, however, was more difficult of
execution than Helen, in the innocence of her heart, imagined. Even the vivacious society of her father, which
was particularly agreeable to Mortimer, failed of producing
its wonted effect ; his mirth seemed misplaced ; his " gallant, gay" proceedings now appeared to Mortimer almost
ridiculous ; and he felt an awkwardness — a difference, in
fact — in the mode and topics of their conversations, which,
unlike their intercourse in other days, were seldom reduced
to a *tête-à-tête*. Jack, who was sufficiently alive to passing
circumstances, saw the change, and felt it ; but attributing
it to the one " great cause" which he had established in his
mind, and communicated to Helen, it had but little effect
upon him, and he rattled and flirted and fluttered away,
with more than his usual activity.

" Pray, Helen," said Mortimer, " as I presume you to
be in your father's confidence, which of the two ladies down
here under his patronage is the object of his ambition —
the mother or the daughter ?"

" How *can* you ask, my dear Francis ?" said Helen.
" If my dear pappy were to hear you imagine a doubt, he
would die of the shock : — the daughter, to be sure."

" Oh !" replied Mortimer — " then he is not so wise a
person as I supposed : — true, the mother's jointure reverts
to Miss Laura at her death, but ——"

" Laura," said Helen, " is not so young as she looks,
and I think will make a very respectable mother-in-law."

" I think her detestable !" said Mortimer. " Flippancy and pertness in a woman are qualified in a certain degree by youth and beauty ; but when the one is past, and the other does not exist, an off-hand tone of superiority, such as Miss Thurston thinks proper to assume, is, at least to *me*, exceedingly offensive."

" Her mistake is excusable, Francis, even upon your own principle," said Helen ; " for she does not consider herself old, nor think herself plain."

" Well," said Mortimer, " self-deception is a vice, or folly — whichever you please — of a most extensive character, if a woman of *her* age and appearance can still believe herself what she so decidedly is not. I confess, if I were condemned to he chained to either, the dowager would be my choice."

" Papa prefers the lesser evil."

" Evil, indeed !" said Mortimer with a sigh, and then relapsed into one of those fits of abstraction, from which Helen did not venture to awaken him.

" I shall not shoot to-day," said Francis, after a pause ; " Magnus and I are going to ride over to Worcester. I will go, however, before we start, and make arrangements for those who like to go out, and you will make your party for the morning as you please."

" Are you going on business, Francis ?"

" Why, yes," replied Francis, " partly — but we shall be back long before dinner ; so try and live without me for a few hours."

These words, accompanied as they were by a " chaste salute," were delivered in a tone by no means agreeable to Helen's ear ; and what made them still less acceptable was, that by an almost unconscious feeling they became mysteriously associated in her mind with the conversation she had had with the Countess St. Alme, as to Francis's insensibility to the value of the treasure which he possessed in *her*."

" I will try," said Helen ; " but, dear Francis, it will be a trial, for when can I be so happy here as when you are here too ? "

" Ha, ha !" said Francis, " you are a dear, good girl,

and, if the world does not spoil you, will mellow down into a most domestic wife : — only," added he, " don't cry ; don't dim those bright black eyes by weeping, even if Magnus and I *should* be too late for dinner. I should have felt some compunctious visitings in leaving you to manage the wide world of a country-house ' all alone by yourself,' but as ' pappy,' as you call him, is here, he will relieve you from all that embarrassment ; he can make himself ' at home' anywhere."

And the tone in which *this* was spoken was not harmonious. The remark of the countess again flashed into her mind. — " What on earth has made him dissatisfied with my father ?" thought Helen. " My father is a cleverer man than Francis ; my father is——"

Hold, temper, hold ! Has the adored Mortimer, the admired of all admirers, already sunk thus in the estimation of his wife ? It is not doubt of his affection that has produced all this ; it is, first, an air of command which he has assumed, which a woman of ardent feelings cannot brook ; this, combined with his abstraction — and this again with the countess's observations — and all this again and again with her father's injunction, not to make a confidante of the countess. Well !——

" Yes, Francis," said Helen, " my father *is* a very agreeable person, and you always thought him so ; and I believe your first beginning to like *me* was, because you esteemed and admired *him ;* that is my pride and pleasure."

" Who upon earth, Helen, said or thought I did not ? " said Mortimer. " I merely observed, — and unless you were disposed to quarrel, my observation would have passed unnoticed except by a laugh, that your father made himself at home everywhere. I meant nothing offensive ; and certainly, if there be any house in England where he may do that most effectively, it is in *this,* where his daughter is mistress, and rules all hearts."

Again the sneering manner of Francis worried Helen, but she felt herself above the influence of anger — she never *had* felt anger towards Francis — and above the reach of anything, strange to say ! except the observation of the Countess St. Alme, — "He does not value you; he does not know the worth of the treasure he possesses."

Poor Helen ran over in her mind all the things she had said and done which could have been likely to excite Mortimer's ill temper, of which she began to fear he possessed somewhat more than an average quantity, but she could tax herself with nothing. Did her liveliness offend him? — impossible! because he himself had spoken, if not harshly, at least strongly, as to his suspicions that the liveliness of the Countess St. Alme was objectionable to *her*. She had been civil to his guests; she had, and he knew her motive, endeavoured to make the place gay; nor did he exhibit anything but the greatest kindness to her in company, — perhaps a somewhat too watchful kindness in its way. The real misfortune of the match was, — and she began to discover it thus soon, however much too late it might be, — that Mortimer, who as a "dandy" of some twenty years before, had established a character for talent and accomplishment, founded chiefly upon buoyant spirits and a fine person, did not, in fact, however much he might deceive himself into the belief that he did, possess one single attribute likely to attract or chain a mind like Helen's.

Well then, when to this unfortunate incongruity and want of sympathy were superadded the gnawing regret and cankering remorse, on the part of Mortimer, for deeds of other days, it did not seem very unnatural that he — also too late — discovered that his project for reform and regeneration into a new life of domestic happiness and respectability, was not so likely to turn out well as he had anticipated. There certainly was something in his manner as he left Helen upon this occasion which was painful in the extreme to her.

What still increased this feeling, — although she dreaded to know more of the cause of his strange behaviour than developed itself so disagreeably on the surface, — was, the admonition of her father as to the countess, who certainly had excited *a* feeling in Helen's breast, not perhaps a strong one, by throwing out hints that Mortimer was not so happy as he ought to be in his domestic circle. Helen

resolved to dress her bright beautiful countenance, in
smiles; and when she rejoined the party nobody could
have guessed what was passing in her mind, unless perhaps it was the Countess St. Alme herself, who, when the
mistress of the mansion announced that its master was
going on an excursion that morning, accompanied by Colonel Magnus, and that she should be sole monarch of the
day, gave her a look which she felt was understood, and
which implied that even with a host of friends about him,
there was something more attractive out of Sadgrove than
in it. Helen saw the glance, and felt its import; but
dashing away the black ringlets from her snowy forehead,
as if typical of casting from her mind all dark thoughts,
she turned from the scrutinising eye of the more than
half Frenchwoman to the smiling countenances of her
other visiters, in order to make arrangements for putting
them all into motion in the most agreeable possible manner
to themselves.

Batley, as far as he was concerned, proposed having the
negative satisfaction of remaining " at home ;" for, according to Mortimer's just view of his character, so did he designate Sadgrove. Helen soon discovered his reason for
this announcement of his domestication ; Laura Thurston
had got the head-ache, — Lady Melanie would stay with
her. Batley saw in the head-ache a *ruse*, because, Batley's own ways being tortuous, he never believed that anybody ever said or did anything without a motive. He
had expressed a sort of half intention at breakfast of not
shooting, — Laura after breakfast had a head-ache, — " put
that and that together," (as the wicked woman said to the
red-nosed justice), it makes something ; and, accordingly,
Batley, the Evergreen Batley, found, in the sudden announcement of the young lady's (young by courtesy) malady, more of sympathy than sickness, and that she had
merely fashioned her complaint to the purpose of the moment, and having previously given sundry indications of a
desire to come to an explanation of his intentions, cousidered that day a fitting opportunity for him to make his
declaration.

There is nothing in the world so curious to look at as

the mind of a cunning man, — not a conjurer, but a man who thinks he is carrying on his schemes, and manœuvring and keeping everybody else in the dark as to his intentions. Addison says that " cunning is only the mimic of discretion, and may pass upon weak men in the same manner as vivacity is often mistaken for wit, and gravity for wisdom." When Batley heard of the head-ache, his cunning made him certain of his point, and he smirked and simpered proportionably; although, in fact, whatever might have been Miss Thurston's feelings towards him, the poor thing had a real *bonâ fide* head-ache. Batley's own practice of the art in which he thought himself an adept, and in the exercise of which he preferred getting at an easily attained object by a circuitous road than by a short one, convinced him that this was a plan, that the heart of the lady was more affected than the head, and that this day was to be *the* day " big with the fate" of himself and Laura.

What the object of Mortimer's visit to Worcester might be, Helen no further sought to know ; nor would she have cared about it, but for the look of *that* countess who became a greater object of interest since pappy had warned her not to make a friend of her.

There is an old story of a man, probably something like Mortimer, who had married a girl something like Helen, and who had a friend probably something like Magnus, and the friend was sceptical somewhat as to the obedient tendency of the young wife's disposition, much to the dissatisfaction of the Benedick, who warmly asseverated that his will was law, and that she never by any chance disobeyed any wish or injunction of his.

" Have you ever tried her in that respect?" said the friend: " have you ever positively desired her *not* to do any particular thing ? for *that* is my point, since you tell me she never refuses to *do* whatever you desire.

" No !" said the affectionate husband, " I never have found occasion to desire her *not* to do anything, but——."

" That's it ! as the old women say," cried the friend, " female obedience is proved by negatives ; tell her *not* to do any particular thing, give her no particular reason why, and see if she does not do it."

" Ridiculous !" says the husband.

" Try !" says the friend.

" Well, replies the husband, " agreed ! we are going away for the day :" — just as Mortimer and Magnus were, — " what proof shall I put her to? what shall I tell her *not* to do? play her harp, sing, or draw? — tell me what you want me to prohibit her doing, and I stake my life she does it not."

" Oh no !" said the friend, " drawing, and singing, and playing the harp are things which she might abstain from without a murmur, or, what is more essential to the affair, a wonder; because she has sung, and played, and drawn a thousand times ; it is an injunction not to do something *she never has done before,* — for instance, tell her when we go, not to climb some particular hill, for reasons which you do not choose to give; or, by way of carrying the principle out to its fullest extent, not to attempt to ride on Neptune's back."

" Neptune's back !" said the husband.

" Yes !" replied the friend, " on the back of this most valued Newfoundland dog, the bravest and faithfullest of his breed."

" Ride on a dog's back ! — how *can* you be so absurd? — as if ——"

" Ah ! there it is," said the friend " as if, — now, take my word for it, if you issue the injunction without giving her any reason, Harriet will break it."

The most incredulous of men rejoiced at the idea, which he felicitously ridiculed, and resolved upon trying the experiment in order to establish his Harriet's superiority of mind, and his friend's exceeding silliness.

He parted from his Harriet, and with tender fondness she clung round his shoulder, as he said in quitting her —

" Harriet, dearest, we have seldom been separated since our marriage, — I shall be back soon — take care of yourself, love, — but, just attend to one thing I am going to say, dear; don't try to ride upon Neptune's back while we are away."

" What !" said the laughing Harriet, " ride upon Neptune, — ha, ha, ha! what an odd idea!—why, what a ridiculons notion!—why should you tell me that?"

"That, my dear, is a secret; all I beg of you is, not to ride upon Neptune."

"Ride upon Neptune!" repeated the lady, and she laughed again, and they parted.

When Benedick and his friend returned to dinner, the laughing Harriet did not as usual present herself to receive them ; there was a sort of gloom pervading the house; the footman who opened the door looked dull; the butler who came into the hall looked as white as his waistcoat; the lady's own maid rushed down stairs evidently to prevent a scene.

"Where is your mistress?" said Benedick.

"Up-stairs, sir!" said the maid, "there is nothing the matter, sir, — nothing in the world, sir, — only my mistress has had a fall— quite a little fall — on the walk in the flower garden — and has cut her face, the least bit in the world, sir ; all will be well in a couple of days."

"A fall!" said Benedick.

"Humph!" said his friend.

And up-stairs ran the anxious husband.

"What has happened?" exclaimed he, catching her to his heart, and seeing her beautiful countenance a little marred, — "how did this happen?"

Harriet cried, and hid her face.

The explanation never came altogether clearly before the friend or the family ; but the accident was generally thought to have arisen from Harriet's having endeavoured to take a ride upon Neptune's back.

The Countess St. Alme was the Neptune of Sadgrove ; the warning Helen had received, coupled with the other odd circumstances which have been already noticed, excited the fated lady of the mansion to increase rather than diminish the intimacy which already existed between them ; and, resolving to lose no time in ascertaining the justice of the paternal admonition, proposed, as one of the arrangements of that very morning, to drive the countess in the pony phaeton herself.

Thus while the daughter had determined to try the

temper of her friend, the father had decided to essay his fortune with the object of his choice; and a very nice morning's work it was, all things considered.

There is an axiom, for the perfect truth of which every living man and many living women can safely vouch; and this axiom says, " Wrong never comes right." No community in the world could be better cited in illustration of its wisdom than the little circle at Sadgrove; the errors of foregone days cast their baleful influence over even the healthiest branches of the family tree; and as it is invariably the case that one falsehood begets ten thousand, so the delicacies and difficulties connected with the occurrences of Mortimer's earlier life led to a series of little tricks and manœuvres which were considered necessary to keep the blemishes out of sight.

The drive took place; and Mrs. Mortimer, having parcelled out her party, and paired those who wished to be together, with all the *bienséance* of London life, started with her friend on their little expedition.

" What," said the countess, " has taken Francis to Worcester ? "

The recurrence of her husband's Christian name in the conversation of her fair friend at all times sounded harsh, and to-day particularly so; probably, because the manner in which the question was put seemed to tally with the spirit and expression of Mortimer's remarks upon her father previous to his departure.

" I have not an idea," said Helen; " I never presume to inquire into his proceedings."

" I suppose he and his *friend*" (with a particular emphasis) " have some very interesting engagement."

" I believe they are gone on business," said Helen, wishing to stop the course of the inquiry, which, although she disdained to show it, agitated and annoyed her.

" What business they can have at Worcester, except to buy you a service of porcelain, a packet of gloves, or a pocket of hops, I cannot guess: perhaps they are gone to visit some friend of other days. By the way, dear, — did Francis ever show you his picture of Amelia ? — it was a wonderfully fine likeness."

"No!" said Helen, and her voice faltered; — she thought the question rather extraordinary and strangely timed; she was not surprised that he never *had* shown it to her, and yet now she felt discontented that he had not, since he knew she was aware of all the circumstances connected with his first marriage.

"You have seen her monument, Helen?"

"No!" said Helen.

"It is immediately at the back of your pew," said the countess; "I wonder you never noticed it."

"I seldom notice anything at church, countess," said Helen.

"Oh!" replied the countess, "I am quite aware of your devotion, of the abstraction it induces, and all that; but I should have thought you would have felt an interest in looking at *that*, apart from idle curiosity: — shall we go there now? — do, — I should like you to see it; it is in the best possible taste, and I think Francis will be pleased to know that you have seen it."

Helen was extremely puzzled how to act; she felt a dread of complying with her companion's suggestions, and a fear of opposing them. She thought she should like to see the monument, but she thought that Francis would be displeased by her visiting it with the countess, or rather, without *him*, since he had never referred to the subject, which, nevertheless, she was told, was nearest his heart.

"No!" said Helen; "I differ with you there, countess; if Mortimer wished me to see the monument, he would either have spoken of it to me, or shown it me himself."

"He would give the world to do so," said the countess, "but he cannot muster sufficient resolution to look at it; if once that struggle were over, he would again visit the church as usual, his absence from which is not calculated to allay the prejudice which exists against him in the neighbourhood."

"Is there a prejudice against him?" said Helen, listening with fearful anxiety to her companion, who seemed of late to take especial pleasure in detracting from Mortimer's merits.

"Prejudice!" said the countess; "why, my dear Helen, you are not blind to that? what else makes Sadgrove as much a desert as it was in the time of its late mistress? not one of the county people come near it."

"No!" said Helen, "because Mortimer declines their society, which bores him, and prefers *that* in which he delights."

"And does he really make you believe all this?" said the countess: "pray, my dear girl, how has he manifested his disinclination to receive them in his house? have they ever made any advances for him to repulse?"

"As for *my* part," said Helen, "I hate neighbours, and I hate travelling out to dull distant dinners and dowdy dances, — so I have told him, and for that reason ——"

"——He would no doubt decline the civilities of the county people," said the countess, "*if* they were offered; but no — even the family of the clergyman, so much here as *he* is on business with Francis, have confined their attentions to a call when they were certain you were out, which you and I returned when they were not at home."

"I know," said Helen, "Francis told me, he thought it best not to invite them here."

"—— Because he could not have borne the mortification of a negative answer."

"Not the least!" exclaimed Helen, in a vindicatory tone; "they would be too happy to come, but he thought it better to postpone the invitation till some of our London guests were gone, and *that* partly at my suggestion; for I declare, good as he is, and all that sort of thing, there is something so eminently absurd in the countenance of the worthy doctor, that I dread a day of them.".

"Well, then!" said the countess, "you will not go to see the tomb this morning?"

"No!" said Helen, "on Sunday after church I will look at it, and will tell Francis that I *have* looked at it; I have no disguises from *him*."

"Poor dear girl!" said the countess, in a tone which could not be mistaken: — "here, I declare, is your most excellent parent and the Thurstons taking a particularly domestic-looking ride, after all the history of the head-ache

and staying at home,—it would be the height of barbarity
to join them; therefore turn short to the left, down this
lane, and leave them to their interesting conversation."

Helen did as she was bid, not that she would have been
at all sorry if the interesting conversation in which she
herself was engaged with her companion had been put an
end to. As, however, she felt that it would, " under existing circumstances," be more agreeable to her father to be
left with his companions to pursue their ramble, the ponies
were wheeled round and trotted away along a beautifully
wooded road which Helen had never before traversed.
Emerging from the trees which shaded the first part of it,
they came upon a sort of terrace cut along the side of
a gently rising hill and overhanging the Severn, which
rippled and glittered at their feet most beautifully.

" What an extremely pretty drive!" said Helen. " Our
meeting papa was quite fortunate, since it sent us in this
direction."

" Have you never been this road before? " said the
countess.

" No," replied Helen, " I seldom attempt to explore:
I keep the beaten tracks."

" But did Francis never bring you this way? " said the
countess.

" No," replied Helen.

" You surprise me," said the countess;—but, to be
sure, it is all part of the same delusion. Drive on, and
when we come to that gate on the left, turn in, and you
will see the prettiest spot in the whole of Sadgrove."

Helen obeyed the instructions of her guide; and when
they reached the gate, and the servant rode forward to open
it, the countess, whose free and easy manner in commanding every member of the household was more remarkable
than agreeable to Mrs. Mortimer, inquired " if he knew
where the key was? "

" They keep it, my lady," said the man, " at Willis's
farm-house."

" Go forward then and get it," said the countess, " and
we will drive round by the shrubbery and meet you."

A touch of his hat was Stephens's practical reply, and off he cantered.

"What place are we going to?" said Helen, who saw that it must be some well-known *endroit*, from the manner in which its key was spoken of, and the knowledge the man possessed as to the place of its keeping.

"I'll not tell you till you see it, dear," said the countess; I like to surprise people. Go on — drive gently — and here to the right, into that copse, and down this *tonnelle* — it is rather steep — but is it not charming, — those glimpses of the river shining through the underwood? — Now, now, to the left — there!" exclaimed the countess in a tone of ecstasy, as the little phaeton stood in front of a picturesque building which she announced to Helen as "The Fishing-House."

So well did the countess know the country, that Stephens, and an old woman from Willis's farm with the key of this fishing-house, reached the spot at the moment of their arrival. With curtsies most respectful, and that flurry which an unexpected visit always causes in humble life, the poor old body, with trembling hand, applied the key to the door.

"I am so sorry, madam," said she: "this is almost the only day this year I haven't regularly opened the Fishing-House in the morning; but to-day — dear, dear me — I am so sorry! I wo'n't be a minute opening the shutters, — deary me!"

"Oh!" said the countess, who always took the lead, "don't hurry yourself; we will get out, and walk round to the terrace, and by that time you will have got it all ready. Come, Helen, dear, — let us leave the phaeton here, and I will take you through the prettiest flower-garden in the world."

Helen wondered, but almost instinctively obeyed her guest.

"How extremely beautiful this is!" said Helen.

"I thought you would admire it," said the countess. "Come — this way."

And she led her through one of the sweetest parterres that ever bloomed, to a terrace-walk of no great extent, which led to what might be considered the front entrance of the building. By the time they reached it, the poor old body had got the shutters open, and was employed in dusting this, and putting right that, labouring under all the horrors of an imputation of neglect of duty.

The Fishing-House consisted of a circular room divided into six compartments, in three of which were windows overhanging the river. In the one opposite to the centre window was a fire-place, on either side of which, occupying the remaining two compartments, was a door ; one led to a kitchen and offices, and the other to a suite of apartments containing a sleeping-room, and a boudoir or dressing-room, as the case might be. The view from it was exquisite, and there was a brightness and a clearness sparkling around it, and a stillness and serenity within it, which might have made the greatest and gayest sigh and say,—

—— " If there's peace to be found in the world,
A heart that is humble might hope for it here."

But no : — the tranquillity which its natural attributes offered were destined neither for humble hearts nor proud ones. The thatch which covered this " gentility-aping " cottage, as Mr. Southey has it, was a mere superficial coating to its well-slated roof, and as little indicated the residence of happiness within, as the humble bearing of its master towards his dependents exhibited the real temper of his mind. The place was lovely — the furniture and decorations, though appropriate, elegant and convenient ; and as Helen cast her eyes around, the countess whispered ——

" Is it not strange that you should not have been here before ? "

" Does it belong to Francis ? " said Helen.

" Belong to him ! " said the countess, " why, my dear love, it used to be his principal residence when ——

" — I understand," said Helen, who thought she observed the old woman somewhat attentively listening to the remarks of the countess.

" I concluded you had been here," said the amiable lady, " or I should have proposed a drive hither a week ago."

" No," said Helen, feeling her cheeks burn with humiliation that she should have been indebted to her friend for
the induction into so lovely and so popular a portion of
her domain.

The countess saw what was passing in Helen's mind.

" Why, my dear," said she, " this used to be the favourite retreat of her who is gone ; and here Francis and
she passed, during the summer months, the greatest portion of their time : indeed, the view which it commands is
so much more beautiful and extensive than that from the
house, that to one to whom seclusion was natural it must
have been extremely agreeable."

" It *is* beautiful !" said Helen.

" Since you were here last, ma'am," said the old woman
addressing the countess, " *my* old man has cut down them
two larches there at the end of the walk, which lets in the
view of the church tower, as you said it would."

" Yes," said the countess, looking remarkably confused,
" Yes — I recollect — yes — it is a great improvement."

" We did not expect to see you so soon again, ma'am,"
continued the unsophisticated rustic, ". or we would have
had that hedge-row clipped, as you desired."

" Oh !" said the countess, " it looks very well as it is."

" What !" said Helen, " have you been here lately ?"

" About — how long is it since ? " said the countess to
the old woman.

" Thursday-week, I think, ma'am," replied the rustic :
— and had she gone no farther, all might have been extremely well ; but the rustic added, — " and then Mr.
Mortimer said he did not think he should be here again till
next Saturday."

Helen heard all this, and felt her head whirl, her eyes
swimming, and her tongue clinging to the roof of her
mouth.   What ! had Mortimer, who dared not venture to
take *her* to this favourite retreat of his former wife, brought
the countess hither, and not one syllable said of the visit,
— no, nor even of the existence of the Fishing-House
itself ?

" — But," continued the old body, " if you wish, ma'am,
to have those curtains which I showed you, put up, instead

of the crimson ones, they can be done in 'three or four days."

What ! ordering furniture — making arrangements — giving directions ! — Helen could bear this no longer : the spirit was roused.

" Pray," said Helen, firing up, her cheeks dyed with the hot blood of indignation, — " pray, for whom do you take this lady ? "

" Mrs. Mortimer — my master's wife," said the simple body, who, although she had partaken of the roasted sheep, and of the flowing ale, on the festive day, had never — probably from the potency of her imbibitions of the latter article — made herself sufficiently acquainted with the person of the squire's new lady to recognise her on her second appearance, and who, being one of those humble grubs who in the midst 'of their work have no time left to be vivacious, considered as a matter of course that the lady who came in Mr. Mortimer's phaeton to Mr. Mortimer's Fishing-House so soon after his return to Sadgrove with his new wife, was that happy individual.

" How 'very ridiculous !" said the countess : — " why, my good woman, *this* lady is Mrs. Mortimer !"

" Dear, dear, deary me !" said the poor old body, looking at the countess with an expression in her countenance indicating a sort of fear that she had made some most serious blunder.

" I wonder, as you see us at church," said the countess, " that, you should not have known."

" — Dear, dear, dear !" said the old woman, " I'm sure, ma'am, I beg a thousand pardons ! — I hope, ma'am, you won't be offended."

" Not in the least," said Helen with a toss of her head ; " the mistake seems to me the most natural in the world."

" There," said the countess, " you may go ; — we will walk round the terrace."

The countess saw that the fire had been kindled, which it would take some time to deaden ; and as she did not wish the old body from Willis's farm to be a spectator of the scene she anticipated, she despatched her as speedily as possible.

Helen said nothing, but she felt as if she were dying,—
and die she would, she resolved, before one single symptom
of what was passing in her mind should exhibit itself.

"What a curious *contretemps*," said the countess,—"it
always happens so: now, I am sure, Helen dear, it must
seem extremely odd to you that Francis and I should have
been here together, and that you should not even know of
the existence of this beautiful retreat: the truth is, we had
a design upon you, and it is *my* fault that it has failed.
We came here to give directions that it should be all put
in nice order to surprise you; and my impression was,
that all the arrangements had been made; but these stupid
people ——"

"Countess," said Helen, shaking the tear-drops which,
spite of her resolution, stood upon her long black lashes,
"I am not pleased with surprises like this. If Francis
could not hear to revisit this favourite retreat with *me*,
what circumstances rendered it less irksome to come hither
with *you*? Of what use was the concealment which kept
from my knowledge the very existence of such a retreat?
The place has no charms for me except those which it derives from Nature, and the fact that it belongs to my husband. I could have felt no difficulty in visiting it; no
painful associations in my mind were connected with it;
and nothing but common delicacy could have been necessary to have kept me from thinking of it as my own loved
place of rest.

"Dear Helen," said the countess, "I am aware how
easy it is to render by a combination of circumstances the
most innocent actions suspicious if not odious. It was I,
who rallied Francis upon his gloom, and told him how
much better it would be if he at once resolved to familiarize
himself with the scenes of other days, and visit those favourite spots in which he had passed so much of his time:
— this was one — he declared the impossibility of his ever
seeing it again. I persuaded, entreated him, for *your*
sake, to come hither,—and at last succeeded. I further gave
such directions to the woman here as might as much as
possible alter its general appearance, and hence at his own
suggestion the change of furniture and other arrangements:

why this poor woman should have mistaken *me* for *you*, it is impossible for me to surmise, except that she happens to be particularly stupid."

" I am quite satisfied," said Helen ; " only I *do* think that if the task of obliterating past recollections were to be assigned to any one, the wife of him who ———"

"—No !" interrupted the countess, "not in this peculiar case. Mortimer's mind is a curious one ; I have known it from his youth. To you he cannot speak on this matter : he is even ignorant how far your knowledge of the circumstances connected with the affair extends. He considers it impossible to touch upon the question ; most of all upon its details, which must have been involved in your conversation with him if you had visited this place together without some preparation."

" Could he not have come hither alone ? "

" He never *would* have come hither alone, and you are indebted, my dear Helen, to *me* for the recovery of this lovely bower."

" I could have lived without it," said Helen mournfully, — " and better so, than have recovered it thus."

" I have but one condition to make with you," said the countess, — " that you will not mention one word to Francis of our visit here to-day."

" Why so ? " said Helen, — " more hypocrisy ! why, countess, am I doomed to live a life of dissimulation, which I abhor ? "

" You do not know his temper," said the countess ; " if he knew that I had anticipated the arrangements we proposed, and frustrated his design, he would be outrageous."

" Then why, why," said Helen, " did you bring me hither ? If my husband, to whom my heart is open as the day, can keep so closely hidden from *me*, thoughts and actions having reference to comparatively trifling matters like these, what confidence — what security can I have that I am trusted at all ? "

" What, then," said the countess, " if everything goes on smoothly and the days pass happily, it matters little whether you know all that occupies your husband's mind !"

" Oh, countess, countess !" said Helen, " if that had

been my creed, I never would have become a wife. I am sure," added she, " that in all that has happened about this place, which, beautiful as it is, I now shall hate, you are not to blame; but I think *I* should be very much to blame if I permitted this evening to pass over my head without telling Mortimer that I had been here, and all I know upon the subject."

" Do as you like, my dear Helen, judge for yourself; I only spoke of expedience, and from a fear of irritating Mortimer."

" — How can he be irritated," said Helen, " by my coming hither, if he were so anxious to prepare the cottage for my reception ? "

" I repeat, dear Helen," said the countess, " I have done. I think I might have been indiscreet in anticipating him in the pleasure he proposed to himself in showing you the place; it remains entirely for you to adopt whatever course you think proper; only acquit me of any unfair motives. I only say, I have known Mortimer longer than you have, and have hoped since I have been here to restore him to himself and you, from whom he seems to me so much estranged."

The conversation here subsided into a calm; but Helen's heart was bursting. The countess appeared at once to dismiss the whole affair from her mind; and, after a nervous walk, or rather saunter, along the terrace, the ladies remounted the phaeton and returned to the " Hall," not much having been said on the road homeward by either, as to the adventure of the Fishing-House, or indeed anything else. What had been doing at Sadgrove during their absence we shall see hereafter.

END OF THE FIRST VOLUME.

---
VOLUME THE SECOND.
---

## CHAPTER I.

It may be supposed that Helen's feelings were not a little
excited by the disclosure made to her by her amiable friend;
not that she was so much mortified by having become acquainted with a fact for the concealment of which there
seemed no adequate cause, but because, being in possession
of that, which for some reason or other Mortimer had chosen
to make a secret, it would be impossible for her any longer
to affect an ignorance of his favourite retreat; for, even if
she endeavoured to conceal the knowledge she had so unintentionally acquired, she was certain it would, even with
the constant watchfulness over her words which such a
course would demand, sooner or later "come out," as the
children say.

Helen felt the necessity of deciding, before her husband's
return, whether she should admit to him her having been
at the cottage or not. If she did not tell him as soon as he
arrived, or at least as soon as he inquired how the day had
gone off in his absence, the time would be past for speaking
of it. He could not be angry — he must have intended her
to go to it at some time or other : besides, she had not
sought it — she had been taken thither by *his* friend. It
seemed absurd to make a point of such a trifle — she
*would* tell him ; — and yet — a dread of something, what
she scarcely knew, shook her honest resolution.

In the midst of these conflicting feelings she determined
to avail herself of her father's presence, and take his advice.
Nothing pleased Batley more than being consulted ; no
matter what the subject, he flattered himself that he could
arrange anything for anybody, however perplexing ; in fact,

the greater the entanglement, the more he was delighted, as it afforded him a better opportunity of exhibiting his diplomacy. Helen rang the bell, determined to lay her case, which she had worked herself up to believe one of great importance, before her sire.

In this design she was, however, foiled, inasmuch as it appeared that, after due and diligent search made, her father was not to be found. The delay which would arise before, she could consult him was, however, rendered inconsequential, by the fact that Mortimer would certainly not return — if to dinner — until so late as to afford her an opportunity of submitting her difficulties for the consideration of "pappy" long before the subject could possibly come under discussion with her husband.

While therefore, Helen, as Carey says of Chrononhotonthologos,

" Unfatigues herself with gentle slumbers,"

and prepares for her toilet, we will draw attention to the occurrences which had taken place at Sadgrove during the fair lady's involuntary " voyage" of discovery.

Batley having concluded his ride with the ladies, and gallantly assisted them in dismounting at the door, found himself left *tête-à-tête* with Lady Melanie ; and, somewhat exhilarated by the extremely kind and lively manner of the gentle Laura, thought it no bad opportunity of pressing his suit, certain from sundry indications, which a man of the world can never mistake, that he would be instantly accepted. Upon his established principle, however, he thought it as well to ascertain the views of the mother of his intended upon the point, as, if she should exhibit any symptoms of distaste, he could shape his attack on Laura in a more romantic manner, and win her in opposition to the maternal mandate.

" My dear Lady Melanie," said Batley, " you have no idea how happy I feel, domesticated again in a family circle. The sudden deprivation of a mistress to my house by Helen's marriage worried me sadly ; and though I tried to laugh off my solitude by rallying friends round me, I found myself, after my little parties had broken up, still more gloomy than before they had begun : — rely upon it, that without the soothing, calming influence of female society, the world is a blank."

" With such opinions," said Lady Melanie, " I wonder you do not again try your fortune in that most interesting lottery, matrimony."

"— Ah! there it is! I assure you that thought has long occupied my mind, — and — only, to be sure, I am not very young ——"

" No, nor very old, Mr. Batley. For *my* part, I think there is a greater chance of happiness in a marriage at more matured years, than in one formed at a time of life when the mind is made up to expect perfection which never exists, and when jealousy and all sorts of worries agitate the heart, for no reason upon earth."

"— Do you really think so?" said Jack, drawing his chair nearer to the sofa on which his companion was seated. " I am delighted to hear such opinions from a person of so much taste and judgment as your ladyship. Is it likely that you might be induced to give a practical corroboration of these sentiments?"

" My dear Mr. Batley," said her ladyship, evidently startled by the emphasis with which the question was asked, " what *do* you mean?"

" I mean," said Batley, "if a man of my time of life were to make such a proposition as you seem to think natural for a man in such a position to make, would you act upon the principle you appear to advocate?"

" Why," said Lady Melanie, " agreeing in your original view of your own particular position, as you call it, I think I should."

" Then," said Batley, with increasing animation, " you *can* and *will* make me the happiest man living."

Saying which, Batley seized her ladyship's hand and pressed it to his lips.

" Dear Mr. Batley!" said her ladyship.

" Dear Lady Melanie," said Mr. Batley, " you must have been aware, I am sure, of the existence of a feeling of the tenderest nature on my part towards one in whom I have flattered myself I saw every quality combined to en-

sure my happiness.    I hesitated, and doubted, more particularly as your opinions and feelings were so deeply concerned.
You know the extent of my fortune ; the place I hold in
society ; my house and establishment are familiar to you ;
and it would ill suit a man of *my* time of life to say more
than that as you seem to have anticipated my object, and
are disposed to make me happy———"

" Why," said Lady Melanie, " I confess I have sometimes thought I saw a disposition towards something of this
sort, — but I doubted, — and ———"

" I felt that you were conscious," said Ja k, — " I rejoice to find you propitious ; and I assure you, Lady
Melanie, that if the most assiduous efforts to secure the
happiness of a second wife, strengthened by the recollection
of the excellence of a first, are likely to be successful, those
you may rely upon."

" Really," said Lady Melanie, " I — cannot — indeed
the difficulty of answering — is ———"

" Of course," said Batley.    " If dear Laura should make
any objections — they may be overcome.    In fact, I merely
took the opportunity — the first I had — of throwing myself at your feet ; — but if, however kind and gracious you
are, and however ready you may be to listen to my petition,
and confirm my wishes, still, if Laura objects — I give you
my honour, nothing like force must be used.    If the gift
be not a free gift, it is none ; so let it be left entirely to
her decision."

" I am sure," said Lady Melanie, looking sweeter than
honey, " I am sure, Mr. Batley, that Laura will not oppose
her mother on this point ; — indeed," added her ladyship
with a still more benignant smile, " Laura herself has anticipated this ; — *I* certainly did *not* — but I suppose, being
more sensitive at her age, she saw the progress of an attachment of which I confess I was not aware.    I so much
esteemed you, and was so much pleased with your conversation, that I easily fell into constant association with you,
certainly not prepared for such a termination of it."

" Then," said Batley, catching her hand again, and
again kissing it, " may I hope ? — all I fear is Laura's —
eh ! — she may ———"

" May what ? " said Lady Melanie, " I tell you she herself first noticed your attentions ; she confided her suspicions to me ; — besides, Mr. Batley, if she *had* scruples, as
a child of mine she would soon overcome them."

" Yes," said Batley, " my dear lady, I agree entirely
with you ; still, if there should be any repugnance ———"

" — Repugnance ! " said her ladyship ; " on the contrary, I do not think you do my girl justice. You should
hear her talk of you in your absence : I do not — upon my
word, I am not joking — I do not think that there is any
dandy of the day — no — not the best of them, who stands
so high in her estimation."

" Why," said Batley, " under the circumstances, I hope
not — eh ! — I should not like to play second fiddle.
However, as I have said, you have made me the happiest of
men.— I may then, dear Lady Melanie, flatter myself"—
and he again kissed her hand — " that — in fact, you consider the matter settled."

" Why," said Lady Melanie, drawing up, " I think,
Mr. Batley, that having permitted the affair to go thus far,
you can have little doubt on that point. I assure you,"
added her ladyship, " that my esteem, I may now call it
admiration, of your character is unbounded ; and when I
recollect, in addition to my personal regard for you, the
advantage which my daughter will receive from the connection, I am not ashamed to own the pleasure I feel in the
result of this conversation."

And Lady Melanie wept, and Jack drew quite close to
the sofa, and Lady Melanie leant her cheek against his
shoulder and wept more.

" Calm yourself, dear Lady Melanie," said Jack; " your
emotion is natural. I can only say, that to secure the happiness of your daughter will be the object of my life : tell
her not to fear that in my new character as affecting *her*,
she will ever experience anything like austerity, or jealousy,
or indeed anything but a tender devotion to her best interests,
and that *her* feelings and *yours* will always be consulted by
me upon every occasion."

" You are a dear kind creature," said Lady Melanie to
Jack, suiting the action to the word, and bestowing upon

his sinister cheek a salute, chaste as Dian's, but which was evidently to be considered the seal of the compact.

" I confess," said Batley, " that it would complete my happiness to know that dear Laura —— "

" Rely upon it," said Lady Melanie, " I would not deceive you ; she is prepared for this : and as to her consent, if I ordered —— "

" — Ay," said Jack, " but, as I have said, compulsion is not the course for me ; — I —— "

" Well, then," said Lady Melanie, " I will put you at your ease, for I do believe you are a little fidgety ; I will go and bring Laura here. I shall only keep you waiting while I take off my habit ; and then you shall hear the meek, the beautiful, and dutiful submission of the young lady herself : — will that satisfy you ? "

" Perfectly," said Jack ; — " satisfy is not the word — it will enrapture me."

" Calm your raptures, and wait," said her ladyship, who, in quitting the room, gave his hand a squeeze which presented to his view a legacy of everything she had to leave to the gentle Laura.

As the door closed, there arose a bright vision before the mind's eye of the imaginative Batley. He never had doubted that Laura was *his* — snared — trapped — bagged ; but he was not prepared for the ready acquiescence of her lady-mother. Mothers have strange notions about daughters ; and coronets and other mystical charms fly about in their day dreams, which circumstances not unfrequently dissipate. Laura was a blue — odious, as we have seen, to Mortimer, but not to Mortimer's father-in-law, in consideration of certain " appliances and means to boot," by which he might, as an Amphitryon — that was his line — work into a position ready for political fight at the earliest opportunity.

It would be impossible to follow the fancies in which Batley indulged during the absence of his future *belle-mère* — the *éclat* of his marriage — the sensation it would make — the triumph he should enjoy over all the whiskered and unwhiskered dandies of London, in the possession of the rich Miss Thurston ; whence he descended into all the details of the marriage, carriage, &c., similar to those which had been exhibited on the morning of the Mortimeration of Helen, and thence into a disquisition as to the most suitable retirement for the honeymoon, and, in fact, into all the *minutiæ* of the most interesting ceremony that can possibly take place in the whole course of a man's life.

He was aroused by the appearance of the gentle Laura, accompanied by her mother.

" Here," said Lady Melanie, throwing open the door — " here is the child herself."

" Dear Laura," said Batley, catching her in his arms, " this is too kind, too good."

" Not at all kind," said Laura, " not at all good. Don't be cross with me ; but, as I love candour and truth, I don't mind — I have expected this for the last month. Mamma says that you imagined that I should frown, and look angry, and say no — dear me ! you ought to have found out by this time that whatever mamma decides on is law with me."

" Angel !" said Batley.

" I only wish that you had spoken to me first; for I own I should have liked to have been the bearer of the news to mamma, so much do I know she esteems and regards you."

" Delicious girl !" said Batley.

" Now," said Lady Melanie, " now you see how little you had to fear from any disinclination on *her* part — no, no, Batley, she never would run *contre* her mother's wishes."

" On the contrary," said Laura, " I do assure you my wishes run ever before yours, and I am delighted to see the result."

" Heaven bless you !" said Batley, catching Laura round the waist, and giving her one of those animated salutes which are perhaps not unnatural under such circumstances, but which young ladies sometimes hesitate to accept " before company."

" I beg pardon, Lady Melanie," said Jack, " I beg a thousand pardons, but one cannot always restrain his feelings. I am perhaps the happiest man in the world, and that must be my only excuse — is it a good one ? "

"Perfectly good," said Lady Melanie, "and I am sure dear Laura will accept it."

Whereupon Laura looked down and simpered, and Jack delighted accordingly.

"Well," said Jack, in a soft under-tone, taking Laura's hand, "I have not been deceived in you — your mother told me I should not be."

"No," said Laura, "I — what can I say ? — I am but too happy."

Whereupon John Batley, Esq. gave Laura another chaste salute.

"Oh dear, Mr. Batley !" said Laura, "you are really too good."

"Not I !" said Batley, jumping up, and twisting himself round in a pirouette; "this is but a momentary transport: I trust, Laura, dearest, we shall be the happiest of the happy."

"But," said Laura, laughingly, "you must not be so *very* civil to *me*. Mamma, I suppose, will not allow so much of your kindness to be bestowed upon *me*."

"Your mamma," said Jack, "is the most amiable of her sex; and in confiding to me the care of a treasure like *you*, convinces me, dearest Laura, of her just estimation of my unceasing desire to make you happy."

"La !" said Miss Thurston, "I never doubted it — why should I ? I have no fear of being tyrannised over — no dread of your temper, which I never saw ruffled — no anticipation of scoldings — not a bit of it. I am sure I can love you without one particle of fear mingling in the feeling to qualify its warmth."

"Angel !" said Batley. What a treasure you have given me, Lady Melanie — to me, who have so recently lost the bright ornament of my house, my darling Helen."

"I trust," said Lady Melanie, "that all will be sunshine and smiles."

"Can there be a doubt ?" said Jack, throwing his well-disciplined eyes so as to bear full upon the not-particularly beautiful face of Laura.

"— And," added her ladyship, " I do hope, since I have acceded to a proposition of the sort, which I really think ' the world' will consider not unreasonable, that Laura will make herself extremely happy under the new arrangement, and that we may all live together."

"Nothing can be more agreeable to *me*," said Jack. " I see no difficulty — not a bit: Laura and I can make it out with the greatest satisfaction, and as for your living with *us*, nothing can be more comfortable."

" Ha, ha, ha!" said Lady Melanie, "what a droll creature! — it is your fun that makes me delight in you. I suppose you would not suggest that Laura should engross the management of our house. No, my dear Mr. Batley, nothing will give me greater satisfaction than proving to you how perfectly Laura shall be under your control."

" Nor anything give me greater pleasure," said Laura, " than submitting most dutifully to so agreeable a father-in-law."

" Father-in-law!"— If Stonehenge had fallen upon his head all in a lump, Batley could not have been more completely smashed, squashed, annihilated, than he was by those words. — What did they mean? — what did Laura mean? — what did Lady Melanie mean? " Father-in-law!"— the word rang in his ears. What was next to be done? — what to be said? — what could he do? — what was the next move?

" You could not have a better," said Lady Melanie.

" I know that, dear mamma," replied Laura; " and it will not require much trouble to be obedient to such a parent."

" 'Gad," said Jack, " I — upon my life! — eh! — why — I — really — there seems — eh! — I don't know — I ——"

" Do not doubt my allegiance," said Laura. " I do assure you I will be as dutiful a daughter as if you were my own father."

" Yes," said Batley, " but — the fact is — it is the most perplexing thing — there is a mistake — a — in fact — I never ——"

" No," said Lady Melanie, " no mistake. I told you you would find her ready to join in my views; and that so far from any desire to oppose your wishes, she would chime in with all your desires."

" Yes," said Batley, " but — really — this is — I — eh ! — I ——"

" What *is* the matter ? " said Lady Melanie. — " Have I mistaken you ? — What upon earth do you mean by this conduct ? "

" I mean," said Jack — " I mean nothing — only that — my object — my view — my intention was — by Jove I — you see — I meant — that is — yes — I meant to propose for Laura."

" Ha, ha, ha !" screamed Laura — my poor dear mamma ! Why I, after all, am the object of Mr. Batley's love and affection ! Oh, what a horrid discovery ! What *has* been the cause of all this *tracasserie ? "*

" I really do not know," said Batley — " but the fact is — I admit the truth ——"

" You *do*, Mr. Batley !" said Lady Melanie, firing up ; — " come then, Laura, let us leave the gentleman to his own reflections. I only regret that compassion for his melancholy position, as he described it himself, induced me to listen to suggestions which I ought perhaps to have crushed in the outset ; but when he ventures to outrage me by making proposals to my child, he puts himself in a situation only to be treated with the contempt which invariably follows folly and presumption. Come, Laura."

Laura obeyed, and on leaving the room, turned round to Batley, and, holding up her finger, burst into a fit of subdued laughter, and said *sottô vocé,* " Oh, you vile deceiver !" The laugh resounded along the lobby after the door was closed, and Batley stood aghast.

It was clear that, after this, Batley could not remain at Sadgrove ; or at least that the Thurstons and he could not both continue their stay ; and as it is an understood point; under such circumstances, that the ladies are to remain as if nothing had happened, it is equally clear that poor dear Batley must forthwith abscond — the which he did, leaving a note for Helen, stating that he was forced to start for town on business, and in such haste as not to be able even to take leave of her.

This note poor Helen, (who of course knew nothing of what had occurred about the Thurstons,) coupled with the absence of Mortimer and Magnus, began to consider a sign of some horrid embranglement of her husband and father; and it may easily be imagined, that when she met her guests at dinner she was in no particularly good humour for conversation.

The long-nosed little Count St. Alme took the presidential seat, and the gay people sat down ; but there was a gloom pervading the scene, which, though natural under the circumstances, everybody felt to be painful, without comprehending exactly why.

The sensitiveness of poor Batley was such, that he could not endure the thought of submitting his discomfiture to Helen so shortly after his expressed certainty of conquest, nor trust to her turn for ridicule, the *rapport* of the mistake into which Lady Melanie — " the figure-head of the Fury " — had fallen ; thus, in the flurry of the moment, he sacrificed his daughter's peace of mind to a personal vanity, which, considering the relationship in which they stood to each other, he might have moderated in her favour.

Ladies who are themselves charming, and who fancy that the men at table are not altogether disagreeable, feel no disinclination, especially in country-houses, to linger long before they " retire : " it is only your very modest, very foolish, or very vulgar person who bestirs herself to get away from an intercourse which every intellectual Englishwoman ought to prolong. In French society, the whole coterie rise together like a covey of partridges, and therefore it makes no great difference at what particular moment they go ; but, with all our translations of foreign fashions, we shall be long before the national prejudice of sitting a little after dinner, subsequently to the departure of the bright stars of the firmament, is generally abandoned. We love to drink their healths when they are gone ; we love to talk of them and all about them : — and then " Bull " must have his politics — the topic in every circle where nothing about the real state of politics happens to be known. Why men and women should separate after

dinner for any lengthened period, certainly requires a solution ; but as English custom has, time out of mind, made
it law, all we can say is, that the longer the mistress of the
house stays at table after dinner, the more benefit she does
to society, and the more rational amusement she and her
lady friends enjoy.

English people get sociable only round a dinner-table,
(and any dinner-table except a round one, we presume, is
rarely seen in these days.)   Strangers who (if a man is
weak enough to be in time to witness its miseries) seem, in
that melancholy stage of purgatorial dulness, the quarter of
an hour before dinner, absolute monsters, become by half-
past eight o'clock generally endurable— sometimes pleasant ;
and only conceive, just as this sort of congenial feeling is
coming on, to catch the inquiring look of the lady of the
house directed towards the leader of the throng, and see
the whole bevy take their departure in melancholy array !

When you go to the drawing-rooms — if you do —
the thing is all to be begun over again ; it is a new field.
Rely upon it, that nothing gives so much play to English
society, high or low, as the aid of a dinner-table : it gets
rid of an awkwardness with which the islanders are, more
or less, universally affected ; it puts them at their ease ;
and however cold and stiff the affair may be in the outset,
it rarely happens but that before the dessert is put down,
all is going well. The best proof of the truth of this axiom
may be exhibited in the supposition of what the same
twelve people — we mention twelve as an extreme number
to be comfortable at a round table — would do, if it were
possible to allow the said table suddenly to sink, like the
cauldron of the "weird sisters," and leave them sitting round
the outside edge of the circle it had occupied.

It might, in some societies, be dangerous to perform this
experiment too suddenly ; but done with due precaution, it
would unquestionably produce on the *convives* a most extraordinary revolution of feeling.

On this particular day, Helen, who always protracted
her stay at table whenever there were present those from
whose high talent, or knowledge of the world, she felt
she could derive either information or amusement, hastened

her departure. She noticed that Lady Melanie, who had precedence, was fidgety, and that Laura looked "extremely odd," during a discussion respecting the untoward departure of Batley ; and Helen, who had last seen her father intimately associated with them, began to suspect that they knew something of the cause of his departure, and that it was connected with Mortimer's absence : this again set her too active mind wondering and weaving a web of mystery — and misery.

" My dear child," said the countess, as they entered the drawing-room, " you are worrying yourself to death about nothing. I know your thoughts ; you fancy something terrible is happening to Mortimer. Make up your mind to this sort of thing ; he will be home long before we retire for the night."

" Yes," said Helen, " but it seems so strange that my father should have gone."

" Oh !" said Lady Melanie, " don't let that worry you."

" Oh dear, no !" said Laura, " *that* needn't trouble your mind. Ha, ha, ha !".

Whereupon Lady Mary something, a crony of Laura's, re-echoed the laugh, which promised to be general, but that, as Helen saw, it was checked by the countess.

This naturally set her wondering more.—What was the influence this presuming woman possessed, to regulate the degree of mirth with which the visitors of Sadgrove chose to visit the departure of her parent ?

It was clear to Helen, that whatever had happened during the course of the day, everybody in the house was better informed as to the particulars than herself ; and, certainly, if the sensation of being, as the phrase goes, " basketed," is never very agreeable, it must be doubly irksome when the " basketed" one happens to be the mistress of the house.

The moment suspicion is allowed a place in the mind, " trifles light as air" contribute to strengthen it ; and though it differs in character from jealousy, inasmuch as it arises from self-love and an apprehension of some plan against the " patient" himself, the progress of the disorder is not very dissimilar. The difficulty of Lady Melanie's position in the family, outraged, as she felt she had been, by the bad taste of the father of her hostess, and the offended vanity of her daughter, piqued at what *she* considered his presumption, and subdued only by a sense of what was due to " the lady of the house," kept them both in a state of artificiality throughout the evening.   They spoke little; and when they did speak, their answers were evasive; and there was a nervousness in their manner, which Helen, never glancing at a rejection of her agreeable parent's offer, still attributed to a knowledge of something in which they knew Mortimer was engaged; for even when the ladies laughed, and when they had, jocosely as they evidently meant, begged her to dismiss all apprehension, the whole performance was undoubtedly an effort.

It would be difficult to describe the anxiety of poor Helen.   Vain were the assurances of the countess that the absence of her husband was in no degree connected with the disappearance of her father; for though, of course, neither Lady Melanie nor her daughter had dropped a hint of the *contretemps* of the morning, the countess was not altogether uninformed of what had happened.   The activity of an accomplished French maid generally procured her all the secret intelligence connected with the society in which she mingled; and on the present occasion, though the particulars had not been distinctly stated, she was aware that an offer had been made and declined.

All these awkwardnesses went on: music was tried — it did not answer: the men joined the ladies, and one or two parties of *ecarté* were formed; but everything went on heavily until about eleven o'clock, when Mortimer, apparently in better spirits than usual, returned.   Helen ran to receive him, and was not repulsed; a kind of reproving look, however, seemed intended to moderate her enthusiasm; and as his eye glanced round the room, Helen saw it first fall on Lady Melanie and her daughter, and then rest significantly upon the countenance of Madame St. Alme.

" Your father has left us, I find," said Mortimer, again looking towards the Thurstons.

" How did you hear that?" said Helen.

"He was himself the herald of the news. He was changing horses at "The Hop-Poles," as we were going into the house; we therefore detained him, and now he and Magnus are gone up to town together."

"What in the world took him away in such a hurry?" said Helen.

A look, in which gravity, admonition, and a comic expression of mock melancholy were blended, astonished Helen.

"He has special business in London," said Mortimer, with another frown, which unfortunately was perceived by Miss Thurston, who was thus made aware of what she could scarcely have doubted,—that Batley had communicated the scene of the forenoon to his friends Mortimer and Magnus. The young lady looked at her mother, but her ladyship affected to be too much engaged with her ecarté to what was going on.

"Well," said Mortimer, "and how have you made it out during my absence?"

"We rode in the morning," said Miss Thurston.

"— And," said Lord Harry, "I and Harvey went fishing. We had no sport, but a beautiful excursion. The view of Sadgrove from the other side the river is charming; by the way, your boat-keeper pointed out one of its beauties of which we have hitherto lived in a state of ignorance unblest.'

"What may that be?" said Mortimer.

"One of the prettiest things in the world," said Lord Harry,—"a fishing-temple."

These words, simple enough in themselves, produced a most extraordinary effect upon several of the company. Mortimer coloured, his lip quivered, and his eye unconsciously sought that of the countess, whose look, to his surprise, as suddenly fell upon Helen.

"Yes," said Mortimer, "it *was* a very pretty thing once, but it has got out of order."

"But does it belong to *you*?" said Lady Mary.

"Yes," said Francis.

"Then, Mr. Mortimer, we must go there," said her

ladyship, " to-morrow ; — to-morrow, Mrs. Mortimer. —
Have you never seen the Fishing-House ?"

" No," said Mortimer, anticipating the answer, " I did
not wish her to see it till I had got it to rights ; however,
if to-morrow be fine, we will send our luncheon there, and
bury ourselves in its seclusion. I meant to surprise Helen
— to-morrow shall be the day.

Accidentally, and by his own anxiety to account for his
wife's ignorance of this favoured spot, Mortimer had
forced her into the very position in which no power on
earth would have induced her to place herself. He had
answered for her, that she had not seen it ; she knew she
had : she knew that silence at that moment was falsehood,
— and yet (not without a warning frown from the countess)
had not the courage to admit that she had that very day
been there. It would have exposed her to a scene, — to
some outbreak of Mortimer's temper. The moment was
past when she ought, if ever, to have said she *had* visited
it ; and now, what had she in view ? — a struggle of hypocrisy from that instant until the hour in which she first
should see it with him.

" What do *you* say, Lady Melanie," said Mortimer,
going to the *ecarté* table, — " will to-morrow suit you ?"

" Why, my dear Mr. Mortimer," said Lady Melanie,
" we *must* run away to-morrow. We have two or three
visits to make, and ——"

" —— My dear Lady Melanie," said Lord Harry, " going
to leave us !"

" Oh, dear !" said Mrs. Mortimer.

" Oh ! we must," said Laura. " Mamma is expected at
the Dumbletons to-morrow."

A look of Mortimer's at Helen was not lost upon the
countess.

" If you must," said Mortimer, rather archly as Helen
thought, " why there is an end ; but we should be too
happy if you would stay much, very much longer."

" The more reason," said Lady Mary, " for our going
to the Fishing-House to-morrow : a change of scene will
divert our thoughts from those who are gone.

" Yes," said Mortimer somewhat mournfully ; and again Helen saw his look rivetted on the countess.

" Is it of any extent, Mortimer ?" said Lord Harry.

" No, a mere summer-house : there are two or three rooms attached to it, and a kitchen ; so you shall have your soup hot."

" I am sure you will like it," said the countess to Helen, by way of effectually stopping what she fancied would be a declaration of their visit, ready to break from her lips.

Helen said nothing, but shook her head mournfully, and looked down.

" I am delighted," said Mortimer, whose spirits seemed better than usual, excited perhaps by some adventitious exhilaration, or by the ride, or — no matter what ; at all events he appeared to enter into the projected excursion with warmth and interest. That he was pointedly affectionate in his manner to Helen was unquestionable ; and it seemed to the countess, that even that effort to unbend was part of his preparation for the visit of the morrow. His knowledge of Batley's proceedings, which he had confided to him, but of which he perceived Helen was ignorant, had created a new interest ; and when the party separated for the night, there was but one aching heart in the whole collection, — that was Helen's.

The moment had passed when the natural impulse of her artless mind would have led to the plain straightforward ingenuous declaration, that she had been at this fishing-temple : it was impossible to recur to it ; she was therefore, as we have seen, destined to live on a feverish life through all the night and part of the following day ; and when they retired to their room, and Francis gave her an animated description of her father's discomfiture, she listened without feeling absorbed in what else would naturally have awakened her filial sympathies — the one sad thought still weighing upon her heart, that, trifling as the circumstance was, she had a concealment from her husband.

If such a person as Helen could have indulged in strong language, — and I am not sure but that, upon reasonable

provocation, she might have done so, — it would be difficult to set down the terms in which she would have
anathematised the fishing-temple, and the countess who
dragged her there.   The night was one, to her, of horror
and remorse ; a thousand times she resolved to awaken
Mortimer and tell him the truth, but as often·was she
checked by the fear of his anger, — a fear instilled into her
mind by the hints and innuendoes of her dangerous friend
the countess.

Generally speaking, where that unreserved communication exists between men and their wives, without which all
hope of domestic happiness is vain, the time of retirement
from the " million " is the season of confidence : to this
period, on all former occasions, Helen had looked forward
for what, in her lively way, she used to call a " talk over"
of the people and the incidents of the day ; and it must
be owned that she had the faculty of hitting off characters
with a quickness and truth which stamped her mind as
one calculated for greater things than those which in all
probability were destined to occupy it.

Different, indeed, was the feeling which actuated her
during this night.   While in her dressing-room, instead of
speaking good-naturedly to her maid, as was her wont, her
thoughts were devoted to what she felt was a wrong she
had done.   The questions of her attendant, as to the arrangements of her dress for the morning, passed unnoticed ;
and her manner was so abstracted, that the poor *soubrette*
began to fancy she had done·something to render herself
obnoxious to her mistress.

It was not so ; Helen was not angry with the maid, but
with herself ; and remorse for what she had been induced
rather to permit than do, preyed upon her with accumulated force from the dread she entertained of Mortimer's
alluding to the conversation which had passed in the
drawing-room.

Luckily, Mortimer did not revert to the subject after
they retired ; the truth being, that it was one which he
could not well approach without admitting that he himself
*had* visited the scene of his former seclusion without his
wife, and with her visiter.  · Thus both these persons were

kept in an apprehension lest either should allude to what
— if their conduct towards each other had been regulated
by the candour which alone ensures mutual happiness in
married life — would have formed perhaps as innocent a
topic as any upon which they might have chosen to discourse themselves to sleep.

Mortimer's feelings were of a totally different character
from Helen's : in his anxiety to avoid the subject, there mingled recollections of crime and sorrow, and a consciousness
of wilful deception towards his bride — for the reader may
be satisfied, that although the agreeable master of Sadgrove
could not refuse to accede to the proposition of his guests
to make a party to the Elysium which some of them had
discovered, it had not been his intention, at all events so
speedily, to familiarise Helen with its beauties ; and he lay
trembling lest her questions might be such that he could
not answer with a due regard to truth, without laying open
more of his former habits, or of his reasons for not taking
her there before, than would be likely to increase her affection or respect for him.

She, on the contrary, through the kind communicative-
ness of the countess, was already apprised of all that he
was most anxious to conceal ; and that knowledge of past
events, blended with the *secret* excursion of the morning,
now evidently not to be revealed, made her miserable.
Fortunately, however, owing to his expedition to Worcester, and the extra exhilaration of spirits which we have
noticed, and which Helen, perhaps not injudiciously, attributed to the effects of wine, of which, ordinarily speaking, Mortimer never took more than ultra-dandy allowance,
or, perhaps, to the very anxiety of which we have spoken,
Mortimer felt little inclination to talk of anything, and
fell into a profound sleep, after having enlightened Helen
as to the real cause of her father's flight, the colloquy ter-
minating by her exclaiming — " Poor dear pappy ! "

The relief to her mind afforded by the certainty that
Mortimer slept without reverting to the one dreaded subject was great, — but she closed not her eyes ; she lay
thinking and considering how she should best arrange the
party for the morrow. If she went with *him*, she could

not act sufficiently well, to affect surprise as the beauties of
the place gradually broke in upon her; and, if she were
able to do so, she could not condescend to deny having
been there before: no, — Francis should drive one of the
ladies, — the countess? — perhaps not, — some one — any
one, — and she, Helen herself, would ride: thus mingled
in the group of horsemen and horsewomen, the conversation would be general, and Francis should go on first in
the phaeton and receive them; and so deception was to
follow deception, — for what? — to humour a whim of the
countess, of whom Helen had become as much afraid *as
her husband actually was.*

For one moment we may be permitted to inquire, why
Mortimer ever sought to renew his acquaintance with that
lady, or why he still endured an association with her, which
evidently embittered his existence; — there must be something in it more than we have yet discovered.   He has, we
know, positively denied to his bosom friend, Magnus, the
justice of his amiable sister's suspicions, as to the nature of
his early friendship for the lady for whose sake, it nevertheless appears, he has consented to relinquish that sister's
friendship; for, though for some time after his return to
Sadgrove, their correspondence continued, it had at the
time of which we now speak ceased entirely.   Time may,
perhaps, enlighten us as to the real causes of Mortimer's
conduct in this respect.

When morning and breakfast came, Helen felt at ease.
The preparations for the departure of the Thurstons, and
the departure itself, would occupy the attention of the group
until it was time to start on the expedition; and, now that
the lady of the house was informed of the real cause of their
evanishment, she saw at once the propriety of their not
longer remaining in the house of the daughter of the gentleman who, with all his accomplishments, had made a shot
so desperately bad, as to wound the vanity of the elder lady
of the two without so much as scratching the heart of the
younger one.   She was accordingly unremitting in her attentions; and, when Lady Melanie's travelling chariot drew
up to the door, the whole population of visiters escorted
her ladyship and her daughter to the steps of the chariot,

and waved their hats and handkerchiefs in gay adieux, until the going guests were out of sight ;—all these tokens of friendship and esteem being returned by similar signals from the carriage windows.

"What a bore that woman *is?*" said Lord Harry, as the party were returning *en masse* to the morning room ; "I think the way she talks up her dear Laura is something beyond the common run of things."

"Oh, and Laura's harp !" said Lady Mary ; "upon my word, it is the most awful affair imaginable."

"I must confess," said Mortimer, "that the incessant harmony becomes after a day or two rather overpowering."

"Yes," said Lord Harry, "and if one ventures to whisper, the old lady looks daggers, while, as everybody knows, the only use of music is to give freedom to conversation."

"Somebody told *me*," said the Captain, "that Laura was going to be married."

"I doubt the fact," exclaimed Lady Mary : "first, I doubt there ever having been an offer ; and, secondly, I doubt still more poor dear Laura's being able to say no if there had."

"Then," said the countess, "you are mistaken."

"Well, countess !" said Helen, "let us live in blissful ignorance ; there *are* secrets in all families — so — shall we think of making preparations for our departure ?"

"If you please," said the countess. "Pray, dear, did you read the description of the flower I talked to you about, in the 'Annual Register,' where there is a long account of it ? I sent it by Hannam to your room."

"No," said Helen, "I have not had time to open the book, but I *will* when we come back."

"Now," said the countess, taking Helen aside, "be sure you do not betray by word or look your having visited the fishing-cottage. I know *his* temper ; besides, you would involve me in a quarrel with him, for I know he never would forgive me for having taken you there, even if he overlooked your going with me."

"Oh, countess, countess !" said Helen, "why *did* you take me there ? why am I forced to play the hypocrite,

when, if we had acted fairly, there could be no necessity
whatever for deception ? —this sort of life will kill me."

" In *this* world, dear," said the countess, " men of the
world are to be met with their own weapons. Candour on
one side is no match for duplicity on the other ; however,
don't let us preach, but get ready."

The laugh with which the countess followed up this
sally rang discordantly in Helen's ear.   There are countenances which, even in playfulness, are demoniacal ; and
the smile which gleamed over this lady's features was characterised, at least as Helen thought, by a triumphant
satisfaction at having, as if inadvertently, inflicted a fresh
wound.

Helen hurried to her boudoir, from the door of which
she met Mortimer issuing ; he was pale and agitated, and
his looks betrayed a violent agitation of mind which
alarmed her.

" Good Heaven, Francis!" said she, " what is the
matter ? — what *has* happened ? "

" Nothing, nothing," said he with a tremulous voice;
and a look more of sorrow than of anger ; " it is natural,
—but cruel : would to Heaven I hadn't known it!"

" Known what ? " said Helen.

" Here, here, Helen !" said Francis, " come in, come in
— we are observed — they are looking up at us from the
hall, — let us have no scene, for mercy's sake !—I will
go in with you."

Saying which, he re-entered the boudoir ; and Helen,
fancying that he had discovered the history of her visit to
the Fishing-House, threw herself into a chair pale as death,
or as her husband,—for *he* looked like a spectre.

" Helen," said he, labouring under deep emotion, which
he strove earnestly to master, — " Helen, you need not
have let me see how anxiously you seek out my evil deeds
— how greedily you swallow all that can militate against
my character."

" Francis ! what do you mean ? —what have I done to
deserve this ?   If I have been inadvertently led to do that
which is painful or unpleasant to you, rely upon it, it has
never been of my own free will.   I wish to know nothing

more than you think fit to trust me with; indeed I do not."

"Then," said Mortimer, "why take such unequivocal steps to bring to your mind the evidence of my guilt?" .

"What on earth do you mean?" again said Helen, sobbing convulsively; "if I have erred, I aske your forgiveness."

At this moment she had resolved, in spite of 'the countess's persuasions, to confess the visit, and to state the truth, which nothing but Mortimer's own interruption the night before would have stifled; for to falsehood Helen's proud heart would never have stooped.

"Hear me!" said she.

"Be calm, be calm!" said Mortimer; "I am not angry, but I am wounded, deeply wounded; the sight of this book curdled my blood,—nay, Helen, Helen, it drove me mad. To think that from the whole library you should have selected this particular volume, stung me to the quick; in it you see me degraded, debased, reviled, and insulted: even if it gratified you to read such a record of my faults, you might surely have concealed the proof of your disposition that way, from my sight."

"Of what book are you speaking, Francis?" said Helen; relieved from her first apprehensions, but bewildered by the new allegation.

"This, Helen," answered he, taking from the table the volume of the "Annual Register" which the countess had sent to Helen as containing a paper on botany, treating minutely of a then newly discovered flower, of which there were at the present time several varieties in her conservatory.

"I have never opened it," said Helen.

"Why is it here?" said Mortimer; "you know its contents; you know that in its pages are published to the world the particulars of that trial whence I came scathed and blasted in reputation and character: there, in its pages, are recorded the savage philippics of the foul-mouthed highly-fee'd advocates paid to blacken my fame, and hold me up to hatred and contempt; and this book is the single solitary one selected from thousands, free for your special amusement and gratification!"

" Oh, Francis !" sobbed Helen, " think better of me :
believe me — trust me — I repeat, and solemnly — that I
have never opened the book.   The countess sent it me that
I might read an account of a flower which ——"

" The countess sent it you !" said Mortimer, his face
flushing from deadly white to crimson ; " *she* sent it to
you, and for the purpose of — not for the — eh ?"

" For what I tell you, dearest," said Helen.

" Helen, Helen, my dearest girl !" said Mortimer, drawing her to his heart, " I believe you.   I see it — I see it
all ; forgive me, sweetest ! — The countess sent it — Merciful Powers ! — say, Helen, — I am subject to these horrid
fits of frenzy, — say, you forgive me."

" Forgive you, Francis !" said Helen ; " what is there
to forgive ?   If I could have been guilty of such a meanness, if I could have harboured so base a feeling as that of
which you thought me guilty, I should have deserved your
curse : — but no — I have told you the truth."

" Of that I am sure, Helen," said Mortimer, again
pressing her to his heart : " sure, you *have* no disguises
from *me ;* — why should you ?"

Again the visit to the Fishing-House flashed into her
mind ; but now she dreaded to confess, lest her admission
as to *that*, might weaken his confidence in the truth of
what she had now told him.

" It is indeed," said Helen, " a singular accident by
which the countess ——"

" Accident !" said Mortimer : " Helen, rely upon it
that nothing the countess does is done by accident ; she is
a perfect woman of the world ; — do not offend her : say
nothing about this ; read the paper to which she has
pointed your attention, and send her back the book : I will
trust you as to avoiding those pages a perusal of which
can do no good, but which perhaps in the playfulness of
her imagination she thought might do some mischief."

Hearing Mortimer speak thus of the woman whom, spite
of herself, he had made her like, and had selected as her first
visiter at Sadgrove, the impulse of her heart would have
been to have strengthened his opinion of her motives by
repeating all she had said of *him* to *her ;* but her father's

caution, added to that which Mortimer himself had given her, not to offend her, kept Helen silent.

"That will be best," said Francis, calmed down to reason by the conviction of his young wife's ingenuousness and truth; "take no notice of what has passed."

"Take you the book, Francis," said Helen; "carry it away,—take it out of my sight!"

"No, no," said Mortimer, "I must not appear in the affair: *you* return it when you have read what she means you to read; or rather when you have not read what she really means you to read, but that which she *says* she means you to read. Come, Helen, dear; these people are waiting for us: your eyes look red; do not come down till all traces of this sorrow are gone: I will keep them engaged till you are ready. You *do* forgive me, Helen?" added he.

"From my heart and soul!" exclaimed Helen, with a warmth so genuine that Mortimer's heart beat with pleasure that he was blessed with such an amiable wife.

He went down into the hall, and Helen rang for her maid; but the more she thought of the brief storm just past, the more she wondered at the influence which the countess evidently possessed over Francis. That he knew her faults and vices, as Helen held them, was evident; for he spoke of her conduct, even in the very last affair, as being full of design and duplicity, — "rely upon it, Helen, nothing ever happens with the countess by accident."

Helen was dressed, her habit was on; her fine countenance was filled with an expression more thoughtful than usual, but not the less beautiful for that. She descended the staircase with an air of ease, *selon l'usage du monde*, and by the time she had reached the bottom, the sunshine of her eyes resumed its brightness, and for the "world's" sake Helen looked the happiest creature on earth.

While arrangements were making for the departure of the merry party, Helen watched Mortimer's movements with a degree of curiosity which perhaps she had never before felt upon the opening of any similar excursion. Her dress proclaimed her intention of riding, for in this part of

her design of avoiding a protracted piece of acting she.
persisted.

"What!" said Mortimer, as gaily as he could, "you
are for riding, Helen?" Who then goes with me in the
phaeton?"

There was a brief pause, it was *but* brief; all the ladies
were prepared for riding, except the countess: "I suppose,
my dear countess, I am to have the happiness of your
society?"

The countess gave a look of acquiescence, and said, "If
I do not bore you."

"Not particularly," said Mortimer, with a look so full
of regard that Helen shuddered; not because she was
jealous; not because she wished to restrain the friendly
feelings of her husband, or check their expression; but
because the look itself, and the manner in which it was
given and received, were so totally at variance with the
feelings Mortimer had so recently expressed. To be sure,
his civility might be offered upon the principle which he
strove to impress upon his wife — of not offending her.
However, Helen determined *not* to think, but to be as gay
as she could upon this, to her, important morning — made,
in fact, important by a series of incidents in themselves of
no importance whatever. Important, however, it eventually
proved; and from its termination may be dated much of
that through which the reader has to penetrate.

Lest, however, we should hurry him, or her, as the case
may be, too rapidly to the *Ultima Thule* — the catastrophe
— we will take the opportunity, while all these very gay
and happy personages are tittuping along upon their sleek-
skinned horses to the Paradise of Sadgrove, just to cast a
look towards London, covered as it is with its brown
blanket of atmosphere, which, at ten miles' distance, points
it out as the region of sea-coal, if not, as generally said, of
sin.

## CHAPTER II.

WHEN Batley encountered Mortimer at Worcester, his first impression — worldly — was not to say one syllable as to the real cause of his sudden flight from Sadgrove; but Mortimer and Magnus led him on to a full confession of the facts, he being never the wiser as to what carried them to that city; for, however assiduous *they* were in finding out *his* little involvements, they remained upon their own business as silent as Gog and Magog during the animated discussions which take place in the Guildhall of the city of London.

Whatever *had* been the occupation of the morning on which those two worthies had busied themselves, nothing transpired except the result, which was a resolution on the part of Magnus to start for London forthwith: that this had been either premeditated or reasonably anticipated, it was not difficult to discover, from the fact that Magnus's carriage had been sent to Worcester from Sadgrove, with his servant, in the morning, under the pretence that, if the night should turn out wet, it would be so comfortable to have it there — a precaution rendered, however, somewhat suspicious by the fact that the imperial was filled with the gallant colonel's clothes, while his dressing-case, pistol-case, writing-desk, and half-a-score packages of travelling comforts, were all stowed away within.

There was a mystery in all this, as indeed there seemed to be in everything connected with the family: nevertheless, Jack Batley, who was the readiest of men at availing himself of anything that was going, either for amusement or advantage, found his account in the proceeding; and therefore, although he might be supposed to be interested in what looked like a decisive movement on the part of the most intimate friend of his son-in-law, he asked no questions, but answered one which was put to him by Magnus, whether he should prefer a corner in his carriage to a hack chaise by himself; for as Batley had gone down to Sadgrove in Lady Melanie's roomy chariot, he had no conveyance at hand but a "yellow and two," or the stage-coach, in which he would most probably have deposited himself in the morning, if he had not fallen in with his son-in-law and his friend in the afternoon.

It is scarcely worth while to detail the conversation which the triumvirate enjoyed at " The Poles," as the house, in its own vicinage, is called : it is merely necessary to observe that Batley opened his whole heart to his companions ; and that the three being, to a certain extent, elevated by a long sitting over tavern wine after an early dinner, he swore a great oath,—not profanely, for it was by some heathen god or goddess, no matter which, — that he would revenge himself upon the Thurstons by marrying the first pretty girl he could find in the humour to accept him ; if he did *not*, he should feel himself dishonoured : and in this sapient resolution this long-headed politician was greatly supported by his son-in-law and his son-in-law's friend, who, though he did not say much, observed that nothing could so completely obliterate a defeat as the speedy occurrence of a victory.

In this strain the three gentlemen continued till Magnus's carriage driving into the gateway, according to order, he and Jack threw themselves into it, resolving to go to Oxford that evening ; unless, tempted by the quiet comforts of " The White Hart " at Chipping-Norton, they might be induced to sleep in that calm and peaceable town, of which horse-cloths are the staple commodity.

Whether this happened, or whether they reposed at " The Star," in other days a bright one, — or at " The Angel," now in great feather, — seems immaterial ; the certainty is, that they arrived in town the following afternoon, heartily sick of each other, — Magnus bored to death by the fluency of Batley, and Batley worn out by the pomposity of Magnus. They parted friends, which was something ; and Jack, spite of all his former repulses — such is the force of habit—resolved to go in the morning and tell his tale of sorrow to brother Jacob, certain, however, of the reception he should meet with.

Jack went about his house a melancholy, miserable man ; he looked at the empty rooms, dingy with London dust and smoke, and redolent of the indescribable vapour, if it may so be called, for which there can be found no suitable word except one, which is not in any English dictionary, —*frowst*. It is peculiar to our great metropolis, and is produced upon furniture and in rooms by the incessant depositings of minute particles of filth upon every object exposed to the operation of what is usually called "the air," and which is in itself a wonderful combination of filth, smoke, fog, gas, and various other results derived from gutters, kennels, decaying vegetables, putrid meat, the chimneys of glass-houses, distilleries, brewhouses, melting-houses, boiling-houses, &c. &c. &c., which in combination constitute that pea-soup atmosphere, of which already notice has been taken, and in which a certain million or so of people contrive to exist nevertheless and notwithstanding.

Batley's house had been shut up to exclude this horror; the remedy was worse than the disease: and, after having breathed the pure air of Worcestershire for a few days, the smell of soot, carpets, and canvass-bags, all equally "frowsty," sickened his stomach, while the desolate appearance of the rooms themselves pained his heart. Jack, however, belonged to two or three clubs; and having decided that "The University" was the best for dinners, thither he repaired, meaning to pass the evening in "reading-up" the newspapers for the two days he had lost by leaving Sadgrove in the preceding forenoon.

Amongst the grievances of clubs are, as in every other place in society, bores; but no bores are so serious or so inevitable as club-bores. To a man much in the world as Batley was, the hope and comfort of dining at a club is, that one may be left entirely to his own solitary cutlet and pint of wine, either, as Batley proposed to do, to read up newspapers after a day or two's absence from town, or to think over matters peculiarly interesting to oneself.

No man, we presume, who has a house of his own and a tolerably large circle of acquaintance, dines at a club, except as a matter of convenience, — always excepting house-dinners and trials of skill in gastronomy. It should therefore be held, if he sit down to dine alone, that his object is to *be* alone; and no man should take the step of inviting himself to dine with him, unasked, any more than he would in his own house. If the originally planted diner begins the colloquy by an invitation, what can be better? but, as it appeared to Jack, the most active self-bidders — the chair-placing offerers of themselves to the unhappy *solitaire*, who desired of all things to dine alone, — were uniformly the greatest bores of the whole community.

" If," said Jack to himself, upon the occasion to which we now refer, " the rule in clubs were, that men should hold the little table at which one dines sacred, and that, until they were asked, they would not ' make one ' at it, all would be well : in all other respects this club-house is my house in common with others ; but my little table is as much mine, individually and exclusively, as my larger table in Grosvenor Street. To-day I like to dine alone ; I am not in the humour to talk, or laugh, or drink, or eat, — and here I am by myself. If I want a companion, there are plenty to join me ; but till *I* say, " Wo'n't you sit down ? '—' Wo'n't you come and dine here ?' or use some such provocative, I do expect to find myself as much alone as if I were in my own dinner-parlour."

" How do you do, Mr. Batley ?" said a most respectable fellow of Ma'dalene, drawing his chair to the table where the repulsed Lothario was sitting.

" How do you do, Doctor ?" said Batley.

" Pray," said the doctor, " have you heard anything lately of poor Dick Dowbiggen ?"—and then, turning away, without waiting for an answer, added, " Waiter, bring my glass of negus *here*."

Batley wished him in——his college, at least.

" No," said Jack, " I haven't heard of him for some time."

" He's going," said the doctor, " very fast ; gout — asthma — and a touch of erysipelas : — why, you know, Batley, we can't last for ever. He must be about your standing, I think."

" My standing ! " said Batley, and all his hopes of ma_trimony rushed into his mind ; " he is *my* senior by twenty years, doctor."

"Oh! perhaps so," said Dr. Bottomly; "I may mistake;—but you were both at Ma'dalene together."

"Ah!" said Batley, "but he was at least old enough to be my father. Why, he was a fellow when I was an undergraduate."

"Probably," said Dr. Bottomly; "but you were always old-looking of your age."

To Batley, with the curly wig, the uncommon stock, the extraordinary waistcoat, and the sort of coat he wore, this was hateful.

"Waiter," said Jack, "my bill!"

"Are you going?" said the doctor.

"Yes," said Jack; "I have an engagement at ten, and it wants only a quarter. I thought you were going yourself."

"No," said the doctor, "no: I purposed having half an hour's chat with you about old times over my negus."

"I don't care much about old times; I always keep looking forward, doctor."

And Batley went off in a strain which quite astonished the venerable fellow, and led him to suspect that his companion was not altogether in the possession of his right senses; after which exhibition of principles and opinions, he disbursed his four and sixpence for his cutlet and pint of sherry, and took leave of the snug corner in which he had ensconced himself to be quiet, but out of which he had been driven by the goodnature and attention of his reverend and venerated friend.

Jack quitted the little club-house, the *beau-idéal* of prettiness (in spite of its marble window-shutters and the equivocal door in the centre of its staircase), and scarcely could muster courage to go directly home;—and yet Crockford's was empty, and Brookes's torpid.—What was he to do?

What he did,—whether he went to the play, or recreated himself in any other pursuit,—makes no difference to the reader: all he needs to know is, that at some period of the night he found himself with his head upon his pillow in his bedroom in Grosvenor Street, resolved to visit Lillypot Lane early the following day. .

According to this predetermination, Jack had no sooner
despatched the ordinary business of his morning than he
betook himself to the city in order to consult Jacob; a
course he the more confidently adopted, inasmuch as not
intending upon that occasion to ask for anything but that
which every man, probably conscious of its value, is extremely liberal in giving,—namely, his advice,—he thought
he might meet with a somewhat more fraternal reception
than he could have anticipated if he had been going on
one of those numerous errands which had so frequently
proved unsuccessful.

In undertaking this expedition, Jack thought proper to
take the precaution which sundry magnates of the west end
of the town are in the habit of adopting when forced to visit
the dens and dungeons, filled with desks and drudges, in the
obscurity of which are made the profits on which they dis-
port and display themselves in what they call their proper
sphere of society, and accordingly ensconced himself in a
hackney-coach; and, having directed the driver to stop at
the corner of Lillypot Lane, he hastily drew up the cracked
glass of the vehicle, and, throwing himself into one of its
corners, began to arrange the materials for a dialogue with
his eccentric relation.

Arrived at his destination, the excited Batley hurried to
his brother's counting-house.   King Charles on his steed
at Charing-Cross, or King James on his pedestal in Privy
Gardens, were not more certain fixtures than Jacob at his
desk in Lillypot Lane, from nine in the morning until
'Change-time; except on Sundays or holidays, when he
indulged himself in a walk to the " west end," as he
quaintly called it, or when any special business required his
personal attention in those parts.

Upon the day in question there he was, poring over
huge books, and files of letters, with as much earnestness
and assiduity as if he were just beginning business, and
had a host of ravenous relations to provide for after his
death, instead of possessing one only traceable connection
in the person of his brother.

" Jacob," said John, pushing open the swing-door of
the sanctum, " how d'ye do?"

"John," said Jacob, looking up, and instinctively shutting the drawer of the table in which lay his cheque-book, "how d'ye do, John? — eh? — what d'ye want?"

"Nothing," replied John, "but half an hour's talk with you."

"Oh, that's all," said Jacob; "I can't spare half an hour now."

"Well," asked John, "when can I have that pleasure?"

"Any time after four," said Jacob.

"Where do you dine?" asked the affectionate brother.

"At 'The Horn.'"

"May I join you?" said Jack.

"If you choose," said Jacob, "share and share alike; only the dinner wo'n't suit *you*, I dare say, nor the hour — half-past four; bit of fish plain boiled, and a rump-steak."

"Nothing I should delight in more."

"Very well," said Jacob; "call here at ten minutes after four; we'll go together, else I suppose you'll not be able to find your way."

"I will be punctual," said John. "But you don't inquire after Helen."

"I am afraid to ask," said Jacob: "I know what the answer *will* be some day, and, though it don't make any personal difference to *me*, anything wrong *there* might hurt my credit."

"Oh, there is nothing wrong, I assure you," said Jack; "Helen is well, and I trust as happy as she ought to be."

"Ah, that'll do," said Jacob; "now go, there's a good fellow; be punctual, for I sha'n't wait: and—here—Mr. Grub!"

"I am off," said Jack; "rely upon my being here to the minute."

"Umph!" muttered Jacob to himself, as he replaced his spectacles on his nose; "something in the wind—no man does anything without a motive: why should he take a fancy to a four-o'clock chop if he did'nt expect to get something by it?—Here, Mr. Grub!"

The faithful Grub stood at his side, and again the prudent Jacob fell to business.

John, having looked at his watch, began to calculate how he could contrive to kill the two hours and a half he had before him: a very little consideration assured him that there were plenty of modes in which that desirable operation might be performed. His first descent was upon the Tower, where two or three of his friends of the Guards were quartered; here, however, to use his own expression, he missed his tip, for those whom he knew best, and with whom he meant to have taken luncheon, were, what they call, "gone to town." Thence he bent his steps to the Custom-house Quay, as one of the liveliest, and, to a speculative eye, the most interesting localities of the metropolis. Leaving this busy scene, he permitted himself to be jostled westward until he reached St. Paul's, just as the afternoon's service was beginning: having gratified his passion for church music in the choir, he lingered amongst the fast increasing monuments of the cathedral until it was nearly time for him to retrace his steps to Lillypot Lane.

"Punctual!" said Jack, as he again made his appearance.

"Every man is punctual," said Jacob, "when he wants anything."

"I assure you," said John, "I want nothing to-day but your society, and perhaps a little of your advice."

"Advice!" said Jacob, "I never take advice; I'm not very likely to give it: however, if I do, it must be after I have dined: I hate conversation at dinner; I like to be jolly and have no talking. — Come, Mr. Grub! call Alexander to help me on with my great coat; good folks are scarce, and the evenings in October sometimes set in sharpish. — D'ye hear?"

"Let me do it?" said Jack, suiting his action to the words.

"No," said Jacob, "I pay Alexander for waiting on me: I know what it costs — and no favour: I hate to be beholden to anybody."

Accordingly, Alexander, or, as he was called by Mr. Grub, Alick, performed the operation of great-coating his master, and, having carefully smoothed it down, presented him his hat; a quarter of an hour being expended in preparing the merchant against the probable severity of the evening of a sunshiny day.

"Now then," said the worthy man, "if you are not too fine to be seen walking with me, here I am, ready and willing, and as hungry as a hunter; so come. — Alick! I shall be in by ten; and, if anything particular comes, I shall be down at the old shop."

Alick bowed obedience, and the brothers sallied forth.

"You never were at 'The Horn'?" said Jacob.

"No," was the reply.

"I can't think what carries you there to-day," said Jacob.

"I have told you, I haven't seen you for some time, and I wish to talk with you."

"Ah!" said Jacob, "all your fine birds are flown, so now you can condescend to join *me*. When are you to be married? not that I care: I only ask."

"Why, it is upon that point I ——"

"Oh, ah," interrupted the worthy citizen, "I thought it was something of that sort; why, is the matter with Miss — what's her name you told me all about? — is that off?"

"That is just what I wish to explain."

"Ha, ha, ha!" said Jacob, "what a fellow you are — always finding mares' nests! — I have heard people say of a mad speculator that all his geese were swans; but, as for you, it's the reverse — all your swans turn out geese."

"Why, there *has* been a little mistake," said Jack, obliged to bawl out his confidential communication in a voice of thunder to out-roar the noise of the carts and other conveyances with which the streets were thronged.

"Mistake! ha, ha! I never make mistakes; nobody need make mistakes, if they will but take a little trouble: I never pity anybody who makes a mistake. Here, turn to the left; there, keep this side!"

And accordingly the relations diverged into Paul's Chain, and, descending towards the river, just as they had passed the end of Knightrider Street, Jacob called a "halt;" and at the moment found himself at the door of a tavern affording in external appearance little inducement to enter it, but which was the chosen *restaurant* of his wealthy brother.

" Is *this* the place? " said John, evidently surprised at Jacob's selection.

" It is," said Jacob, " and a deuced good place too: there, go in ; push open the grain-baize door — there. — I hope they have got a bit of fire — October afternoons are chilly, eh? — they *have*, by Jingo! that's right: — all done for *me ;* other people think it too hot, but what do I care for *that ?*  Well, well done, Thomas! — nice fire, eh? — dinner ready? "

" In two minutes, sir," said the waiter, placing a chair for John on one side of the table, standing in the corner between the window and the fire-place, Jacob's seat being opposite and against the wall.

The look of dismay which overspread John's countenance as he entered the small and somewhat dark apartment, relaxed into a more complacent expression as his eye glanced over the snowy whiteness of the table-cloth, the shining cleanliness of the plate, and the comfortable appearance of the arrangement altogether.

As the reader is already apprised of Mr. Jacob Batley's aversion from conversation at dinner, we will pass over the history of the meal summarily ; there was salmon *au naturel*, a broiled fowl with mushroom sauce, and a rump-steak ; the sherry was good, the cooking good, to the full extent of its pretensions : and when Jack, who did not think it right in the " world " to drink port-wine, tasted one glass of Mr. L.'s favourite vintage, he sipped and sipped again, waiting for an opportunity to begin his interesting conversation until the four or five other diners had taken their departure, seeing that the coffee-room was too small to admit of any confidential intercourse without the certainty of being overheard.

The few visiters, however, were there habitually, and Jacob knew them all, and they all knew Jacob ; and John Batley grew gradually to like them, inasmuch as each of these men, for whose intellect he began by having no respect, exhibited in the course of conversation after dinner, which, from the circumscribed size of the apartment and the acquaintance of the parties, became general, knowledge and information which astonished the theoretical man of public business. Here, in this small unpretending room, was he associated with men whose innate talent and industry had honourably realised for themselves thousands upon thousands, and who were, each in his way, masters of subjects of which Batley had learned only to think superficially; and he at last worked himself into the faith that there might be not only wealth and enterprise eastward of Temple Bar, but knowledge, and gentlemanly feeling, stored in the darkest recesses of Lillypot Lane and Watling Street; added to which, he admitted to himself there might be comfort at " The Horn," though the introduction of cigars after dinner certainly staggered him. However, " nobody " was in town, and therefore " nobody " would be annoyed upon his return to his own propher sphere; and as he found Jacob in a good humour, he determined not to be betrayed into a bad one, upon the occasion of having, for the first time, beheld his brother in a position in which he was looked to as somebody of importance by persons who, never expecting any favour from him, did not care for, if they saw through, the selfishness of his disposition, but who paid that regard to assiduity crowned by success, which, in a mercantile community, cannot fail to command respect.

By nine the rest of the company had quitted the room, and John having in an " unworldly " manner suggested another bottle of port, Jacob objected point-blank, and proposed a glass of punch " in lieu thereof," to which proposition John, the younger brother, the *verd antique,* assented, and drawing his chair nearer his relative and the fire, made preparations for opening his subject.

Thomas the waiter, who had never seen John Batley, and did not know in what degree of relationship he stood to the " constant customer of the house," felt an unaccountable jealousy of the ease and familiarity with which he thus placed himself in juxta-position with Jacob. An elderly gentleman, known to be rich, is uniformly surrounded by a certain *clique* of expectants : they call on him in the mornings ; dine with him in the afternoons ; they

sit with him in the evenings; do all his little biddings —
go of errands for him, buy him sixpenny presents, affect
the greatest assiduity in his service, shut doors that are
left open behind him, pull down blinds that are left up
before him, stir the fire for him, write letters for him,
and, in short, fetch, carry, fawn, and cringe, like so many
daggle-eared spaniels. Thomas the waiter was not, of
course, admitted to a degree of familiarity which could
entitle him to such gentlemanly subserviency; but Thomas
had a notion that Jacob would leave him something "very
considerable" when he died, and therefore it was that
Jacob's fish was better dressed, and Jacob's rump-steak
tenderer and more carefully cooked, than those of any
other frequenter of "The Horn." This feeling was
nursed and cuddled up in the mind of the respectable
attendant; nothing, therefore, could annoy him more than
the sight of a stranger to *him*, taking, as he considered,
such extraordinary liberties with Mr. Jacob Batley, except,
indeed, the extremely placid manner in which Mr. Jacob
Batley seemed to admit them upon this special occasion.
Nothing is more diverting than this sort of irritable
anxiety upon such points; as if the rich man, in his
senses, does not duly appreciate the fulsome attentions
that are paid him by people who care nothing in the world
for what he is, but for what he has, to the attempted
exclusion of those who really love and respect him, but
who abstain from forcing themselves upon his kindness or
intruding themselves upon his hospitality : — not that either
of these two last attributes could with any degree of truth
be made applicable to Jacob.

"Well," said John, when the company was gone, the
green-baize doors shut, and the punch on the table, "I
have something to say, brother, which I want you to
hear."

"Oh !" said Jacob, "about the mistake and the marriage?"

"Exactly so," said John; "the story is brief, and you
shall have it."

And so he had; but as we have been at Sadgrove,
where Jacob had not been, it shall not be repeated here :

the blunder was a strange one — the result, as we know, decisive.

"Well," said Jacob, "I never heard such a thing in my life. I know nothing about female hearts, and all the stuff you talk about; but how the deuce you could go on with your fine talk to one woman — ha, ha, ha! and make the other — ha, ha! If I had done that! — no matter — no. I don't know anything about it, — and don't care; but *you*" ——

"Don't laugh at me!" said Jack; "for, whatever else I can endure, I can't bear ridicule. I feel conscious that I have made myself absurd, and that 'the world' next season will have the whole story, and I sha'n't be able to show my face. There is but one course; nothing can save me but marrying somebody else — *coute qui coute:* upon *that* I am resolved, or I perish. A lady, and with money; — if little, something, — if much, more."

"Umph!" said Jacob, stirring his punch, and then sipping; "that does'nt seem so unreasonable: on the contrary, if you are afraid of being laughed at by what you call 'the world' — of ·St. George's Hanover Square, and the surrounding streets, — I think that is the best plan: but it's ticklish work; to have anybody to care about, must be an infernal bore — eh? — and the quarrels and squabbles — eh?"

That would be *my* affair," said Jack; "but I never shall forget the hyæna-like laugh of that Laura Thurston, who, I give you my word, was, or at least seemed to be, as fond of me as ever woman of thirty could be of" ——

"Thirty, was she?" said Jacob.

"I should think little less," replied John.

" — And not married — eh? — why, for what reason, with *her* fortune?" said Jacob.

"I don't know," said John, "except that she is deep blue."

"Oh!" said Jacob. "Ah, well, that *is* something; but, however, in course she is altogether out of the question now — eh?"

"Quite entirely," said Jack.

"Why," said Jacob, sipping his delightful beverage,

"if you really have resolved upon marrying again, — and now it seems a matter of spite" ——

" Yes, I confess, more pique than passion."

" — Why not," said Jacob meditatingly, — why not turn your thoughts towards Mrs. Catling, that very pretty widow who dined once or twice with Helen and you in Grosvenor Street; and who is — why, I cannot say — so very much delighted with *you*?"

"What! that pretty creature," said John, "with those bright blue eyes and that lovely fair hair, up in the Regent's Park?"

"Don't talk so loud," said Jacob, "waiters always listen; and as what you are praising so much is not altogether in my regular line of business, it might do me harm if it were overheard; but," added he, leaning over his tumbler to speak confidently to John, "she *is* — — you may rely upon it."

"She certainly *is* very handsome," said Jack, "and extremely lady-like. Her late husband was your greatest friend, — that's something; and she is of a good family."

"Family!" said Jacob, "if you will step over to Bennett's Hill, not twenty yards from this door, the Heralds will give you such a history of her as will make your hair stand on end: — she is one of the two last of the noble race of Fitz-Flanneries of Mount Flannery, in Monaghanshire — quite the gentlewoman; — and as for what you call accomplishments, — she draws like a cart-horse, and sings like a tea-kettle, as the man says in the book."

"Now don't joke, brother," said Jack. "I remember thinking her extremely agreeable; — and — it would be such a triumph to marry off-hand after this contemptuous rejection, — and a handsome woman with property, too."

"Property!" said Jacob; "her late husband, Kit Catling, who made mints of money by madder, died of dropsy just eighteen months ago, and left me trustee, sole executor, and residuary legatee — all, everything in my own hands, — more fool he! — but that's nothing. I didn't care a straw for *him*, — but so it is; it is of no use caring for anybody, it never does any good. His will, like his wife's pedigree, is within a hundred yards of us — Prerogative Office, just round the corner; — arms one side, leg's t'other — eh ? — there's a joke for you! Convenient neighbourhood — what ? — I think she would be a capital match for you. I know, as I have told you, she likes you; I know she wants to be married; and I know she likes. what you call, and what she considers, ' the world.'"

" Has she a jointure or _____ ?" said Jack.

" Jointure !" replied Jacob; " seven hundred and fifty pounds per annum of her own for life, let her marry when she pleases; all snug — requires nothing on your part — pleasant addition to your income. Give her two hundred a year of her own cash by way of pin-money, and let her have the balance back again for jointure if she survives you : I can manage all that."

. " Upon my life ! brother, this sounds well."

" I think so too," said Jacob. — " Thomas !" — (Thomas came.) — " Ditto punch."

· Thomas " understood the call," and as speedily as possible re-appeared with two more glasses of " the same," which in Jacob's facetious manner he called " warming it up again."

" Well," said Jacob, apparently taking much greater interest in John's affairs than usual — which John naturally attributed to the influence of the " drink," and which, moreover, made him deeply repent that he had not at an earlier period of his life more readily fallen in with the habits of his eccentric relative, whose liberality appeared to him to possess, in a great degree, the mercurial quality of expanding in proportion to the warmth of the atmosphere by which it was surrounded — " well, now really — I am serious — I think Mrs. Kit Catling would suit uncommon well; you would, as I have said, have your life-interest in her seven hundred and fifty — short the pin-money."

" I recollect admiring her very much," said John, warming with the subject.

" She is a charming woman," said Jacob: " you'll be a happy man if you get her."

N ·

—"And you think there is a prepossession?" said
John.

"She has told me as much," said Jacob; "but, as I
never meddle nor make in matters of that kind, I didn't
take the trouble to say any thing about it: it is nothing to
*me*, you know; however, I tell you my mind."

"And I thank you sincerely," said John.

—"And I tell you what," added Jacob, evidently excited by his potation, "I'll do something for you unasked
—and I do it, Jack, because you didn't come to see me
to-day, merely because you wanted something — I'll stump
you down a thousand pounds the day you get her consent,
just to give you a start. It is not for *your* sake so much
as to show those women, the Thirstys — what d'ye call
'em? — people of 'the world,' which I hate — friends of
Mortimer — eh? — that we can do without 'em: so, there's
my hand, and a thousand pounds in it when widow Catling
says 'yes' to the bargain."

"My dear Jacob," said John — for, for almost the first
time in his later life he had called him by his Christian
name — "how can I sufficiently thank you! I am resolved — her seven hundred and fifty pounds a-year added
to my income will do all we want: — you are sure she has
*that*?"

"I tell you I am sole executor," said Jacob, "trustee,
residuary legatee, and every thing else under the will. I
told Kit that I wouldn't have any thing to do with it if I
hadn't it all my own way : — no colleagues for me!"

"Then," said John, "the sooner this is concluded the
better, and a thousand thanks to you for your kindness!"

"A thousand pounds, you mean," said Jacob: — "and
now let us have our bill, and go. Walk home with me
and we will talk this matter over further, and to-morrow
set to work about it."

"Waiter!" said John, "bring the bill."

"Put it all to my account," said Jacob.

"No my dear brother, I — " said John.

"Will you allow me to do as I please? — *my* bill —
you understand, Thomas."

"Yes, sir," said Thomas, and walked away admiring

the extraordinary liberality of the millionaire in not making his brother pay some seven shillings and ninepence three farthings as his share of " the reckoning."

The brothers then left " The Horn," and Jack was too delighted to accompany Jacob to Lilypot Lane, astounded at his warmth, and liberality reaching in its expanse from seven shillings and ninepence three farthings to a thousand pounds; but as they walked, so the more earnestly did Jacob confirm his resolution as to the liberal gift of the latter sum, and the more fervently did John resolve to carry into effect the proposal which should insure it.

Now, as to the facts of the case: — The Mrs. Catling in question was, as both brothers agreed, sufficiently pretty for all the purposes of this world; a lady by birth — a circumstance which weighed considerably with Jack — being the youngest daughter of the youngest son of the first cousin of an Irish baron glorying in the name of Fitz-Flannery. To say that she married the late Mr. Christopher Catling, of Cateaton Street, for his money, would be to admit that she was mercenary as well as poor: but that she *did*, as she considered it, sacrifice herself for the advantage of her mother and sister, is not to be doubted, inasmuch as Mr. Catling did not, either in person, mind, manners, or accomplishments, possess any of those qualifications likely to engage the tender affections of a " lady" of gentle blood and modern education.

During the lifetime of her gentle helpmeet she remained secluded in his suburban residence in the neighbourhood of Highbury Barn, a villa with a brass plate on the door, and a gas-lamp over it; and, although her connection with the peerage was with difficulty ascertained, she was acknowledged in all the little parties of that neighbourhood as the lady to be taken out first.

Of Catling's family stump — for tree it could scarcely be called — nobody knew much, not even himself; — nobody cared — for, let him *have been* what he might, they all knew what he *was* — an opulent, honest, good-natured man; and, as the tablet erected in Islington church by his inconsolable widow remarks, " as he lived respected, so he died lamented." He had, however, been preceded to the

grave by his wife's mother, Mrs. Fitz-Flannery ; and, at
his death, his widow and her sister, after a due attention
to the rules of decorum, removed from Highbury to the
more genial region of the Regent's Park, where, on one of
the banks which constitute its neighbourhood, she and her
companion, at the period to which we now allude, resided.·

The extraordinary confidence with which the late Mr.
Catling had honoured Jacob, and the complete control he
had given him over his property, placed the widow in an
extremely embarrassing position. During her husband's
lifetime she regarded Jacob with a jealousy founded upon
his evident power over her husband ; a jealousy rendered
not milder in its character by a suspicion that the old mis-
anthrope, as she considered and called him, was securing
Mr. Catling's confidence in *him*, by endeavouring to shake
his confidence in *her*.

When she found herself a widow, left literally at the
mercy of the man whom, to say the least, she could never
bring herself to like, she grew peevish and nervous ; and,
not being blest with more than an average proportion of
sense, she worried herself, and felt degraded at being obliged,
in case her expenditure upon any extraordinary occasion
happened to exceed her available resources, to apply to her
trustee for an advance. The truth is, that the will of her
husband was neither more nor less a memorial of *his* mistrust, than *her* tablet in Islington church was a perpetuation
of his merits and virtues : which of the two was the most
sincere, we leave the reader to surmise.

It was in the second year of her widowhood that Jacob
(before the invasion of Grosvenor Street house by Mortimer
had occurred), the trustee and sole executor and residuary
legatee, had asked Helen to invite Mrs. Catling and her
sister to dinner. The long-oppressed lady seemed to breathe
again, in the air of the western part of London ; and the
party happening to be small and agreeable, and John in
high spirits, she was delighted with Helen, with Batley
(wondering that two such men as he and Jacob could be
brothers), and with the society in general. She saw the
manner in which John treated his daughter ; she saw the
devotion of Helen to her father, and thence justly argued

in favour of his kindness of temper and disposition, upon which alone such mutual feelings could be founded : then she looked round her, and thought what a remarkably nice establishment it was, and how agreeable it would be to be mistress of it; especially when Helen, by marriage, should leave that mistress in the enjoyment of undivided control, to mix with that class of society to which, by birth, she herself really belonged, but from which, adverse circum-cumstances, and her later connections, had in a great degree excluded her.

Over these thoughts she brooded ; but she had few op-portunities of improving her acquaintance with Helen, or repeating her visits, for she was not after Helen's heart ; and, when Mortimer came, the unqualified exile of uncle Jacob necessarily involved the exclusion of Mrs. Catling : nevertheless, it may be naturally inferred that, when Jacob mentioned her name to his brother as a " sure card" if he chose to play the game, he had been led to do so by what he had gathered in conversation with the lady herself, with whom he generally dined on Sundays, and by whom he was received with that equivocal hospitality which springs rather from fear than affection, and which is exhibited more in the hope of soothing than of satisfying the visitor.

" What can this mean ?" said Mrs. Catling to her sister Margaret Fitz-Flannery, as she came into the parlour of Shamrock Cottage, No. 120. South Bank, the morning after the dinner at " The Horn ;" " old Batley has sent to invite himself to dine here to-day."

" La, T'resa ! you don't say so ! — what d'ye mean to do ? not let him come, I hope."

" How upon earth can I avoid it ?" said Teresa, " it is not wise in me to offend him — and — it's exceedingly worrying ; — Sundays I bargain for, and there is only one Sunday in a week, and one knows the worst ; but here —— "

" Oh !" interrupted Margaret, " send word we are en-gaged."

" But, my dear child, replied Mrs. Catling, " he will know that we are not ; our visiting list is not so long as one of our visiting tickets, and he knows the name and residence of every one of the half-dozen select acquaintance we really happen to have. No — come he must; and perhaps you will not be so violent in your objections when you hear that he proposes to bring a friend with him."

" A friend!" said Margaret — " what! a gentleman friend?"

" Sure yes," said Mrs. Catling.

" That's very handsome of him, considering," said Margaret; "can you guess who?"

" No," said Mrs. Catling, "but he puts 'a friend' — a gentleman who is very desirous of improving his acquaintance with you."

" I'd lay my life," said Margaret, " it is either Mr. Grub, his head-clerk, or else that young Haddock, the alderman's nephew."

" Well, there's one comfort," said the mistress of the house; "Grub, or Haddock, or any body else, will be better than having him all alone by himself."

" What is this postscript?" said Margaret, turning over the note; " did you see this?"

" No," replied Mrs. Catling, taking the note from her sister; " which?"

" ' P. S. — Tripe is just coming in; have some for dinner.   Let the cook wash it twenty times over; boil it in milk, and serve up with lots of onions.' "

" Tripe! T'resa," said Margaret.

" Onions!" cried Teresa.

" I hate tripe," said Margaret.

" And I can't endure onions, and he knows it."

" That makes no difference in the world to him," said Margaret.

" No; self, self predominates," said Teresa, "from objects of the greatest importance down to things of the smallest consequence.   If, however, tripe is to be had, it must be got; whoever he brings will of course know his ways; besides, he will not fail to boast of his authority in controlling my table, so that at all events we shall not be blamed by the stranger for being the projectors of such a dish."

Having, therefore, soothed their excited feelings, and

,moderated the anger which the indelicacy of his favourite
dainty had induced, Teresa wrote a kind note, expressing
her delight that " dear Mr. Batley " was so good-natured
as to favour them with his company, and that they should-
be charmed to receive any friend of his ; and begging him
to come as soon as he could ; that dinner would be punctually ready by half-past four, and that the tripe should be
smothered in onions as he desired. Then came Margaret
uniting in kindest regards, and Teresa subscribing herself
his faithful and sincere; and all this was written on a sheet
of pale pink note-paper, redolent of musk, then poked into
a straw-coloured envelope with an embossed border of
shamrocks, and closed with a seal on which was engraven
a funeral urn with cypress twisting over it; and all this
again was directed to " Jacob Batley, Esq. Lilypot Lane,"
and consigned to the custody of the "young man" who
had brought his letter, and the sisters proceeded to consider and wonder who the stranger would turn out to be.

As for Mr. John Batley, as was his wont whenever he
started a new object, his whole heart and soul were in the
pursuit. With a vivid imagination, which would have almost discredited the judgment of a boy of twenty, he proceeded, during the night of the eventful day when the subject was first opened to his notice, to build castles of the
most fanciful order: he saw domestic comfort restored to his
house ; he should exhibit his fair wife to " the world," a
triumphant refutation of any gossip which might get abroad
as to his recent defeat ; then it would be such a delightful
thing for Helen to have so nice a person at Sadgrove —
one so preferable to Madame St. Alme ; totally forgetting
in the hurry of the moment that Helen had been more than
ordinarily severe upon the widow Catling, and that he himself had been compelled to admit that, however lavish
Nature had been in giving her personal beauty, she had
not been equally attentive to her mental qualifications.

It was near one before Jack received Mrs. Catling's
answer to his brother's note ; for, to save time, Jacob had
directed his " young man," Alïck, to take the lady's reply
direct to Grosvenor Street, so that John might be informed
of the order of proceeding, and whether the ladies would

receive them.   He took the note in his hand, and felt a
little disheartened.   Finery and tawdriness are so at variance with good taste and good sense, that the straw-
coloured envelope staggered him; he proceded, however,
to break the melancholy seal.   When he beheld the pink
note itself, musky as it was, his heart failed him, a pink
note in a yellow cover, with an embossed border, and
sealed with putty-coloured wax — all contrived to announce that the tripe should be cooked according to order,
and smothered with onions.

Now, abstractedly, there are few things so good as this
particular dish; and nobody was more ready to subscribe
to its excellence than Jack Batley, when out of " the
world," from which it is affectedly proscribed: but not
being aware that his worthy brother had made his conditions, or directed the preparation of this one favourite
viand, it did seem to him a somewhat unsuitable topic to
be conveyed through such a " beautifully elegant " medium.
However, his resolve was taken; the note was transmitted
to Jacob in one of his own, announcing that he should be
ready, when his brother called, to accompany him to
Shamrock Cottage.

That Jacob *did* call, and that the brothers *did* go, we
shall in due time be informed; but as some little time must
elapse before the affair can be concluded, it may not be
amiss to draw the reader's attention from the anticipations
of the ardent aspirant for the lady's favour, — to a retrospect of what occurred at Sadgrove since he left it, or
rather after the departure of the party from the Hall to
the Fishing House.

## CHAPTER III.

THE day was delightful; everybody seemed in spirits —
most of the party *were;* those who were *not*, assumed a
gaiety suited to the occasion.   To Helen, the sight of
Mortimer driving the countess in the phaeton was blissful,
compared with what her own position would have been in

the countess's place. As it happened, during their progress, neither of those who were on either side of Mrs. Mortimer asked one question about the Fishing House; which, however important to everybody as the cause of an agreeable ride and a pleasant luncheon, nobody, save three of the party, cared one farthing about. The lions of a neighbourhood are visited as a matter of course by everybody staying in a country house; but, however much the geologist, the naturalist, or the antiquarian may delight in the research, the idlers run their eyes over a ridge of rocks, a tract of country, or a heap of ruins, merely as the accessories, if not the immediate cause, of an agreeable excursion. In fact, the conversation near the "lady of the house" turned chiefly upon the merits, or rather demerits, of the departed Thurstons; it being a remarkable fact — or one might better say, a fact worthy of remark — that, whether it be in public or private life, the fluency of vituperation against any individual object becomes infinitely more powerful — playful perhaps it might be thought amongst what Mrs. Trollope calls "*La Haute Volée*" — the moment that the absence of the parties implicated is ascertained to be certain and likely to be permanent.

One thing contributed to relieve Helen's mind — the absence of Magnus. There was something in his manner and in the distant coldness of his behaviour towards her, which his friends — the few he had — attributed to shiness; but which was so like the result of pride and sullenness, that it required a greater degree of intimacy with him than it seemed probable Helen ever would arrive at to ascertain its true character: and, moreover, Helen had taken into her head — erroneously perhaps — that Mortimer had appointed his trusty friend to the office of guardian-dragon of his Worcestershire Hesperides; in fact, that the consciousnes of his own demerits, and the natural suspicion of his character, had induced him to invest his high-minded friend with the chivalrous character of domestic spy.

If Helen could have satisfied herself that this were the case, it is impossible to guess what course she might have taken; for, generally speaking, that sort of *surveillance* is

sure to lead to the result which it is meant to avert.
Nothing short of implicit confidence satisfies a woman;
doubt her ever so little, and the chances are a hundred to
one that she will eventually justify your suspicions. The
absence of Magnus was therefore a relief to her, she
scarcely knew why; and she laughed and talked gaily and
merrily as they wended their way to the beautiful bower.

The conversation being all pure " London," nobody
paused to exclaim as the scenery burst upon the lively
party, and Helen was consequently spared the necessity of
acting novice: indeed, little was said germane to the
matter till they arrived at the temple, on the steps of which
stood Mortimer and the countess waiting to receive the
." company."

" Well, Helen dear," said Mortimer, addressing himself
specially to his wife, " what do you think of this snug-
gery ? "

" What I have seen of it is charming."

" Come this way then," said the animated husband, who
seemed resolved to be unusually cheerful; " I think I shall
surprise you."

Saying which, he threw open the door of the circular
room in which the banquet was spread, and took her to
that window which commanded the most beautiful view of
the rich valley through which the Severn rippled brightly,
skirted in the back-ground by the Malverns. The deep-
ening tints of October had already beautifully varied the
foliage: and, as the fresh breeze blew on Helen's flushed
cheek, she pressed the arm on which she was leaning, and
said half unconsciously, " It is indeed lovely."

" I knew you would like it," said Mortimer; and turning
to the countess, who was close behind them, added, " I told
you, countess, that Helen would be pleased."

" I never had a doubt of it," replied the lady, in a tone
evidently meant to imply something — what, Helen could
not divine.

" Isn't it charming, Mrs. Mortimer ? " continued the
worldly woman, throwing an expression into her countenance
of triumph at the successful manner in which they were
deceiving her husband.

Helen seemed to shrink at the sight of this odious look, which, though not understood by Mortimer, was neither unseen nor unfelt. It had the effect of curdling all the suavity which he seemed to have stored up for this particular occasion. Its meaning was as mysterious to Mortimer as the countess's previous glance at *him* had been to Helen: but it evidently had a meaning; and the little, little doubt which it engendered so counterbalanced all his hopes of temporary happiness, that he seemed at once to fall back into the morbid melancholy by which he was so frequently oppressed.

This tone once given to his mind, his memory recurred to all that had happened in the same scene years before. The bright expectation, that, by again familiarising himself with his once favourite retreat with Helen, he might again enjoy its beauties, blest with the possession of a being as much devoted to him as she had been who in other days had shared its charms, faded in an instant. Either Helen did not like the place, or, liking it, had been prepossessed unfavourably against it by the countess — or — it mattered not what the alternative was — there was something hidden under the surface, and his peace of mind was gone for that day. Sure it is, as the vulgar man fancies that everybody who laughs in company is laughing at *him*, the guilty man fears in every look, and every observation, however vague the one, or general the other, an allusion to his own particular case. Mortimer turned from his wife and the countess, and with a deep sigh, which he did not mean Helen to overhear, joined the group at the other window, at which Lady Mary, who was so near-sighted as not to know her husband three feet off, was descanting largely upon the delightful view which the temple commanded.

" Surely, countess," said Helen, " Mortimer isn't well ! "

" Oh," said the countess, " nothing — don't mind him ; he is only thinking of other days: that willow which now overhangs the bank so gracefully was planted by poor Amelia. I dare say something struck him — don't think any thing about it ; nothing makes him worse than taking any notice or making any remark."

" I almost wish we hadn't come," said Helen.

" Oh, never mind," said the Countess St. Alme;
"sooner or later you must have come, and never could
there be a better time than when we have a merry party
here."

" Yes," said Helen; " but if Francis is sad, their mirth
is no pleasure to me."

" Oh, it will all blow over: my delight is, how admirably you acted your surprise at the prettiness of the
place."

" Oh, countess !" said Helen, pushing gently past
her, towards the group where Mortimer was, but looking
at the moment as if she had stabbed her through the
heart.

" Good God !" thought Helen, " what is the spell this
woman has over me? Why am I made to deceive my husband
without the least cause? Why driven to embitter the
moments of one to whose happiness my whole soul is devoted ? — This *must* be conquered."

The moment Helen joined Lady Mary's coterie, Mortimer left it on a pretence of showing Captain Harvey a
particular sort of boat which he had built for his fishing
excursions ; but it was evident to Helen that her approach
had been the signal for his departure. She felt a sort of
wild determination to follow him : it seemed as if she were
to lose him for ever if she did not make an exertion at that
moment ; if she admitted for once the possibility of her
presence being repulsive, she admitted all that could render
her miserable for life. Her eyes swam ; she felt her cheek
flushed, and seemed, for the moment, imbued with a giant's
strength.

" Come, Lady Mary," said she, " let us go and see this
famous boat, too; why should the men have it all their own
way ?"

This was said with apparent gaiety, and a laugh, in
which, alas ! there was no mirth. Lady Mary, who
took things as they came, thought Helen had some reason
for wishing to see the boat, about which her ladyship
cared no more than she did for its hospitable owner ;
and, accordingly, taking the arm that Helen offered,

they " trotted off," to use her ladyship's own expression, to the boat-house where this wonderful bark was resting.

The countess saw this movement; and having, what the world calls, "all her eyes about her," saw also that she had wounded Helen's feelings, and that Helen really cared for Francis a great deal more than she thought she did: this, for some yet undiscovered reason, rendered the unhappy Helen—for such she seemed destined to be—more hateful to her than before; and, while the anxious wife was gone on a journey of love to her captious husband, her charming friend was calculating the means of undoing all the poor girl hoped to do in the way of conciliating him.

When Helen found the truant, he seemed surprised and pleased at her pursuit, and chided her jestingly for her fear of losing him.

" I assure you, dear Francis," said Helen, " I was wondering whither you had flown; and, as everybody seems ready for luncheon, I enlisted Lady Mary to be my comrade in overtaking and apprehending the deserter."

" I am sure, dear, it is very flattering to be so hunted," said Francis. " Where is your friend, the countess?"

" *My* friend !" said Helen in a tone unlike that which she usually adopted when speaking of her intimate associates. —" *your* friend, Francis."

The sunshine of his countenance was gone in an instant; a frown again contracted his brow; and turning away, hastily, as if to conceal his feelings, he proceeded to point out to Harvey some peculiar advantages derivable from the particular construction of his vessel.

" Why, my dear," said Lady Mary in a sort of whisper, " what sharp lectures you can give in a few words !"

" How ?" said Helen.

" I mean, the way you snubbed your husband about *his* friend the countess."

" I—I snub !" said Helen ; " my dear Lady Mary, I assure you I am not at all a lecturer. I merely said what was true : Francis introduced me to the count and countess, and they *are* his friends, not mine."

" Yes," said Lady Mary, " that's all very true; only ——
Did you ever see young Blocksford, her son ? "

" Yes," said Helen, " he has been staying here : those
two drawings I showed you in my boudoir were done by
him."

" Yes, I know," said Lady Mary; " but I did not know
whether you had seen *him :* that's all.   I —— Oh ! here
she comes."

—And so she did come, accompanied by her husband.
But what Lady Mary had said sounded very odd to Helen;
she could not comprehend it; and yet it seemed to be meant
to have a meaning, and somewhat of an ill-natured meaning
too, as regarded the countess, whom Lady Mary hated
most cordially."

" Dearest countess," said Lady Mary, " are you come
to bear witness to this pretty pilgrimage of love ?   Helen
has been husband-hunting."

" I hope," said the countess, " she has caught her dear,
for we are all starving."

" Yes," said Helen in a subdued tone, above which she
somehow felt she could not raise her voice; " he is coming,
I believe."

" Well," said the countess, " as *you* are here, we need
not wait for *him :* so, come, let us rally; I think we shall
all be the better for something to eat."

—"And a leetle to drink of de champagne," said
the count; which was all he said during the whole of the
day.

" I should like to wait for Mortimer," said Helen.

" I'll go and fetch him," said the countess; and suiting
the action to the word, she proceeded to the boat-house.

Helen felt a chill run through her veins as this was said
and done : but what her feelings were cannot be described,
when, upon raising her eyes from the ground, she beheld
those of Lady Mary fixed upon her, with an expression
of surprise at the free and easy manner of her friend, and
of the quiet way in which Helen seemed to endure her
domination.

All Lady Mary said was, " Well ! "—but her looks conveyed an idea that she thought a great deal more.

Strange to say, however worried, however excited, however vexed by the countess, Helen never before had entertained the slightest suspicion of that which, for her misery, at this moment flashed into her mind. It was clear as light; Lady Mary, a woman " of the world," was' aware of it: Helen was looked upon by her own guests as a victim — a duped, deceived wife — and the countess —— But was it probable, was it possible, that in the first month of his marriage with *her* he should seek not only to renew an old acquaintance with this woman, but bring her into a constant association with his young wife? The thing would not be believed even in a novel; yet ——

And then came the collecting in her mind the ten thousand nothings — the " trifles light as air," which had occurred during the countess's domestication at Sadgrove;—the visit to this very fishing temple :—but no, no —it must be calumny — it must be the jealousy which women cannot repress —the envy they cannot control;—and yet, why should Lady Mary be envious of the Countess St. Alme? Still, the look she gave!—and then the manner of the men who were staying there, while addressing her —there seemed to be an ease, an almost boldness, in their conduct towards her, totally different from that which they observed towards herself, or Lady Mary, or any other of the visitors. Then, the rooted hatred of Mortimer's sister for her — for of this she was made aware by the necessity Mortimer felt for giving some strong reason why Mrs. Farnham refused to join the Sadgrove party: in fact, all in one moment were conjured up, by the glance of Lady Mary's bright blue eyes, visions innumerable, doubts, suspicions, dreads, and alarms, to which Helen had yet been a stranger.

Helen's spirit was a proud one: she would bear with patience all the ills and sorrows of mortal life to serve, to soothe, to save the being she loved: nay, marrying Mortimer as she did, with a knowledge of his character, of the follies, and even vices, of his earlier life, she was prepared to make allowances, and to look over with kindness what-ever circumstances connected with his former marriage might militate against their happiness; but the moment she fancied that she was made a dupe of, and that " the world " pitied her blindness or meanness in enduring a rival, all other feelings sank into shade.

Candid and open-hearted as she was, how was she to smother this volcano in her bosom ?—how was she, who never knew, until lured into it by this very countess, what deception meant, to conceal from him to whom she was devoted the dreadful thoughts which had been created in her mind ? How could she bear to look upon the countess ? —how, to see her the usual companion of her husband ? And yet, so did it happen, that as she turned from Lady Mary, and while yet all that has been written was flashing, lightning-like, through her brain, she saw the countess gaily approaching them, leaning on Mortimer's arm.

Whether Lady Mary saw how her blow had told, or not, one cannot ascertain : she certainly followed it up in the most skilful manner by saying, with all the carelessness imaginable,—

" Well, dear, although *you* went out to hunt your hus-band, the countess has secured the prize."

" So I see," said Helen—and she drew her hand ra-pidly across her eyes — perhaps to brush away a tear : " let us be revenged, Lady Mary, and leave them to follow us."

Lady Mary was as much a woman of the world in her way as the countess in hers, and duly appreciated this forced piece of gaiety on the part of Helen ; however, as she had carried her point by enlightening her fair hostess, she, of course, entered into the little divertisement with the greatest alacrity.

The luncheon served, the soup, according to the treaty, hot, the champagne cold, the party seated, the windows closed, and the snug circle formed, everybody seemed at home. All the sight-seeing part of the morning being past, the refreshment after labour, alike essential to free-masons and the " profane," seemed to put everybody in good-humour, excepting two persons, by whom was all the gaiety provided. Mortimer and Helen were the only two compelled to act a part ; they were both wretched : Mor-timer, for a thousand reasons connected with the present and the past; and Helen, because she was under the spell of a sorceress, to whose influence she had been subjected by her husband, and by whose arts the confidence of that husband had been already, to a certain extent, shaken.

What position could be more painful than that of this man and wife? Devoted to each other, if their affections had been allowed fair play, they were, without the slightest reason, estranged; here were two hearts, in which were sown the seeds of mutual love, throbbing in this hour of gaiety with pain, with grief, with doubt, with jealousy.

It is said, that it is "better to be at the end of a feast than at the beginning of a 'fray;'" now, as Sterne says, "That I deny." Nothing is more agreeable to the eye than the gay brightness of a *déjeûner à la fourchette* like this of Mortimer's: look at it when its "hour is past," the ruins by no means splendid, viewed, too, after the appetite (which, *par parenthèse*, is always better at luncheon-time than at the supper-hour of modern dinners,) has been gratified — the mutilated jellies, the abandoned legs of fowls, the scattered lobster salad, the desolated piles of prawns, and all the rest of it. Things had arrived at this point, and the listlessness of the flushed guests manifested itself by their rising from table, and beginning to feel chilly, and talking about the carriages and going back again. There it is — all pleasure must end in this sublunary world; and, accordingly, orders were given for making preparations for the departure.

" I cannot go," said the countess, " without seeing my poor dear nice old woman. — Here, sir," continued this most amiable of her sex, speaking to one of the footmen, " go, and send Willis's old woman here — the guardian nymph, as I call her, of the fishing temple."

" Poor old soul!" said Mortimer; " I really believe that she is as proud of her post here as a governor-general is at Calcutta."

—" And," whispered the countess, " Amelia gave her the office."

Helen did not hear the words, but she saw the action. Mortimer raised his hand towards his face, and seemed, in what might be called friendly anger, to repel the remark by motioning the countess from him.

Helen, not daunted by the feelings with which circumstances had inspired her, joined her husband and his friend, who, with a cunning inherent in her nature, had, during the repast, felt that something *had* occurred to change Helen's views of her position in the family, and who seemed proportionally more resolved upon mischief. It would be invidious to notice how many glasses of champagne she drank at luncheon, but there seemed to be in her manner a restless anxiety for something to happen at this moment, for which Helen, who noticed her agitation, could not account.

. The side-door of the round room was opened; and in walked, " as nice and as neat as a new pin," our old friend *La Curatrice.*

" Well, old lady," said Mortimer, " how do you get on? You are one of those evergreens upon which time and seasons have no effect. Are you comfortable and happy ? "

" Yes, sir," said the old woman ; " quite so, thank you, sir. I hope, ladies, you are quite well," added the grateful rustic, addressing Mrs. Mortimer and the countess.

" Quite well, thank you."

" Here, my good woman," said Mortimer, slipping a sovereign into the wood-like palm of her shrivelled hand : " you must not forget our first visit to the Fishing-House."

" Thank you, sir, thank you," said she, dropping a courtesy, from which it appeared improbable that she would ever recover.—" I hope, ma'am," added she, addressing Helen, " you like the way I had those muslin curtains put up : I could not get the man to send home the pink ones which you told me to get cleaned."

Helen felt as if she should sink into the earth. Mortimer looked astounded.

" Why," said he, " what are you talking of ? — this lady has never been here before. Are you dreaming ? "

" No, sir, dreaming ! — I never dream till I go to sleep, and not often that now. My lady there ordered me to get the curtains which used to be in the inner room ———"

Mortimer looked at Helen, who hid her face in her hands, and sank on a chair.

" There," said the countess, bursting into a laugh; " that will do, old lady: nobody *can* have secrets in this world.— Go along. Here is a pretty discovery, Helen dear."

" God help me!" said Helen.

" What does all this mean?" said Mortimer. " Have I been duped — made a fool of? — taught to bring Helen here as a surprise — as something to delight her — and she has been ——"

" Oh! Mortimer," said Helen, " do not ——"

" My dear Mrs. Mortimer," said the countess, " pray consider: do not make a scene. I'll explain it all to Francis: you are not in the least to blame; it is all *my* fault."

" Let me go in," said Helen: " I cannot face these people. Oh! Francis, Francis, have mercy upon me!"

" This is most extraordinary!" said Mortimer.

" Let me lean on you, Mortimer."

" Countess," said he, " lead her in."

" No, no, no, Mortimer," sobbed Helen —" you, you!"

She leant on his arm, and he did lead her to the door of the boudoir; but, as he went, he cast a look at the countess, which, if she had possessed the common feelings of humanity, would have wrung her heart: — but no; she turned from his gaze with an air of triumph, and, joining her particular friend Lady Mary, merely said, in answer to an inquiring simper,

" A little domestic happiness — that's all!"

The manner in which Lady Mary received this explanation might have satisfied the countess, and perhaps did satisfy her, that the character of her influence in the family was not altogether agreeable to the ladies who visited Sadgrove: however, there is a certain class of adventurous women in the world, who, after having run a long career without having been actually " found out," seem resolved to fight the whole battle, and defy the usual prejudices of society — as wicked or foolish ministers endeavour to bolster up their worst or weakest actions by heaping rewards upon those who have been the active agents for carrying their ruinous designs into execution.

She turned from Lady Mary, and, affecting a solicitude in which she knew neither Mortimer nor his wife would put faith, inquired at the door of the boudoir how Helen was.

Helen was leaning her burning forehead on Mortimer's bosom : he had placed her on a sofa, and drawn his chair beside it. The circumstances, the innocent disclosure made by the poor old woman, the surprise it occasioned him, and the fearful agitation of his poor wife, filled him with wonder and alarm; but when Helen, hearing the countess's voice, clung closer to him and held him fast, he felt that the course he was pursuing, and the line of conduct his hateful friend was adopting, was one which must be abandoned.

" Do not, do not let her come in," whispered Helen.

" No, no," said Mortimer, almost terrified into submission ; " I will speak to her myself."

" Francis, Francis dearest, do not leave me !" said Helen.

" But for one moment," said Francis.

And in that brief space he communicated to the countess the necessity for keeping Helen quiet ; nor did he fail to express by his manner his almost abhorrence of her conduct in making his innocent wife a party to a deception in the exposure of which she seemed to delight.

Certain it is that the countess was by no means pleased with the manner in which her kind attentions to Helen were dispensed with by Mortimer ; and the look she gave him convinced him that, however much his natural feeling for the peculiarity of his wife's position under the influence of such a woman might in fact predominate, it became a matter of policy, for reasons known to himself, to conceal, if possible, the resentment which he could not help entertaining towards the author of the mischief which had occurred.

" Francis !" said Helen, violently agitated, " Francis, acquit me of this deception ! It is no act of mine ; it is ——"

. —"Stay, Helen," interrupted Mortimer. "I am ready, and most willing, to make all allowances; but surely no human being, man or woman, ought to usurp that confidence which is of right a husband's. It is true that the book I saw this morning in your room was sent you by the countess; I do not doubt it: the coincidence as to its contents is curious. I have no doubt either that the countess brought you to this place; it must be so: — but what then, Helen?—why conceal the truth? If you had not some particular reason, it would have been the most natural thing in the world to have told me of your visit."

"I should have told you all, Francis."

"Should! but you did *not*, Helen, say one syllable about it. You suffered me to tell our visitors that you had never been here, that this day should be a surprise to you: you never checked me — never said you had been here. What will these people think——"

"These people!" said Helen: "oh! Mortimer, my beloved Mortimer! what these people think or say matters nothing to me: it is to you alone I look; it is for what *you* think, I alone care. I was warned by the countess not to tell you; and, if I could make you comprehend all I have endured since we were here yesterday, you would pity me."

"But, dearest," said Mortimer, "where in all this is the evidence of that strength of mind for which you have been so remarkable? What right has man or woman to the allegiance of a wife, when coming in competition with a husband? The pure ingenuousness——"

"Oh, spare me, Mortimer! spare me; I am wrong — I know it; but indeed — indeed I was misled; I *was* influenced."

"Well," said Mortimer, "I should have thought you could have resisted the influence of Madame St. Alme in my favour."

"Francis," said Helen, clasping her hands, "why — why did you ever render the trial possible?"

"It was by your own invitation they came here," said Mortimer.

"How, and by whom suggested?"

" I thought you would find society agreeable here," said Mortimer ; " and I ———"

" What society did I ever wish for but yours, Francis?" said Helen ; " besides, have we not plenty without fixing ourselves so decidedly with one family ?"

" Perhaps," said Mortimer, " any old friends of mine are objectionable to you."

" No, no," said Helen ; " but you — you yourself, not four hours since, spoke to me of the countess, not as if you loved her."

" Loved her !" said Mortimer.

" I mean liked her," said Helen.

" To be sure," muttered Mortimer ; " what else should you mean ?   Loved her ? — who has been talking to you in this strain ?"

" In what strain, dearest ?"

" Dearest," said Francis, " your mind has been unsettled ; some devil has been at work here : — what do you mean by my loving the countess, Helen ?"

" I merely used the word," said Helen, terrified at her husband's manner, " as one uses it in common parlance."

" This is all wrong," said Mortimer ; " the train is fired — every thing is deception ; the ground we tread is mined — hollowed.   Who has been poisoning your mind against me ?"

" No one," said Helen, growing calmer and more determined as she saw her husband's anger rise.   " I have spoken of you to no human being except the countess, who has known you so long.   Mortimer," added she, rising from the sofa on which she had been reclining, " you do not know me yet.   I am too proud to make confidences ; and all that I have heard, and all that has been insinuated by your friend the countess, I have treated with disdain : and now you shall see how this proud heart that you continue to fancy capable of deceit and meanness shall bear me through this struggle. — Let us join our *friends ;* they will wonder why we stay so long from them : and, if I perish in the struggle, no tear shall dim these eyes, no sigh shall heave this breast ; and, since I *can* dissemble, Francis, I will make the effort now, that these hollow-hearted guests of ours may not be gratified with that which of all things would please them most — a domestic quarrel. But mark me, Francis; I have been led into this by *your* friend : let me be released from her influence, and I shall be happy."

Saying which, she hastily put together her hair, which, after a ride and stroll upon the Severn's banks, was not likely to be in the best order ; and playfully, almost wildly, said, —

" Give me your arm, Francis. Do not degrade me ; I do not deserve it : — let these people know nothing of this."

Mortimer was startled by her manner, utterly overcome by the occurrences of the morning, and driven to an extremity by the demand of his wife with regard to the countess : but, although convinced that she had been the victim of that artful woman's cunning, the conviction had taken full possession of him that he had, nevertheless, fallen in her estimation ; that his influence over her was now only secondary ; that other persons had stimulated her in what he considered a rebellion against his will ; above all, he felt that the woman who, under any circumstances in the world, could deliberately conceal a visit made the day before to the spot to which her husband was ostensibly to take her for the first time, would, upon a more important occasion, play the hypocrite with equal skill.

Mortimer, however, obeyed Helen's suggestions, and they rejoined the party as if nothing had happened ; the countess having, however, been good enough to throw out insinuations quite sufficient to counteract the effects producible by Helen's triumph over her feelings. The arrangements for the return were made. The countess again mounted the phaeton, and Helen again joined the equestrians.

What the conversation might have been which passed between Mortimer and the countess on the road it is impossible to say, or what art she might have exercised to fashion the events of the morning after her own will ; but one thing is certain ; on that morning were sown in the heart of the master of Sadgrove the seeds of a mistrust which germinated luxuriantly, and produced a harvest of evils for which the gathering time has not yet arrived.

---

## CHAPTER IV.

NEVER had Helen entered Sadgrove with feelings like those which oppressed her this day ; and surely, never, taking all the events which seemed likely to result from the unsettlement of Mortimer's mind into the calculation, did there arise a more dreadful illustration of the principle, that great events turn upon small ones. The whole affair of the fishing-house, with all the concomitant proceedings, was one of the most trifling nature , but it involved a spirit of insincerity which alarmed and grieved him. It might be true — nay, the countess admitted and protested that it was — that she was the sole cause of the visit ; but, though her candour upon this part of the transaction was most laudable, it did not go the length of avowing that she also was the cause of the concealment of that visit. She left Mortimer to put his own construction upon Helen's silence, which he, instead of attributing to the influence of her dangerous friend, laid to the account of her abhorrence of the scene of his former happiness ; and this, coupled with his previous discovery of the book, roused in his breast the ever latent feeling, that he was hated and despised for his former crimes by her to whom he had looked for consolation and an oblivion of the past.

Helen, who had made up her mind to a quarrel on their return, was almost painfully disappointed by beholding the sullen calmness of her husband throughout the rest of the day. She was all spirit and animation : she would have vindicated her conduct, explained its causes, and, even if Mortimer's anger had been roused, would have borne it all with the certain assurance that she should eventually convince him of her innocence, of every thing, except — submission to the influence of the Countess St. Alme ; — but no: Mortimer's brow was overcast, and he seemed melancholy and unhappy, but he was studiously polite towards his wife when he did address her during the day; but the affection and tenderness dear to her heart were absent. The well-bred gentleman could not endure the idea of " a scene ;" and, though he engaged himself generally in conversation, no eyes except those which were accustomed to watch with tender anxiety every turn of his countenance could have detected the change which to them was but too evident.

In this state Helen could not bear to exist: the idea of living, as it were, upon sufferance — upon the negative, the conditional affection of her husband — was worse than death.

" Mortimer," said she, when they retired for the night, with difficulty suppressing her tears, " I cannot endure the change in your manner. If I have offended you, tell me so ; if I have been guilty of any disobedience — of any fault either of omission or commission — chide me, and I will willingly submit myself to your judgment ; but to be neglected, slighted, shunned — I cannot, indeed I cannot bear it."

" I know of no fault," said Mortimer, " I feel no anger ; I may, perhaps, be a little surprised at the skill which you exhibited in acting this morning. I know no reason why you should have taken the trouble to deny that you had visited the fishing temple."

— " I never *did* deny it, Mortimer."

" No," said Mortimer, " I grant you *that ;* but your tacit admission that you never had — your dissembled surprise when I pointed out its beauties — in short, every part of your conduct was, as you know, meant to deceive me into the belief that you were, till then, a stranger even to its existence."

" That is true," said Helen ; " but you do not ask me why I permitted myself to adopt the course of which you complain, and not unjustly either. I admit the fault ; but I acted under an influence, and in the belief that I was doing *that* which would most conduce to your tranquillity and pleasure."

" How could you believe, Helen," said Mortimer, " that I had any object in concealing from you the existence of this pretty toy, except that of surprising you by a visit to it when the fit season should have arrived ?"

" I *did* think so, or, trust me, I never should have acted as you say I have."

" That seems strange !" said Mortimer, in a tone of doubtingness, which to a heart like Helen's was unbear.able.

" It is *not* strange," sobbed his wife : " I was taught to think so, by one who seems, or pretends at least, to know more of your temper and character than any one else."

" What ! are you jealous, Helen ? "

This brief question gave a sudden turn to Helen's thoughts and feelings and a dialogue, for which Mortimer was scarcely prepared.

" Jealous !" said Helen, turning crimson — " jealous, Mortimer ! — no : if I were jealous, God knows what I might do; but I am *not*. No, Francis, never till this moment did I think—did I fancy___."

" Hush ! dearest Helen," said Mortimer, " I only joked: I___"

" This is no time for joking, Mortimer. With a heart all your own — a devotion such as woman perhaps never felt for man — with an earnest and unceasing desire to gain, not your love only, but your esteem and respect — I have been led in half-a-dozen instances to conduct myself, not, as *I* thought, according to your views or wishes, but in strict conformity with the opinions of the Countess St. Alme as to what would most conduce to your happiness and tranquillity."

" Did she use the word tranquillity ?" muttered Mortimer.

" I merely echo her expression," said Helen.

" *She* never told me *this*," said Mortimer abstractedly.

" *I* tell you, Mortimer," said Helen ; — " and," added she, looking bitterly indignant at the sort of doubt of her veracity, which, if not expressed by words, seemed half implied by her husband's tone and manner, " I suppose I am at least to be believed."

Scenes like this, dialogues like this, and the feelings

whence they took their rise, are too painful to be long
dwelt upon: a brief glance at them exhibits all the misery
which presently exists, and which is for the future to be
apprehended.

Let the veil then fall over the rest of this discussion: it
ended in Mortimer's conviction that Helen was all truth
and ingenuousness, and that she was the dupe of the Countess St. Alme. But, in the midst of this conviction, there
grew up a jealousy indescribable by words, and almost in-
calculable in thought — a jealousy that racked his heart
— not that which he himself felt, but which he believed
Helen to feel towards the lost, fallen Amelia! The plain,
straightforward step which would have insured his comfort
would have been, the banishment of the countess from his
domestic circle. Intriguing, complex and manifold, characterised that vivacious lady; and, while she remained to
keep alive the recollection of other days, nothing like happiness could be expected; the more especially as, if any
human being could have searched her heart, they would
have ascertained that whatever might be her present feelings towards Helen, her detestation of Amelia Lady Hil-
lingdou was ten times more powerful and invincible.

It has already been said, that Mortimer, at the end of
the discussion which took place upon this occasion, was
convinced that Helen *had* been deceived and betrayed by
the countess; but that conviction was rendered less satisfactory by the evidence adduced from events of the readiness of Helen to lend herself to what could be considered
neither more nor less than deception, negative or positive,
of the man to whom her devotion was unquestioned; and
so, out of her anxiety to conform herself to his character
under the control of the countess, there was created in his
imagination, besides the sensitive jealousy to which we
have before alluded, a vision of weakness on her part, or
rather a facility of complying with the opinions of others,
with regard to his conduct, which tormented him even
more, perhaps, than the conviction that she had, of her
own free-will, deceived him would have done.

To do this extraordinary man justice, it must be admitted,
that in the morning the thought which ought first to have

suggested itself to his mind did glimmer there; he *did* begin to think that the stay of the countess had been sufficiently protracted: yet, how to remove her?—what say to induce her to leave the place she liked most, the place where, in England, if truth were to be told, she could alone conduct herself as she did.    The difficulty was overcome by circumstances; circumstances which in their combination operated most curiously to meet the views of various persons, the gratification of which, a few weeks before, would have been thought incompatible with the arrangements of the family.

Ten days passed away after the excursion; one or two visitors went, one or two new ones came: but the Countess St. Alme rémained in the circle, fixed as steadily as the flag-ship in Portsmouth Harbour; and there she probably would have remained much longer but for the arrival of the following letter from Jack Batley to his daughter, which, as it involves a description of every thing essential that occurred after his receipt of the pinky-rosy, musky, putty-sealed missive from Mrs. Teresa Catling, will serve to enlighten us not only as to what has happened in the Regent's Park, but what is likely to occur at Sadgrove Park in Worcestershire.

" Grosvenor St., Nov. ——

"   " My dear Helen,

"   " What I am about to write may perhaps surprise you; though, I know enough of matrimonial happiness to know that family secrets are no secrets at all, and that therefore through Mortimer, if not by other means, you are by this time, and have been long before, perfectly aware of the ridiculous mistake I made with regard to the Thurstons.

"   " I declare to you, my dear child, that I had not courage to explain to you the nature of the miscarriage of my suit with that amiable family; nor should I have touched upon the subject had I not assured myself of the certainty of being able to place myself in a position not only to overcome the small obloquy which might attach to a venial error, but to present you with a mother-in-law, of whom, I am sure, you will be as fond as I am proud.

"   " You will recollect, my dearest girl, a remarkably pretty, sprightly, blue-eyed, fair-haired widow, of the name of Catling, who, just out of her weeds, dined with us twice last season in Grosvenor Street. I think, somehow, you did not quite sympathise with me in my admiration of her: — *I* thought her charming: well, *n'importe !* — you are settled brightly and happily, and therefore her dominion cannot in any way affect you. The fact is, we are en_ gaged: she has a pretty jointure, not large, but enough, with what *I* have, to make us quite happy for life ; and I shall be enabled to secure her an equally good income with that which she now possesses, after my death, if, as the common course of nature indicates, I should go first.

" This, I think, will please you — at least, dearest Helen, I hope it will : for my success in this proceeding involves, as I look at it, no small degree of respectability to my personal character. To me the pleasure of seeing you and Mortimer at the celebration of the marriage would be great ; and though I am aware of his disinclination to my brother, still he has been upon the present occasion so kind and liberal, that I should consider his meeting Jacob on the wedding-day a personal favour.

" I cannot explain all the particulars of Jacob's con_ duct, but it has been such as to justify me in putting him forward ; and, although he affects a perfect indifference, I think he would feel pleased at finding your husband and yourself so far disposed to approve of his proceedings in this affair as to sanction its conclusion by your presence.

" In the negotiations for my marriage, I gave Teresa several reasons for my anxiety that they should be perfected with all possible expedition. I admit to you that the real one was not communicated to her ; and though Jacob was in the secret, such has been his friendship and discretion that he has never even remotely alluded to it, his only joke being that I was in so great a hurry to get married because I felt I had no time to lose ; this she took in good part, and, I must do her the justice to say, seemed to participate in my proposal to expedite our settlement as much as pos- sible. The result is, that we are to be married on the twelfth, that is to say, Tuesday se'nnight. The old pro- verb says, ' Marry in haste and repent at leisure ;'' the

falsehood of which we shall practically expose: but, having
gained so much, and carried my point, so far as I am myself concerned, I am now anxious with regard to the arrangements to which the attention of 'the world' is to be
called.

" Of course we shall be married by special licence; the
expense is nothing, compared with the *éclat*. Then for
bridesmaids, Miss Fitz-Flannery, Teresa's sister, will be
one; and, I think, Miss Rouncivall, Lady Bembridge's
niece, another. If I can lay hold of a bishop at this
season in town he shall officiate; if not, we have a dean
certain: but even with this, and some twenty persons for
the *déjeûner*: — and in November one must scrape hard to
muster so many — the affair would be *manqué* without
you and Mortimer: your presence would give a character,
a respectability to it, especially as the wound I received was
inflicted at Sadgrove: your being at the wedding would at
once show to the world the nature of your feelings and
Mortimer's, and put down every whisper against the rea-
sonableness of my conduct."

In this way Batley contrived to fill four sides of his
letter, arguing that the memory of one absurdity is to be
extinguished by the commission of another; not seeing,
in the hurry of his vanity smarting under its wounds, that
nothing could more glaringly proclaim the heartlessness of
his intended offer to Miss Thurston, than his almost immediate union with the widow Catling. As to that step
being the consequence of despair, it was not likely that
any woman would believe *that*. Because, although spite
might drive a man to such an extremity, it was no doubt
taken in the hopes of happiness with another, to the certain
exclusion of a chance of realising it with the original
object. However, Mr. John was off upon one of his
" slap-dash " enterprises, and nobody could have stopped
him, had anybody been so disposed; knowing which, and,
moreover, seeing no " just cause or impediment " why he
should not "follow his own vagary," Helen contented herself with showing his letter to Mortimer, gently arguing in
favour of acceding to the wish expressed in it.

There can be no doubt that her principal motive in undertaking the advocacy of her parent's cause was the desire that he should be gratified, not perhaps unmixed with a kindly leaning towards her uncle, who had always evinced more kindness, perhaps one might more properly say less indifference, towards her than towards other people ; yet, if her heart had been laid open, the chances are, that, with all these hopes and wishes, there would have been found mingled the expectation that such a move as her father suggested would have the effect of unsettling the count and countess, who, though the party was broken up, and all but one or two men were gone, still remained as calmly domiciled as if they were in the château St. Alme, on the Loire, instead of being guests at Sadgrove Hall, on the banks of the Severn. In fact, from some hints which the countess dropped, Helen began to think that their stay would be protracted till after the end of the term at Oxford, when Francis Blocksford would be able to join them on their return to France, where the count proposed to keep Christmas, and whither she felt afraid that Mortimer would suggest their accompanying them.

This chain of events, galling as Helen felt it even by anticipation, she fancied might be broken by her father's wedding : the mere change of scene for a few days would be a relief, inasmuch as it would withdraw her from the immediate influence of the woman whom she was taught at once to hate, to doubt, and fear, yet compelled to seem to love. Her eloquence, therefore, in setting forth the justice of her parent's views, the duty she owed him, the pleasure it would give him, and the gratitude he would feel to Mortimer if he acceded to his request, was most remarkable. The marriage of her father was eulogised as prudent ; the widow-bride was depicted in glowing colours, her beauty heightened, and her wealth increased ; her worth and accomplishments were put in their brightest array, till Mortimer began to listen to the proposal, which he at first treated with ridicule, with something like patience, and even an incipient desire to be present at the ceremony.

He *had* business in town : they could stay at an hotel, or in Grosvenor Street ; and——

"Why not offer them Sadgrove as a retirement for the honey-moon?" said Helen, half jokingly and half in earnest.

"No, no," said Mortimer, "that would involve us in a longer stay in London than I should like; besides, what should we do with the St. Almes?"

It is impossible to guess what might have been Helen's answer if she had felt it convenient to offer an opinion; as it was, the question itself was an ample answer to her "previous question," and she received it accordingly with a sort of doubting expression of countenance and a considerably prolonged "w-h-y;" leaving Mortimer to supply whatever else might be necessary. So much, however, was achieved by this manœuvre, (and let us only look at the prospect of happiness in a family where manœuvring was the order of the day, after a few months only had elapsed since its establishment,) as went to empower the lady at this critical juncture just to inquire how long he expected the St. Almes to stay.

Upon Mortimer this question, its causes, its objects, were not lost; yet he would have been better pleased if it had not been asked. He was conscious, not only that the presence of the countess produced exactly the effect upon Helen that Helen described, but that he himself was anxious to see her depart; but he could not, for some reason known, as it appeared to himself alone, or, if not, to the countess and himself in partnership, hasten or hurry in any rough or unseemly manner that departure.

"No," said Mortimer: "I am sure, Helen, any thing that can gratify you, or your father, I am most ready to do; and as we cannot be pestered by the coarsenesses of 'uncle Jacob' for more than one day, I shall be glad to do what your father calls 'honour his nuptials with our presence.'"

"And the St. Almes?" asked Helen.

"Oh," answered Mortimer, "we will leave them here: we shall be away but four days at most; and if we should have anybody down here — I forget if any people are engaged to us — that week, the countess can do the honours during your brief absence."

That she might be perfectly able to do so, Helen did not mean to dispute; neither did she, beginning as she did to understand Mortimer's disposition, propose to dissent from the lady's appointment as regent of Sadgrove during her own absence, inasmuch as, besides not wishing to ruffle the serenity of her lord and master, who, according to that same countess's description, was as different when angry from what he was when he was pleased, as the rippling sea on a summer's day is from the mountainous and foaming alternation of coal-black hill and valley in the boundless ocean — her great object was to carry the point of being present at her father's marriage, for that she knew was *his* point; and, weak or strong, what mattered to *her*, since it was the desire of a parent — the only one she had ever known, to whom her love was devoted, as was his to her.

Therefore did she content herself with the gracious permission to go to the wedding, and followed up the somewhat questionable consent of Mortimer by touching upon the details, as to whom they should go; whether to Grosvenor Street, or to an hotel, or ——

"Oh," said Mortimer, "there is time enough for all that: say we will be there."

The words were music to her ear.

—"As to the precise time or place, that shall be determined hereafter: but mind, Helen, you are to consider that this infraction of my rule — never to subject myself to an association with your extraordinary uncle Jacob — is to be held by you as a special grace and favour."

Saying which, he drew his Helen to his bosom, and gave her one of those kisses which go direct to a heart anxious to have the feelings with which it is overflowing appreciated.

After this conversation and consent, Helen was as nearly happy as she could be so long as the countess remained at Sadgrove.

One can hardly picture the delight with which she sat down in the morning to describe to her father, in an affectionate letter, the ready acquiescence of Mortimer, and to inquire into particulars, as to whether there would be accommodation for them in Grosvenor Street, whether he wished them to go to his house, in fact, touching every point relative to the "exhibition" which, knowing her volatile parent's character, she felt assured he was anxious to make.

As to the proceedings of the vivacious bridegroom elect they were most prosperous. No sooner had Jacob opened the subject to Mrs. Catling in his own peculiar manner, the abruptness of which saved a world of trouble and an age of time, it was charming to see how readily she acquiesced in his suggestions. This was natural enough; for, besides being really prepossessed in favour of Jack, and feeling a general anxiety to be married again and brought forward in the world, she had been taught to consider old Jacob in the light rather of an absolute monarch than an ordinary trustee, and to measure his influence by the confidence which her late spouse had reposed in him, and the extent of power over her with which he had invested him.

In the association of Jack and his intended, during the short space which intervened between the beginning and the ending of their "courtship," there was nothing sufficiently romantic to render the details interesting. At this season we shall, therefore, take only a hasty glance, although it is necessary that the reader should know how delighted John was with Mortimer's acceptance of his invitation, a circumstance to him of first-rate importance. The announcement of his intention was received by Jacob with one of his most uncourteous grunts, and a hearty declaration that, "come, or stay away, it was all one to him."

The second title selected for the narrative before the reader will naturally have led him to anticipate the occurrence of several of those events by which the three principal epochs of life are distinguished; and therefore he will not be disposed to quarrel with the writer for shortening the details of the second "marriage," which it becomes his duty to record. Certain circumstances connected with it, however, are perhaps worthy of remark.

The preliminaries were very soon arranged: the gaiety and vivacity of Jack were the theme of the widow's admiration, and the little dinners in Grosvenor Street, which, by degrees, two or three of his dearest friends were allowed to join *en petit comité*, were quite charming ; Lady Bembridge came and made the *aimable ;* and Miss Rouncivall and Miss Fitz-Flannery began to be friends ; and all went on delightfully, Jacob having already handed over to his now happy brother one moiety of the promised thousand pounds. Just tipping Cupid's wings with gold, if the precious metal does not clog them, makes them flap most agreeably. The judicious application of even five hundred pounds, makes a wonderful difference in the general aspect of affairs ; and when Mrs. Catling returned to Shamrock Cottage, after an agreeable, or, what she called, an " elegant" evening at the house of her intended, — which house, moreover, was intended for her, — she dreamed herself into a new region, and saw all her hopes on the point of realisation.

In the mean time Jacob was doing the more important business connected with the affair. The worldly part of the arrangements, and the legal proceedings, were confided to the care of his faithful counsellor, Brimmer Brassey, of Barnard's Inn, who, though the most agreeable of attorneys in his own estimation, was so odious in Jack's eyes, that he could scarcely endure a dialogue of ten minutes with him even when business required an hour. Brassey had the entire management of Jacob's concerns ; and it had more than once struck Jack that a great deal of his brother's churlishness towards him arose from prejudices awakened in his mind by the attorney, whom he never could be prevailed upon to invite to Grosvenor Street, even although Jacob's hints that way tending had been by no means few or obscure.

" I tell you why I like him," said Jacob; " he has a short, off-hand way of doing business, after his own fashion; no bills — no running up — no instructions — no consulting about this, or advising about that, or conversing about t'other ;— does every thing for me by the job. ' Brassey,' says I, ' I want to do so and so ; — can I, or can't I ? — How much will it cost?' He says yes, or no, as the case may be — fixes his price — does it : I give him a cheque for the whole, and there's an end."

" He seems quick," said Jack.

" Quick ! — psha ! lightning's a slow coach to him !
See how he managed matters at Mudbury — and here, with
all those settlements and things.   Why, one of your fine
tiptoppers would be a month haggling at three-and-fourpence
a minute : not a bit of it with Brassey — all done at a blow.
I just give him the heads : — seven hundred and fifty per
ann. ; — two hundred settled on self — at death of husband, jointure from first marriage returns to her, in addition to what may be left ; — eh ? — All plane-sailing —
no jiggamaree stuff !   *He* drew Catling's will, don't you
see ? — knows all the particulars.   Well, now, for fifty
pounds all that will be done, which, of course, I pay."

Jack bowed.

— " And what happens ? — why, the day of the wedding, nothing remains but sign the settlement, and all safe.
No worries about references and consultations — does duty
for both clients ; I have known him, under the rose, act
half a dozen times for plaintiff and defendant in the same
cause ; — it simplifies matters.   Besides, when one *has* got
hold of an honest lawyer — eh ? — it's as well to keep him."

" I leave all this to you, brother," said Jack ; " you
have a longer head than I."

" You shall be taken care of.   I always take care of myself — *you* don't.   Brassey shall get all ready, and you will
have nothing to do but sign ; so, set your heart at rest."

Jack's delight at being relieved from any lengthened
intercourse with Mr. Brimmer Brassey was great ; but it
was somewhat qualified when Jacob suggested that it would
be considered " uncommon rude" not to invite him to the
*déjeûner*.   Jack felt the strongest inclination to demur ; but
Jacob was so important a character in the drama about to
be enacted, that he had not the courage to " speak up."

" My reason for pressing it," said Jacob, " is this :
Brassey doesn't think small beer of himself ; and although,
as far as he personally is concerned, I shouldn't care three
straws if he were hanged to-morrow, so that my accounts
with him were all square — which, please the pigs, they
are every Saturday night — I think it might give him a
better idea of *me* to see me amongst the lords and chaps
whom I despise, but whom he worships."

"Oh! there can be no difficulty : the invitations will all come from Teresa ; I dare say she will have no objection."

"She !" said Jacob with a contemptuous sneer ;—" no, I think not : *her* objections wouldn't go for much with *me*. I look to myself — eh? — that is *my* principle. What I think right must be right with those who think it worth while to keep in with me; and when I say worth while, you perceive, Jack, I am not such a bumpkin as to suppose that anybody *does* keep in with me but for what he can get. Catling, to be sure, did leave me a lump of money ; but then he had advances, at reasonable interest, during his life. If he hadn't paid me, somebody else would : he was but a noodle-pie after all — eh?"

Jack never permitted himself to differ with Jacob ; and, as he certainly could not sympathise with him in feeling or principle, he allowed him to have it, as *he* called, " all his own way." He was sure that he was on the safe side while Jacob espoused his cause in the financial arrangements ; and, as the fact was truly stated by him, that the preparation of a settlement, by which the gentleman had nothing to give, and the lady all to confer, the said gentleman could lose very little ; Jack conceded the point, and Mr. Brimmer Brassey, the ambidextrous attorney of Barnard's Inn, was commissioned to do the whole business, though Jack had at the very moment resting upon a shelf in a leading solicitor's chamber in Lincoln's Inn one of those brown cannisters of which mention has elsewhere been made, upon which his name appeared painted in white letters, perfectly legal as to length under the last act for regulating the descriptions of owners of carts and caravans, and which might have secured a dealer in " Marine Stores" from the penalty to be pounced upon by some common informer, in regard to the dimensions of the characters which over his door announce the character of the owner of the house. In fact, the isolated Jacob had succeeded in establishing a kind of dogged influence over everybody around him — certainly not obtained by conciliation or fair means — which had the effect of putting down all opposition to his will, unless it happened, as it had occurred in the case of Mortimer, that his subjects rose into open rebellion and threw off the yoke altogether.

However, it must be confessed that every thing looked smilingly, as far as the union of John and Teresa — (the Christian names make it sound more romantic) — was concerned ; and it was this perfect harmony of all things in concatenation accordingly, which so completely divested it of real interest.  Jack did nothing but laugh ; T'resa laughed from morning till night ; and Margaret couldn't answer the commonest question without bursting into a fit of noisy mirthfulness : even Jacob chuckled, Mr. Brimmer Brassey tittered, and the infection became so general, that Mr. Grub, the head and confidential clerk, could scarcely keep his countenance seriously inclined while regulating the ledger in Lilypot Lane.

In the midst of all the arrangements, Jack was particularly anxious that Colonel Magnus should also be present at the " nuptial ceremony ;" not only because he was somebody in *his* way, but because he was the particular friend of Mortimer : not but, if he had known the real truth, he might have felt less disposed to cultivate or cherish his acquaintance, since the first important difference that had ever arisen between him and Mortimer occurred upon the particular point of Helen's marriage,  Fortunately for the world, its inhabitants are not omniscient ; and Jack took Magnus for what he seemed to be, and held that he would be ornamental as one of the party.

" I guess," said Mr. Brimmer Brassey, as he was sitting after dinner at Shamrock Cottage with Jacob and his brother — for *there* John Batley was forced to endure him — " I guess, as the Americans say, that Colonel Magnus wo'n't show : his paper is a good deal about.  I think — only, of course, we professional men say nothing except where we are not ourselves concerned — I have seen his name in queer places ; and I think that, although he ought to be in his own country, he is on the other side of the Channel."

" What !" said Jacob, " hard up ?"

" Chock, block, and belay, sir," said Brassey.  " I heard of his having been at Worcester a fortnight ago trying to raise money — I think I could guess by whose assistance ;

but, of course, I say nothing : — no harm done to anybody, for he couldn't do it."

Jack was convinced that Brassey was right as to the period of his visit to that city, and also of his return in company with him to London ; and thence concluded that all his facts were equally accurate.

" I know," said Batley, " he was at Worcester at the time you mention, for I saw him there with my son-in-law, and came up to town with him myself."

" Ah ! " said Brassey, putting his finger archly to his nose, " that's just it, sir ! I keep my eye upon him, for I am concerned for one or two establishments where he is dipped a good deal ; and, by not hearing from him lately, we are fearful he will fall into bad hands, and get into the X, Y, Z line."

" Brassey," said Jacob, acting as interpreter, " Brassey means, into the hands of advertising money-lenders."

" I see," said Jack, not without a sort of unpleasant consciousness that he was in the company of a gentleman who, from his calling, and the general course of his practice, might have seen *his* name in some of the places in which that of Colonel Magnus had figured ; " but I understood that Colonel Magnus was a man of considerable property."

" Probably you heard himself describe it," said Brassey, who, as all vulgar-minded men do, grew familiar and impudent as he warmed with his subject. " Great talkers, Mr. Batley, are the least doers ; and those who flourish most in words, are the least flourishing in fact. No : depend upon it, you will not get him to the breakfast or dinner, or whatever it may be."

" I had no idea," said John, " that the case was so bad."

" Nor anybody else," said Brassey, " but we, sir — we who know and see, and work the wires that make the puppets dance. Bless you ! I could show you such things about your tip-topping friend — only, of course, *we* of the profession are sealed — as would astonish you."

Jack, who had always hated Brassey, began to find his aversion gradually increase as the man's familiarity progressed, and already had satisfied himself that his first impression of his character was the just one ; nor did he

altogether rely upon his own judgment, for he had mentioned his name to his own solicitors, and they had, without
descending to particulars, sufficiently corroborated the prepossession he entertained in his disfavour.   The high, the
honourable, and respectable solicitors of London are as completely the antipodes of the sneaking, jobbing, dirty attorneys, as the *élite* of St. George's, Hanover Square, are of
the inhabitants of New Zealand; so that every sentence
Mr. Brimmer Brassey uttered reduced him one step in Jack's
estimation.

It is said that there never was a book published which
did not contain something worthy notice; it may be that
there does not exist a man from whose conversation something valuable may not be extracted.   Hating and despising
Mr. Brassey as John Batley did, he had certainly received
an enlightenment from him upon the subject of Magnus's
circumstances which was at once curious and interesting.
With all his activity of mind, his thoughts had never taken
*that* turn; and when he became the companion of the
colonel in his journey to London, he certainly did not
entertain the slightest suspicion that his removal from
Worcester was the result of the failure of an attempt to
raise a sum of money in that city upon Mortimer's credit:
nor, to say truth, did he feel at all obliged to Brassey for
enlightenment on the subject; on the contrary, the flippancy with which he spoke of Magnus, and his alleged
pecuniary connexion with Mortimer, in direct violation of
that confidence which forms an essential part of the compact between lawyer and client, disgusted him; for though
Magnus might not have been in direct communication with
Brassey, it was evident that he had become familiar with the
state of his circumstances, and the course of his proceedings, by some professional intercourse with those who had.

As the evening advanced, and Mr. Brassey " passed the
bottle," which he did with surprising activity, he became
more lively and loquacious, and proportionably more odious
to Jack.   He described at length the pleasures of a weekly
dinner of a convivial club, as he called it, to which he belonged, where there was always a remarkably good "spread,"
and where, he ventured to say, they had the best port in

the parish ; and where Bob Simmons used to sing the drollest songs after dinner ; and then, at nine, the smoking began ; — and so he went on, until Jacob, taking fire at the mention of smoking, rang the bell for cigars, and punch, and Jack made his escape to his intended.

Hapless swain ! little did he anticipate that his fair Teresa would be ordered by her obdurate trustee - to prepare with her own hands the beverage he loved so much. As Mrs. Catling the wife of his friend, she had been taught to compound it according to an approved recipe ; and, as Mrs. Catling the widow, he expected her to continue her services. Jack, of course, bore all this philosophically ; and while his intended was gone to the fulfilment of what she seemed to consider her duty, he and Margaret remained talking over Mr. Brimmer Brassey, who, it seemed, was more than half convinced that the said Margaret was in love with him — which, if it be true that women endeavour to conceal their affection by abusing the object of their devotion, he could not have doubted for a moment, after having heard the young lady's analysis of his extraordinary merits.

Batley had a sharpish battle to fight with his pride, which revolted against what he considered not only a great want of consideration on the part of Jacob, but a degradation of his intended wife in the eyes of the establishment. The idea of the future mistress of the mansion in Grosvenor Street being compelled to "make punch," and, in order to do it *secundum artem*, to retire to the butler's pantry — was so revolting, that it was with difficulty he smothered his indignation, and endeavoured to divert himself with tumbling about the contents of Margaret's workbox, over which, in order to exhibit at once her industry and "gentility," she was busying herself about nothing : but it cost him an effort. To be sure, a few days would change the whole arrangement — and Jacob was omnipotent ; he had only yet got the moiety of his thousand pounds, and had not yet secured the lady ; and therefore must he patiently endure what was exceedingly galling : and as the infliction was characteristic of his brother's selfishness, he

resolved to put a good face on " the business," and seem
satisfied with what was going on.

The nectarious compound having been judiciously con-
cocted, and then deposited on the table by the fair widow
herself, who uniformly acted Hebe upon such occasions, she
joined Jack and her sister in the other room, leaving the bear
and the boar to revel in all the luxuries of smoking and
tippling, while the more refined portion of the party were
enjoying the calmer delights of coffee and conversation,
till the little clock on the chimney-piece that never went
right, struck ten.

" Well, Brassey," said Jacob, knocking away the end
of his cigar, " you have read over the draft of the settlement to Mrs. C. ? "

" Does a duck swim ? " said Brassey, giving forth a
puff which would have made the funnel of a steam-boat
jealous.

" And she —— "

" Is as she always is," said the attorney-at-law with a
smirk, " quite agreeable. I am not surprised. Your brother, Mr. Batley, is uncommon pleasant — easy to deal
with — no buckram — a great favourite with the sex, no
doubt ; and what I call quite the gentleman."

" Umph ! that's it," said Jacob ; " and a very fine gentleman too, as I always tell him."

" I'm afraid," said Brassey, giving another puff, " that
Mr. Mortimer will get entangled with Colonel Magnus —
eh, sir ? — there's something going on in the accepting
line."

" I don't care three brass farthings what happens to
*him*, or anybody else," said Jacob. " He is another fine
gentleman — a fine race, eh ? — friends as they call themselves — I always knew how these matters would end —
what do I care ? "

" No," said Brassey, " I don't see why you should,
sir ; " — he always called Jacob " sir ; " — " only I was
thinking something might be done in the way of business
with the kites that are flying ; — I shouldn't mind dab-
bling a bit ; besides it might be of use to the parties."

· "Never you mind that," said Jacob, filling his glass: "take my advice,—put yourself out of your way for nobody, nobody will ever put himself out of his way for *you*; stick to your six-and-eightpences, that's your mark. You have read the settlement over to Jack too?"

"Of course," said Brassey, "and he is equally pleased with the lady."

"Well done!" said Jacob, "that's something: there, you see, I please two people by pleasing myself;—all comes to that,—eh? Now, Brassey, another glass? this is very pretty tipple. We shall shift our quarters to Grosvenor Street soon—nearer at hand than this London-gone-out-of town place; that's one of my objects: I shall get my Sunday dinner without having so far to go for it."

"Colonel Mortimer is coming to the wedding," said Brassey, in a tone which implied his knowledge of the fact, although he was merely fishing.

"So I hear," said Jacob; "and of course his wife. I would rather she was coming by herself."

"I hear, sir, that Mrs. M. is in the way which ladies wish to be who love their lords."

"What way is that?" said Jacob: "hang me if I believe any ladies love their lords now-a-days: but Mortimer isn't a lord."

"No," said Brimmer; "what I said is a delicate allusion out of a play, sir. I meant, that Mrs. Mortimer is —as I hear—in the family way, sir."

"Oh, ah," said Jacob, "very likely; I'm sure *I* don't care; I suppose the live stock must be kept up, and it's all very right: I haven't heard any thing about it, and can't say; it's nothing very remarkable any way."

A pause followed the ungracious snub which Jacob had inflicted upon Brassey.

"Have you managed about the carriage for me?" said Jacob, after two or three puffs.

"All settled, sir," said Brassey; "Mr. Perch will take the old one at the price named, and two years' credit for the new one."

"Right!" said Jacob—"money is money; I see no use in keeping a chariot in a coach-house to wear itself out:

besides, there's interest for two years. That's a good bargain — eh ? — for *me* at least. Monday, I shall hand Jack
over the other five hundred — get *that* off my mind —
nothing to repent of there ; — when are the things · to be
engrossed ? "

" Three days will do the needful, sir."

" I have nothing to do with the stamps."

" Nothing, sir," replied the attorney ; " and on the
wedding-day we will sign, seal, and deliver."

" Just so ; and I'll tell you what ———"

What that was, the reader is not at this moment doomed
to know, inasmuch as the servant entered the room at the
instant to inquire whether Mr. Batley would like to have
any cold meat, or broiled bones, or any thing to wind up
the evening.

" Odds bobs !" said Jacob, " what! is it getting late
enough to ask that question ? No — nothing — nothing
more to eat. — Is tea over ? "

" A long while ago, sir. My mistress's compliments,
would you like a little more punch ? "

" What d'ye say, Brassey, — eh ? " said Jacob ; " warm
it up again — eh ? "

Brassey inclined his head and smirked, as much as to
say with Bombastes in the tragedy,

> " Whate'er your majesty shall deign to name,
> Short-cut, or long, to me 'tis all the same."

" As you please, sir."

" A leetle more, William," said Jacob ; " about half as
much as before ; and — d'ye hear ? — put it in the drawing-room with two clean glasses ; we'll go and sit there —
the fire is getting low."

William obeyed.

" Shan't we disturb the lovers, sir ? " said Brassey, with
an arch look.

" Lovers ! " said Jacob, making a' face, " Pooh, pooh !
Mr. B. what have they to talk of that we mayn't hear ?
Why, the one's a widow, and the other, according to your
account, very near being a grandfather — hey ? No — no,
come along ; I dare say Jack wo'n't dislike our interrup-

tion: if he does, I can't help it; I can't let myself get cold to please anybody: so come—let us move."

And move they did: nor was their appearance in the slightest degree annoying to the Philander of the evening, who, with all his resolution to be pleased, found it rather a toil to keep the conversation going.

This discovery did not much disconcert him, inasmuch as he had seen numerous examples of domestic happiness in cases where the intellectuality of the wife ranked vastly below that of the husband: nor did he entirely disapprove of the principle of relaxing his mind, when quiet and at home, by bringing it to the level of that of his fair partner —not altogether losing sight of the satisfaction to be derived from a consciousness of superiority over a companion in whose eyes he wished to appear something better than the common run of men.

Mr. Brassey, a little elevated by his potations, brushed up his greasy hair, and seated himself next Miss Fitz-Flannery, who had been again reduced to the task of doing the honours, and making herself agreeable, in consequence of Jacob's second demand upon the services of her sister. His conversation upon this occasion was made up of inquiries whether Miss F.-F. had been at the theatre, whether she had seen Mr. Tidmarsh in Othello, what she thought of Miss Pumpkin in Juliet, and a lamentation that the "fair sex" could not be members of the Slap-bang club to which he belonged, where he was sure Miss F. would be delighted with the singing after supper.

When Jack's carriage was announced, Jacob engaged places for himself and his legal adviser; it could set Jack home first, then take him to Lilypot Lane, dropping Brassey at Barnard's Inn. The arrangement was particularly inconvenient to Batley, who had no intention of going home so early; but Jacob's will was law, all was done according to his bidding, and, at eleven, the triumvirate took their departure from Shamrock Cottage.

## CHAPTER V.

I⊤ must not be supposed that, during the period which had elapsed since Mortimer's marriage, his sister had ceased to watch with solicitude the course of his proceedings. She was, in every sense of the word, exemplary; and the love she bore her brother was the real cause of the apprehension, of which she could not divest herself, as to the happy issue of his second marriage. The correspondence between them had ceased; but, without adopting any unfair means of ascertaining the real state of their domestic affairs, Mrs. Farnham was not without information as regarded the proceedings at Sadgrove: one of its visitors was an old friend of hers; and from *her* she learned enough to render her extremely anxious for the future happiness and respectability of her brother.

It appeared to Mrs. Farnham, from all she could hear, that the position of her new sister-in-law was one the least calculated to secure her from what the politician would call " pressure from without." She had received descriptions of her character from one who had known her from childhood, and who was fully alive to the peculiarities of her temper, which, although based upon high principle and uncompromising candour, seemed, in her eyes, fearfully conducive, at some period of excitement, to dissolve the bond of union which held her to Mortimer, whose temper so far resembled that of his wife, that, the moment he fancied that efforts were making to deceive him, his rage would know no bounds.

Mortimer was conscious of his own weakness; and never did man struggle more earnestly against the workings of his mind than he did: but informed, as his sister was, of Helen's independence of spirit and impatience of control, her apprehensions were the more awakened to the peril of their happiness by the circumstance that Helen had no real female friend—no experienced counsellor—who might point out to her the course of conduct by which she might conciliate, and so eventually reform, the husband who had sought, in his marriage with her, the restoration of his peace of mind, and a gradual oblivion of past indiscretions. On the contrary, having been brought up without a mother, placed early in the control of her father's house, and accustomed to associate with his companions, she had, as has already been remarked, no female friends whose advice she could seek; and, as if to make this evil the greater, her husband had supplied the place of such an associate by domesticating in his house the Countess St. Alme.

Why he did so, Mrs. Farnham could not imagine; but when, in reply to her disinterested remonstrances, she received an unkind answer, she ceased to press a matter upon which she was plainly told her interference was not required; that Mortimer was master of his own actions, and that he did not feel disposed to ask or accept advice as to the regulation of his conduct; that it was sufficient for his sister to know that the countess was one of his oldest friends to induce her to denounce her; and that, since she had refused to afford Helen her countenance and friendship when he had expressed the warmest wish that she should do so, he must beg to be left unmolested in the course, which, under the circumstances, he had considered it best to pursue.

If ever the blindness of a man of the world were made evident, it exhibited itself in this proceeding. It is not at this moment our business to dive into the particulars of the intimacy between Mortimer and the countess, nor to ascertain the real cause of the influence over him which she unquestionably possessed: suffice it to say, that he knew her as a worldly woman — an *intriguante* — daring and insincere — and that yet she had the power to make him believe that, from her perfect intimacy with all the circumstances of his former marriage, as well as with the peculiarities of his own character, she was, of all persons in the world, the one to soften down any difficulties which might arise in the development of the truths connected with his former attachment, and accustom Helen to the occasional gloominess of temper to which he was subject, and which had its origin in the recollections which her sweet influence was destined to overcome.

How the countess fulfilled the task we have seen; why

she acted as she did, we have yet to learn : but, let her
motives have been what they might, their results were not
unknown to Mrs. Farnham, who began to repent, when
she felt it was too late, that she had sacrificed to friendship
and a feeling of distaste, which she now thought she ought
to have overcome, the chance of securing her brother's happiness.

She had even heard the intelligence to which Mr. Brimmer Brassey had so "genteelly" referred at Shamrock
Cottage, which increased the interest she felt in her sister-
in-law, and led her to look forward to the period when the
attentions of one so nearly connected with her as she was
might be most valuable to Helen : in fact, she repented of
having withstood her brother's invitation, and resolved to
overlook the harshness of his last reply, in the hope of res-
cuing those who were dear to her from a fate which she
considered inevitable, if the visit of the Countess St. Alme
were permitted to continue. This design the amiable Mrs.
Farnham lost but little time in putting into execution. She
wrote to Francis, and told him that her friend and family
had resolved to visit England earlier than they had intended; that she proposed accompanying them; and,
having fulfilled her engagement to them, should be happy
to offer herself for a visit to Sadgrove.

—"And," added she, "tell your young and beautiful
wife, for so I hear she is, that I shall press her to my heart
with the feelings of a mother rather than a sister. The
difference between your age and mine, dear Francis, has
always given me a sort of semi-maternal authority over
you; and, as Helen is still *your* junior, why may I not
cherish a sentiment towards her which will necessarily
involve that care which, at no great distance of time, may
probably be acceptable to her? Bid her think of me, then,
as if I were the parent she has lost; and do you, dear
Francis, teach her to love me as you think I deserve to be
loved by one who is so nearly and dearly allied to you."

Francis read his sister's letter. He threw it from him.
"This," muttered he to himself, "is trick — artifice
—design. Some tattling gossip-monger has been plying
her with news of my misconduct; or else she thinks me

incapable of preserving my own honour without *her* assistance. It is evident her opinions are changed; she is willing *now* to come to Sadgrove — ready *now* to do that which a few months since I vainly implored her to do. She finds that I will not endure her literary lectures, and so has resolved to settle herself here to preach them personally. No!—all that I sought to do has been done: Helen knows the whole of the history, which I feared might startle her, and heeds it not. Emily would undo all this: — if it had been her pleasure to come to me in the outset — but no — not now: she then inflicted a wound which this offer cannot cure. Nay, she herself has pleaded against the very course she now proposes to adopt, by fixing herself in my family to act the part of mother to my wife, when her own letters distinctly deprecate such a system, and uphold the undivided dominion of the mistress of the house as ——."

Mortimer's thoughts glanced towards the countess, who, in fact, was playing the very part which Mrs. Farnham proposed to undertake, but in a different manner, and with very different motives. His sister had warned him of this intimacy—had expressed her disbelief in the possibility of its existence: the intimacy continued. Was it not that very circumstance which had induced her to alter her resolution of remaining abroad? — was it not that which had roused her to take a step inconvenient to herself? It was certain that the Countess St. Alme and Mrs. Farnham could not meet; the very acceptance of her proposal would be the signal for the removal of the other; the countess being sufficiently a woman of the world, even if she had not been made acquainted with Mrs. Farnham's feelings towards her, to render any explanation unnecessary: the tacit understanding being, on the part of Mrs. Farnham, that, if the countess did not go, she would not come; and, on the part of the countess, that Mrs. Farnham would not come if she did not go.

Francis gave the letter a second perusal; and then (a circumstance which may pretty well explain the course of affairs at Sadgrove) proceeded to the morning-room, where his wife and the countess were sitting, and handed the despatch *to the latter* to read.

"An offer of a visit, Helen," said Mortimer. "I give you leave to guess from whom."

Helen, seeing that the letter, the contents of which the countess was eagerly devouring, in all probability announced the fact, felt startled by being permitted to surmise about an event *officially* confided to his guest.

"I cannot imagine," said Helen:—"not my father?"

"No," said Mortimer, "not exactly; but from a lady who is good enough to wish to perform the part of mother to you. I suppose she imagines that you are not able to take care of yourself, and that I am not able to take care of you."

"Who is that? I was not aware that anybody was sufficiently interested in my proceedings to take such pains in my behalf."

"The lady is no other than my most reverend, grave, and potent sister," said Mortimer—"a lady who has the quality of acidulating every thing she approaches; who looks upon everybody as doomed to eternal destruction who does not act up to what she considers propriety, rectitude, virtue, &c. &c. &c., and is the completest wet blanket that ever was thrown upon the warmth of a domestic fireside."

"Mrs. Farnham!" said Helen—and the tone in which she repeated the name was not exactly in accordance with the sketch which Mortimer had drawn of her. Helen had heard her spoken of in the highest terms; and even the countess herself, who hated her, had taught Helen to understand that the real cause of her sister-in-law's absence from England and the wedding was a scrupulous sensitiveness with regard to Mortimer's former errors, and a nervous doubtfulness of the success of his scheme of reformation; so that, although Helen had been taught to fear, and even dislike her by the countess, she had learned from other reports — probably enough, from the very friend who had communicated to *her* the details of what was passing at Sadgrove — to respect and revere her.

—"And *will* she come?" said Helen, feeling at the moment a fervent hope that she might.

"I should think not," said Mortimer:—"how should

she? We shall go to France in December, and she does not propose coming to England until the end of November."

"Do you really mean to go to France?" said Helen, wishing to be informed as to the strength of his resolution.

"So the countess says," said Mortimer.

"What does the countess say?" said the countess herself, laying down the letter.

"That we are to be your guests at Christmas," said Mortimer.

"I understand it as settled," was the lady's remark; "but Mrs. Farnham's pilgrimage may alter your determination. Do not let us interfere with her proceedings."

"May *I* see the letter?" said Helen, with an air of humility not quite so well acted as her surprise at the fishing temple.

"Have you finished it?" said Mortimer carelessly to the countess.

"Oh! yes, *I* have done with it," replied the lady, tossing it to him across the table.

"Then," said Helen, "I presume I *may* see it."

All that had passed between her and Mortimer on the subject of the countess (much more than the countess herself suspected) flashed into the minds of both husband and wife; but Helen struggled successfully with her feelings, and took the letter to read, as a matter of course, and thus escaped the sight of an interchange of looks between Francis and their lively guest, which would have excited any other than pleasurable feelings.

"I suppose," said the countess, with a pert toss of her head, "we are bound to make way for your sister, Mortimer; and that not only we must retreat, but you must abandon your intention of visiting us, to receive her."

"I have *said*, countess," replied Mortimer, "we are engaged to *you*."

"But why," said Helen, putting down the letter for a moment, "is it necessary that one engagement should destroy the other? Is there any reason why you should not receive your sister before the count and countess leave us, and then we might go?"

"No," said Mortimer, "that wouldn't answer."—And

Helen *did* see the look at the countess which followed this declaration.

"But wouldn't you like that Mrs. Farnham should come here?" asked Helen. "I am sure her letter is full of kindness."

"Yes," said the countess, "she is all kindness to those who happen to come up to her notions of propriety; but her benevolence is extremely circumscribed. I believe I am not upon her list as one of those who can be preserved from destruction, merely because I do when in Rome as Rome does, and have been guilty of going to a play on Sunday in society where it is thought no sin. I know she thinks me a most abominable person."

Helen looked at the lady, and felt the force of the contrast which the words then glibly flowing over her roseate lips afforded to those contained in her sister-in-law's letter; but she saw that Mortimer was determined, and that the lively countess's influence would prohibit the visit of the amiable widow.

This circumstance weighed upon her mind. She appreciated the affection which evidently had prompted Mrs. Farnham's forgiveness of Mortimer's letters to her; and, anticipating the difficulties which she was destined to encounter, dwelt painfully upon the decision which would deprive her of the support of so amiable a being. It was, however, of no use. The answer to Emily Farnham's offer was brief and almost harsh, conceived in the spirit which dictated her brother's first remarks upon it when he received it, and couched in terms little more considerate.

It was impossible for Helen not to be conscious of the triumphant air of the countess when this refusal had been given, or that *her* power had outweighed that of the woman she detested, and whom Mortimer ought to have loved; and for the next two or three days she joked Helen on the possibility of doing without her volunteer mamma, who was probably more anxious to assume the character in jest, from never having filled it in earnest. Nor was Helen better satisfied with this *playfulness*, by seeing that it pleased her husband, who seemed to seize every opportunity of supporting the countess in running down his nearest relative.

Time, however, wore on, and the day of Batley's marriage drew near. The question was, whether the St. Almes should remain at Sadgrove during the absence of its owner and his lady, or that they should all break up, and remain in London for a week or two, until they should take flight for France; an event which depended chiefly upon the emancipation of young Blocksford from his labours at the university: and it must be admitted that, pending the discussion, Mrs. Mortimer leant very much to the latter scheme. She felt that, quitting her house, and leaving her establishment under the control of a lady for whom her affection certainly did not increase, was something like a degradation, and even a sort of admission of ownership, which every action of the lady herself tended to assume. As for Mortimer, he appeared to have forgotten all that had passed on the subject, and seemed, less from regard for the countess, than from some indescribable power which she had over him, to become fascinated — in the real rattle-snake sense of the word — and subside into a passive obedience to her will, which even his earnest desire to conciliate his wife was not sufficiently strong to counteract.

A new difficulty, however, arose, inasmuch as the countess, who had a great fancy for "patronising," and who, reckoning upon her "title," such as it was, imagined that she gave *éclat* to whatever she condescended to sanction ; and, therefore, as soon as the arrangements for their all going to town were in a state of forwardness, she addressed herself in some of her sweetest tones to Helen, and, dressing her vivacious countenance in its brightest smiles, suggested that, as they should be in London at the time of her father's marriage, she should be extremely happy to attend, if he felt that it would be agreeable; " for," added she, " he is a very charming person, and I wish him all sorts of happiness ; and besides, Helen dear, he is *your* father."

Now it so chanced, that in a letter from her father, that very morning received by Helen, in answer to one which she had written, speaking of the probability of going to town *en masse,* he had written thus : —

" One worry appears to me probable from the general dispersion of your party, and its general movement upon London — I mean as relates to the Countess St. Alme. She will, I suppose, naturally expect to be invited to the wedding, and I would not have her there upon any consideration. I have engaged the best of the few folks who happen to be in town, or passing through it; and, although I have no doubt of her amiability, and sociability, and all other ilities, there *are* people who carry their dislike of her so far as to consider being brought in contact with her an offence. It would be the most unpleasant thing in the world to have any thing of that sort happen upon such an occasion; yet how can I exclude her, unless by some extraordinary bit of good luck they should be engaged? Try to manage this; for, I declare to you, I cannot have them with any thing like comfort to myself."

The lady's expression of her intention to honour the *nóces et festin* with her presence, coming so immediately after Jack's declaration of the impossibility of receiving her, was a sad puzzle for Helen, who dared not call her husband into council, inasmuch as she was assured the whole history would be told to the St. Almes, and in all probability induce Mortimer to decline being present himself.

" I am sure," said Helen, " papa will be too happy, if his arrangements are not all made. I believe the party will be very small, and confined entirely to relations."

" Oh dear no, I have heard of half-a-dozen people who have been invited, and *I* believe it is to be as gay a thing as the time of year will permit: however, don't bore yourself about it; I will write to your papa myself."

" Do," said Helen, hoping by this means at least to shift the responsibility of getting rid of her; " you will hear what he says."

" I should think," said the countess, tossing her head in a manner peculiar to herself, " he can say but *one* thing. — It is not often I volunteer myself."

And so this brief colloquy terminated, it appearing to poor Helen that every succeeding day entangled her more and more in difficulties, from which she ought, in fact, to have been perfectly free; and she proceeded to her boudoir to write an account of what had passed, to "pappy," recommending the management of the matter to his care and discretion.

This incident, in itself trifling, would have been hardly worth recording, except as showing the perilous state in which Helen was placed. The wish of her father confidentially expressed, she dared not communicate in confidence to her husband, under the apprehension that that confidence would be broken in favour of the woman in whose society she was forced to live, and whose influence she was hourly made to feel — and yet without any show of unkindness on the part of her husband, who seemed to think the domestication of the countess in his house as much a matter of course as that of his wife.

Little did Batley dream of the actual state of affairs at Sadgrove: indeed, the active preparations for his own happiness superseded all other matters, and the payment of the second moiety of Jacob's liberal gift put him so completely at his ease in the way of outfit, that Grosvenor Street looked gayer than ever. A second seasonable application of two or three hundred pounds brightened the prospect, and the smiles of the fair widow amply repaid him for all the trouble and expense which were bestowed upon the repairings and refittings to render his *bijou* of a residence worthy of her reception.

When, however, Jack received his daughter's letter, which came by the same post as the countess's offer of patronising his nuptials, he was, as the saying goes, "struck all of a heap." What was to be done? a man of the world in a dilemma is a moving sight; and see what the consequences to him would be arising from this *contretemps!* Besides several extremely respectable persons, the bishop who was to marry him, and his wife and one of his daughters, had promised to breakfast with them; and the Countess St. Alme was no company for lawn sleeves. This he knew; but if he did know it, he ought long before to have objected against Mortimer's retaining her as a visitor in the house of his daughter. If he now evaded her visit, having before tacitly admitted her respectability, &c. what would *she* say? — what would Mortimer say?

He had certainly so far committed himself to Helen as to beg she might not be of the party, but he had given no specific reason, nor perhaps could he have given any; but it was not a question of morality, or propriety, that worried him now — it was how the thing was to be managed so as to offend nobody. Nobody hears names at parties, and the countess's person was by no means well known in London, therefore it might all pass off quietly; and even if, through the officiousness of the butler or Gunter, the names of the Count and Countess St. Alme *did* creep into the Morning Post, there they would be together, husband and wife — and what more could the most fastidious require? — At all events, it seemed impossible to avert the blow; and so away went a letter to the lady, full of delight and happiness, and "nothing could be so kind, and nothing could make him so happy as presenting his amiable Teresa to her; and nobody could be so charmed to have the honour of making her acquaintance," and so on; and these honied words travelled side by side in the Sadgrove bag with a brief but animated scrawl to Helen, depicting all the parental anxieties in terms the most glowing and most pathetic.

What a world it is! Further on in our narrative we shall perhaps take occasion to let the principal actors in this domestic drama stand forth and speak for themselves under circumstances where their candour will be unquestionable: for the present we content ourselves with the rare specimens of worldly sincerity afforded us in the two letters despatched at the same time from Grosvenor Street to Sadgrove.

"Well," said the countess gaily, after luncheon, "I have done what I said I should do, and have got my answer."

"From whom?" said Mortimer, "and about what?"

"Mr. Batley's marriage," replied the animated lady. "I resolved to patronise it, wrote accordingly, and have received a most gracious reply: so we shall make an agree-able party of ourselves, let what may happen."

"I do not think," said Mortimer, in a manner indicative rather of grief than of any captious disinclination to be present, "that I shall be there."

"My dear Francis!" said Helen, "pappy will break his heart if you disappoint him."

"*You* can go, dear Helen," answered Mortimer, in a tone of kindness; "it is *your* company he desires: we will all go to town, and you can make some excuse for *me.*"

"I know," said Helen, "why you hesitate; it is on account of my poor ill-mannered uncle."

"No, Helen," said Mortimer; "to that I had made up my mind; but it is — in fact, I think these ceremonies tedious, and one always seems *de trop*, and — in fact, I dislike ——"

"Well, then," said the countess, "if Mortimer does not choose to go, *we* can go without him, and dear St. Alme here will take care of us both — wo'n't you, love?"

"Certainly, to be sure, *ma chére*," said the count; "whatever you ask of me."

"I think," said Mortimer, "Helen had better go alone; she will naturally feel an interest in the marriage, and we can all be with Batley and his bride-elect, and dine with him the day before, and make the lady's acquaintance; it is the ceremony I would avoid."

"And now, pray, let me ask why?" said the countess.

"Oh!" said Mortimer, "there is a fuss — and worry — and dressing in the morning — and — in fact, I must decline it."

"But," said Helen, "my dear Francis, you promised ——"

"Yes," said Mortimer; "but your father is resolved to be so very fine, that a common good parish priest will not suffice him — he must have a bishop to tie the knot."

"What!" said the countess, laughing, "are you frightened at a bishop? What bishop may it be?"

"The Bishop of Dorchester," said Mortimer, fixing his look on her animated countenance.

"And is he such a dragon of piety that you dare not face him?" asked the lady in a laughing tone of voice:

" I have no such fears. . What is the name of this most
formidable prelate — for, not living in England,. I am not!
well informed as to English episcopacy ? "

" His name," said Mortimer, slowly and· distinctly, 
without moving his eyes, which seemed riveted on hers—
" his name is Sydenham."

In an instant the whole expression of her countenance
was changed ; its animation was gone ; a death-like pale-
ness left the rouge on her cheeks a palpable pink, ghastly:
and unnatural ; she gazed with an unconscious stare · on
Mortimer, who remained motionless before her, resting his
chin upon his folded hands.

" My dear countess," said Helen, starting up, " surely
you are are very ill.   What *is* the matter ? — Mortimer
dear, what is it ? — Here, give her some water, count."

" Yes," said the count, rising, and walking slowly to
the table from which she had retired, and filling a glass of
water, " she is sometime often so when somsing is not·to
disgest."

The look Mortimer cast upon the poor little man expressed, to Helen's perfect dissatisfaction, that he was
thoroughly aware how much of mind mingled in the lady's
disorder.

She soon rallied, thanked Helen for her care, believed it
was the heat of the room, and begged St. Alme to ring for
her maid.   All· this was done ; the bell was rung — the
maid came — the countess retired ; she recovered — dined
at table, and was as lively as ever : — but she did *not* go .
to Mr. John Batley's wedding.

Nobody can doubt that these frequent developments· of
innumerable little somethings which she did not comprehend had the effect of keeping Helen's mind in a constant
state of unsettlement ; still, though fits of gloom occasionally affected Mortimer, she had no cause to complain of his·
conduct towards her ; on the contrary, whenever he had
exhibited any symptoms of a ruffled temper, she had been
— unconsciously it will be admitted — to blame : but this
last scene, taken in conjunction with her father's evident.
dismay at the countess's approach, led her· more than.ever
to feel the necessity of again urging on her husband the.

necessity of relieving her from an association, which, though the countess, when she chose, was a delightful companion, she felt to be painful and disreputable; although, of course, she knew nothing of the real cause of her sudden abandonment of her design about the wedding.

It is extraordinary with what readiness people of the world contrive to find some excellent reason for suddenly changing their minds, when the alteration has become necessary. It was but two days after this affair that the countess received a letter from her son at Oxford, in which, as she said, he reported himself so extremely unwell, that he had been advised to go off to Cheltenham; and that he had taken his departure for that Montpelier of England, where, he trusted, his mother would contrive to visit him, if it were only for a few days.

Never did indisposition seem more sympathetic than that of mother and son in this instance; nor ever one more agreeable to all parties: it relieved the St. Almes from the difficulty, whatever it might be, which hindered their being at Batley's marriage; and it got rid of the awkwardness which Helen had dwelt upon to her husband, of leaving them in possession of Sadgrove. Thus were all their little asperities smoothed; and the day that the Mortimers left home for London, the St. Almes took their departure for Cheltenham, at which place Francis Blocksford was to meet them, in consequence of a letter written by his mother expressive of her anxiety to see him there on very particular business, and in which not one syllable about health or change of air was mentioned.

It is impossible to express the relief which Batley experienced when he heard of this determination; he was himself again: and not prepared for the defection of Mortimer, which seemed but too probable, he danced and jumped about with the greatest imaginable activity, and with his bride elect and her sister continued his mirth day after day, till that arrived which was to seal their destinies.

That day, as all days will, at length came; and all the ceremonies, which we have anticipated in description, were performed upon the most liberal scale.

In the first place, it should be understood that Mortimer

and his lady dined with Batley and Mrs. Catling and Miss
Fitz-Flannery, the day before the wedding : nobody else
was there; and Mortimer was extremely agreeable and
gracious ; and Helen felt extremely odd at finding herself
a visitor in Grosvenor Street House, though, as yet, it had
not passed into the hands of another mistress ; but Helen
made up her mind to like her new mother-in-law, and behaved, as she could when she chose, so as to engage and
win all hearts.  It struck her that the rooms looked
smaller, the hall narrower, that the sky was darker, the
atmosphere thicker, the little garden behind the house more
miserable, and the sparrows that hopped about it much
blacker than they used to be ; and the rattling of the
coaches astounded her; a knock at the door, which could
be heard in the dinner-parlour, startled her; and, when
she returned to sleep at the hotel, the air seemed less pure
and fragrant than she used to think it when stepping from
Almacks to her carriage, breathing the incense of sundry
link-boys, or curtained within Lady Bembridge's five-feet
square box at the opera, she inhaled the odour of gas, and
the breath of some two thousand exceedingly warm ladies
and gentlemen.  Habit is second nature ; and the return
to scenes, now for some months abandoned, only served to
show her to what people must submit who are resolved to
live in "the world."

The after-dinner conversation of Mortimer and Batley
upon this occasion was what might be expected from two
men of the "world" in their relative positions — a sort of
extremely friendly interchange of thoughts and sentiments;
in which not the slightest approximation was made to the
actual state of affairs.

" I was sorry," said Jack, " that your charming friend,
the countess, is unable to honour us with her company to-
morrow, as she had kindly promised."

" Her son is unwell," said Mortimer.

" She is a most agreeable person," said Jack, " quite an
acquisition in a country house."

" Extraordinary spirits," said Mortimer : " she is a very
old friend of mine ; her husband was a worthy man."

" The son is a fine youth," said Jack.

" Yes, very like his father, I think."

" I don't remember ever to have seen him," said Jack. " Pray, Mortimer, when do you expect Magnus in town?"

" That I don't exactly know; he has been obliged to go to a sick aunt, or cousin, in France: —exceedingly inconvenient just at present; but he is so kind-hearted that he sacrificed every personal consideration to the desire expresed by his relative."

" It was quite unexpected; the day we came to town, he knew nothing of it."

" No," said Mortimer; "it is impossible to describe his activity, slow as he seems, when he is actuated by any sympathy which touches his heart. By the way, Batley," continued Mortimer, "what a prize you have drawn in the lottery of life! — a favourite expression, I remember, of Lady Thurston's, on the same subject; — your widow is charming!"

" Upon your honour?" said Jack, holding his glass in his hand in a state of suspense; "really — eh? — do you think so?"

" Quite charming," said Mortimer, "perfectly handsome; and so extremely natural—nothing *maniérée*."

" I think she is all *that*," said Jack, sipping his wine, and looking diffident; "there certainly is no pretension about her: and, I think, the more you know of her, the more you will like her."

" They are nice people," said Mortimer: "the sister is very agreeable — lively."

" I am delighted to find you think so," said Jack. " I really look forward to a very nice family circle. I *do* think we may not be very unacceptable guests at Sadgrove."

" Nothing can be more delightful than the anticipation," said Mortimer.

And so these two men of the world went on deceiving themselves into the belief that they were deceiving each other: Batley "buttering" the countess, whom he detested; and his son-in-law praising the widow, whom he dreaded — upholding the benevolence of Magnus, whom he knew to be a bankrupt in fortune, and vouching for the extraordinary likeness of Francis Blocksford to his deceased

parent, to whom he bore no more resemblance than Julius
Cæsar. did to Sir William Davenant: and, to crown the
whole as it were triumphantly, Mortimer wound up the
dialogue by promising that he and Helen would be at the
door punctually at ten o'clock in the morning; he knowing,
at the moment he said so, that he would not face the Bishop
of Dorchester for ten thousand pounds.

They joined the ladies, and it was not unamusing to
Helen to see "pappy" playing the lover on the same scene
in which she had a few months before performed the cha-
raeter. now enacting by Mrs. Catling.   Batley's agreeable
manner and juvenile appearance favoured the illusion ; and
nothing could seem more happy than the bride and bridegroom elect.

When the party separated for the night, Helen entertained not the slightest suspicion that Mortimer intended to
absent himself from the ceremony, and subsequent *déjeûner;*
indeed, never having been separated from him since their
marriage, the idea of its being possible that she could go
anywhere without *him,* or without a *chaperon,* had never
entered her head.   .She never yet had exerted the power of
that independence which is the privilege of the married
woman, and felt as if she should sink under the heavy responsibility of acting entirely by herself.   Mortimer was
aware of her unsophistication touching this point, and
therefore never dropped a hint of the possibility of his not
fulfilling the engagement for which he had expressly come
to town.   By the course he purposed to adopt, all beseech-
ings, and remonstratings, would be avoided ; and the indisposition which he intended to plead as an excuse would be
of so extremely slight a nature as not to alarm his tender
wife's fears ; while his desire that she should punctually
fulfil her father's wishes he was sure would. be acceded to,
as the performance of a double duty to both husband and
parent.

The morning dawned brightly on the second marriage
which it is our duty to record, and in its details the event
very closely resembled the first we had to notice.   Lady
Bembridge and the one bridesmaid, and Mrs. Catling and
the other, with Helen, formed the female group.  .Jacob

Batley, Mr. Grub the clerk, and Mr. Brassey the attorney, being, with the exception of Lieutenant Horseman of the Life Guards, and the curate, who assisted the bishop, all the men whom in the then state of London he could secure. The defection of Mortimer, and the excuses of some five others, left him thus painfully deserted ; while, with the exception of Lady Bembridge, pledged on account of her niece's official character in the proceedings of the day, all the fair promisers had broken their faith. Poor Batley was exceedingly annoyed, not more by the absence of those who stayed away than by the presence of some who came. Brassey, vulgar as he was, was a necessary evil, and Jacob had both his near relationship and great wealth to plead in extenuation of his appearance ; but Grub surely might have been omitted : however, as the whole affair originated with his brother, of whom Grub was the special favourite, it was useless to repine ; a few words of explanation to the bishop would set all that to rights. But the failure was most painful : nevertheless, it ought to be considered that his disappointments were all attributable to the season, the emptiness of town, and the absence of all the " world" in the country.

When Mortimer, in the morning, imparted to Helen the impossibility of his venturing out, in consequence of a sore throat which had suddenly and violently attacked him in the night, she, as he had anticipated, declared her going without him to be impossible ; that " pappy" would break his heart ; that she should be so miserable, she could not bear the idea ; and so on : — for all of which he had prepared by ' having called in the nearest apothecary, who assured the lady that, though the gentleman would run great risk in exposing himself to the cold atmosphere of a church, there was no doubt but the confinement of even one day would restore him. This assurance, backed by a grave asseveration on the part of the same judicious practitioner, that he would not answer for the consequences if the " gentleman" went ; and enforced by the supplication of Mortimer, that she would go without him, Helen, more readily than he anticipated, acquiesced ; and accordingly dressed, and proceeded to the mirthful scene, where she was the expected ornament.

The reader probably has discovered by this time that Helen Mortimer was a person of strong mind and quick perception ; and though the tactics of " the world" in which she had been trained, had not in the slightest degree injured her own principle, or deteriorated her own single-mindedness, they had afforded her an aptitude of forming opinions upon very slight grounds, and deducing great results from trifling occurrences. Strange to say, however painful to her the refusal of Mortimer to accompany her to Grosvenor Street on the wedding morning might be, the surprise at his not going was by no means great. From the moment in which the Countess St. Alme exhibited such unequivocal signs of emotion at the mention of the Bishop of Dorchester's name, Helen felt assured that *she* would not, even after volunteering, present herself. The manner in which, upon that occasion, Mortimer pronounced the name of the bishop, convinced her that he was fully aware of reasons which existed for *her* not going to her father's wedding : thence she inferred, she scarcely knew why, that the name of Sydenham was somehow connected with the circumstances of their early lives, much of which she knew, even without the friendly enlightenment of Lady Mary, they had passed together ; from that moment she anticipated that Mortimer would not endure the meeting to which it was evident the countess either could not, or would not, submit herself.

It was perhaps this *pressentiment* that induced Helen the more readily to agree to the suggestion of going alone : she had a duty to perform to a father whom she loved, and who affectionately loved her ; and she believed, more especially after the declaration of the apothecary, that her original suspicions had been just, and were now justified by the sudden ailment of her sensitive husband. This was not what it ought to have been, but it was natural that it should be.

Now to the point : — the carriages — the bride — the bridesmaids — the friends, the select few — and the pro-

·cession to· the church, where ,the bishop met the *cortège*.
The ceremony was performed : there was no crying ; the
affair went on without sensation ; and the party returned
.to Grosvenor Street, bishop and all — the bishop's lady,
however, being unable to join the party on account of a
dreadful cold.

Down they sat. Gunter had been active, and had done
his best on Jack's limited scale : there were high baskets
and low baskets, and silver absurdities and tinsel absurdities,
and pink fooleries and white fooleries, and all the other
trasheries out of which a fashionable confectioner contrives
to make a fortune, drawn from .the pockets of an aristocracy
whose best-paid tradesmen are generally their bitterest political enemies : and the thing went .on, or rather off, extremely well, and the new Mrs. Batley looked marvellously
pretty.

The bishop seemed to watch Helen, and listen to her
conversation, with an interest which excited a deep interest
in *her*. He was a man in all respects qualified for the
high position in society which he filled. Mild and amiable
in disposition, benignity and benevolence beamed in his fine
countenance. Beloved by his family, in which he was the
best of husbands and happiest of fathers, he was venerated
by his inferiors ; and whosoever passed through the vicinity
of his palace heard the blessings of the poor implored upon
his head, as the most excellent of masters and the most
charitable of men. Born of high blood, he was full of high
principle : — not suddenly elevated from a sordid lust for
gain, but devoted to the sacred profession to which he had
voluntarily, anxiously, and conscientiously devoted himself,
and which he graced and honoured by his virtues and his
talents. Such was the Bishop of Dorchester ; — such was
the bishop that Mortimer did not dare to confront ; — such
was the bishop upon whom the eyes of the wife of Mortimer were fixed in admiration.

Mr. Brimmer Brassey, who cared no more, spiritually
speaking, for a bishop than a beef-eater, loved.him out-
rageously because he was. a lord ;..and therefore contrived,
by one of those manœuvres which such men sometimes
perform, to get next his lordship at the *déjeûner*. Helen

R

doing the honours, the bishop sat on her right, the bride on his lordship's right, and next the bride, Brassey. The bride shortly disappeared to prepare for her change of costume, and the party still remained: thus came Brimmer Brassey next the bishop.

The bishop poured a few drops of wine into his glass, and, rising from his chair, proposed the healths of the newly-married couple. How the toast was received, nobody can doubt. Jacob, who had never been in company with a bishop before — except in the shape of a tankard of burnt port wine, with a roasted Seville orange stuck full of cloves swimming in it — did not know how to get on: not so, Brassey. His lordship having agreed to wait until the " young people" took their departure for St. Leonard's, where they proposed to pass the honeymoon, Brassey, finding himself so conveniently placed, in the first lull of a conversation not particularly lively, looking the bishop full in the face, twiddling one of his horse-hair whiskers with his finger and thumb at the same moment, said, *à propos* to nothing, and in a tone of perfect confidence, —

" I say, my lord, what does your lordship think of the voluntary principle — eh ?"

The bishop looked a good deal surprised, and began folding and unfolding the napkin which he held in his hand: after a moment, he bowed, smiled graciously, and said — " I really am not prepared to answer that question. I —— "

Batley, who had, previously to the *déjeûner*, undressed and re-dressed for the journey, looked, as the sailors say, "marling-spikes" at the attorney; but *that* did nothing : he had got hold of a bishop to work, and a lord to talk to.

" — Because," continued he, " my lord, what I wanted to say to your lordship is this, my lord :— if, my lord, your lordship will only put your lordship's nose out of your lordship's *charrot winder*, as your lordship goes down to the House of Lords, your lordship will see, if your lordship will but look —— "

" I believe," said the bishop, " Mrs. Batley is waiting for us; at least, the carriage is —— "

"Ay, ay," said Brassey, "that's it, my lord. I never can find one of your lordships to——"

"I appeal to you, Lady Bembridge," said the bishop, "if we ought to talk or think of any thing this morning but the happiness we anticipate for our friends."

"Why," said Lady Bembridge, "I never give an opinion; but, when a ceremony of this sort takes place, it is certainly understood that the object of the meeting is confined to the particular celebration of the —— Oh! dear, here comes our charming Mrs. Batley!"

Luckily, the appearance of the widow-bride, in a morning dress which became her infinitely, stopped this charming conversation; and, the carriage being announced, the affair seemed at an end, and everybody prepared for a start.

Batley felt agitated and excited: he had undergone certain mortifications as to the party;— in fact, there was nothing to relieve what might be called the absolute vulgarity of the company, save and except the bishop's wig and Lieutenant Horseman's *moustaches*: the rest was painfully below Jack's mark; and, to say truth, besides all those anxious palpitations which, of course, must agitate the hearts of bridegrooms, Jack felt as much relief in dispersing his ill-assorted party, as in finding himself so very near the exclusive possession of his second Mrs. B.

Everybody was now on the move: the functions of Lady Bembridge's niece were at an end, and she brooded under her aunt's wing; Miss Fitz-Flannery was to remain with Miss Rouncivall for two or three days: the horses were pawing the pavement, and the cockneys were standing in a group before the house-door:— inasmuch as even the simple fact of calling a hackney-coach and getting into it, or stopping one and getting out of it, will infallibly collect spectators in the metropolis, in which, it is supposed, the great mass of the people have not a moment to spare.

"I beg your pardon!" said Brassey to Jack, who shrank from his appeal with a horror the most sensitive — "Mr. Grub, will *you*?"

What was to happen Jack did not justly understand.

"It is just merely to sign the settlement-deed," said

Brassey. " Will you ask Mrs. Batley to come ? — it is all ready in the back parlour. Grub will be witness."

" Oh ! to be sure," said Jack, delighted that something like business gave the horrid Brassey a momentary claim upon his attention ; — " shall I call her ? "

" If you please," said Brassey, doing up his hair with his fingers.

Batley called Teresa, and Teresa came — and so did Jacob ; and then there were Teresa, and Batley, and Jacob, and Grub, and Brassey ; and there was the deed of settlement ; and Jack signed it, and Teresa signed it, and Grub witnessed it, and Brassey certified it : and then Jacob kissed Teresa, and so did Batley ; and so did Brassey, which Jack did not much like ; and so did Grub, which Jack did not like at all : — however, it was all settled, and the carriage was ready — the man and the maid packed up in the rumble.

The bishop stepped forward, and, offering his arm to the bride, led her to the steps.

" By Jove ! sir," said Brassey to Batley, " what a fortunate man you are ! — that woman — eh ? — and her devotion to you !"

" Yes," said Batley, " yes," in a sort of pooh-pooh-ing way, and endeavouring to shake off his toady.

" — But, Mr. Batley," said he, with an expression which attracted his attention, " you do not know, as I believe, how much you really do owe her ; and I ought to tell you."

" How do you mean ? " said Jack.

" A proof of her devotion," said Brassey, " which is unequivocal. That kind-hearted creature had a jointure of fifteen hundred a-year so long as she remained a widow, to be reduced one half when she married again : that, Mr. Batley, she has sacrificed for *you ;* and I was sworn never to let you know of her disinterestedness till the affair was irrevocable."

" Sacrifice half her jointure !" said Jack — " excellent woman ! — this *is* a proof of affection. But to whom does the other seven hundred and fifty pounds per annum revert ? "

, " *To your brother Jacob,*" said Brassey.

" Come," said the bishop good-humouredly, walking into the room — " come ; the bride is in the carriage and waiting."

" Thanks ! my lord," said Jack ; " here I come : so, good-by l and a thousand acknowledgments for · your kindnesses ! — So, that's the story, is it ? "

Mr. John Batley was forthwith buttoned up with his new wife, and away they went. The party almost immediately separated ; but, in addition to the rest of his liberality upon the occasion, Mr. Jacob Batley gave a snug dinner to Messrs. Brassey and Grub at " The Horn," at half-past four, with an extra bottle of Mr. L.'s port, to commemorate the day upon which he had insured the happiness of his brother and a charming lady ; and had, at the sacrifice of one thousand pounds, secured to himself an additional seven hundred and fifty pounds· per annum out of the estate of his late friend Kit Catling.

---

## CHAPTER VI.

To a man of Batley's character, nothing on earth could be so ill-timed as a surprise like that caused by Mr. Brimmer Brassey's intelligence. He was, to use a colloquial phrase, " struck all of a heap " by this fresh evidence of his worldly brother's self-love ; and, if his vanity had been somewhat mortified by the defection of his aristocratic friends from his wedding, his *amour propre* was infinitely more wounded by the conviction that he had been made the dupe of his relation, for whose intellectual qualities he did not entertain the highest respect, and to whom he was perpetually in the habit of offering advice, based upon the soundest principles of diplomacy.

But above all, and more acutely, did he feel the extraordinary position in which his wife's sacrifice of half her income out of sheer affection for *him,* had placed him with regard to *her.* He never had, never could have expressed, his high sense of such a mark of attachment, inasmuch as

he never had been made aware of the fact till the moment
before he stepped into the carriage. She must nnques-
tionably have considered him strangely insensible to her
kindness, inasmuch as she never could have given him
credit for ignorance upon so striking a feature in her conduct ; even now, he could not endure that she should become acquainted with the fact, that the circumstance had
never been imparted to him, or that he had suffered himself to be so completely outwitted by Jacob.

But above all did he feel the loss of the moiety of the
lady's jointure, arising, as it did, from the extraordinary
propensity for " grasping," which could induce one brother
to act so towards another, as Jacob had acted towards
him. The reflection that, possessing the influence which
he evidently did possess over the widow, he might, by
waving the penal condition of the will, have put fifteen
hundred a year into his possession for life, without the
positive sacrifice of a shilling of his own, rendered the
mere loss of the additional income a secondary grievance.
Now was it that Jack solved the problem of the thousand
pounds bonus ; now did he account for all the hospitality
and welcomes he received at his brother's hands the moment the scheme of marrying Mrs. Catling was started ;
and, to add to the unpleasantness of his position, all these
facts, circumstances, incidents, plots, contrivances, and
arrangements crowded into his mind at the very moment
when his thoughts should have been exclusively employed
in expressing to his fair companion the happiness he
enjoyed in the attainment of the object of all his earthly
hopes.

Mrs. Catling — or rather Mrs. Batley — was not slow in
discovering the change which had taken place in her dear
Benedict's manner ; and, to do him justice, no small part
of his abstraction arose from the difficulty he felt in devising a scheme to make her understand how highly he
appreciated the sacrifice she had made for his sake ; for,
after all, Jack was not mercenary. He sought a wife, to
soothe his wounded vanity ; and, having made up his
mind to marry, considered it prudent to get one who
would bring to their common stock a sum adequate, to

the increased expenditure of his establishment; beyond that, now that Helen was settled in the world, he cared nothing : — but *then,* the deception practised by Jacob — the mean, low, peddling selfishness of the lord of Lilypot Lane, created feelings which it was impossible for him entirely to conceal.

Upon the mind of the now Mrs. Batley, the effect produced by the change which had been so unequivocally wrought in the spirits and manner of her spouse, might be considered something like the disappointment experienced by the noble lord who bought Punch, and found, when he got him home, that he could not make him squeak ; or that, which the lady, who had united herself to a wag, the fiddle of the company, felt when she found, as the old story goes, that, once domesticated, her facetious partner used to hang up his fiddle in the hall with his hat. Your very lively and agreeable creatures in society are by no means so vivacious when at home, where, as " monarchs of all they survey," they feel the full force of the authority which empowers them to bestow all their dulness, or even ill-humour, which long bills, heavy expenses, and a small revenue, are by no means ill calculated to generate, upon their near connections. And, as for high spirits, the bow must be unstrung sometimes : — the people whose feelings are most excitable by mirth, if their feelings be worth any thing, are always, as Moore poetically tells us, the most susceptible of compassion and sorrow.

To be sure, in her first matrimonial experiment, Mrs. Batley had not succeeded in acquiring a companion calculated at any time to afford any very striking contrast between his home and foreign conduct ; for, if ever there lived a matter-of-fact man upon earth, Catling was one — incapable of taking as of making a joke, his conversation, when lively, turned upon what he called the pleasures of the table, and the modes of cooking certain high esteemed dishes ; and, when of a graver character, was directed to the development of his own prudential schemes for getting money ; — eating and accumulating being the great objects of his ambition : the results now attained, his own repose

under the floor of Islington Church, and his widow's second
marriage, with the loss of half her jointure.

But though Teresa had lived this life, and gone on
" never minding it," hoping for brighter days — a hope
which will perhaps not bear any very minute examination —
she felt that she deserved a better fate. She loved gaiety,
and gaiety of a higher sphere than that to which she had
been dragged down by her weighty partner afforded; and
having, as she thought when she rose on the morning of
her second marriage, secured the society of a man whose
taste and feelings seemed entirely to assimilate with her
own, it may easily be supposed that the consciousness of
the sudden alteration of his look and manner, which has
been noticed, caused a pang in her bosom which she was
ill prepared to feel.

" Are you ill?" said the lady, looking doubtfully at
Jack; — there might have been a slight dash of reproach-
fulness in the glance.

" No," said Jack, " not ill:—no, my dear Mrs. Catling,
— not ill."

" Mrs. Batley," said Mrs. Catling, drawing up coldly and
somewhat indignantly.

" I beg a thousand pardons!" said Jack, " but — really
— I have just heard — something so very surprising — so
very mortifying — that — upon my word and honour —
I ——"

" What does it relate to?" said Teresa.

" Why," said Batley, more puzzled than before, " why,
that's it: it is something so extremely strange — and so
particularly delicate — and so very abominable — I never
can explain; —it must explain itself."

" How very strange!" said Mrs. Batley. " I never saw
you so agitated before. Is it bad news? — tell me, as the
first proof of your confidence. If you don't, I shall fear
I have done something, or that you have heard something,
calculated to lower me in your esteem."

" No," said Batley; " on the contrary, it raises you in
my esteem. It is *there* I feel the difficulty — how to express my gratitude for the sacrifice you have made on my
account."

" Oh !" said Mrs. Batley, whose heart was full of Irish
liberality and spirit, " now I know what you mean — the
condition of Mr. Catling's will — I'm sure that is just what
you mean. Why think of that just now ?"

" Why," said Jack, " it is but five minutes ago I was
made aware of the circumstance : — and there is the difficulty — to think how insensible of your kindness I must
have appeared, never to have expressed my thanks for your
giving up — in short — it seems so strange !"

" What !" said Teresa, with a look of comic astonishment, " did Mr. Brassey never explain that to you ?"

" Never till the instant I left the house."

" Oh !" said the lady. " And what difference does it
make in whose name the money is paid, so as we enjoy it
together ?"

" Enjoy what together ?" said Jack.

" It is all one," said Teresa ; " we wo'n't quarrel about
that, rely upon it : you are quite welcome to call the other
half yours. I dare say you wo'n't stint me nor starve me."

Hereabouts Jack became more mystified than before, and
it took eighteen miles of moderate travelling to make the
case entirely clear to the comprehension of the " high con-
tracting parties ;" but when, after two hours had been
expended in discussion, it appeared that Mr. Brimmer
Brassey, as solicitor on her part, had represented that Jacob's liberality towards his brother was such, that, although
she nominally must forfeit half her jointure by the marriage, he should take care that her husband should receive
it ; while, as solicitor for Jack, the same Mr. Brassey had
entirely omitted any mention of such disposition on the
part of Jacob : and thus, by playing the game for both
hands, the worthy trader had completed his design, satisfied from the delicacy of the lady, and the thoughtlessness
of Jack, that the parties themselves would come to no
explanation ; a circumstance rendered certain by Jack's
frequent expressions of gratitude for his brother's liberality,
which she, without venturing to touch the matter further, was
convinced referred to the sacrifice of the other seven hundred
and fifty pounds a year, which, with a generosity equal to her

own, he had nobly' given up in order to bring about the much-desired marriage.

It was droll to see — or rather would have been had there been a third person present — how gradually ·Teresa and her husband advanced in the avowal of their hatred of Jacob's avarice, and in their abuse of him generally. Teresa, of course, went slowly at first, for fear of wounding her new husband's feelings ; and Jack was gentler in his remonstrances, lest *she* should be annoyed by his reprehension of the friend of her old one : but as they warmed with the subject, and as Jack's spirits rose in consequence of having unburdened his mind, their abuse of the curmudgeon knew no bounds ; nor did the attorney get off with much less vituperation. A sentence of exile from Grosvenor Street was on the instant pronounced against them both, the more especially as Mr. Brassey — a fact already alluded to — had made some unequivocal manifestations of a desire to be received as the suitor of Miss Fitz-Flannery.

It was, however, fortunate for the peace of mind of the bride and bridegroom that the explanation had been come to. He was charmed to be assured of the warm-hearted disinterestedness of his fair partner ; while she, in being able to account for a depression which at first excited her alarm, entreated him to think no more of the unhandsome trick which had been played off, but to believe that, poorer or richer, she could never be happier than at the then present moment.

And so the sunset of the wedding-day was brighter than its rising, and, during a stay of three weeks in retirement, each hour seemed to add to their affection for each other; and though, as has been surmised, Mrs. Batley the second was not remarkable for any high intellectual powers, she was gay in her manner, handsome in her person, gentle i her blood, and good-humoured beyond question : and Jac walked up and down, with his pretty wife on his arm quite satisfied with his gain, and wishing every minute o the day that Miss Thurston could only just . see ho charming a partner he had secured for life.

At the end of ten days Miss Fitz-Flannery joined the

at St. Leonard's, and there, for the present, we will leave
the trio ; Jacob being not a little surprised at never receiving a line from any of them, but, as usual, not caring
enough about them to trouble himself to inquire into the
cause. He might have guessed ; and, if he did guess, it
is probable that he and his legal adviser might have agreed
that it would be best to let the transaction remain, without
inquiries which might produce replies.

As to Helen, who, of course, was informed by her father
of the conduct of her uncle, she felt herself, for the first
time, at ease, and mistress of her own house. The absence
of the countess was a positive relief to her : Mortimer devoted himself to her society, and appeared as if, like herself,
he was delivered from some influence which 'seemed perpetually to keep him in a state of alarm lest he should appear
too much devoted to the society of a wife wholly devoted
to *him*.

Two days after the marriage they had returned to Sadgrove, Mortimer's inquiries of Helen concerning the ceremony being chiefly confined to the conduct of the Bishop
of Dorchester. Whatever were the ties which connected
this exemplary man with Mortimer — whatever the reasons which existed for Mortimer's absence from the ceremony — it was clear to the perceptive mind of Helen that
they were equally powerful as far as the countess was
concerned ; and this conviction satisfied her that, whatever
it might be, some bond of union existed between her husband and the lady, the nature of which she did not permit
herself to question. In fact, the principle of action which,
as we have 'already seen, she had in the outset of her
married life adopted, was that of never seeking to inquire
into events connected with Mortimer's early career, nor of
permitting herself to believe that, let them be what they
might, they were likely to interfere with her own happiness. It should also be remembered that, upon all the
occasions when she had broken through this golden rule,
she had been led to its infraction by the very woman who
seemed, as far as one could judge, to have the strongest
possible reasons for not recurring to days that were gone.

But the calm was of short duration : Mortimer again

became nervous, gloomy, and irritable. It is scarcely possible to describe the anxiety which seemed to affect him
when three or four days had passed, because it is scarcely
possible to explain — scarcely to understand — the doubts
and apprehensions which kept him in the most unenviable
state of mind. It was not jealousy of others that excited
this perpetual fear; as has been before stated, it was jealousy of himself that tormented him. The slightest and
most unintentional reference by Helen to any thing that had
occurred while the house was full of guests, struck to his
heart; and, before the week of domestication was over, he
had satisfied himself that the great design of his life in
marrying Helen had failed. In fact, the delight which she
experienced during the first three days of those seven, in
finding herself shut out from the world with the man she
loved, gradually faded in proportion to the increasing evidence of his mistrust; and, truth to be told, she did not
regret hearing that Colonel Magnus, whom personally she
disliked, was expected; nor that Mr. Francis Blocksford
had invited himself to pass a few days at Sadgrove at his
mother's particular desire.

"Dear Mrs. Mortimer," writes the countess, "the count
feels so much benefit from the waters and the air, or probably the regular and abstemious life which the Cheltenham
doctors enforce as an auxiliary to both, that I have resolved
on remaining here, although it is not the usual season,
until we take our departure for France. Mortimer and
you will, of course, arrange as to our meeting — the *point
de réunion* and all the rest of it; but, in the mean time,
Francis, who absolutely raves about you and Sadgrove and
all its *agrémens*, wishes to be allowed to look again at the
first English country-house he ever saw, at a different time
of the year from that in which it first won his heart; and
so he will be with you to-morrow. If Mortimer can give
him a little shooting, so different from the *chasse* with us
at St. Alme, he will be delighted. He is really a kind,
open-hearted boy; and, although his present figure and
appearance make *me* look rather old, it is not because I
wish him to go from me that I have encouraged his disposition to leave Cheltenham, but because I wish him to .

go to *you*. I know you will like him'; he deserves to' be liked; and his godfather, young as he was at 'the time when he undertook the sponsorial duty, will, I think, not be. displeased at showing him a little English sport."

Amiable, plausible, fascinating countess! What! knowing that Mortimer and Helen were alone, did she fear that they might find their own society so agreeable as to induce them to do without the infusion of external gaiety? — or did she wish Francis her son to become the associate of Francis her friend, before their departure to the Continent?

When Helen gave the countess's letter to Mortimer to read, watching, as she always did, every turn and change of his expressive countenance, she did not think, from what she saw, that he was altogether gratified by the proposition of the lady or the volunteer visit of her son: indeed, he did not leave his feelings upon the occasion to be guessed at.

"Umph!" said the master of Sadgrove :: — "this is not altogether convenient. Surely, if we are so soon to join the St. Almes, she might have waited to improve 'my acquaintance with her son till we were all together."  ·  ·

The tone in which these words were uttered, and the short personal pronoun by which Mortimer somewhat emphatically designated the lady, convinced Helen that her sensitive husband was what the vulgar call "put out of his way" by the proposition.

"Oh," said Helen, "poor, dear fellow! why shouldn't he come if he likes?"

"Ah!" said Mortimer, "why not, indeed!—But if *I* do *not* like."

"But he is your godson, Francis."

"I am quite aware of that fact," said Mortimer; "but, whatever my duty towards the young gentleman may be, it is extremely inconvenient having him just at this time. I expect Magnus; and he and I have things to talk over, —matters of business—and ——"

"Well," said Helen, "all *that* you can talk over in the mornings. Give Francis Blocksford a keeper and dogs; and, while he is amusing himself in the woods, you and the colonel can be managing your state secrets."

" Who told you, Helen, that my friend Magnus and I had any secrets?"

" Nobody, dear Francis," said Helen, alarmed at the manner in which the question was put—"nobody, except yourself this moment."

" I !" said Mortimer.

" Yes," said Helen more firmly, and in a tone which, if he had properly appreciated her character, he would have known indicated a resolution to maintain her ground in any discussion of such a nature as that which he seemed not particularly anxious to avoid. " You told me that young Blocksford's visit is particularly inconvenient just at this moment, because Colonel Magnus is coming, and because you and he have subjects to discuss."

" Ay, subjects, but not secrets."

" Ay," said Helen proudly, and perhaps in a more imitative tone of voice and manner than he had ever seen her exhibit before; " but if subjects that cannot be discussed before a third person are *not* secrets, what are?"

" Indeed !" said Mortimer, looking surprised - at the earnestness of his wife; " why, Helen, you take high ground upon this question. Is young Mr. Blocksford really so very charming a person, that his proposed visit can make you at once so eloquent in the cause?"

Helen uttered no word—no syllable; but she fixed her bright black eyes upon the pale countenance of her husband, and looked as if she waited for an explanation of words the meaning of which she did not understand:—this was what her look conveyed. He was at no loss to comprehend its meaning.

" I tell you," continued Mortimer, beaten at his own weapons, and driven from the line he was about to take by the firm resolve, and look of dignified, and yet indignant, affection which Helen assumed— " I tell you, Magnus and I have no secrets, but we have matters to talk over; and, perhaps, he may bring a friend with him—and— I ——"

" Oh !" said Helen, in a manner which fluctuated between the submissive and humble, and the scornful and ironical, " any friend of such a person as Colonel Magnus must surely be a suitable associate for the son of the Countess St. Alme."

" I don't know *that*, Helen," said Mortimer; " at least, you can be no judge of such matters : it is extremely unpleasant to me."

" I have done," said Helen, who was not sorry to find any proposition of the countess liable to such a reception. " I have only to write, and say we are unluckily prevented by circumstances from receiving her son."

" *You* write! " said Mortimer, in a tone which cut Helen to the heart; not because it was calculated to arouse her to a sense of her helplessness and inferiority, but because it served to carry fresh conviction to her mind that, be its origin what it might, there did exist a power of control in the countess over her husband, which, although the lady might choose to conceal it, in the present instance, by communicating her wishes about Francis Blocksford to *her*, she had no power to resist.

" If he come, Helen," said Mortimer, lowering his tone of positive refusal to one of conditional acquiescence, " the task of entertaining the young gentleman must devolve entirely upon *you* : " and his eye followed the conclusion of this sentence to that of Helen, who felt her bosom heave as his looks fixed themselves upon her face, and her heart beat rapidly ; but she would not believe that she understood what his manner implied.

Mortimer saw he had inflicted a wound, and in an instant repented.

" The countess," said he, " treats us, I think, *de haut en bas*. It is all extremely well her fixing *herself* here ; but making my house a hotel for her son, and putting my preserves at his disposal, is a little too much."

" Well then, Francis," said Helen, earnestly and sincerely, " if you think so — decline the visit. Let us not go with them to France. My father and his wife can come to us, and so get rid of the St. Almes at once."

" Ha, ha, ha! " laughed Mortimer, if that could be called a laugh which sounded almost sepulchral. " So, because the countess worries me by offering her son as a visitor at au unsuitable period, I am to relinquish the oldest friend I have in the world. No, no. I will not tell the countess of your suggestion, Helen; but do not make it again."

The manner in which her husband disclaimed the intention of making the communication led Helen to believe that he would make it the first opportunity; and she almost repented of her ingenuousness.

" He must come, of course," continued Mortimer, in a tone indicative of the positive necessity of submitting to the will of his mother; "and then, I suppose, we shall all meet at some given point preparatory to our start:— London I should prefer. London, in my mind, is the nearest way to every place in England from any other; so —-write, Helen — say how glad we shall be to see him: tell him he need bring neither guns nor any other implement of sport—he will find every thing here: and give my best love to his mother, and so on — you understand the *façon de parler;* — and, as you say, Magnus and I must transact our business in the morning, and — yes, yes, we shall make it out, ·I dare say. Write this afternoon," added Mortimer, as he quitted the room; "and, dearest, give direction for Magnus's room to be got ready, and a room for his friend — if he bring one; and if he should not, which I sincerely hope may be the case, there's no harm done."

As the door closed, Helen's eyes remained fixed upon the space which her husband had so recently occupied. What was her destiny—what was to be her fate?— Every hour afforded fresh evidence of the unsettled state of her husband's mind, and of the restlessness of his feelings. He seemed to live a life of constant apprehension —of care and watchfulness; and when the fit was on him, his words, hastily uttered, and his manner, flurried and discomposed, combined to assure his devoted Helen that her affection was questioned, and her sincerity suspected.

The tears, which pride had checked while he was present, chased each other down her cheeks now that he was gone: she felt alone in the world, as in truth she was. As has been remarked, the circumstances of her youth, and the mode of her education, had left her without female friends of her own age and standing. She looked round, and saw no one to whom she could appeal for advice or support: there seemed no alternative but the countess, whom, if she liked as a companion, she feared as a woman, and could not bring herself to trust as a friend. She found herself daily approaching a period at which, as her exemplary sister-in-law had said, the care and tenderness of a· female relative would be valuable and important, and saw no prospect of sympathy or consolation even in the distance. Worlds would she have given, if Mortimer could have been persuaded to accept Mrs. Farnham's offer of a visit. But no: that was interdicted, as she believed, at the countess's suggestion — and why? Because Mrs. Farnham was too good and too devout. Strange reasons for keeping her apart from her sister-in-law, but so it was.

When her father first imparted his design of marrying again, Helen joyously acquiesced, thinking that, by securing his own comfort, he might bring into the domestic circle an agreeable companion and friend for herself. He *had* married; but though *his* part of the design might have been accomplished by his union, his daughter's hopes were not likely to be realised. The lady had nothing in manner or character likely to attract Helen to her; and though she would have been' delighted to make up a Christmas party at home, which might have included her father and the two ladies, rather than fulfil the engagement to the St. Almes, she feared that even a more intimate knowledge of their qualities would not, in any great degree, conduce to the increase of her affection for them.

She made an effort to stifle her grief, and proceeded to fulfil the duty assigned to her by her husband, of writing a worldly letter to the "dear countess," setting forth, in affectionate phraseology, the happiness which the visit of her son would afford Mortimer and herself; in fact, putting into conventional language all her husband had suggested.

: When she had finished the despatch, she carried it to her lord and master in the library. He was occupied in writing, and appeared somewhat confused by the sudden appearance of his lady; and with an abruptness meant to look accidental, contrived to cover, with other papers, thé letter upon which he was employed. He might have left it as it was: neither curiosity, nor any desire to know more than he chose to tell her, would have led Helen to question him as to the object of his labours. He took the task he had set her, and read it; and, as his eyes followed the lines across the paper, his lip curled with a sneering smile of inward satisfaction; how excited, Helen, who watched every turn of his countenance, could not exactly comprehend.

"Will that do, dearest?" said Helen, when he had finished.

"Admirably, my dear Helen," replied Mortimer: "you write with as true a semblance of sincerity as you can act. Who would suppose that this cordial letter was the production of a young lady who, five minutes before she sat down to write it, suggested the utter rejection from her visiting list of the lady to whom it is addressed?"

"I spoke, Mortimer, for myself, I have written for *you* : — I may have my feelings, my thoughts, and wishes. I know it is my duty as a wife to repress them, and act in obedience to one whose judgment may be more matured than my own, and, above all, whose will in this house should be law."

"Upon my word! Helen," said Francis, "you are almost as good in tragedy as in comedy. I did not mean to vex you; I merely made an observation generally applicable."

"I am no actress," said Helen. "Heaven knows I never was accused of deceit or hypocrisy: still, still that hateful day and its events haunt your mind! What object could I have had in all that affair, but, at the countess's desire, to shield her from your anger?"

"You are a dear, kind-hearted girl!" said Mortimer. "I believe it; but I still maintain that you should not have permitted *her* influence to supersede mine."

"Are we to begin again upon that subject?" said Helen: "I thought it was all ended and forgotten. The influence of the countess is, I know, something irresistible, and affects others as deeply as even I have been affected by it."

. " There, there," said Mortimer — " I have: done. I beg your pardon, Helen! I know she is a very extraordinary woman, and you are quite right in writing thus kindly ; — but," added he, playfully, " you can't bear to be joked with."

It seemed, by the manner in which Helen was agitated by her husband's renewed reference to her " acting," placed in juxta-position with her " writing," that she and Mortimer had formed very different opinions upon the subject of joking. Such, indeed, was the effect he produced by his abrupt allusion to her " hypocrisy" upon the occasion in question, that nothing could have prevented a " scene" but the timely announcement to Mortimer of a visitor in the person of the rector, which terminated the dialogue, and gave Helen an opportunity of retiring from the library.

## CHAPTER VII.

THE reader may, perhaps, think that the frequent descriptions of scenes of this sort are uncalled for, inasmuch as their recurrence leads to no great result ; but reflection may perhaps furnish an excuse for placing them on record, inasmuch as the conduct of Mortimer upon every occasion of the kind, exhibited to Helen, in their true colours, the character and disposition of her husband, disconnected from the occurrences of his earlier life, as they existed at the moment ; and that exhibition convinced her, that never were two minds or tempers more diametrically opposed to each other than hers to his.

Helen, as we have seen, was always candid — except when, to her own mortification, she consented to " act" under the management of the Countess St. Alme. She was open-hearted, powerfully affected by passing circumstances, impassioned, and even violent in her passion ; but the burst once over, and her heart relieved by the outbreak of its feelings, she was calm, placid, and content, and on the tablet of her memory there rested no mark of what had happened: if she had been right, she was satisfied; if wrong, she satisfied herself by admitting her fault; but either right or wrong, she never felt either triumph or resentment beyond the moment. Such a heart, and such a mind, properly treated, would have insured happiness to him who had, in fact, the first training of them in the world.

Mortimer, on the contrary, might forgive, but he never forgot. Subject to fits of deep gloom, he was equally the victim of violent bursts of anger— founded on jealousy — of himself, in the first instance; but when jealousy once gains ground, Heaven only can set bounds to its influence.

In these bursts of anger, all that had ever occurred at any period of his life in relation to the person, their then present cause, flashed into his mind, and found utterance from his lips. He brooded over fancied injuries, and harboured the remembrance of them even though they had been long before explained and expiated; and whenever the chord was stricken which could awake their memory, no feeling of regard, for himself or others, could restrain the reiteration of his denunciations.

The reader will have seen that, from the moment the visit to the fishing temple seized hold of his imagination, no circumstance could occur, no trifling difference ever arise between himself and Helen, but *that* piece of duplicity was raked up to be thrown in her teeth.

Trifling, indeed, in point of fact, as that incident was, his perpetual recurrence to it irritated Helen more than she dared admit even to herself. " I did err," said Helen: " it is true, under the influence of his friend; but my heart was nearly broken by my error. I admitted — I apologised: — apologised! — I implored pardon for it; and that pardon was sealed, as I hoped and believed, with a husband's kiss of love! I cannot bear a constant reference to it whenever the slightest difference of opinion arises between Francis and myself; and then, if I show how much I feel the cruelty of such conduct, I am told I am not fond of jesting!"

In five minutes after Helen left the library, Francis was

as much vexed as she could be, that he had permitted himself again to allude to the event, and listened with the most patient inattention to the pleadings of the rector in behalf of some deserving family, anxious only to get rid, of him that he might seek out his wife and soothe the sorrow which, the moment reflection came to his aid, he felt assured his uncalled-for allusions had occasioned her.

This repentance was all extremely good, and the desire to make · atonement for an injury inflicted, just and honourable; but the negative course of not giving the pain he was so soon desirous of assuaging, would have been infinitely more likely to secure the heart that he had made his own. Helen was yet but a young wife, and regarded Mortimer with something amounting to awe. As time wears on, this may wear off; and if the tenderness of her affection shall become blunted by the shocks to which it seems likely to be subjected, the respect with which their relative situations, and ages, might now inspire her, may perhaps be converted into some very different sentiment, and thus, divested of those restraints which she now imposes upon it, her temper *may* have its way. It is not, however, for us to anticipate.

It seemed, it must be admitted, a somewhat fortunate coincidence of circumstances that, upon the day in question, before the rector had brought his tale of woe to a conclusion, Colonel Magnus, the redoubtable, arrived at Sadgrove, and, as Mortimer grievously anticipated, accompanied by "a friend." The pair, if pair they could be called, were ushered into the library, where Magnus, having gone the length of honouring the rector with permission to touch two of the fingers of his left hand, introduced his companion to Mortimer, whose astonishment, under all the circumstances, at beholding his person and hearing his name, was beyond any thing that pen can adequately describe.

The rector took his leave, and certainly he had no business in such company. It required at least three quarters of an hour's explanation to satisfy Mortimer of the expediency, or even the possibility, of finding the colonel's companion a visitor at his house; at the end of which

period, Magnus (they having retired for the purpóse into
Mortimer's own room) had thoroughly convinced him not
only of the prudence, but of the absolute necessity, of
bringing down to Sadgrove, in his carriage, no less a persoñ
than Mr. Brimmer Brassey, of Barnard's Inn, Gent. —
one, &c.

The very fact of Mr. Brimmer Brassey's confidential
connexion with Jacob Batley, putting aside his personal
disqualifications as an associate, was sufficient to dis-
gust Mortimer with his visitor; and the other fact of his
having been actively and successfully employed in defeating at Mudbury the pretensions of Magnus himself,
seemed to him to render the present confederacy dangerous,
if not disgraceful. However, Magnus had that magnificent
manner of pooh-poohing down all Mortimer's oppositions,
and a despotic way of marching over all difficulties in a
" Nec aspera terrent" style of magnanimity, that, if he
thought Mr. Brimmer Brassey essential to his extrication
from difficulties, and if he employed him as his agent,
Mortimer must necessarily admit that Mr. Brassey was
every thing that he ought to be; and Mortimer, really and
truly succumbing to this influence, whatever his own personal prejudice against him might be, his hostility was at
an end, and Mr. Brimmer Brassey was right welcome to
Sadgrove.

It would be improper, at present, so far to anticipate
occurrences which we may have occasion in due time to
notice, as to make any particular remarks upon the nature
of this visit; but it seems as if the intelligence which
Mr. Brassey had received with regard to the pecuniary
connexion between Magnus and Mortimer, which, as the
reader already knows, he communicated to Mr. Jacob Batley, was tolerably authentic. How far Jacob might have
yielded to the disinterested suggestions of Mr. Brassey, as
to playing with some of the " kites" (as he called them),
which were supposed to be flying about, and in how much
he might have lent himself, or any part of his capital, to
the temporary release of the embarrassed dandy, it is not
for us now to inquire; but it does appear somewhat
strange, that, in so short a time after having so strenuously

opposed the gallant colonel, and defeated him at Mudbury, Mr. Brassey should be found at his side under the roof of his most particular friend, with whom he had so recently made a sort of official acquaintance as the *homme d'affaires* of the man Jacob, whom he hated so cordially.

Everybody has seen how a character for low legal dexterity brings a man forward in certain circles. When talent in this line is discovered, money, of course, will buy it: prejudice or feeling does not influence it — delicacy or consistency does not control it. You might as well charge a Conservative physician with inconsistency for curing a Radical patient, as a Radical lawyer with treachery for serving a Conservative cause; nay, the very fact that an electioneering attorney has, as he would call it, " done his best" for a Whig, to the utter discomfiture of a Tory, affords the strongest possible reason to the next Tory, who wants to beat a Whig, for employing him. Magnus's good opinion of Brassey's talent was painfully established at Mudbury, and his vanity strengthened this conviction of his ability; for, said Magnus, drawing himself up to his full height, " If the fellow could contrive to smash *me*, with all my personal influence and political character, in favour of such a person as Sir Christopher Hickathrift, of Tipperton Lodge, he *must* be something out of the common."

To this feeling, and the consciousness that something must be done further to relieve his necessities, which any person of greater respectability in the profession than Mr. Brimmer Brassey would hesitate to do, may safely be attributed the employment, upon the present occasion, of the worthy in the black velvet waistcoat.

" Have you heard from your father-in-law, sir," said Brassey to Mortimer, " since his start ? "

" No," said Mortimer, nearly paralysed by the question and the manner in which it was put : " Mrs. Mortimer, I believe, has."

" Oh, indeed ! " said Brassey — " I suppose so : — she seems to *me* to be a very affectionate daughter. I hope Mrs. M. is quite well."

" Quite well, thank you," said Francis, with another " look."

" Missed you at the wedding, sir," continued Brassey : " very nice party. The bishop is a very charming man, —very ; and the bridesmaids looked uncommon pretty. Miss F. is a nice young woman — don't you think so ?"

" Miss ——— ?" asked Mortimer.

" Mrs. J. B.'s sister," continued Brassey : —" very nice young woman, indeed. Rather Hibernian — but that's no fault, in my mind : —sweetly lively. I think she would make a very pretty partner for a well-disposed young man in a good line of business."

Mortimer stared, and so did Magnus : they bowed their heads slightly, and Magnus took a very large pinch of snuff.

" Pray, sir," said Magnus, looking particularly dignified, " when shall we be able to proceed in our business? I opened the particulars to Mr. Mortimer in the next room ; he knows that ——— "

" Why," said Brassey, " in a day or two I shall be able to make something like a calculation. I hope by Saturday or Monday to give you an outline of the terms."

" Saturday or Monday !" said Mortimer, in a tone of despondency ; — " not before ?"

" I think not," said Brassey. " I shall have to com- municate with my clerk in town ; and then the insurance ; and then ——— "

" Oh ! well, well," said Mortimer, " I don't mean to hurry on the affair ; and I hope you will make yourself at home while we have the pleasure of your company here. I only ——— "

" Never fear, Mr. M.," said Brassey. " I have a rule for staying at country-houses — ten miles a day, sir. Go ten miles — dine, sleep, and breakfast ; twenty miles — stay two days, ditto ; thirty — three days ; and so on : we are about a hundred and twenty-four from London, which makes ten days and the eleventh morning about the cut — eh? — ha ! ha ! ha !"

" I fancy, in ten days," said Mortimer, " we shall be on the other side of the water."

"What!" said Brasséy, "the Colonel — eh? — in Banco?—ha, ha, ha! Oh! no, Mr. M. we must keep him out of *that*."

The look which Magnus threw across the room at Mortimer was furious beyond measure.

"I hope," said Magnus, "that two or three days will bring our affair to a termination."

"I fear not," said Brassey: "I have to deal with queer old codgers. If *I* had the money myself, you shouldn't be plagued five hours; but, as I say, men who haven't got money are plaguy liberal: those who *have*, like it too well to part with it — what I call slap-dash off-hand — ha, ha!"

"Well," said Mortimer, "as we can proceed no further to-day, perhaps you would like to be shown your room, Mr. Brassey? Magnus, you are at home: I will ring and inquire what room is assigned to your friend."

"You are very kind, Mr. M.!" said Brassey — "very kind, indeed, sir! Ah! I wish we could thump a little of your liberality into your old uncle."

"Uncle!" said Mortimer, opening his large eloquent eyes, "I have no uncle, sir!"

"Not uncle Jacob?" said Brassey.

"Oh!——"

"There's a vast deal of good in him, sir," said Brassey: "uncommon fond of the stumpy—that's true: he likes his own way as much as anybody I ever saw. The proverb says, 'Where there's a will there's a way;'—your father-in-law should recollect that 'where there's a way there's a will.' He should study his brother's humours — that's all, sir. He is easily led; but the Old Gentleman with the hoofs and the horns, and the tail—you'll excuse my mentioning his name—cannot drive him."

Mortimer, who had carefully avoided any allusion to the shabby trick which Jacob had played upon Jack, was particularly desirous of cutting the conversation short, fully aware of the sort of evening that was in perspective, and wishing, if possible, to leave Mr. Brassey that period for the display of his eloquence, convinced that his readiness to talk would be considerably excited by the wine which he

felt certain he would swallow ; being, moreover, anxious to
make his peace with Helen before dinner, lest her serenity
might be ruffled, and her appearance indicate a state of
affairs which, as he was assured that every thing the attorney
saw would be reported to her uncle, he least of all desired.'

Mortimer even yet did not know or appreciate Helen's
temper. He sought and found her: no lurking frown
contracted her brow ; no pouting lip proclaimed a " lingering grudge :" all that had occurred when they last met had,
as usual, passed from her mind ; and when she saw her
husband approaching her with a countenance neither in
sorrow nor in anger, but lighted up with an expression of
good-humour blended with what might be called " comic
distress," caused by the unexpected arrival of Mr. Brassey,
she ran towards him, charmed to see him animated, and
anxious to know who Magnus's companion was ; for, though
the arrival of the colonel had been announced to her by
her maid, nobody seemed exactly to know the name of the
" little gentleman in the black velvet waistcoat, who came
with a carpet-bag, and had no servant."

" What on earth can he be come for ? " said Helen.

" Ay, there it is," said Mortimer ; " that is one of our
secrets."

Does not the reader perceive in this trifling observation
the still existing disposition which was perpetually vexing
Helen. True, Mortimer was playful, kind, and good-
humoured ; but even in his gaiety and playfulness and
good-humour he could not omit to remind her that the
words she had used in some previous conversation were
treasured in his memory.

" Oh ! then I shall inquire no more about him. Has
he heard from papa ? "

" I never asked him," said Mortimer, " although he
asked *me* if I had heard. In fact, the business he is here
upon is so totally disconnected from any concern of ours
— I mean as relates to the family — that it did not strike
me. It is necessary, for the sake of my friend Magnus,
to be civil to him, but that is all."

Helen felt that she would give the world not to dine at
table with the new guests, and a sort of desolation in

having no female companion, even upon ordinary occasions like this, not to speak of the more important circumstances before noticed.

The party did not meet until just before the second bell had been rung, and Brassey, never having visited Sadgrove before (his being there then was one of those surprising things which oftener happen in society than people ·imagine), blundered about the lobbies and passages, and having, after many "bad shots" at different doors, found his way to the principal staircase, followed his nose down into the hall, and was saved all further difficulty by the groom of the chambers, who opened the door of the small drawing-room in which people usually assembled before dinner. This act of civility being performed by somebody so much more like a gentleman than himself, or any of the bodies with whom he was in the habit of associating, produced not only one of Brimmer Brassey's smartest bows, but when Jenkins stood with the door in his hand to usher him in, provoked the still more polite address of "Oh! dear, after *you*, sir !"

This mistake may be considered by some a *gaucherie* of the first order; but looking round the world, whatever may be one's inherent respect for high blood, it must be confessed that on many occasions the democracy of the second table have much the personal advantage of the aristocracy of the first : and it did once happen to the narrator of this small history, at a party at which the attendance of blue coats and white waistcoats was profuse, to send a gentleman so clothed, three or four times, for soup; lobster-salad, jellies, and other nourishing supports, the absolute necessaries of life for ladies after dancing, until, at length, having borne with ineffable good-nature the toils which he felt conscious were inflicted on him by mistake, and in the "service of the fair," the aforesaid gentleman, upon a fifth demand, delivered in the ordinary tone of — "Here, sir, get this lady some Macedoine"—quietly turned to the narrator, and said, — "No, no : I have got all you asked me to get for your friends five times ; now it is time I should get something for myself." It is needless to add (as the jest-books say), that your narrator was ab-

solutely annihilated — stammered an apology, the more
difficult to make, as what had previously happened practically inferred his belief that the suffering gentleman
was, in fact, a servant. The suffering gentleman, however, seemed perfectly aware of the mutual embarrassment, and behaved very like a gentleman who did not deserve to suffer by taking his seat next the narrator, and
proving his claim to " guestship" by finishing with the
said narrator at least one bottle of champagne, not to speak
of the moral to the fable in the shape of two verdant, spiry
glasses of Roman punch, which cockneys think it right to
translate into " *ponche à la Romaine;* " believing, to a
certain extent, that it was invented by the late eminent
preacher of that name — and more shame for him !

Having reached the *terra incognita* of the drawing-
room, Mr. Brimmer Brassey found himself alone; his
punctuality having brought him to the ground before any
other one of the small family party with which he was
destined to pass the day. He looked at every thing he
saw with extreme curiosity; but at himself, in the glass
over the fire-place, with the greatest satisfaction; still
there dwelt on his mind a sort of embarrassing doubt why
the very elegant gentleman who had given him precedence
did not join him in the room. At length Mortimer
arrived, and relieved him from the embarrassment of being
alone, which is said to be, to a certain class of legal prac-
titioners, a disagreeable circumstance.

Mortimer, whose manners were, when he chose, agreeable almost to fascination, felt it his duty, hating Brassey
as he did, to put him perfectly at his ease in his own
house, and immediately on joining him began to inquire
whether he shot with caps or flints, regretting that, it being
late in the season, he was afraid he could not give him
quite such sport as if he had favoured him earlier; hoped
that Mr. Blocksford, a young friend of his, would be down
to-morrow evening, and that they might have some tolerable
amusement on the following day; and, in short, exhibited
himself under the roof of Sadgrove in a character so different from that in which he had appeared at Batley's, that
Brimmer was astounded. If he had been told that he was

deceived, or, as he would have said, "humbugged," by his host, he would have angrily denied the imputation. The fact is, that Mortimer was a gentleman, and under whatever circumstances a guest once passed his threshold, his feeling, his taste, and his tact were to put that individual upon a perfect equality with the rest of his visitors; in fact, the smaller the legitimate pretensions of that guest, the more particular was his attention to bring him to the general level of the existing society.

When the elegant gentleman, whose society Brimmer Brassey so deplored, threw open the door for the admission of Mrs. Mortimer, the attorney was as much astounded at his mistake as at the appearance of the lady of the house. She bowed good-naturedly to *him ;* but his anxiety was, to be exceedingly polite to her. He did not exactly know how to achieve this; but his first attempt was reasonably enough made in reference to the events of " pappy's " wedding : a mild, placid reception of something, which he meant to be facetious, stopped his further efforts in that way ; and a subsequent sudden turn round, from a sort of whisper which might have done remarkably well for the wives and sisters of the members of the " Slap-bang" club, which Helen effected in favour of Magnus, (whom she avowedly disliked, but who was, at all events, incomparable with Mr. Brassey in every point of view,) left Mr. Brassey looking excessively uncomfortable.

Dinner was announced, and Mrs. Mortimer took the colonel's arm — Mortimer bowing to Brassey, who, in the excess of his civility, said, as he had already said to the groom of the chamber, " After you, sir," a difficulty which Mortimer got rid of by clapping him on the shoulder and pushing him before him, in order to let the servants suppose that his ignorance was merely affected, and that he was a particular friend of the house ; it being, as we have already said, his invariable rule to put up the man who most needed putting up.

The party consisted of only the four, and nothing could be more dull. At dinner, of course, Magnus sat on Helen's right hand, and the attorney of Barnard's Inn on her left. In pursuance of his established principle, Mortimer paid

him every due and undue attention. While under the excitement occasioned by handing about the *entrées*, Brassey
was somewhat subdued; and his astonishment when Mrs.
Mortimer put the *carte* before him was by no means small.
Mortimer's cook was a *cordon bleu*, who piqued himself not
only upon the variety of his dishes, but upon their novelty
both of name and nature; but Brassey, who had never
seen a *carte* placed upon a table, except, indeed, a *carte à·
payer*, was terribly confused — first, by its appearance generally, and then by its contents particularly : and although
he collected — which, with his quickness, it was natural he
should do — that the paper described what there was to be
eaten, the difficulty lay, not only in choosing between
dishes, the characters and qualities of which he did not'
understand, but in pronouncing the names which custom or
the cook had assigned them. However, the infernally per-
severing assiduity of servants, who offer every thing that
ever was put down upon a table to everybody who sits
round it, released him from his embarrassment *that* way ;
and after half an hour, and a few glasses of champagne,
Mr. Brimmer Brassey became almost as vivacious as at the
" Slap-bang" club.

Things went on tolerably till dinner was over, and,
luckily, all the servants were gone, except the butler, whom,
by a mistaken notion of saving his guests trouble in putting
round the wine, Mortimer retained in the room. Now, of
all men in the world, Mortimer, being the most particular
as to the character of the conversation which took place at
his table, one would have thought, would have been the first
to discard the melancholy restraint imposed upon society by
the double-refined invention of keeping servants in waiting
to pass the bottles. If there be a moment in which men
unbosom themselves, no matter upon what subject, it is in
the hour, or even half hour (if custom and fashion so say),
after dinner : and if any thing can kill and entirely ruin the
genial interchange of feeling and sentiment, the confidential
avowal of opinions upon men and things, for which the
said hour or half hour seems to be the season, it is the presence of a circumambulating menial, who derives the only
satisfaction for his trouble, from listening to the convers-.

ation, of which, however discreet he may be in the "u.e s. of his knowledge, he becomes perfectly master; and which is completely at his disposal, either for love.or money, as the case may be.

Mr. Brimmer Brassey, in the outset, had been confused and worried, but he bore his infliction well. It is true, he ate mustard with his *soufflet*, and covered his *fondu* with sugar; but he joked and laughed and went on upon the only subject of which he knew any thing which could interest Mrs. Mortimer. All he talked about was the wedding — and the bride — and Miss Fitz-Flannery — and the bishop — and his great delight at having sat next a bishop at the *déjeûner;* —" he had no idea what pleasant people bishops were :" — which most luminous remark, followed by a loud ha! ha! ha! gave Helen the strongest possible indication that the period was rapidly approaching at which she ought to retire.

This she accordingly prepared to do, but, as she was rising to leave the room, Mr. Brimmer Brassey, gallant beyond her warmest hopes, jumped up, and exclaimed in a sort of mock-heroic manner, " Oh! Mrs. M., don't run away yet !"

The awful silence with which Mortimer and Magnus, the aristocratic Gog and Magog of Sadgrove, received this little bit of liveliness, fell heavily upon Brassey's heart; and when Mrs. Mortimer, without taking the slightest notice of the attorney's " Slap-bang" civility, made a sign to Mortimer that she should *not* expect him in the drawing-room, Magnus gave an approving nod to the suggestion.

" Come, sir," said Mortimer — " Magnus, come up. The nights get cold: we'll have some logs put on these coals, and draw round the fire. Now, Mr. Brassey, don't you think that will be more snug and comfortable?"

Brassey had not as yet been long enough in the house to form any distinct idea of " snug and comfortable;" nay, such was his innocence that, totally unprepared for being marshalled to his chamber, his small mind was at present employed in considering (charged with champagne as it already was) how he should get to bed; and yet, such are the circumstances of modern society, that this man, who lived in a sort of terror during his temporary exaltation, was considered worthy to be the associate of those who endured his presence merely because he was necessary to one of them as a means of saving his — pecuniary reputation.

Mortimer having, by one of those conventional signs which exist, and will, we hope, for ever exist between men and their wives, ascertained from Helen, that, as she should not expect them, she would go quietly to bed, felt no inclination to balk Mr. Brassey's evident disposition to sit and drink for any given time and of any given quantity. The object of Magnus, as may be conceived, was to gratify him to the fullest extent; and so Mortimer, whose convivial qualities, as far as an active participation in Bacchanalian revels went, were extremely limited, desired Jenkins to bring a particular sort of claret; having obeyed which order, he was dismissed from attendance.

The claret was excellent, and Mr. Brassey swallowed it; and if the Severn itself had flowed in such a "regal purple stream," he would have gone on drinking it so long as he could sit. That period, however, was past long before even his host expected the downfal; for after having assured both Mortimer and Magnus that the business he had in hand would succeed; after having pronounced Mrs. Mortimer a charming woman, and gone the length of smacking the back of Colonel Magnus, and proclaiming him a devilish fine fellow, he suddenly lost his balance and measured his shortness on the carpet, whence he was carried to bed in a state of glorious insensibility.

At breakfast in the morning he did not show. To Helen this did not give any particular uneasiness. Mortimer had not only ordered every attention to be paid him, but had visited him himself: the symptoms of his complaint were not such as to excite any alarm, the greater part of his disorder appearing to arise from the lately-arrived conviction that he had exceeded his usual quantum.

When he himself awoke to a consciousness of his real position, his apprehension was great, lest he had permitted the real object of his solicitude, or rather that of his client, to be of use in relieving Colonel Magnus from his difficulties, — difficulties of a nature so intricate and peculiar, that nothing but an immediate supply of ready money could rescue his property from ruin, — to have escaped him during the discussions of the previous night.

Nothing can be more dreadful than the uncertainty in which a man who has accidentally drank so much of claret, or any other stronger potation, wakes in the morning, as to what *has* happened the night before. In fact, the visit of Mr. Brimmer Brassey was — harmless as it seemed — fraught with the ruin of more than one of the party present; and, from the character of this " Gent. — one," &c. it may be imagined, that, when the point to be gained was important, he would not stick at trifles.

Is it not strange — for this he did not know when he awoke — that, during all the absurdities and vulgarities of which he was guilty, until, unable to remove *himself,* he was literally carried to his bed-room, not one allusion did he make to the business upon which he came down; not one reference to his client (or, as he sometimes called him, his principal)? — nor did the smallest hint escape him touching the name, character, or circumstances of that client. Does not this lead us to believe that men have two minds, — an outer mind and an inner mind? Statesmen get drunk — at least they did before these no-drinking days; (some probably even now;) yet the hilarity of the convivial evening never seems to affect the ministerial recesses of the brain. There never was, that we know of, an instance of a cabinet secret slipping out, tipsy as might have been any member of that important conclave.

Certain it is, that, whenever Magnus or Mortimer endeavoured to draw Brassey to *the* point which alone interested them, after he had finished his second bottle, he evaded it altogether, or touched upon it with as much caution as before he tasted his first spoonful of soup; nay, not five minutes before he tumbled off his chair, with which feat the entertainments of the evening concluded, he was descanting with the most pertinacious propriety as to the precise value of a stamp necessary to a certain deed which had accidentally become the subject of conversation.

Little, however, did Mr. and Mrs. Mortimer anticipate

the results of Mr. Brassey's dissipation. As the day wore
on, and the attorney did not put in his appearance, the
master of Sadgrove directed his man to visit him, and
inquire whether he would like anything in the way of
luncheon, or, as he privately added,—medicine. But no:
all was in vain: — no remedies they could apply, could
stop the *fiat* which Nature had issued. The blow had
fallen ; Nature had issued a writ of *ca. sa.,* and Mr.
Brimmer Brassey was relieved from all other worldly ills
by the unquestionable commencement of a fit of the gout.

" The gentleman is very bad, sir," said the servant, who
had returned from the visit.

" Magnus," said Mortimer, " your friend has got the
gout."

" The gout ! what's to be done ? "

" The gentleman says," continued the man, who seemed
to possess the universal failing of all servants, — the desire
to make everything appear as bad as possible, and to lay
all manner of blame upon people who make visits to
country-houses with a carpet-bag instead of a valet, — " the
gentleman says he is afraid it is one of his periodical fits,
which generally lay him up for a month or six weeks ;
and his doctor never permits him to check them."

" Well," said Mortimer, " I will go up to him myself."

The servant withdrew.

" This is one of the most agreeable incidents that ever
occurred," said Francis.

" Yes," said Magnus, " and to *me* particularly delightful, inasmuch as it not only puts a stop to our business,
but leaves on my shoulders the onus of having brought
the fellow here : the inconvenience which it may occasion
me is but a secondary consideration."

" There is no inconvenience to *us* in the matter," said
Mortimer, — " There is his room ; I will send for our
apothecary, assign him a servant to attend him, and eventually leave him in possession of Sadgrove, if the fit hold
till we take our departure for France."

: Even to his friend, Mortimer could not permit himself
to hint, or to show by his manner, — that nothing could
be more disagreeable than the circumstance which had oc-

·curred. The patient was his guest, and the friend of a guest; accordingly the gracious host proceeded to his room to offer all the consolation he could, and take his pleasure as to anything he might wish to have done with respect to his professional business.

Brassey was all gratitude, — but the most miserable of men. It had been found necessary to confide to the foot-man, to whose care he had been consigned, the key of his " carpet-bag," which contained so small a supply of shirts, stockings, &c. as to betray the economical character of his wardrobe; while a file, as he would have said, of collars and fronts, with holes in them for his emerald studs, gave evidence of the superficiality of that delicate dandyism which dazzled the eye with its snowy whiteness. One tooth-brush twisted up in a piece of ·whitey-brown paper; a razor by itself — razor, tied with a piece of red tape to a round pewter shaving-box, (enclosing a bit of soap,) with the top of its handle peeping from the bottom of a leathern case, like the feet of a long-legged Lilliputian sticking out of his coffin; a remarkably dirty flannel under-waistcoat, edged with light blue silk and silver; one pair of black silk socks, brown in the bottoms; an ill-corked bottle, half full of " Russia oil; " a very suspicious-looking wiry hair-brush, and one shaving ditto, were amongst the most striking items of the omnium gatherum. Pandora's box, or the green bag of more recent celebrity, could not have contained so much of mischief to anybody as this carpet envelop of Mr. Brimmer Brassey produced to him.

The gout!— it was nothing to the pain which this involuntary exposition occasioned: though, in truth, the gout had nothing to do with the disclosure; for it was while he was insensible to the things of this world that the man had opened the " bag," in order to hunt for the various articles of drapery necessary to establish him for the night, and who, with a mixture of attentive civility and *méchanceté*, had taken the trouble to lay out and spread on the table, in the adjoining dressing-room, all the articles which Mr. Brassey deemed essential to his personal comfort. ·.There were, however, greater difficulties in the way. than at the first blush presented themselves to view. However active the mind of the man of business might remain, it was clear that the body was immoveable. That part of his duty which involved the attendance of a surveyor, was, of course, impracticable ; and the fact that his correspondence with his client must pass through intermediate hands in its way to the post-office, rendered it necessary that he should enclose the communications he had to make to his own clerk, a person of matured years, and by some imagined to be the parent of his respectable employer. Even the great Lord Chesterfield's unquestionable dictum, that gout is the gentleman's complaint, while rheumatism is distinctive of hackney-coachmen, could not reconcile him to the embarrassment in which he found himself involved ; yet he dared not appeal to Wilson, Colchicum, and Co. — inasmuch as Dr. Doddle, his own physician, had pronounced sudden death the inevitable consequence of any such application.

"Of course," said Magnus, when they returned to the library, "we must not kill the man ; because one might have some qualms of conscience ; but I really think that it would be more advisable to try some other channel through which matters might be managed."

"If it does not press imperatively," said Mortimer, "I should advise you to keep things where they are : every fresh attempt opens the business in a new quarter ; and if, as you seem to think, this will answer your purpose eventually, you shall not, my dear Magnus, be inconvenienced by any temporary pressure."

"No, Mortimer, I will not hear of this," said Magnus. "With a fortune like mine, and an influence the extent of which you know, it seems absurd to be *géne*'d in the smallest degree : but West Indian property has been so entirely demolished by the saintly white-washers of Aldermanbury, that if it had not been for the compensation which they gave me for that which they had rendered utterly valueless before, I should have been, as far as that source is concerned, completely gravelled. Now, the object I have ——"

"My dear Magnus, say no more," interrupted Francis.

" The plain fact is, you want money at the moment; at the moment it is within your reach, an unexpected event occurs which draws it away from you : — come into my room ; let me sign a cheque on my banker, and you fill it up to the amount you require for present use, limiting yourself only to a sum which you think the worthy Sir Anthony — than whom there never lived a better man — will honour by draft."

" My dear Mortimer," said Magnus, " you are a noble-hearted fellow, and the kindest of friends ! This is not the first time I have profited by your generosity ; and although, I declare to you, it is most painful to me to ——"

—— " There, there, my dear Magnus, you shall tell me the particulars hereafter. Come, — come along, and do what I desire."

Suiting the action to the word, he led, or rather gently drove him into his room, where, according to his solici-tation, Magnus mentioned two thousand five hundred pounds as the ultimatum of his temporary necessities.

By dinner-time the doctor had pronounced Mr. Brassey's fit to be decided : everything was going on well ; nothing out time, patience, and flannel were now requisite. If by an additional quantity of the latter article the proportions of the two former could have been diminished, Mortimer would probably have felt extremely pleased ; but evils that cannot be cured must be endured ; therefore, applying an admixture of good-breeding and philosophy to the case, Mr. Brimmer Brassey was desired to ask for, and to order, what he pleased ; and at a quarter before ten o'clock, Co-lonel Magnus, having had a long audience of leave of his " legal adviser," took his departure from Sadgrove, bearing with him what was to be considered merely an advance on account of the larger sum which Brimmer Brassey was eventually to procure.

There is something in the succession of visitors at a country-house which produces a mingled sensation of plea-sure and pain. The gratification arising from what may be called a " fresh infusion," is sometimes counterbalanced by regret at losing an agreeable companion ; and it some-

times happens, when the visit does not exceed a week, that
it is not until the fourth or fifth day that one gets really
to like the individual who is destined to go on the seventh;
because, in fact, people know nothing of each other who
merely meet in London society. There do, of course, exist
friendships, especially between women, in London, but
those have been established either by family connection or
early association : it is only by the constant intercourse —
the juxtaposition produced by the unstarched (as Helen
would have said) intercourse of a country-house, that
the real qualities of mind, and temper especially, can be
tested.

Scarcely had the wheels of Colonel Magnus's departing
carriage ground the gravel in front of Sadgrove Hall before the light britscha of Mr. Francis Blocksford was
whisked up to it. The person and manner of Magnus
did not offer a stronger contrast to those of Blocksford,
than did the arrival of the animated, youthful Blocksford
to the departure of Magnus. Magnus, with a look fixed
as marble, a pace which might have suited the march of
an emperor to his throne, gravely, grandly, and gracefully
stepped into a remarkably low, large, heavy chariot, covered
with caps, tops, imperials, &c., having below it a well of
vast dimensions, leathern-covered chains, drags, and all
the paraphernalia of extensive travelling, and which four
horses found quite enough to do to move off with, at a
decent pace. Blocksford, in his light, open carriage, —
December as it had just begun to be, — with a pair of
of rattling nags, skimmed along the road, and — hear it
not!—with a cigar still smoking in his mouth, leaped
from his seat, dashed away his burning comfort, and, running up the steps of the house, bounced into the presence
of his host and hostess, and stood before them

" Like Mercury new lighted on a heaven-kissing hill."

"Ah! Francis," said Helen, jumping up with unaffected pleasure at his unexpected arrival,—for at the
moment it was unexpected, — " how glad I am to see
you!"

,They shook hands; and I believe, by the motion of his head, or body, or arm, Blocksford implied the possibility of her conferring a mark of friendship upon him which, in France, he had been taught to consider " nothing at all :" nor am I quite sure that Helen, who really liked him, and who scarcely knew whether he had quite outgrown his boyish privilege, did not look as if she did not think it would have been dreadfully indecorous to have given him so cordial a welcome : nor is it quite clear that the inter- rogative look which she gave Mortimer, while all these things were flashing through her mind, might not have in one instant curdled his temper, and induced, on his part, the coldest acknowledgment of Francis's warm inquiries after his health. He certainly did shake hands with him, but his manner of doing so struck to the heart of his wife, not perhaps so much on account of Blocksford, whose coun- tenance betrayed no feeling of vexation, as on her own. She saw she had transgressed, and though she could forget, in one sense of the word, she could not, in another, cease to remember the manner in which her husband had before alluded to her having the task of entertaining the son of his oldest friend, if he arrived during the stay of Magnus and his companion.

Young Blocksford, checked in his natural vivacity by his reception, looked to Helen as if for some explanation. Mortimer never turned his eyes towards his wife.

" Have you dined, Mr. Blocksford ? " said he, without moving a feature of his face.

" Oh ! yes," said Francis ; " I thought you would have done dinner before I could possibly get here, so I dined at Worcester. I don't know how it is, but my mother kept me so long waiting for her commissions, that I did not get away from Cheltenham till near four o'clock. I have got lots of letters and books for you, dear Mrs. Mortimer, and a whole heap of loves and remembrances."

" Helen," said Mortimer, without seeming to pay any particular attention to the speech of his young friend, " perhaps Francis would like some tea ; we will go into the drawing-room when you send for us."

Helen rose ; Francis Blocksford rose too, to open the door. Mortimer rang the bell. Helen felt all that was passing in her husband's mind, and was ashamed—not of herself.

END OF THE SECOND VOLUME.

---

VOLUME THE THIRD.

---

## CHAPTER I.

THINGS seemed to go crossly at Sadgrove. It appeared that one feeling wholly occupied the mind of Mortimer; and that anything which irritated or provoked him, acted immediately upon it. The first thing that had worried him during the day, was the fit of the attorney; the second, Magnus's acceptance of his proffered aid: the rest was made up of little contradictions on the part of Helen, and domestic disagreements with tenants and servants, all tending to keep his bile in motion; and when he saw, at the close of his day of worries, the reception his wife gave Blocksford, the train was fired, and we have the result.

Now, if the reader should have become interested in this narrative, it is natural to suppose that he might wish to hear how the attorney got through his gout; how Mortimer endured the society of Frank for the next two days; when Batley and his bride came to Sadgrove; and when the St. Almes went to France; "with many things of worthy memory which now shall die in oblivion," and, as Grumio sayeth, "he return unexperienced to his grave."

In the conduct of my story, the reader will observe, that at this moment two years and a half have elapsed since the day of Mr. Brassey's attack of the gout: — two years and a half and more have flown during the interval between his laying down my second volume and opening my third; and that, therefore, instead of dwelling upon events which this *hiatus* renders comparatively remote, he must be prepared to find himself — at Sadgrove, it is true — its inmates being under very different circumstances from those in which he last saw them, — placed in different positions, and exerting and obeying new influences.

I have said that it was my intention, at some period of this history, to let the characters speak for themselves. That period has arrived; and I know no better method of enlightening the reader as to what has occurred during the past two years and a half, and the *now* actual state of affairs, than putting at his disposal the contents of the letter-box of Sadgrove Hall, as they were prepared for despatch on a particular day in the month of April, when a select party was assembled under its roof for the purpose of passing the Easter holidays.

Upon these documents comment is needless. A country-house is the world's epitome, as everybody knows. Here is the box, and speaks for itself.

It may perhaps be necessary to enumerate the persons from whose pens the position of affairs is to be. judged. The party consisted of—besides Mortimer and Helen—Mr. Francis Blocksford; Lord Harry Martingale, a regular periodical visitor; Lady Mary, as before; old Lady Bembridge, and her niece (still Miss Rouncivall); Captain Harvie; Mr. Pash, a millionnaire and *gourmand, determiné;* and, professionally, for two days, again, Mr. Brimmer Brassey,— a circumstance worthy of remark, as indicative of the gradual influence attainable on the score of business by such personages.

The under-plot, as it may be considered;— that is to say, the correspondence of the second table, was carried on by Miss Mitcham, Mrs. Mortimer's maid; Mr. Swing, Lord Harry's man; Mr. Fisher, the cook; Wilkins, Mortimer's most trusty right-hand adviser; and sundry other persons in the "domestic" line.

## No. I.

*From Mrs. Mortimer to John Batley, Esq. Grosvenor Street.*

Sadgrove, April 3. 18—,

"My dear Father,— I am not satisfied with the accounts you give of.your.health, nor.do.I think Teresa herself is at her ease about you. It is all perfectly right, and quite according with the customs of society,.to submit to the advice of a physician of eminence without suggesting the propriety of calling in other assistance ; but if you really have not an unbounded confidence, or entertain any question as to the accuracy of his view of your complaint, all such punctilios should be overlooked. I really do wish' — if I were where I was three years and a half ago, I think I should succeed in enforcing the wish — that you would send for somebody else, — of course not without mentioning your intention to Dr. Z. : — nothing would be in worse taste than to attempt concealment from him of your proceeding. Let us do whatever we may consider best for ourselves, but let it be done openly and fairly : disguises and contrivances and deceptions I cannot endure ; and certain I am, if he be the sort of person I have always heard him represented, considering the place he holds in his profession, that he will feel no illiberal jealousy if you suggest calling in additional advice. Do, dearest father, for my sake, — for Teresa's sake — for your own, (and I put that last, because I am sure you care more for me and Teresa than for yourself,) — do what I ask.

" You may easily imagine, with such unsatisfactory accounts from you, how irksome the effort to be gay here is. I am dreadfully worried by my visitors, who, for the most part, are not altogether after my own heart : Lady Bembridge does not improve with age, and her niece is anything but agreeable : what I think of Lady Mary you already know ; but as she and Lord Harry are not only old friends of Mortimer's, but of each other, they are to be looked for here as regularly as the recurring seasons.

" Mr. Pash, a new ally of Mortimer's, — for what particular merit I have not been able to discover, — is intolerably vulgar, talks loud, and laughs loud at what he himself has said. He passes one-half of his time in descanting on cookery, and the other in eating the 'delicacies' upon which he has previously lectured ; one of his favourite morning strolls being to the kitchen to inquire of Mr. Fisher, our cook, how the *carte* is to be varied for the day, and even to instruct him in the construction of certain peculiar dishes; his principal boast being, that he has given his name, in Ude's book, to some ' Sauce à-la-Pash,' which has been pronounced *impayable* even in Arlington Street.

" There are gradations in everything, and Mr. Pash is
preserved from my denunciation as the most odious person
I ever saw, by the unexpected presence — for but a short
time, I trust — of Mr. Brassey, my uncle's attorney : of
course, I have no right to say one word to Mortimer upon
matters about which he must know so much more than I
can ; but there is something about Mr. Brassey, totally
apart from his assurance and vulgarity, which makes me
dread his presence.    Knowing, as we do, the implicit reliance that my uncle Jacob has upon him, and how impla-
cable his hatred for Mortimer is, I cannot disconnect, in my
mind, the object of his visits here with some plan to annoy
my husband ; for I know so much as to be convinced that
while Mr. Brassey is occupied with Mortimer about Colonel
Magnus's affairs, he is playing some under-game with my
uncle.    He never mentions his name ; but every now and
then I see an expression of triumphant satisfaction lighting
up his impudent countenance, which conveys a meaning to
my mind, that he feels conscious he is in some way carrying his point in deceiving Mortimer, and is anxious to
make me understand that *I* am a person for whom he has
a very high regard.

" As for Mortimer, every year seems to draw him farther
from me with respect to that which I have all along so
earnestly desired — a confidential reliance upon me — a
singleness of thought and intention.    My life is spent in
endeavouring to secure the wished-for certainty that I am
trusted and beloved.    I deserve that reliance :— but no —
let what may happen, I am never told of it until some
third person informs me.    The advertisement in the papers
of the sale of an estate which Mortimer parted with last
year, was the first announcement to me of his intention to
dispose of it: on the smallest as well as most important
arrangements, except those purely personal, I am never
consulted.    Why this is, I know not.

" I had hoped that this reserve, which is growing almost
into coldness, would have given place to some more congenial feeling, after his recovery from his long and dangerous
illness.    For seven weeks I never quitted his bed-side, except when at intervals he got a little sleep.    I watched him

day and night, and prayed for him as he slept. I hoped to prove to him how devotedly I loved him ; and when, by Heaven's goodness, he recovered, all I longed for, was that confidence which I feel I never yet have succeeded in obtaining. Do not, my dear father, think that I mean to trouble you with my grievances, at a time when you should be kept quiet : it is no new theme. All I desire is to be trusted :—I am not ;—I feel myself therefore degraded.

"Under this affliction, for I call it nothing less, Providence has sent me consolation and support,—my two dear children are the constant objects of my care. Francis is growing fast, and like his father, who really seems fond of him. The dear child almost begins to talk, and is one of the most engaging babies, as Teresa says, that ever lived. Rosa is yet too young to give me the slightest idea of what she will turn out ; but they are to me treasures dearer than life ; and yet, I think, Mortimer is not pleased that I am so much in my nursery. Oh ! that I could but discover the means of engaging his mind,—of securing his sympathy ! But I will not complain ; the day *may* come, and I am resolved not even to murmur, except to you, my dearest father. I will do my duty rigidly and righteously, and I am sure, in time, I shall triumph over the discontent which now seems to triumph over *him*.

"Tell Teresa that my new maid Mitcham answers extremely well : she is so ladylike in her manner, that I feel scarcely able to consider her as a mere servant. She has been educated—too well, I should say, for her station ; but, as the unexpected bankruptcy and death of her father are the causes of her being thrown upon the world, no blame can attach to those who, in her earlier and better days, afforded her the ordinary advantages of girls in her own sphere. I did not know the family was so large,— three sons and four other daughters. I feel extremely interested about her : she tells me her sisters are much better-looking than herself ; of course, I did not express any opinion as to their relative merits that way, but I doubt very much whether anything as regards expression of countenance can exceed her own. You must not suppose, my dear father, that I am so dazzled with beauty, as not to see

the failings of its possessor; but, as I think Mitcham's
good looks might have exposed her to danger and difficulty
in the world, I rejoice to have had the opportunity of
giving her a respectable situation and a comfortable home.

" Francis Blocksford is here, gay as usual: his pencil is
in constant requisition in the morning, and his guitar in-
the evening.  He is really a charming person, and so I
believe Miss Rouncivall thinks; but she is considerably his
senior, and has no fortune, which I fancy will not particularly suit the St. Almes; and, moreover, I suspect that
Francis has left his heart in France.  I had a long letter
from his mother the other day, and not one word of coming
over to England.

" You ask me if I have heard anything lately of Mrs.
Farnham.  Alas! no.  I fancy the correspondence between
her and Mortimer has ceased altogether.  The report you
have heard of her arrival in England may be true, for her
name is never mentioned here.  I wish she *would* return;
it might perhaps lead to a reconciliation between her and
her brother. His disinclination from her is another instance
of his sensitiveness upon the subject of his early life.  Oh!
if I could but teach him how much better it would be to
assure himself .of the efficacy of repentance, and a resolution to be good for the future :— but no !

. " My dearest father, I have written a volume; and I
could still go on,—for with whom can I converse as I can
with you?—in whom can I confide?   I will not ask the
question, it brings me back to the one painful subject by
which I am worn down.  If it were not for my darling
children, I do think I should sink under it; but as it is,
Mortimer and I are the civilest couple in the world before
company; nay, he allows me to rally him, and joke about
him, and looks contented, and even pleased; and I believe
I have therefore established a reputation as a wife dominant.
Ah! father, how truly do I now illustrate all the theories
I used to hold about worldly comforts and appearances.   I
am ardent and enthusiastic, I know; and that ardour, and
that enthusiasm, would secure the happiness I seek, and
even think I could confer.  But energies are damped; the
anxiety to please is mortified, and the warmth of affection

chilled, when we are conscious that our feelings are *not* reciprocated. Still, father — dearest, best of fathers! — fear not for your child: she gave her heart to the man she loved, and no disappointment of her early hopes shall wean her from that love, or draw her from her duty.

" Write to me, and tell me you have done as I desire. If I do not hear by return of post, I shall write to Teresa, to whom, dearest father, give my best of loves; and believe me ·

" Your affectionate and devoted child,

" HELEN MORTIMER."

No. II.

*From Charles Calley Pash, Esq. to Lord Rumford.*

Sadgrove Hall, April 3. 18—.

" My dear Lord, — I was extremely glad to get your letter. I shall make a point of being there. I have been here now nine days, and a change of pasture is becoming necessary. This is to me an extremely dull place. I see no beauty in country excursions, and the people here seem to be all out of sorts. Mortimer himself is mortal dull, and stalks up and down, scowling about, and looking very like his grandfather's picture just stepped from its frame.

" His cook, upon whom he rather piques himself, is a failure—a monotonous mountebank, who has not a spark of genius. I have taken pains with the man personally, and have really obtained for the society here a little hitherto unknown variety. I do not think Mortimer cares much about it. The man's name is Fisher, and he is an English-man.

· " Old Lady Bembridge is here, cheating at cards, and making herself as great a fool as ever ; and her niece, whose case is growing desperate, is making *beaux yeux* all day long at a Mr. Blocksford, who seems to be quite at his ease in the family : — not so his host, who appears to me to watch the young gentleman with a sensitive anxiety. I never saw anybody so gone off as the lady of the house must be. She is amiable, and all that, but nothing like what you taught me to expect from your description of her before her marriage: she seems much addicted to her children, so until dinner we see but little of her.

" Lady Mary Sanderstead is as gay as usual, and quite as full of scandal. How lucky it is for the peace of society that there is no such place as a Palace of Truth in England: to hear her talk *of* others, and see her talk *to* Lord Harry, is as amusing a *spectacle* as one can find in a country-house.

" I do not know if you recollect our seeing an attorney at Epsom races in a particularly awkward scrape with some of the ' legs,' and something closely resembling a horse-whipping being the result: *he* is here, evidently doing a little dirty work for somebody. I certainly was a good deal surprised at his appearance at table yesterday: however, I find that he is professionally occupied, and that he goes the day after to-morrow: he was condescending enough to invite me to the billiard-table, but a violent rheumatism, which I never had in the whole course of my existence, prevented my accepting the gentleman's challenge.

" Taken altogether, I think this is one of the very worst arranged houses I ever yet have been sent to, — for so I consider myself to have been: but it is always the case where the master has no turn for living, and is nearly as careless of the cellar as of the *cuisine*. In combination, this sort of thing is terrible. If I stayed here another week, I should be starved, without even being able to adopt the woodcock system of living upon suction. I have no faith in Fisher.

" You told me that I should be delighted with a fishing-temple in a romantic glade on the banks of the Severn, and lured me into an anticipated liking of the place by describing the gaiety of the parties made to visit it. Deluding friend ! After two or three dull mornings, diversified by discoursing Mr. Fisher on the shape of his *croquets*, and the consistency of his Macedoine, not to speak of instructing him in the *fabrique* of the *Sauce à-la-Pash*, I made inquiries about this bower, when my gloomy host informed me that it was pulled down two years since, and the gardens surrounding it ploughed up for the benefit of the agriculturist. I am afraid there is some history attached to its demolition, by the way in which the *enfans de la maison* looked at each other when I asked the question.

" As to the negotiation about the property I talked to you of, it will never proceed farther : the place is altogether too small. However, I am equally obliged to you, and if things had been in better order here, I should have been very much obliged to your friend Mr. Mortimer ; as it is, however, there is a great deal of pleasure to be enjoyed by my visit, entirely derivable, however, from the certainty of getting away in eight-and-forty hours.

" I must tell you one smart thing which the little attorney sported yesterday after dinner. Lady Bembridge, who was sitting opposite to him, looking at him as she would at a toad, anxious either to satisfy herself, or to mortify *him*, asked him if his grandfather did not once live at some place, I forget where, in Devonshire, and if he were alive or dead.

" ' My lady,' said Mr. Brassey, ' I really cannot answer your ladyship's question accurately. I remember hearing that my grandfather disappeared many years since, just about the time of the county assizes, and I never made any farther inquiries upon the subject.'

" Lady Bembridge, who is perfectly matter-of-fact, believed the story, which may probably be true enough. If it be, the way in which it was told does infinite credit to Mr. Brassey's imperturbability.

" At half-past seven on Saturday, then, we meet ; till when, believe me, my dear Rumford,

" Your faithful and sincere<br>" C. PASH."

From these two letters, the reader will begin to perceive the actual state of affairs. The more of the correspondence he sees, the better he will be able to ascertain the probability of happiness for Mr. and Mrs. Mortimer.

## No. III.

*From Miss Rouncivall to Miss Grover.*

Sadgrove Hall, April 3. 18——.

" Dear Fanny,—I long since hoped to have heard from you, but I suppose you have been busy in preparing for your excursion. I wish I could persuade my aunt into a similar expedition ; but so long as she can get her *ecarté,* she thinks little about scenery, or any change except that which she gets for her counters.

" This is a delightful place : nothing can be more lovely ; and I, who really like the country in the season at which it looks greenest and prettiest, feel myself in paradise.

" We have a small party here. Lady Mary Sander-stead you know ; she is here, and, of course, Lord Harry, —and a Captain Harvie. A little lawyer, who is my aunt's aversion ; and a monster of a man of the name of Pash ; he is, I believe, what they call an " East India Director,' whatever that is : where he comes from I have no idea : that he is going on Saturday is by far more important to my comfort.

" Mrs. Mortimer is extremely agreeable and kind, but so changed that I scarcely should have known her : it is nearly ten months since I last saw her, and so great an alteration in so short a time I could hardly have imagined. I think she worries herself too much about her children : they are nice little things enough ; but when children *are* so little, I feel no great interest in them. I suppose it is necessary that all men and women should begin in that small way ; but to *me,* till it can talk and walk, a child is almost a nuisance.

" Mrs. Mortimer, however, devotes herself to her nursery ; and, I think, Mr. Mortimer feels rather vexed that she does. She does not take a sufficiently active share in making up our little morning parties ; indeed, she scarcely shows herself, except at breakfast, until dinner. You have no idea how pleasant Lady Mary can make herself in a quiet circle like this. She is full of fun and anecdote ; and being some five years my senior, I gather traditional jokes from her against my contemporaries, which are extremely amusing.

" Pray, tell me, dear Fanny, have you ever heard more about the ' *aimable Henri?*' I know exactly what you will say,—and that you will either laugh at my question, or be angry; but, seriously speaking, I think him particularly agreeable,—not, my dear girl, to your prejudice, for he would not deign to cast his diamond eyes at such a being as Miss Rouncivall: nevertheless, do tell me. A little sincerity is a charming *cadeau;* and I pique myself on the possession of a stock of that commodity.

" I told you, some two years since, that I acted bridesmaid, by aunt's desire, to the widow-bride of Mrs. Mortimer's father. It was, as I mentioned, altogether a ridiculous affair: the affectation of the lady, the widow of some city shopkeeper, and the affected juvenility of the bridegroom, never have left my recollection. The poor dear bridegroom of that day is, however, dangerously ill, which, of course, adds to Mrs. Mortimer's dulness. Oh! Fanny, if the option were offered me to die, or marry Mr. Mortimer, supposing he had not married before, I think I should prefer death, and a decent funeral, to such a union.

" Now, you will ask me why?—He is handsome,— agreeable,—accomplished, and though, perhaps, (because between you and me there cannot be many secrets as to age,) twenty years my—may I say *our*—senior, he is in society most fascinating, still there is something about him —I cannot explain—this is entirely *entre nous*—which is odious. He seems to me as if Old Nick had some claims upon him; and that, while his bright eyes are sparkling, and a sweet smile is playing over his features, there is something beyond our ken, which holds him, if not to another world, at least to some other train of thoughts and feelings. Mark my words,—Mrs. Mortimer is not happy. She does everything she can to make us believe she is the most entirely delighted wife in the world; but I am sure it is not so. Aunt Bembridge has never said anything on the subject; but, from some of her hints, I am certain she is of my opinion.

" Mrs. Mortimer appears to be as much changed in mind as in person since I first knew her. She is now so very good, that she even goes the length of repressing any joke at the expense of her absent friends, which amounts to the absurd: still, she is all kindness to her guests. There is none of that off-hand smartness — that sort of character-sketching, in which she used to excel, and which made her so many enemies. One thing, I think, she has done, which is injudicious; she has brought into the house, in the capacity of her own maid, — who is to grow into a nursery governess when the babies require such a servant, — one of the prettiest young women I ever saw: it seems she is the daughter of respectable parents, who have met with reverses, and Helen has therefore determined to patronise her. I do not think this wise: the young woman appears all diffidence and submission, but I should say — *why*, I shall *not* say — that I think her far too engaging for her situation; and I much doubt whether her mistress will not repent of her kindness: however, I may be wrong, and one ought not to be uncharitable.

" Let me beg you, my dear Fanny, to write: you would not, I am sure, think of leaving England without bidding me good-b'ye. The Dartnells have taken a house at Exmouth for the summer: poor dear Mrs. Dartnell, who is really a kind-hearted woman, has done this because she thinks it will be good for Caroline's health, and because dear good Dr. James Johnson has advised it. Caroline writes me word that she detests the scheme, and that all her anxiety was to remain in town till the end of August, but that she dare not rebel, especially as George Walford will be quartered at Hounslow, and she knows that her mother would attribute her unwillingness to leave London to her anxiety for a chance of seeing him after his banishment from the house. Mrs. Dartnell is very shortsighted, but thinks herself prodigiously wise, and honours me with her correspondence, in which she entreats me to exert the influence I possess over Caroline to make her in love with this Devonshire rustication, which, of course, I have promised to do; but which, as I am sure the attempt would be useless, I certainly shall not try; for Caroline, though a dear amiable creature, has a temper and a tongue, neither of which, with all my regard, I have any desire to rouse.

" Young Walton has proposed to Louisa Barton, who, to the astonishment of a 'numerous circle of friends,' has refused him. She wrote me the whole history, and it really was so absurd, that I could not help reading a part of her letter to Lady Mary, who was exceedingly amused by the reasons which led her to the unexpected conclusion. *I* cannot understand it: he is agreeable, with money,— and though not an Adonis, like ' *Henri*,' still quite good-looking enough; she, plain, not very young, (seven years our senior,) not rich, nor anything else very fascinating, discards him. I ought to be extremely obliged to her for detailing her reasons for so doing,— not that I needed the confession : however, I wrote her a letter full of approbation of what she had done; for, though I think it exceedingly foolish, and am quite sure she will regret it hereafter, there could be no necessity for my making myself disagreeable by finding fault with a measure which was irrevocable.

" I have no other news for you, nor room to say anything more but that I remain, my dear Fanny,

" Yours affectionately and sincerely,

" J. R."

" P. S. — I forgot to tell you that we have here Mr. Blocksford, a son of that odious Countess St. Alme by her former husband. He is handsome, and highly accomplished; very young, and I should say giddy; but his singing to his own guitar is very charming : he draws beautifully, and is a pattern of good-nature. It might sound vain to you, dear Fanny, to say that I think I am his favourite; but it is not of my seeking. Mr. Mortimer appears to be extremely attached to him,— I suppose, for ' his mother's sake.' However, thank our stars! she is not here. Young Blocksford treats Helen Mortimer as if she were his sister; and her husband treats him as if he were his son. People do say strange things, but I never listen to tittle-tattle,— only he certainly *is* very like our elegant host, and his name is Francis; but then he is Mortimer's godson, and ' that accounts for it.' I think, if you saw him, you would say that he rather transcends the '*aimablé Henri*' in looks; only you know that, to me, personal appearance in a man is a secondary consideration: Francis Blocksford, however, *is* very handsome. When you write, tell me if you have ever seen him."

---

As these letters are given exactly as they turn up in a box, it may appear a by no means unhappy coincidence, that the very next which comes to hand is one from this "Adonis of the woods," Mr. Blocksford himself, addressed to his most intimate friend, Robert Gram. It does not present an unacceptable *pendant* to the epistle of Miss Rouncivall; for, if not equal in worldly knowledge, it is at least superior in sincerity.

## No. IV.

*From Francis Blocksford, Esq. to Robert Gram, Esq. C. C. Oxford.*

Sadgrove Hall, April 3. 18—.

" My dear Gram,— I am either the most fortunate or most miserable of mortals. During all my former visits to this place I have been charmed with the urbanity of my host, who, as an old friend of my mother's, has put me quite *à mon aise,* and has indeed given me a more unlimited control over the establishment than I feel I have any right to. As to his charming Helen, who really seems to me the *beau idéal* of a perfect wife, I never in my existence have seen a woman who appeared to blend all manner of kindness and good-humour with prudence and amiability in so delightful a manner.

" I have now known her for three years, and, of course, in the earlier part of our acquaintance she treated me as a big hoy growing into manhood, and seemed rather to encourage the transition from the chrysalism of ' hobbledehoyism,' by a sort of sisterly feeling, which I duly appreciated. Dear soul! nothing can be better or more delightful than she is, and you know how much I appreciate her goodness, and that of Mortimer.

" The party here is this year, at least to me, flat, —
accustomed as a boy to the gaiety of Paris, and not in the
least understanding in France what the society of a country-house meant, inasmuch as we have no such comprehension. I have been enraptured with the *réunions* at
Sadgrove; but, this year, I declare it is melancholy.
There is a Miss Rouncivall, a well-preserved old beauty,
about thirty, who is, I confess, oppressively good-natured
to me: she makes me draw everything upon the face of
the earth or the waters for her in the morning; forces me
to walk with her in the gardens, to ride with her in the
park, and, in short, to do every thing which decorum and
her aunt permit; whilst I am unfortunately devoted to
what some people may call a pursuit.

" My dear Gram, this dear friend of mine, Helen
Mortimer, has, in the plenitude of her benevolence, taken
into her establishment such a creature — come, no frowns
— as her maid; how long she will remain in that character
I do not pretend to say: she is called Miss Mitcham.
Now, just picture to yourself a creature with the most
symmetrical figure, very little favoured by purchaseable
in-and-outishness; with feet almost as small as our beautiful friend, who shall be nameless; eyes the most brilliant,
yet full of all sorts of expression; a mouth only just
sufficiently opening, when it smiles, to show two rows of
teeth, which to compare with pearls were an absurdity,
inasmuch as the best pearls are not always the whitest; and
an air that would dazzle a duchess. I never saw such a
being.

" Hear me, Gram: this girl is well-born and well-bred;
I suppose my excellent mother would cut my legs off if
she thought I could be so grovelling in my views as to feel
a real passion for a person in such a position; but, on my
soul! I do believe that the girl is so far above her state, in
mind and accomplishments, that Helen herself feels a
difficulty in preserving their relative positions.

" This divine creature puzzles me; I can think of
nothing else. I declare, if I could prevail upon her to
quit a service — ay, Gram, that is the word — for which
she never was designed, I would risk the censure of the

world, and my lady-mother into the bargain, and go the whole length of marrying her.

"Oh, Gram, Gram! she is so beautiful! — I wish you could but see her! It sounds, of course, ridiculous, and I dare say you will think me mad, and say in your answer, — 'Give her twenty guineas, and she will be very good-natured.' No, no, Gram: I declare to you, whether I am mad, as I begin to think I am, or not, I do not care, I love her to distraction; — I do: and yet, Gram, I would not that she should suffer *by* or *for* me—no; — but I think nothing can turn me from this love, for it is my first — my first real love.

"My dear friend, — my dear Gram, — I shall be one-and-twenty next week: see what a line of years are before me, if I marry this young, innocent creature, well educated! Helen says all that of her; — for, whenever I can get Helen out of her nursery, I take her to walk in the garden, and, accidentally as it seems, bring her to speak of Mary Mitcham. Whether she is aware of my admiration —whether Mitcham, as they call her, has told her, (I am never sure of what these women do,) I don't know, but she seems to humour me in the conversation; and never do we part, after one of these *tête-à-têtes*, without my being more assured, upon Helen's own showing, that this beautiful Mary Mitcham — recollect, Gram, a gentlewoman born— would make an excellent wife.

"Am I romantic, Gram? — am I wild? I see nothing before me but paths strewed with flowers, — an Eden which only wants an Eve: I do think, indeed I do, that I have found her. Dear, blessed innocent! she knows nothing of the strength of my feelings. My dear Gram, I love her devotedly, — devoutly! Am I to blame? — all this is perhaps Fate. Darling — she is an angel!

"The party here is as usual, I suppose, agreeable; — but, as I tell you, to me it is all a blank. I taste nothing, see nothing, hear nothing — my beautiful Mary is a servant! — think of that, Gram: she who can talk and sing as well as any of them, and looks ten thousand times better, is excluded as a servant! I am sick at heart! All my resource is, when I am unable to see her, — and I

scarcely ever can, except in the nursery,—is getting into
the woods and throwing myself under the trees, and thinking of her: — but she knows of my love — yes, yes ! —
and does not kill my hopes! Now, Gram, I trust you will
not show me up to Ward, or Hall, or Martyn : — raise a
laugh at my expense, Gram, and it shall cost you dear ! —
But you won't—I know you won't : you are my friend,—
my true friend! You have told me stories of yourself;
and, by Jove! if you betray me ! — But if you could but
see this creature, — this lady, for that is the term, — this
beautiful lady ! — you would agree with me in all I say.

. " Dear me ! how sickening is all the detail of what is
here called gaiety ! — and, oh ! that Miss Rouncivall—how
she pesters me ! And then, poor Mary Mitcham ! ten times
handsomer, and twenty times cleverer, comes in sometimes
with a shawl or a bonnet for Helen, while I am subser-
viently doing Miss Rouncivall's biddings : — and then the
dinners, and all the rest of it; and the music, and the
ecarté for Lady Bembridge, who patronises me ; and then
the flirtation of Lady Mary Sanderstead and Lord Harry.
I wonder they are not tired of the same performance,
which I recollect, night after night, ever since I first saw
them. Some people say Lord Harry will marry her when
old Sanderstead dies ; but I should think, after a decided
flirtation of twenty years, of the nature which everybody
imagines theirs to have been, they may both seek variety
with somebody else when the veteran drops off.

" I tell you Mary Mitcham is something like — that
beautiful girl we saw at the ball at Cheltenham, only infinitely more delicate ; her eyes are so much fuller of
expression. And then, my dear Gram, to think that she is
doomed to the enormities of the second table ! Oh, Gram,
I wish you could but see her ! — and yet I would rather
you should not — her figure is so exquisite. I don't like
to say much to Helen about her, but — oh, my dear Gram,
I am mad !

" I am not quite sure that Mortimer is altogether insensible to her beauty, — but then he is devoted to Helen :
besides, he is an old fellow now, more than forty ; and, of
course, has given up gallantry : but I have observed, when

I praised Mary to him in our rides, he snubbed me —
nipped me in the bud. I shouldn't be surprised if the old
fellow had cast a look that way himself: but all that is
dissembling; I am in earnest. I see Paradise — Paradise !—Heaven before me; because, as our dearest poet
tells us, —

        ' Love is Heaven, and Heaven is Love.'

  " My dear Gram, I have but one subject to write upon:
If I could but get a lock of her hair ! — but I cannot —
how can I ?  Oh, she is so lovely ! — really and truly there
never was anything like it, — and so innocent ! Tell me —
write to me — advise me : I care for nothing — think of
nothing but her : and what a delight it is to have a friend
into whose bosom one may pour one's inmost feelings !

  " I cannot tell you how kind Helen, as I always call
her, is: she is all sweetness, and so fond of her dear
children : I suppose that all is right : and I hear the
women call them fine children, and pretty children ; but,
as far as I am concerned, I am like the man in the book,
who declared he never could see any difference in babies,
they were invariably the same, all so soft, and so red, and
so very like their fathers. Mary Mitcham, by the way,
sings sweetly ; — I heard her yesterday ;—oh ! a thousand
times better than Miss Rouncivall, who is cried up as a
great *cantatrice*. I have made half-a-dozen sketches of
Mary, but not one of them does her justice. Lawrence
could not have done her justice. I say again, I wish you
could see her, — and yet I would rather you should not;
I should like nobody to see her but myself.

  " Why, my dear Gram,—why would there be anything
degrading in my marrying the only being who could make
me happy ? She is of a most respectable family : where
there is respectability, misfortune enhances the interest
which beauty and innocence excite. Advise me—tell me
what you think ; only do not kill the hopes I entertain.
Bid me follow the dictates of my heart, and make this
amiable creature my wife. Oh, to madness do I love her !
Write, my dear friend, write, and say you sympathise with
me. What in this world could compensate for the loss of

dear, dear Mary! I wait your answer with deep anxiety. Adieu! dear friend; let me implore you to write.

"Yours always truly,

"FRANCIS BLOCKSFORD."

To this ardent appeal succeeds an epistle from Mr. Swing, Lord Harry's man, to Mrs. Swing, his loving wife.

## No. V.

### From Mr. Swing to Mrs. Swing.

"Dear Nancy,—I had hoped to have got away long before, but my lord is still so deucedly constant to Lady Mary, that there is no parting them. To be sure, in an honourable, right-up matter of marriage, that sort of thing is quite laudable, and the like; and I am sure, Nancy, I never by no accident repented of the day when we was made one, because I am never so happy as when circumstances permits us to be together; nevertheless, when there isn't what I call right principle and the church service to bind two people to one another, I do not think it altogether right to see what, in course you know as well as I do, is going on. But I never says anything; I'm as close as wax; and as to my lord, why, if I do sometimes jig a little out of him, I take special care that he shall not be cheated by anybody else.

"He knows *that*, and he knows how careful I am of his reputation. Why, when that Mr. Wattle, which writes the statistical novels, offered me three guineas to tell him about my lord, and where he went oftenest to dine, and when he slept at home, and when he went to the country, I refused the money slap-dash; not only because I wouldn't betray my lord, but, but because I despised the meanness of the cretur', to offer me such a disparaging sum. In course, I told my lord, and he give me a ten-pound note, thus making out the whole adder, that 'Honesty is the best policy;' and so, my dear Nancy, you may depend upon it it is, whenever you can get most by it.

"It is wonderful to see how curious little folks are about great ones. There is a lawyer here — a Mr. Brassey; in

course he is only down for some job; but they let him sit
at table, and all that: nevertheless, he is uncommon low in
the trade; and as I was a-standing just giving some directions about our carriage which was in the court-yard, up
he comes, and begins: 'I suppose Lord Harry travels. a
good deal?.' I give him a look! — (uncommon civil) —
said nothing that little Six-and-eight-pence could lay hold
of — 'Yes, sir,' says I.

"'Did you come down straight from Town?' says
little Nickey.

"'Don't recollect, sir,' says I, and walked off. Up I
goes to my lord, and says, says I, 'My lord, in case that
small gentleman with the sky-blue under-waistcoat, that
sits down at the bottom of the table at dinner, should complain of my being impudent, I 'll just mention the fact.'
So I ups and tells him; and he laughed like anything, and
said I was right.

"Why, bless your soul! Nancy, at that place, Chapel
House, — I don't think much of the place itself, — while
we were a-changing horses, the head waiter comes up to
me, and says; 'How well your master is looking!'

"'Yes,' says I, 'pretty well; how are *you*?'

"'I'm pretty well,' says the snob. 'But,' says he,
'what's your master's name? I have known him a long
time up and down the road.'

"So I wasn't to be had. What d'ye think I said in
reply? 'What's his name?' said I. 'Why, I have
only lived with him eight years, and I never took the liberty
yet of asking him.' I wish you had seen Snob's face.
No, no; there 's nothing like caution.

"Mr. Wilkins, Mr. Mortimer's right hand — not that I
mean to say a word in disparagement of him, for he stands
treat like a Trojan, — and he and Mr. Tapley, the upper
butler, are really liberal fellows in regard of table and all
those arrangements; but he leaks, — lets out things he
ought to keep in. I don't believe he is treacherous, but
his head isn't so strong as it ought to be; and although,
in course, we confine ourselves to claret, after the port
foundation is laid, I have heard him say strange things as
to the unpleasant way in which Mr. and Mrs. Mortimer

live. As for Miss Mitcham, Mrs. Mortimer's own maid, she looks as if butter wouldn't melt in her mouth : but my notion is, she and Wilkins are hand in glove; and that she tells him all about her mistress, and that he tells all he hears from her to his master. Now, that would be all very well if he gets proper remuneration; but he should recollect that all that is in the *enter-nous* line, and that he ought not to speak about such things to other people.

"Wilkins tells me — only, in course, this goes no further — that Mrs. Mortimer is over head and ears in love with a Mr. Blocksford, who is always staying here, — a nice handsome-looking fellow, and as good-natured a chap as ever I saw; and that Mortimer has told Wilkins to keep an eye upon him, which, if he has done, in course, Wilkins ought to keep to himself. And what makes Wilkins think there is a good deal of truth in this is, that Mr. Blocksford is always a-dangling after Mitcham, which is Mrs. Mortimer's maid, and always making some excuse to go and see the children, two little babbies; which, you know, is not likely, because, at his time of life, babbies is not no manner of attraction. So I was rogue-ing Mitcham herself about the young dandy's civilities, and that he was in love with *her;* but the moment I spoke about it, out of the room she went, and never came down no more : and what with that, and her being constantly with Mrs. Mortimer, Wilkins thinks that something wrong is hatching. But, as I said to myself, if Mr. Mortimer really set his man to watch his wife, it was an action which I would scorn, for I think it more calculated to turn her wrong than keep her right; and, at all events, Wilkins ought not to tell tales.

"We none of us like Miss Mitcham, — we call her 'my lady;' and though Miss Nettleship, which is Lady Bembridge's young lady, is as nice a young person as ever trod shoe-leather, Miss Mitcham will not associate with her, nor with Lady Mary's maid, at which I do not so much wonder. But no : Miss Mitcham likes to read books; and she sings songs, and loves to watch the babbies while they are asleep, and the mamma is away, which to me looks like being very fond of their papa; because, to a young

woman at her time of life, I am sure our society, with conversation and cards, and a remarkable nice supper, with all
the etceteras, must be more agreeable than seeing two little
things like them snoozling in a cot, unless there was something in it.

" Now, Nancy, never you betray one word :—my belief
is, that there is more going on in this house than many
people may think — (Wilkins never dropped the smallest
hint of this—that I must say); but what I have taken
into my head is, that Mr. Mortimer himself is taken with
this Miss Mitcham, and so wishes, if he can, to catch out
young Blocksford in something which may make a regular
blow-up. Besides, it is quite surprising to see how fond
everybody in this establishment is of babbies: never an
evening comes but up goes Mr. Mortimer the moment wine
is over,—and he drinks scarcely any — and it isn't good,
moreover, except some that Wilkins gets from Tapley for
our table—however, up stairs he goes to look at the babbies,
and then there is Miss Mitcham watching them. To be
sure, there is Mrs. Horton, which is the nurse, and Sarah
the nursery-maid ; but still — in course I say nothing ; —
and then Mr. Mortimer kisses the babbies, and Miss Mitcham holds the candle ; and then he comes down again,
and goes into the drawing-room ; and then Mrs. Mortimer,
she goes up and kisses the babbies ; and then Mr. Blocksford strolls into the billiard-room and knocks the balls
about, and then out *he* goes up the stairs which lead to his
room, and then, if he sees the door ajar, and Mrs. Mortimer
is in the nursery, in *he* goes to look at the babbies. Something will come of it.

" We are tolerably comfortable. When I first came
down we had muttons for our bed-rooms, but I soon set
that to rights ; and neither Miss Nettleship nor Miss Frowst,
Lady Mary's young lady, now ever thinks of coming to
dinner without having their hair dressed, and no caps.
We have quadrilles in the evening, and do very well; only
Miss Mitcham retires, and hopes that the fiddles won't
wake the babbies: they are not within fifty yards of them,
— but it is what she calls fine and affectionate. She is

playing her game double deep, and, as Miss Nettleship says, if she can but find her out, woe betide her.

"I hope you got the trout safe. It is very early, and if I hadn't got them netted, you wouldn't have had them. Mr. Mortimer is very particular about his trout-streams; but we, who are not so rich, cannot wait till the fly is up, so we net them: also I have sent you some very fine lampreys, ready dressed. I don't think you would like them to eat, inasmuch as they taste very like pitch; therefore send them to Mr. Buffley, the glover, in return you know for what. The little pots of lamperns are a delightful relish, so keep *them*. I am on exceedingly good terms with our cook here, who is a remarkably nice fellow, of the name of Fisher, and will do anything for me: in fact, the lampreys were down in the *carte* for dinner to-day, but the moment I insinuated my wish, out they went, and salmon took their place, which grows in the river at the bottom of the garden; lampreys, ditto. Never mind—let the glover have them.

"And so now, dearest Nancy, no more at present. I hope to be back in a week or ten days at farthest. Remember me to Bill and the rest: I hope they treat you well. And believe me yours most truly,

"JOHN SWING."

Every step we take towards the development of affairs appears to entangle them the more; and so far from clearing away the difficulties with which the family of Mortimer seem to be surrounded, a combination of evils, misunderstandings, and misconstructions arise around us. We have yet one or two letters to open, from more important personages of the drama, which may tend to enlighten us as to the *real* facts of the case, at which the subordinates can only be permitted to guess. We must first, however, allow our friend, Lady Bembridge, to communicate, after her own fashion, some of her opinions to the Dowager Duchess of Gosport, one of her greatest allies, and who was a sort of sister chaperon to Helen in other days.

## No. VI.

*From the Countess of Bembridge to the Duchess Dowager
of Gosport.*

Sadgrove Hall, April 3. 18—.

" My dear duchess, — Whenever a person is sensible of
friendly attentions, and an earnest desire on the part of
others to do them a kindness, it is impossible to quit the
scene of their hospitality without regret : and, certainly, if
ever anybody were justified in feeling grateful for courtesy
exhibited in this house, I am that individual.

" When one sees a couple, who seem devoted to each
other, domesticated in a beautiful retreat, in the enjoyment
of every earthly comfort, it naturally occurs to the observer
of human nature to inquire whether the happiness with
which they are apparently blest is, in point of fact, genuine.
If an intimate acquaintance with the persons, and a consideration of circumstances connected with their marriage,
should lead one to entertain a doubt upon the subject, we
grow naturally apprehensive that some day the calm, in
which they appear to exist, will break into a storm, the
consequences of which may be the wreck of all their hopes
and expectations.

" I would not, my dear duchess, have you infer that I
intend to apply my remarks to any particular case, for I
have always observed, that, if a person, however intimately
connected with a family, venture to meddle in its affairs,
that person becomes involved in difficulties, and generally
incurs the anger of both parties : all I mean to say is, that,
when once the idea of a possibility of such a state of circumstances has taken possession of the mind, it is extremely
difficult to mingle in the domestic life of such a pair without an anxiety incompatible altogether with a perfect enjoyment of their society.

" Should it occur that the Winsburys are able to receive
Harriet and myself next week, it seems probable that we
shall leave this, on a visit to them ; but where a family is
large, and its connections numerous, it is scarcely possible
to be sure of a reception exactly at the time we are pre-

pared to avail ourselves of a general invitation. At all events, if circumstances, unexpected at present, should not intervene, the visit which Harriet and I have so long anticipated will be made out, and we shall present ourselves at Hartsbury accordingly.

" Believe me, my dear duchess,

" Yours most sincerely,

" E. Bembridge."

The next correspondent is Lady Mary, from whom we have more than one letter.

## No. VII.

*From Lady Mary Sanderstead to Lady Alicia Burton.*

Sadgrove Hall, April 3. 18—.

" My dear sister Alice, —Your letter afforded me a deal of amusement. Your description of your party is admirable ; and I can imagine your enjoyment of all that has been going on ; not but that we *have* things to amuse us even here.

" Poor dear Mrs. Mortimer, who evidently remains as fond of her precious husband as ever, is absolutely in heroics if the slightest hint is thrown out as to his agreeable levities. She flatters herself that she has quite reformed him, and seems resolved not to have her eyes opened —*ainsi soit il*, it is no affair of mine ; and as I have enough of my own to look after, I give her up. She is exceedingly fond of her children — not more so, probably, than I should have been, if I had been blest with any ; but I must say, to indifferent persons, it is rather tiresome : of course, if she chooses to hide herself in her nursery, that can be nothing to anybody else, if she would only take a little more pains to make things agreeable for her friends. I believe, after all, that the way she leaves us to ourselves is best calculated for our amusement. We do just as we like — order the horses and carriages when we please, without the slightest demur, for Mortimer is generally eclipsed all the morning — shut up with a lawyer, or else riding, or walking, or fishing with young Blocksford, to whom he appears to pay particular attention.

x

" I cannot quite make this out.   *I* believe he is as jealous of him as ever middle-aged man was of young one ;
whether with reason or not, I do not pretend to say.   The
youth is in love—of that I am certain, and so is Mortimer;
and my belief is, that he makes him the companion of his
rides, not so much, as Lord Harry thinks, to worm out his
secret, as to keep him from the house during the mornings.
I remember Sanderstead's condition, when we married, was,
that I was to change my dandy every week, and receive no
morning visitors.   Mortimer appears to be of poor dear
Sandy's opinion touching this last point.   Mr. Blocksford
seems solicitously attentive to Helen, and his manner this
year is very much altered generally : in fact, he is growing
more into the world ; and, considering who his mother is,
the probabilities are, he will make rapid progress that way.

" I have heard nothing about her, or her annual visit :
indeed, Mortimer rarely mentions her, and looks odd when
anybody else speaks of her.   I think there is some understanding, arising probably out of some little misunderstand-
ing, between the ' happy ' pair, that the amiable countess is
not to be a guest at Sadgrove ; whence arises the awkwardness of feeling manifested when the subject is touched on.

" Colonel Magnus, the odious, is to be here in a few
days, at least so Mrs. Mortimer says.   How she can speak
of that man with patience, I cannot understand !   I really
believe she is too good, too confiding, and too unsophisticated for this world.   Certain am I that she has not a
bitterer enemy than that said Colonel.   The way in which
I have heard him speak of her in society, the contemptuous
tone which he assumes whenever she happens to be talked
of, and the lamentation in which he indulges at the sacrifice his friend Mortimer made in marrying her, provoke
even *me*, who have no particular friendship for her ; — but
I hate deceit ; and whatever her failings may be, I cannot
endure hearing a person, constantly associated with a woman under the roof of her husband, speak of her in terms
of such disparagement as those which he uses.   Whenever
I find a man talking in such a manner, I suspect that
vanity has been somehow mortally offended ; but in the
case of Colonel Magnus, as all his love and admiration are

bestowed upon himself, there is not, I think, the slightest probability of his having suffered a repulse from anybody in the world. *His* coming, however, is the signal for *my* going; and although the cave of Trophonius itself is Almacks', compared with Glumston, I shall fly to its lengthened avenues, its dingy tapestry, and its shining floors, with delight, as a refuge from Colonel Magnus. He once endeavoured to ' make friends,' as they say, with poor dear Sanderstead, but he did not suit Sandy; and if he had suited *him*, he would not have suited *me*. People who have malicious minds and evil tongues should take care before whom they speak. Colonel Magnus, I know, has said things of *me*, which, if I were silly enough to tell Sanderstead, would lead to extremities — horrible things! —But I should be foolish and wicked to put my husband's life in peril by telling *him* all I do know.

" You must let me hear before I leave. I propose staying only three or four days at Glumston, and then to finish the season. Those Fogburys are the most melancholy race alive; but as connections of poor dear Sandy's, I must go some time or other; and the opportunity a visit now affords of escaping my persecutor — the man watches one like a lynx — is the best I can avail myself of.

" You ask me if I like Captain Harvie: — decidedly *yes!* — he is admirably good-natured, and a sincere friend of Harry's. By the way, somebody was kind enough to send me a newspaper, in which there was a paragraph about Harry and *me*. Harry thought, at one time, of prosecuting the people, but by my advice he dropped all idea of it: — there is something very dreadful in having one's name canvassed in a court of law. He then talked of horse-whipping the editor, if he did not give up the author; but this would have been as bad — worse indeed, for 'it might have ended more seriously for Harry; so we agreed to burn the paper, and think no more about it. If our kind friend had not sent it, we should never have known of it; as it is, few people read the thing, and fewer care about it.

" Old Lady Bembridge remains, with that fascinating niece of hers, Miss Rouncivall: as a pair — each in her

·way — they are incomparable. The old lady is so extremely expert at *écarté*, that she can get nobody now to
play with her here but Mortimer, who seems to feel it a
duty to permit himself to be made a victim.    Miss is
smitten with young Blocksford, but to her passion, alas!
there seems ' no return.'    What on earth the master of
the house sees in these people, who are, in fact, no friends
of his, I cannot imagine : I believe he fancies his wife
likes them, the which I take to be an error.    They are,
however, on the move ; so that another ten days will leave
these sylvan scenes deserted, unless their master and mis-
·tress choose to remain in their Paradise, as Miss Rouncivall calls it, where, if they propose to play Adam and Eve
for the rest of the season, Colonel Magnus is admirably
qualified to make the third of the party.

" I have told you before of the little attorney who, two
or three years since, came down for two days' business.
over-ate and over-drank himself on the first, and was laid
·up with a five-weeks' fit of the gout : he is here again,
only for two or three days ; it is wonderful to see how
careful Mr. Mortimer is of his health.    He is the most
ridiculous person imaginable, and not by any means safe.
Only imagine, the night before last, Mortimer saved himself from old Bembridge, and set Mr. Brassey to play
*écarté* with her.    The delight of this delegation was great
·to the little man, but most oppressive to Bem ; however,
so as she wins, she cares little from whom, and they
started.    At about the third deal, after Mr. Brassey had
cut, the old lady went fidgeting about the counters, and
challenged her antagonist's score, which, as she knew, was
perfectly correct.    Having performed these manœuvres,
she took up the pack, and was on the point of beginning to
deal, when the little man, with an energy not to be described, said, —

" ' Stop, my lady, if you please ; your ladyship has put
the wrong parcel at top.    I cut to the right — eh !'

" Bem looked angry, but it was beneath her character to
deny what she knew to be true; she therefore merely said,
in the most dignified manner, —

:. " ' Did I ? — I beg your pardon, sir !' and put the

pack upon the table, to be re-cut at the attorney's discretion. He did cut again ; and, if the matter had rested there, all might have been well ; but, in order to convince Mortimer of the justice of his suspicions, when he had taken off the top packet, and took up the under one to place on the top of that, he turned it up before he deposited it, and, with a sort of wink that I never shall forget, exhibited to Mortimer a king at the bottom of it ! The look of exultation which enlightened his countenance at the verification of his anticipation, was accompanied with a loud ' Umph !' and the application of his fore-finger to the side of his nose. Bem did not, or would not, see this ; but poor dear Harriet certainly did. What a man to have in society !

" Well now, dear Alice, mind and write me a nice budget of Rillesford intelligence. I had a letter about ten days· ago from poor dear Sanderstead ; he was then at Malta, but expected to return to Gibraltar in a week or two. He has sent me some extremely pretty chains, one of which I intend for you, and a profusion of oranges. He writes most affectionately ; indeed, he is a dear good creature, and I sometimes wish I had gone with him ; but he overruled my inclinations, and, to be sure, it would have been rather ' roughing it,' as he calls it.

" I have told Mrs. Mortimer that I have sent her kindest regards to you, so — mind I have. Harry *really* begs to be remembered ; and in a perfect reliance upon hearing from you ' forthwith,' I remain, dear Alice,

" Your affectionate sister,

" M. S."

## No. VIII.

*From the same to Mrs. Fogbury, Glumston Hall, Leicestershire.*

Sadgrove Hall, April 3. 18—.

" My dearest Mrs. Fogbury, — I have been for some time longing to avail myself of your kind invitation to dear Glumston. I never shall forget the many happy hours I have passed under its hospitable roof with my dear hus-

x 3

band.   You will be delighted to know that I have heard
from him at Malta: his letter breathes nothing but affection, and I deeply lament not having gone with him.   He
has sent me some beautiful presents, which I will show
you when we meet.

"I write now to say that I shall be delighted to go to
you next week.   I assure you I look forward with the
greatest pleasure to a visit to your charming family.   I trust
that dear Amelia, and my favourite of all, Elizabeth, are
well.   George and Frederick are, I suppose, from home ;
however, I must take as many of you as I can find:
therefore have the kindness to let me know what day in
next week I may, with least inconvenience to you, join
your delightful family circle.   My stay can be but short, I
regret to say, as I must be in town to present a young
cousin at the first drawing-room after Easter.

"As I shall have the pleasure of seeing you so soon, I
need say no more at this moment, but that I remain, dear
Mrs. Fogbury,

"Yours most truly and sincerely,
"MARY SANDERSTEAD."


"Best loves of all kinds to your dear engaging girls, and
kind regards to Mr. Fogbury.

"I forgot to say that Lord Harry Martingale, a great
friend of dear Sanderstead, will be over at Melton next
week: he is going there to look at a house which he thinks
of hiring for the next season.   I know, as a connection of
my husband, and being in your neighbourhood, he would be
delighted to pay his respects to you and Mr. Fogbury ; and
if you should be disposed to receive him any day during
my stay with you, I shall have great pleasure in making
you acquainted.   He is a most excellent, amiable person ;
and if he takes the house he thinks of, will be a great
acquisition to your neighbourhood."

The next which turns up is from a person in an humbler
walk of life, but who seems destined to perform no unim-
portant part in the play which is acting at Sadgrove.

## No. IX.

*From Miss Mary Mitcham to Miss Caroline Williams.*

Sadgrove Hall, April 3. 18—.

" My dear Caroline, — When I promised to write to you regularly after I came here, I was not quite aware of the many duties I should be required to perform, and fancied that, after Mrs. Mortimer was dressed for dinner, I should at least have the evenings to myself. This is not, however, the case ; for Mrs. Mortimer, whose temper does not suit everybody, has, I believe, taken a great fancy to me, and makes me attend to the two children, in return for which she promises, that, when they are sufficiently grown up to require a nursery governess, I shall have the situation : they are very nice children, the eldest — a boy, in particular. There is a regular nurse and nursery maid, but Mrs. Mortimer seems never satisfied unless I am there too.

" I do not regret this, as it gives me an excuse for keeping away from the housekeeper's room, where I hear and see many things I do not like ; and as Mrs. Mortimer gives me a great deal of needle-work to do, I tell them I have no time to pass in conversation and cards, in both of which they indulge in a way which would astonish you. Mr. Wilkins, who is Mr. Mortimer's favourite, seems to manage everything as he likes ; and yet, with all this power in the house, there is not a word too bad for him to use when talking of his master, of whom he tells such stories as *he* ought to be ashamed to repeat.

" Mr. Mortimer is extremely kind and civil to *me*, and therefore it is very unpleasant for me to hear all this going on. He is very fond of his children, and comes up and sees them regularly every evening. He speaks to me just as if I were here as his equal, and so does Mrs. Mortimer ; but then she sometimes is cross about nothing, and scolds without reason. Mr. Mortimer, the other evening, bade me sit down and tell him about my family ; said, that if he could be of any service in getting William into some public office, he would do all he could ; and bade me not think of leaving, as his man Wilkins had told him I had talked of, which *is* true, but not on account of what is happening here, but because of a letter I received from John Singleton, which has kept me in a state of agitation and uncertainty for some days: however, having made up my mind, I am easier, and shall remain where I am, which, I think, is for the best. If you see John, do not take any notice that I have said anything about him, as it might vex him; and if mother came to know about it, she would be angry, and I would not vex either her or poor John for the world: he is a kind and affectionate young man; but when I last saw him, I could not help feeling that it *was* for the last time.

"Mr. Mortimer was kind enough to say that, if mother would like to come here to see me, she would be quite welcome, and to stay as long as she pleased; but I told him she would not be able to leave the younger children; when he said, 'Well, then, why should not they all come?' which was very good of him. However, I shall not ·tell mother all this, for even if she *could* come, I should not like her, who has been used to such different ways of life, to see exactly what is going on here, which might lead her to take me away; and now that I have determined upon remaining, I should be vexed and sorry to go.

"But, Caroline, you have not heard my secret yet; for I have one, and one which no human being but yourself will ever know. There is a French countess, a great friend of Mr. Mortimer, whom I have never seen, but of whom Mr. Wilkins, and even Mrs. Stock, the housekeeper, speak very strangely, and say, that when she is here, she is more mistress of the house than Mrs. Mortimer; and add, that she has more right to be, if all was known that is true; with none of which I meddle or make: but she has a son by a former husband, Mr. Francis Blocksford. Oh! Caroline dear, I tremble all over when I write his name! For Heaven's sake! Caroline, never mention it—never let my poor dear mother hear it:—he is the handsomest, cleverest, kindest, best of human beings! Mr. Mortimer is very fond of him, and is constantly with him; but the moment he can get away, up he goes to the nursery to inquire after the children. If I am there, he will stay playing with them till Mrs. Mortimer or somebody else comes; and as his room is on the same staircase with the nursery, he always contrives some excuse to see me.

" Caroline dear, I know it is wrong that I should encourage hopes of a fate so far beyond my deserts, but he has told me that he loves me better than life; and when I have bid him not talk so, he has declared, upon his honour and truth, that if I would but consent, he would marry me the day after he is of age, which is in less than a week from this time. What am I to say or do, Caroline? It is hard to struggle against the affection I feel for one so good, and so honourable; but, if I listen to him, what would those who have been so kind to *me* say? ·What would Mr. Mortimer, who couldn't be fonder of him if he was his own son, say? — or what would Mrs. Mortimer, who puts perfect confidence in my steadiness and propriety, think? Might I not even involve *him* in endless quarrels with his mother, whose temper is reported to be most violent? He says he is prepared to meet all *that*, that he has sufficient fortune of his own to justify his making his own choice, and that he never will rest till I have agreed to it.

" What he says, dear Caroline, about it, is, after all, not so unreasonable : it is not as if he were going to marry a person raised from a low origin to a highly respectable situation. The situation I now fill I have fallen to, through inevitable misfortune; that makes a great difference. I once told him that I would consult mother upon it, but he would not hear of it; he apprehended that she would feel it her duty to make the matter known, and that then we should be separated eternally; so I shall say nothing at home. The other day I was singing to the children, and when I turned round, there was *he*, standing listening. He seemed quite delighted·to find that I was in some degree accomplished; and ever since he has left the door of his sitting-room open, and plays so sweetly on the guitar, accompanying such beautiful songs, all on purpose to please me—because, of course, I cannot hear him in the evenings below.

" One day Mr. Mortimer proposed that I should let the

company hear me sing ; but I pleaded so strongly against it, and explained to him how painful it would be to me, who once belonged to at least respectable society, to be let into the drawing-room on sufferance to exhibit, that a compromise was made by Mrs. Mortimer ; and Lady Mary Sanderstead and Miss Rouncivall came up to the nursery, and I sang to them : and that day Francis—I have written it again—Francis came up too, and made me sing a duet with him.   I did not much like Lady Mary's manner : she seemed to take no manner of notice of me ; but she is a fine singer herself, and, I suppose, despised my ' humble efforts.'

" You will see by this, Caroline dear, the way in which I am treated ; give me, then, your advice as to my conduct with regard to the one great step in my life.   Ought I at once to tell Mrs. Mortimer the circumstances of the case, and leave the place, and every hope of future peace of mind ? or can I, without repaying kindness with ingratitude, secure happiness to myself and confer it on another, while I may restore my beloved mother and her dear children to their place in the world, (for this will, by *his* own promise, be the consequence of our marriage,) and ensure me the unfading love of one who has made himself dear to me ? The trial is a severe one : to you, dear Caroline, I submit myself, and by your decision will I be guided.   I own, that I earnestly hope you may decide favourably ; but fear not — do what is right.   Tell me how to act ; and in a firm reliance on the qualities of your head and heart, I will act up to your decision without one sigh or one murmur.   I shall make some reasonable excuse for quitting this, the moment I receive your unfavourable decree : if you determine otherwise, you shall hear further.

" Yours always most truly,
" MARY MITCHAM."

## No. X.

*From the same to Mr. John Singleton.*

Sadgrove Hall, April 3. 18—.

" My dear John,—I was surprised and vexed at receiv-, ing your letter of the 1st; surprised, because I did not expect any letters to be addressed to me here ; and vexed, because it cannot fail to give pain to those who are obliged to inflict it upon others.

"You most truly say that I was delighted in your society, and our constant association made me feel that you were one of our family ; but, my dear John, recollect how differently we are now circumstanced: I have sunk from the place which I then held, humble as it was, and you are grown, like myself, two or three years older. Indeed, dear John, though I always looked upon you as one of ourselves, my feelings towards you were those of a sister ; and never, until I received your letter, did I fancy that I had excited any other sentiment in your heart.

" Dear John, forgive me ; but I am sure candour is best ; therefore do not hate me when I tell you, fairly and honestly, that you have mistaken the character of my affection for you—for affection it was, and is. It is true that I accepted a lock of your hair, and gave you one of mine ; that I always preferred dancing with you to dancing with any-body else, and that I always loved to sing the songs you liked ; but, dear John, this meant nothing more than that, being cousins, we were affectionate cousins, and that I never intended to infer that I was actuated by any feeling beyond that of affectionate relationship.

" Besides, dear John, I say again, consider the difference of my position: I am now neither more nor less than a servant. What would dear Mrs. Singleton say if you were to bring home a wife from a menial situation?—It would break her heart, John ; and as I know your feelings as a son, I am sure you would not hazard her happiness in such a matter, even if I were to admit that which I deny, any previous knowledge of the character of your affection.

" No, dear John, fancy me your sister, having none of

your own, and rely upon me for returning all your regard and love (if you please) in that character—anything more is out of the question ; and as for the violence of your expressions towards the end of your letter, let me entreat you to calm the feelings which have given rise to them. Indeed, John, even if I were devoted to you, I am not worthy of your kindness. You have just entered upon a business of high respectability, and God grant that it may answer your most sanguine expectations! Look round you, and endeavour to secure in marriage some amiable woman, who may possess the means of advancing your interests ; not unless you love her ; but do, for *my* sake, make yourself happy with a wife who deserves you.

" As for myself, it is impossible to say what my fate may be. All I entreat of you is, to think nothing of anything that may have passed between us ; and lest you should imagine that I am trifling with you, dear John, I enclose the only two letters I have of yours, and that very lock of hair of which I spoke : burn mine, dear John ; it is not worth returning.

" This gives me great pain, for, as children, we were happy together ; and I could have gone on, happy in the knowledge of your regard, but you have opened my eyes and forced me to speak the truth : —and yet forgive me— try to separate the love which we *may* feel for each other, from that which you wish to inspire. Be my best friend, dear John : love me, I again entreat you, as a sister ; but forget that you ever wrote the letter which I now return.

" Upon second thoughts, I will still keep the lock of your hair until you tell me that you are satisfied with my proposal. If I consider it as a brother's, I may still retain it. Write, therefore, once more to me, and tell me that you forgive me, and will do as I·bid you.

" Before I conclude, let me beg you, dear John, not to let my mother know that you have written to me. I should be very unhappy if she knew anything about it.

" I am very comfortable here. Mr. and Mrs. Mortimer are kind to me, and so is every body in the house. My health is much improved by this excellent air ; and I want nothing to make me happy, but to hear that you take what

I have written in good part, and that you believe me to be, as I really am, dear John,

"Your affectionate playfellow of other days, and—if you please—your loving sister at present,

"MARY MITCHAM."

It would be invidious to make any remark upon this correspondence, or excite a desire in the reader to institute an inquiry as to the causes which produced Miss Mitcham's missive to Mr. Singleton, or the ultimate retention of the lock of hair, upon the Platonic system, until she should hear whether he were inclined to subscribe to her doctrines. As it has been agreed that all the parties to this correspondence should tell their own stories, it may be best to say nothing, but turn to the next of the collection:—

## No. XI.

### *From Lord Harry Martingale to Mr. Hawes, Melton.*

Sadgrove Hall, April 3. 18—.

"Mr. Hawes,—I shall be at Melton on the 9th: get me some comfortable rooms. I shall bring no horses over, and only one servant. I wish, if there is any house to let, either in or near the town, you would get the particulars, and let me find them upon my arrival. I do not want anything of the sort for myself, but I should like to hear, on account of a friend of mine.

"H. MARTINGALE."

## No. XII.

### *Mr. Brimmer Brassey, " Gent." to Mr. Driver.*

Sadgrove Hall, April 3. 18—.

"Dear D—,We have so much to do in the way of pleasure here, slap-bang, and all that, that I really have no time for writing, although Squire Flat is uncommon sharp, as he thinks, in business, and keeps poring over some ridiculous point for hours, after having given up all I want in five minutes: he is quite one of your camel-swallowers.

However, all goes right: his confidence in M. is wonderful, and it is, of course, my game to keep that up.

"I think I shall get him to sign the mortgages to-morrow. I want to get the thing done before M. comes. I have put all in a right train, and the chances are ten to one, if he come himself, it will all be blown up.

"It would make you open your eyes to see the things that are going on here. Mortimer himself is in love with his wife's maid — dead: she is really an uncommon nice creature, but not fit to be a maid in such a house as this. Only think what a silly person the lady is to have such a girl in the family, knowing what she must know of her husband. Luckily Miss M. does not seem to 'come to corn,' as we say at the 'Slap-bang:' yet she is deucedly good-natured; and, I think, fancies me to be about the best of the bunch.

"I must just tell you. The night before last I was playing écarté with the Right Honourable the Countess of Bembridge, rather an old friend of mine, who is down here; and, by jingo! when I had cut the cards, I saw her take up the pack I had cut off, with the king of hearts at the bottom, and clap it smack under the other, just crossing it backwards and forwards, and leaving it just as it was. 'Hallo!' says I, 'my lady; come, come; fair play's a jewel: take the right pack — no shuffling!' Gad, you can't think how the people round looked; but everybody seemed quite delighted with my presence of mind.

"There is one thing I have to say: if old Batley asks about the Exchequer bills, tell him they are at my banker's; and if he wants any statement of accounts, say you cannot do anything in it till I come to town: from what I hear of his brother he is in a bad way. I suppose he goes there again now, as usual. If anything happens in Grosvenor Street, I think he will find the widow (for the second time) a troublesome customer, for she never has forgiven the trick he played her about the jointure.

"I expect to get away the day after to-morrow; but as it is holiday-time, and the people here try to make it pleasant to me, I do not so much mind for a day or two. Lady Mary and Lord Harry are here as usual, and I suppose it is all right; but there never was anything so plain.

" Mr. Mortimer tells me he is going to write to M. to-day, and I suppose upon *that* subject particularly. I never saw a man so low in spirits : he walks about, groaning, and rolling his eyes like an actor ; and yet, for all I can understand, unless Miss Mitcham is very ill-natured, I see no reason for it ; for if M. *does* let him in for a few thousands, he has plenty to bear that without feeling it.

" I shall write to old Batley to-morrow, and so you may tell him. If Hammond or Wood call, take care that he does not see either of them ; and tell Wood that he must manage about the shares before Saturday ; he will know what I mean.

" If Cornet Tips comes about *his* business, say you cannot settle anything till I return ; but puff up the horses ; don't let him have a trial ; say the owner is in the country. I think, if we can get him to take two of them for a hundred and sixty guineas, charging him thirty for discount and agency, we may do his bill for two hundred and fifty, which will leave him 40*l*. 10*s*. to receive in cash.

" I suppose every thing is alive and kicking at the ' S.-B.' I assure you I wish I was there every night ; for here, though every thing is uncommon genteel, there are no suppers ; and as for a glass of toddy, you might as well look for it in the fish-pond as in the drawing-room. I see Thumpkin's farce was produced on Tuesday. It seems to have made a hit : I am glad of it. Thumpkin stands high with the public already, and this will add to his fame. I was speaking of him here yesterday ; and only think, Mortimer said he never had heard of him ! To be sure, M. lives quite out of the gay world ; but it is surprising to find such ignorance where one should not expect it.

" Mind and remember me to old Jacob. If you hear *very* bad accounts of Jack B., write by return, as I do not want the old gentleman to be first in Grosvenor Street.

" Yours truly,

" J. BRIMMER BRASSEY."

---

The next letter is, we perceive, from Mr. Wilkins to his brother Thomas.

## No. XIII.

Sadgrove Hall, April 3. 18——,

"Dear Tom,—You may congratulate me on the success of my operations with my gentleman. During the last few days he has given me proofs of his confidence, and I have every reason to believe that, if I can get Crawley out, you will see me land-steward of the Sadgrove property. I never could forgive Crawley's attempt to undermine me; and the opportunity of making Mr. Mortimer suspect that all is not right, was too good to be lost.

"You must know, there is one thing which has brought Mortimer and me nearer to each other than anything else could have done, that is, his jealousy of his wife. Now, you pretty well know my opinion of the lady, who, if she had her own way, would absolutely starve the house; and who I know hates *me*, because she thinks I have more power over the master of it than she has. Once or twice she has tried to get me out altogether; and I have found out that she has been warning her maid — that pretty girl I wrote about — against me: she had better warn her against somebody else. However, if I play my game well, I think the chances are, if there is any doubt as to who is to *go*, she is more likely to depart than me. Hear, and judge for yourself.

"Mr. Mortimer, after having been desperately sulky, as I told you, about the lady and young B., has at length resolved on taking some active measures: he is in earnest, because he has spoken to *me* upon it, and asked sundry questions, to which, you may be sure, I did not give careless answers. He began by saying that he did not think it impossible but that he might break up his establishment, and go abroad; circumstances might happen — and so on; and added — 'If that were the case, after what you have told me about old Crawley, I think I should leave you here as land-steward, with Crawley's house and salary.'

"Of course I thanked him; and finding him just in the humour to talk, said I hoped the day was far distant when

he should leave the place where he was so much respected!
— he being, as I need not tell you, hated all over the
neighbourhood: that led him on, till he at last said
that he alluded to my mistress's conduct, which gave him
great pain! *My mistress*, indeed! — the moment he said
that, I was sure I had him. I never knew a gentleman go
down stairs to make a confidant upon family matters, who
was not thrown over. I affected not to understand him:
at last, after again expressing his reliance on me, he asked
if I had not heard what he alluded to spoken of? I
hesitated, and humm'd and hah'd, which hit him harder
than if I had spoken out; and after a good deal of
boggling, he engaged my services to watch and discover
the truth.

"Now, the best of the thing is, it is true that young B.
has been a great deal here since I have been here, and, sure
enough, is extremely free and easy with the lady; but the
change which Mortimer has seen in B., and all his anxiety
to be up-stairs, is owing to his being over head and ears in
love with her maid. Now, if I had told M. this, the
mystery would have been solved, Miss Mitcham in all probability, sent off, and my lady quite cleared, which is not
my game. I can see as far through a millstone as my
neighbours. Mrs. Mortimer's temper is what they call a
very sweet one — when she is pleased; but when it flares
up, I leave you to imagine what it is. Being, as I believe,
perfectly innocent, and uncommon fond of M., and bearing the domineering of his dear friend the countess, the
least thing said to her cross by M. sets her off into a bitter
passion; this I know from Mrs. Woodgate, who was with
her before Miss Mitcham. Now, if I can work up my
respected master to tax her to her face with being in love
with B., you'll see what will happen.

"This is not so difficult to bring about as you might
imagine: it is only reporting to him what B. does in the
way of slinking up stairs, and sitting with his room-door
open, singing love-songs, and going to see the children when
he can get an opportunity, for the purpose of talking to
Mitcham, which seldom happens unless the lady is there
too. *I* need not know that all this is meant for the maid

—- don't you see, Tom ? And more than *that*, if I am not mistaken, the young gentleman has got a trick of writing notes to his beloved — much may be made of this; and what puts me more at my ease, Mortimer himself –is so much in love with Mitcham, and she is so remarkably civil, that he never suspects that B. is after her too, or that she encourages *him*, which she most undoubtedly does. I owe *her* no great deal of affection : she holds herself too high for me, and must have a little pull down too ; that, however, is matter for hereafter. If I can stir up a good quarrel between the two heads, my belief is, that, what with the jealousy of B. on the one hand, and love for Miss M. on the other, — falling in with the lady's high spirit, — I shall do the job, and secure myself the command of this place, which, ten to one, M. will never see again, if such an affair takes place.

" I dare say, you think me a sad rogue ; however, it don't seem to me that you can find fault, considering how you manage to feather your own nest. If I should want an anonymous letter or two to feed the flame, I will send you a copy, which you can write out, as nobody here knows enough of your hand to trace it ; but, I think, B. is so giddy, that I can trap him without much trouble. Colonel Magnus is expected, and I know he will do the scheme no harm. He is about as good a friend of the lady as I am. Some people say that he wished to be very civil to her, and that her refusal of his attentions turned him into an enemy. How that may be, I know not ; but I believe he was always against M.'s marrying at all : he will do me no harm.

" I am exceedingly civil to the old brute Crawley, and get Mrs. Stock to order nice things to be sent every now and then to his daughters. I am particularly kind to the youngest, who, as it strikes me, would have no objection to become Mrs. Wilkins. I shall humour this, because it puts the old fellow off his guard, and makes him believe that I do not know all that he has done to try to get *me* out.

" I believe the lady's father is dying: if this should send her off to Town, something may be done here in her absence. You may take my word for it, she shall get all she deserves from *me* for her past kindness. When you write, get somebody else to direct the letter, in case I should want what I mentioned. Remember me to all friends, and believe me, yours affectionately,

" R. WILKINS."

The reader must begin to perceive that the " wheel within wheel" system, was actively at work. A few more specimens will suffice to put him *au fait* as to the various interests.

No. XIV.

*From Rachael Stubbs to Richard Turner.*

" Sadgrov, April 3. 18—.

" Dere Richud, — I receved yewer kind leather on Fryday, wich fond me in good helth, but not spirts, — for sins yow went a whay i have encresed my sise hand teers. yew was kindust off the kind, and i cud have wukked has kitching-mad from marwn to nite if yew had note gon; but sins yew want away iviry think sims to go rong. Muster Fishir, wich is, ginrilly speking, has gemmunly a Cock as is, scalds me iviry day for nott beasting the jints; hand Missus Stoak says I pays no manor of respict to her for nott gitting their diners better dun, wich I bleve, Richud, his owen to yewer habsence. If I thote all wot yew sed was sinsear hand yew ment it, i wud giv wharning hand go hat my munt; but praps, deer Richud, yew whas only roging me, wich wud be onkind and crule. Tommus Wite is halways laffing hat me about yew, hand says i ham a grate fowl hif I wait for yew, for yew ment nuthink, and says it is eye tim i was marred, wich he wood willinly do imself; but i says, no, Tommus, i likes yew well enuff, but as long has Richud Turner sticks to is bargin, i ham is, hand is aloan.

" Wat i rites now for, his to hask yew wat yew wood lick me two do. my muther, i know, cud neerly funnish a rome for hus, and pot in a Tabbel and chares and a chest of drarers, hand a Bedd, wich is the most Hessensheal hof hall, hand wood be quite haggreable to the mach; hand

Y 2

hif we cood bitter hourselfs buy aving a frunt were we cood sell Hoysters hand srimps, hand red Earings, and sich lick, hin wintur; hand Soddy wattur, hand Pop, hand them kind of harticles, hin summer; i might tunn a peny wile yew wos hin playse, hif yew Kontinewd hin survice, hand hif not, do togither in bisness; wich wud save me from brileing my fayse hin the rosting hand beasting, wich I most do till I leave, or get a cocks playse in a small famly.

"Deer Richud, i ham wiling to wuk day and night opon my ands hand neese to make yew cumfurtable, hand i think we cud be very appy; but do not make a fowl hof me now, hand i will truss yew hall my life; hand my Muther his well to doo, hand wen it pleses Purvidence to tack her will leve us sumthing for a raney day, wich wud be a grate cumfut to me, appen wen it may.

"i pot this hin a buskett, hand have sent yew three fools and a small Sammon cott this mawning, for yewer Sister Lizy, wich altho i never seed hur i ham very fond hof from yewer subscription on her,—hif she will haxcept the triffles i shal be plesed, hand my love; hand wen yew are a heating the fools, do nott forget her wich sent them.

"Hif yew lick, yew can call on muther, wich is the darey at the korner of Jon street, and tawk maters over. i am tird hof life without yew. I have got Tommus Wite to rite the redress, not bonely because he rites a good and, but to show im thatt we hare frends.

"do let me here from yew; and with true love and frenchship, in wich yewer sister is inklewded, beleve me, dear Richud, yewers internally,

"RACHEL STUBBS."

"i ave pade the Courage hand Bucking."

It is painful to think that, as far as we have yet gone, the most sincere and least artificial letter of the whole collection should be that of Miss Stubbs: it is characterised by a candour which the habits of better society refine away generally to nothing. Miss Stubbs, the kitchen-maid, did not feel a warmer affection for Mr. Turner, than Miss Rouncivall did for Mr. Blocksford; but nothing can be more different than the lines taken by the two under similar circumstances. The only resemblance between their letters is, in the proverbially feminine pithiness of their postscripts. We now come to another specimen.

## No. XV.

*From F. Mortimer, Esq. to Col. Magnus.*

" Sadgrove, April 3. 18—.

" My dear Friend, — The postponement of your visit vexes me greatly: every arrangement has been made to put you at your ease. Pray, therefore, do not longer delay your departure from Calais, for I have need of your advice.

" The state in which I exist is too dreadful to describe; and the tortures I endure are in no degree alleviated by the recollection of your too justly realised prophecies. I have long doubted—and feared; but those feelings have given place to something like a horrid certainty, that I am hated by Helen, and that she is loved by another, and that other — Francis Blocksford ! Conceive the fearfulness of the combination.

" I have felt more at my ease since I confessed to you the nature of the *liaison* between me and the countess. Forgive me, my dear friend, for having so long denied the allegations of my sister to you, from whom I ought to have had no secrets; but recollect how many people are compromised by the admission: — and, after all, what *is* the admission ? — for, although I have never dropped a hint to Helen which could awaken her suspicions, I am convinced she is aware of the nature of my thraldom to the countess; yet, from the course she is pursuing, assuredly not to its full extent.

" A fate seems to hang over me, which, at all times, places me in the most painful positions. Conceive that when poor Batley — (I say poor Batley, for I believe he is dying, and, though his conduct and character were never calculated to excite respect, we were once great friends— would the connexion had never been more intimate !) — conceive, I say, that when he took it into his head to marry, he should have selected the Bishop of Dorchester

to perform the ceremony, the only human being who positively knows the secret which binds me to the countess.
We were at Florence — she was dying: he was, like ourselves, a visitor, and the only English clergyman there.
She was given over: he visited her, — and, in the firm
belief that recovery was impossible, she unburthened her
conscience ; and, on what she believed her death-bed, confided to Sydenham the fact, that her only son was not the
son of her husband : — that son, as you know, is Francis
Blocksford.   Imagine, then, that of all the clergymen in
England, this very Sydenham should have been selected
to perform a wedding ceremony at which that Mrs. Blocksford, as Countess St. Alme, and I, as the son-in-law of the
bridegroom, were to be present.

" You will now more plainly than ever see the racking
difficulties in which the follies — vices, my dear Magnus,
is the word — of my early life have involved me. · With
this claim upon me, — for upon *me* the claim was, —
Mrs. Blocksford, feeling sure that when her husband, who
was thirty years her senior, died, she should at least have
so much reparation as might be afforded her by marrying
the man for whom she had fallen.   There was the wound
which burns and rankles !   Instead of treasuring up my
heart for her, the crowning event of· my degradation occurred while yet her husband was alive ; and when Amelia's
divorce was followed by our marriage, Mrs. Blocksford was
again at the point of death !   Her violence of disposition,
acting upon her constitution, had nearly ended her career,
— but again she recovered ; and seeing the impossibility
of her becoming *my* wife, she married the unfortunate
·man who has given her a title, likely to secure her a place
in foreign society which might have been denied to the
widow of an English merchant.

" Strange coincidence, that circumstances, wholly un-
foreseen by me when I left her in Italy, should have combined to make me· marry, — pledged as I felt myself to
her ; and that she, being free some few years after, should
again have married, not six months before I became a
widower !   There is in all this a mysterious· counteraction
of vice : — hopes, sown in guilt, bloom not !   And now, as

a climax to the whole, I am convinced, by a thousand circumstances, my wife is devoted to —— ! — I cannot write the word. Magnus, the true hell for a sinner is his own conscience !

" Can you fancy any human being tortured as I am at this moment ? I associate much with Francis. He speaks of Helen — strangely enough — as if she were a near relation ; and, when they are in society, his manners to her are those of a brother ; but latterly he has become melancholy and abstracted, shuns company, and devotes his attention to Helen's children. This strikes me forcibly : I understand the feeling ; I myself have felt it.

" I have but one person in my whole establishment that I can trust — my house-steward, Wilkins. You know how often I have proved his fidelity. Of course, I should not let drop one word to him likely to imply a doubt on such a subject as this ; but, in speaking on business, something occurred which led to it accidentally ; and though he said nothing, I saw from the honest fellow's embarrassment that the thing is talked of in the family. Now, picture to yourself this ! A suggestion to Francis to leave Sadgrove, reported to his mother, would raise a storm which nothing could allay : a hint to Helen would, as I know, be equally productive of violence, and an open rupture. The countess, relying entirely upon her visits to us for admission into English society, is already furious at not being invited this year. Helen's condition that she should not come, proves to me that she knows more than she ought to know, and moreover that she does not wish to have her here as a restraint upon her son. I fear much, my dear friend, that this state of things cannot long endure.

" Helen is devoted to her children ; but more so, I think, since Francis has chosen to be so fond of them. Dear children ! — why am I not permitted to be happy ? Why —— But I will not write thus. Come to me : *you* might, perhaps, speak to young Blocksford in a way which I cannot — might rally him on his sunken spirits, and even altered appearance. I dare not trust myself to remark upon them to Helen.

" My sister writes me word that she has abandoned her

intention of coming to England, and, as far as I can see,
has resolved upon ending her days abroad.   Her friend
has married both her daughters, — one to an English
squire, the other to a French officer ; and has, jointly with
Mrs. Farnham, taken a chateau, near Beaugency — a pretty
village on the banks of the Loire, nearly midway between
Orleans and Blois.   Helen expresses great anxiety that she
should pay us a visit ; and, if I could feel that she was
acting sincerely by me, I should say it is right that her
sister-in-law should be of our circle, and would write, and
press her to come ; but I feel that Helen is playing a part,
and shall say no more about it.

   " We have but a few people here, and those old stagers.
Lady Mary Sanderstead leaves us in a day or two, and, of
course, Harry ; the Bembridges are also on the wing.   I
am dead-sick and tired of them all ; yet the common ob-
servances of society force me to appear delighted with their
presence.   Brassey will, I hope, be here when you come ;
not because I wish his stay to be long, but because, I
trust, your absence will be short.   Forgive me this letter,
so full of my own troubles ; the only relief I experience is
in telling them to the only person in the world to whom I
would permit them to be told.

                  " Ever yours, dear Magnus,
                                   " F. M."


   In this candid letter of Mr. Mortimer we find him concealing from his bosom-friend one or two points of importance ; which, however, involve conduct on his own part
not to be admitted even in a communication so unreserved.
He dwells with acute sensibility upon the probability of
Helen's attachment to Francis, but sinks altogether his own
unequivocal admiration of Miss Mitcham, to whom he
makes not the slightest allusion.   In ordinary cases there
would be nothing extraordinary in a man not mentioning
his wife's maid in a letter to a friend ; but, considering the
position of the gentleman to whom this confession is confided, it is rather remarkable that one of the leading causes
of the writer's unhappiness finds no place in its pages ;
neither do we find any reference to what appeared by

Wilkins's letter — the commands of the writer to that worthy to keep watch over his wife; nor of the implied reward in the appointment of land-steward : in fact, Mortimer, in the midst of his candour, trusts Magnus only with facts and surmises which affect his own view of the present state of things, and favour the course he seems to have chosen to adopt.

We have nearly come to the end of our letters; but one which follows is curious, as illustrative of the enthusiasm of artists, and of the importance which every man, let his calling be what it may, attaches to the craft generally, and his own share in it particularly. Mr. Fisher, the cook, writes thus to a Fellow of the same Society : —

"Sadgrove, April 3. 18—.

" My dear Sir, — I acknowledge your kind letter of Thursday, which I should have answered sooner, but really have had no time. I thank you for your idea of the *pigeons à-la-maréchale.* I have for several years contemplated something of the sort myself; but the suggestion of frying the *ravigotte* in butter, and moistening it with *consommé* and Spanish sauce, is new to me. The shalots are tempting, I admit; but, in looking at the state of society, I am apprehensive that more than a transient suspicion of their presence must be avoided.

" As to the question you ask with regard to my position, I confess I am not entirely satisfied : there are scarcely sufficient opportunities here of putting myself forward. We have generally the same set of people staying in the house; and it naturally occurs that, when such is the case, a professional man is more driven to his resources to produce a variety, than when the company change more frequently. I begin to suspect that Mr. Mortimer himself has no great taste in art. I often ask if they have heard him express any opinion of such and such a dish, to which I have devoted my energies, and find that he has not even tasted it, but has dined on the roast. This is, I confess, disheartening.

" A Mr. Pash has been down here, who appears to have a good idea of things generally. We had several very interesting conversations on the subject of my *matier,* and he was good enough to favour me with a recipe for *Sauce à-la-Pash,* as, he says, M. Ude has been so kind as to name it, in his general classification.   It is evidently the work of an amateur, but there is a character of genius about it.   I subjoin a copy : — 'Two pounds of veal, three or. four slices of ham, the backs and legs of two partridges, with a quarter of a pint of good stock, — the partridges, of course, on the top, — over a slow fire in stew-pan, to sweat.   When the partridges are enough, moisten with *consommé,* throw in trimmings of mushrooms and truffles, a little mace, a clove or two, three or four allspice, a bay-leaf, and, if you dare venture, two or three young onions.   The whole is to boil till the partridges are enough ; then strain the *con-sommé;* add some bechamel with some game-glaze, and a wine-glass full of thick cream, to keep the colour light : fry some truffles, and put them by themselves in a stew-pan till you want to dish-up your fillets.'   Now, though I detect a little plagiarism, still, for an amateur, it shows research and genius.

" The truth is, I feel mortified at being kept down by a want of ardour in our patrons. ' We hear a great deal of Scott, and Byron, and Wordsworth, and folks talk of Lawrence, and Reynolds, and all the rest of it ; but what is poetry to cooking ?   Painting is an absurdity by comparison.   A Macedoine of mine involves more research than one of Martin's finest pictures ; his is all oil — monotonous : Turner's finest drawing does not cost him so much labour as one of my *omelettes aux fines herbes.* Look at St. Paul's, or Waterloo Bridge, — why, my dear sir, the men who build these things know that, when they chip stones to a certain size, and lay them in certain spots, and bed them in a certain quantity of mortar, there they will stay, and the execution will be exactly like the design, and all will go well ; but with us — bless my soul ! how is it possible to answer with any certainty for the effect of our *feuilletage?* — how ensure the just proportions of a *crocquette,* or the exact flavour of a *remoulade ?*  We work, comparatively, in the dark, my dear sir ; hence the difficulty of making a reputation.

" Greatly are we indebted to M. Ude for his elaborate

history of the rise and progress of cookery. Little did the world think, till that work was published, that Martin Luther was the first great reformer of the kitchen! What does he say too, my dear sir, of Gonthier D'Andernach, who raised the culinary edifice, as Descartes, a century after him, raised that of philosophy? — Both introduced doubts — the one in the moral, the other in the physical world: Gonthier is the father of cookery, as Descartes is of French philosophy. Then came Catherine, the daughter of Lorenzo de Medici. Look at Henry de Valois, — to which illustrious man M. Ude attributes the invention of the *fricandeau!*

" We are much indebted to M. Ude's research : the way in which he puts down Henry the Third of France, and gives thanks to Providence that Charles the Ninth had been preserved by having the immortal De l'Hôpital placed about him. Henry the Fourth justly falls under his censure ; and, in fact, as you know, he dates the art of making sauces from the age of Louis the Fourteenth : till that period, strange and disgusting as it may seem, meat was either roasted or broiled! Now, what I have before said personally about sauces, and the delicacy and difficulty of treating the subject, you will see by M. Ude, that St. Augustin said before me, ' *Omnis pulchritudinis forma unitas est,'* — therefore there must be unity in every good sauce ; there is harmony of taste, and colours, and sounds : if it were not so, why should the organ of taste be wounded by one composition, and flattered by another? To appreciate a sauce, a delicate palate is as necessary as a refined' ear to a musician. Pash has this quality to perfection.

" You will forgive my quoting from our great contemporary ; but I am an enthusiast, and hope some day to make a name which shall last : in fact, my principal motive in worrying you just now, is to ask you to keep your eyes open, if anything should turn up which may suit me. Mine, at present, really is ungrateful work ; and, except for the air and exercise, I could not have endured it so long. We have a nice light claret here, which agrees with me, and Wilkins and I are *d'accord* altogether. Of course, I see very little of the family, but, from what I hear, the lady and gentleman of the house lead a sort of cat-and-dog life; and Wilkins himself, who is in great favour with the latter, is, as he hints, likely to marry one of the prettiest girls I ever saw—a Miss Mitcham—a kind of shabby-genteel dependant of the former. The establishment is altogether *mal monté;* but, if I had more extended means, I could, I think, do myself good in the way of experiment. You know my old principle of always trying my success; so that, as I admit one or two of the presentable people to my confidence, we make an extremely agreeable committee of taste. One thing I would suggest — should you hear of any situation which may suit, altogether sink my having been here. Date back from the duke's; and remember, since I left his grace, I have been in Worcéstershire for the benefit of my health.

" Keep me in mind, and believe me yours,

" WALTER FISHER."

There are still many more epistles; but, what have been submitted are enough to throw a light upon affairs at Sadgrove, and to justify the most censorious -in their opinions of worldly friendships and the sincerities of society.

## CHAPTER II.

THE 3d of April has been so frequently before the eye of the reader, as the date of the letters which have been submitted to his perusal, that it will not require much calculation to ascertain that when the party at Sadgrove assembled at breakfast on the 10th, a week had elapsed since the despatch of that heterogeneous packet.

It may be conceived that seven days' fermentation of such materials had produced something. Magnus had arrived; the Bembridges, aunt and niece, were gone; but Lady Mary Sanderstead remained, and, *mirabile dictu!* Lord Harry Martingale remained too. The attorney had

winged his flight to town; Harvie and Blocksford were
yet at anchor.

It was about half-past twelve, and the breakfast-party
still lingering in inaction, when the Sadgrove bag arrived,
and all its members were, of course, anxious to hear from
their dear friends, and enjoy the fruits of that intercourse,
the sincerity of which they have themselves so satisfactorily
established. Helen, of all of these, was however most
affected by the event; and, in order to conceal the emotion
which her efforts to stifle her feelings had excited, rushed
from the room before she had half finished the letter which
she had first opened.

Mortimer followed her to her boudoir, where he found
her violently agitated, and in tears.

" What is the matter, Helen dear? " said he.

" Mortimer," sobbed the weeping wife, " my poor father
is dying,—he is, he is ! "— and, as she spoke these words,
she felt that, when *he* was gone, she should be in the world
alone, without one friend upon whom she could rely for
counsel. In mind and sentiment her husband, even now,
was a stranger to her.

" What does he say ? " asked Mortimer.

" He ! " said Helen, — " oh, dear, dear father, *he* can
say nothing ! — he is past writing to me ! — he is gone
from me — perhaps at this moment ! — my only parent
that I ever knew, who loved me beyond himself ! She tells
me that he constantly repeats my name — calls on me —
prays for me ! "

" My dearest Helen," said Mortimer, " in Heaven's
name, if you wish it, why not go to him? You have hinted
such a desire two or three times; but the worst of it is,
you never speak out. You know your will is law here.
Do you wish to go to him ? "

" Oh ! Mortimer," said Helen, " do not ask me: the
choice is one of pain and peril. I dread the alternative.
He wishes to see me ; that wish is enough to overcome all
other feelings: but I would rather — I can do no good —
I would rather recollect him, as I last saw him, in all the
gaiety of his kindness and good-humour, than have impressed upon my mind the eternal recollection of his

beloved countenance — changed by the heavy hand of sick-ness—perhaps of death!—And if he *were* dead when I reached town! — Oh, no, no, no; I couldn't bear it!"

"Do as you will, dearest," said Mortimer, in a tone which perfectly conveyed his personal indifference as-to the election she made. "I know enough of the sort of feeling which agitates you now, to question whether you had better not wait the result, and ———"

"The result!" said Helen,—"then he *is* to die! — and if he asks for me — and I am not there, and they tell me of it hereafter, my heart will break — it will, Mortimer, it will!"

And she clasped his neck, and hid her face on his bosom, and her tears flowed again in torrents.

Was hers a heart to wound? — was she a wife to scorn and suspect?

"Why not go, then?" said Mortimer.

"How can we leave our friends?" said Helen.

"*We* need not leave them," cried Mortimer; "I may remain. What can prevent your starting for London two hours hence? Take your maid and a footman; and, if you dislike travelling at night, sleep at Oxford or at Henley, and start again in the morning."

"Leave my children, and go without *you?*"

"*I*," said Mortimer, "could not well leave home: I have a dread, too, of such scenes; and besides — that uncle of yours! — in fact, I should rather be in your way. That you should feel towards your poor dear father as you do, is not only natural, but right and just: the case is different with *me*."

Helen could not help thinking that the readiness with which Mortimer gave his sanction to her solitary journey was not quite in accordance with that sensitive tenderness which she had always fancied, before marriage, characteristic of the devoted husband: but her enthusiasm had been fre-quently damped before; and, as her whole heart and soul were engaged in the anxiety to see her beloved father before he died, she grasped at the possibility of realising her wish at all hazards.

"If it were not for the children, ———"

"Why," said Mortimer, as if the thought had that moment stricken him for the first time, "if you feel anxious about *them*, Mitcham might stay with them, and you might —— "

"No," said Helen, but without even thinking beyond the one object, "I could not do without Mitcham."

"Faith!" said Mortimer, with one of those gloomy smiles which so frequently played over his countenance, "I believe you ladies have as much difficulty in changing a maid as a monarch has in changing his minister."

"But," said Helen, "I have no option: I have no other person at hand to take her place. No: the dear babes have their nurses; and you, my beloved Mortimer, are equally devoted to them with myself."

"Yes," said Mortimer, exceedingly angry at something which Helen could not even surmise, although the reader perhaps may, "I will act as head-nurse in your absence."

"I wish, Francis," said Helen,—"devoutly wish, that I could persuade you to go."

"What!" said Mortimer, with another of those looks which cut her to the heart, "and leave the dear children entirely to the tender mercies of the servants!"

"I know," said Helen, "the natural dislike you have to my uncle; still —— "

"Helen," said Mortimer, "do not talk of him to me: *you* hate him as much as I do; and nothing is so abominable as a hypocritical avowal of affection for near relations for whom one does not care sixpence. That you should desire to see your father is, as I have stated, most natural. My advice is this: it is impossible that you can get clear of Sadgrove before three: do what I before suggested—go on as far as Oxford; rest there; start early in the morning, and you will be in Grosvenor Street before noon."

This plan exactly accorded with poor Helen's wishes; but the more calmly her husband discussed it, the more her heart sank; because, in the philosophical manner in which he treated it, and the readiness he evinced to accede to her wish, and even went into the details of the journey, she perceived fresh evidence of his indifference, not only as to her absence, but as to the fate of her beloved parent, which had so often before agonised her.

"We are reduced to a very small party here," said Mortimer; "and though Frank Blocksford will, no doubt, miss you, Lady Mary will not, if Harry remains. Magnus will amuse the young gentleman, and Harvie and I will make it out remarkably well. I suppose you will not stay till the funeral."

Helen felt herself choking: she was unable to speak — to look at her husband, who, in one sentence, had, as *we* know, intentionally inflicted a thousand wounds. The allusion to Francis Blocksford at such a moment; the triumphant announcement that the (to *her*) odious Magnus was to take charge of that youth ; the inference that he sanctioned under his roof, and in the society of his wife, such a *liaison* as all the world, except Helen, understood to be existing between Lady Mary and Lord Harry—never brought to entire perfection till Lord Harry's father had made successful interest, at his persuasion, with the Admiralty to get her ladyship's husband a ship on a foreign station, for the command of which he was about as fit as the coxswain of the Lord Mayor's barge would be to navigate the Red Sea in a seventy-four. As for the service, that was one thing; all that was wanted was Sanderstead's absence from home ; and, as the Mediterranean was thought the safest pond for him to play about in, thither he was sent.

But if these hints and inuendoes — first, as to Blocksford, which Helen felt, however undeserved ; and next, as to the sort of society which her husband encouraged under his roof, irritated and wounded her, the way in which he spoke of the certainty of a fatal result to her father's illness was still more painful. We, who have seen Mortimer's letters, and know the dreadful character of his suspicions, can duly appreciate the tone and spirit of his remarks, sweetened and softened in manner, and even *that* equivocal: but it would be hard, indeed, to give any adequate description of his unhappy wife's feelings, when she heard him consign to the grave, as a matter of course, the father she adored, and the man with whom he had himself lived for years upon terms of perfect friendship.

The course Mortimer adopted determined her as to that

which she should take. If he had followed up the line upon which she had at first set out, and strengthened her in her view, that it would hereafter be more consolatory to look back upon her father as she had last seen him, than to have impressed upon her mind for ever his image stretched on the bed of death, she might, fearing that all would be over when she arrived in town, have waited the event at Sadgrove ; but the moment she found her unqua_lified love for her parent scoffed at, the certainty of his dissolution established, and the whole affair nearest to her heart treated as a matter of indifference, her filial love was roused beyond control, and she decided, in a tone much more of command than she was generally accustomed to assume, upon undertaking the journey as soon as it was possible to begin it.

"Women are strange creatures!" said Mortimer. "Well, I will order the carriage to be at the door at three ; you will get to Oxford by nine or ten : there I advise you to sleep. If you prefer it, you can get on to Henley ; but, at all events, stop there, because you will save fatigue, and arrive in town at any hour you choose to-morrow, which will be infinitely more convenient than getting to Grosvenor Street in the middle of the night."

" I care for nothing," said Helen, " but reaching home in time to see my dearest father."

" Home ! ha, ha ! So, then, your heart has never been at home here, Helen !"

It drives one half-mad to hear such things said, and at such a time, by a man like Mortimer, to such a being as Helen. She heeded them not, and only said, —

" I call my father's house my home ; surely, dear love, there is no harm in *that*."

" Harm !" said Mortimer, " oh, dear, there is no harm in anything you say, Helen ! But there, I had better give orders about the carriage, and have horses sent for : — and you take Mitcham then, of course ? "

" Of course !" said Helen.

"Which of the footmen shall go — your own or Richard?" said Mortimer. " I ask only because Richard, I think, is the steadiest."

z

" Do whatever you like, dear Mortimer, I shall be ready at three, and I assure you I thank you a thousand times for letting me go, though I would thank you ten thousand times more if you would go with me."

" Ay," said Mortimer, " that is· quite another affair. Well, then, I shall go down and announce your projected departure, and make all necessary arrangements. Let us, however, first look at the babes ; I promise, Helen, to take the greatest care of them during your absence."

Helen, too much delighted to be associated with her husband in such a labour of love, felt grateful to Heaven that it had bestowed on them children, who seemed to form the only real link which bound them together.

They proceeded to the nursery, which opened into Helen's dressing-room ; and as Mortimer gently pushed open the door, Helen following, his eye glanced upon Blocksford, who, the moment he heard the rattling of the lock, was evidently making a hasty retreat. The nurse was there, but not Miss Mitcham.

In one moment the fitful smile which had gilded Mortimer's countenance was turned into a look of the deadliest gloom ; an oath, muttered not so softly as to pass unheard by his wife, escaped his lips. In an instant the children, and everything in the world except the object of his suspicion, was forgotten.

" Wasn't that Mr. Blocksford who went out ? " said Mortimer to the nurse.

" Yes sir," said the woman ; " he generally looks in as he goes by, to see the dear children."

Mortimer spoke not for a moment ; then, turning to Helen, his countenance quivering with emotion, said,—

" If Francis has ascertained they are well, I conclude I need not inquire after them myself. I'll go and see about the carriage."

And away he went with an affected carelessness and gaiety, leaving Helen in a state of surprise and misery, which, however, were greatly modified by her one thought of the impending calamity which seemed to her fraught with the most important consequences : and so in truth it was.

Little need be said, after what has been disclosed, to 'convince the reader that Helen, under the fearful circumstances by which she was surrounded, had a worse chance of coming out unscathed from her trials than even the innocent queen after her walk over the hot ploughshares.

" Rely upon it," said Magnus to Mortimer, when˙ he reached his own room, and imparted what he had seen as to the evanishment of Blocksford, " the case is a bad one. To a person like myself, my dear friend, accustomed to view things on the great scale, and to whom matters of first-rate importance are confided, the underhanded trickeries of small men are immediately evident; of course, when I say small men, in the present case, I mean men of small experience. I say again, the case is a bad one : rely upon it, that sort of open-necked, guitar-playing, song-singing, sketch-making, poem-writing person, at his age, is the most dangerous in the world."

" That is all true, but Helen ――"

" Helen !" said Magnus, ― " Helen married you, as you know, out of pique. Did not that father of hers――"

" Stay," said Mortimer, " he was our friend ; he is dying."

" That is in the course of nature," said Magnus ; " but did he not actually send after you to Brighton ?"

" All that is past ; I speak of the present."

" Well, then, for the present," said Magnus, " Mr. Blocksford is too much here, ― especially after having excited the feelings you so fervently described in your last letter to me. I have carefully watched the workings of his mind : I have seen an interchange of looks between them : her spirits have sunk in due gradation with his : ― he is in love."

" In what a position do I stand ?" said Mortimer. "How am I to act ? A word―a hint―a doubt expressed, would fire the train : ―at this juncture, too, while Helen is oppressed with grief for her father !"

" There is a good deal of acting in that, I take it," said Magnus. " I speak out, because you desire me to do so, and because I would guard you against deception. May she not assume a greater degree of sorrow for her father's illness, in order to cloak the real cause of her depression? May she not seek the journey to avoid the scrutinising gaze with which she must be conscious I watch her actions? She is conscious of *that*, I know; and ———"

"And, after all, we may be wrong," said Mortimer, relentingly. "However, at this period, nothing can be done in the affair. She is plunged in grief, and her feelings must be respected. If, in her absence, Francis could be spoken to, — told that people remark his familiarity — his constant residence here: *I* couldn't touch upon the point, but a friend might."

"A friend *will*," said Magnus. "You have put this affair into my hands: I am resolved to maintain your honour. While Helen is away, I will draw young Blocksford, as you call him ———"

"Hush, hush!" said Mortimer.

"I will draw him, I say, into conversation, and lead it to the topic. He has honoured me by taking a fancy to my society—a family failing,—and, I think, is inclined to place reliance on me. I will discourse him gently upon the caution necessary to be observed in society by attractive young men in their friendships with young married women: in fact, I will advise him whilst I search his mind, and, as I find the fact to be, so shall I act; and if—as I have little doubt I shall—I should be able, from the ingenuousness of nineteen or twenty, ———"

"More than that; he was of age yesterday. I did not touch upon the point, though I recollected it; nor did he, which surprised me."

"There must have been some reason for *that*," said the amiable Magnus: "however, twenty or twenty-one, I flatter myself I shall come at the truth: and then, if in his confessions there should appear anything to justify your suspicions, — not as to himself, but as to her, — I will suggest, as a matter of honour, his making some excuse for immediately leaving Sadgrove, which, while Mrs. Mortimer is absent, will be less noticeable, and stop the matter in time to avoid *éclat*."

"Excellent counsellor!" said Mortimer: "you can,

indeed, do all this, and I may be saved, — Helen may be saved. I may, perhaps, be restored to tranquillity, even by the very course of examination to which you propose to submit him : it may all be innocence and —— "

" It *may*," said Magnus. " Trust to me : it requires a grasp of mind to take these subjects into one great general view."

" But," said Mortimer, " let me entreat, let me conjure you, by no implication, no allusion, permit the slightest hint to fall from your lips which could lead the thoughts of this dreaded object of my solicitude to the fact of our wretched consanguinity. I was mad when I permitted his mother to force him thus upon me : and yet, Magnus, I am not lost to natural feeling. If I dare own the truth to *him ;* — but no, no ! — there falls his mother's reputation ! — there perishes his respect for her whom he now loves ! Oh ! my friend, this is all just retribution ! Let the sinful suffer, but let us save the innocent, — if innocent yet they be ; and spare the countess degradation and disgrace, and keep her son from a knowledge of—— "

" My dear Mortimer," said Magnus, bending gracefully forward, and grasping from his ample box a ' gigantic pinch of snuff,' do you suspect me of any *gaucherie* like *that ?* "

" I think," said Mortimer, (and it is wonderful to see how much the man condescends who, to use Mr. Wilkins' expression in his letter to his brother, goes down stairs to make a confidence,) " I think, from what I have heard, that all may yet be well ; that the extremest point to which our charges can go is indiscretion : but the state of doubt —— "

" Shall be ended forthwith. Leave the affair to me. Rely upon it, this journey is a providential occurrence, and we will take advantage of it. Go, see preparations made for the lady's departure ; stifle your feelings ; check yourself if you feel inclined to abruptness ; seem as kind as ever. Remember, we have yet slight grounds to go upon ; let the fault of harshness not rest upon *you.* I will·go with you, and take my share in the ceremonies of the day."

If one did not, know that all this was true, and~had
happened, would it be believed that a man of Mortimer's
sense and spirit, high breeding and knowledge of the
world, could have consented to talk with any man, no
matter whom, upon such a subject and in such a strain?
— that jealousy, and that most peculiar jealousy of others,
originating, as we have seen, in diffidence of himself —
could so far have debased his mind as to have thrown him
into the power of two such persons as Colonel Magnus, the
mightiest of his friends, and Mr. Wilkins, the meanest of
his domestics?

So it was; and, after what we have seen, it is clear that
the efforts of the subordinate, whose association in the
league Mortimer never mentioned to Magnus, were in no
degree inferior to those of his more important, though unconscious, confederate.

Mortimer, who seemed to have placed himself implicitly
under the tutelage of his friend, acceded to all his suggestions as they related to his apparently affectionate superintendence of the proceedings connected with Helen's
departure; and the Orestes and Pylades of Sadgrove
joined the half-disjointed, half-expectant party, who, unsettled by the announcement of their fair hostess's departure under such painful circumstances, considered it
necessary at least to postpone their arrangements for the
day's diversions till she was fairly out of sight; their tone
of sorrow being taken from their host, who merely
regretted that Helen's feelings prompted her to make the
journey which, from the contents of her mother-in-law's
letter, he felt assured would be too late to secure the object
in view.

And while this scene was acting below, what was passing in the neighbourhood of that nursery, the scene of so
many whispering interviews between Francis and Mary
Mitcham?

Francis Blocksford no sooner heard of Helen's projected expedition, than he resolved that the crisis of his
fate was at hand. Mary was going with her: the thought,
painful as it was of itself, was coupled in his mind with
the certainty of losing her eternally. Left alone with her

mistress, the secret would be betrayed. Won by Helen's kindness, and melted by sympathy for her grief, she would own to her their attachment. The idea was madness. His heart and mind were filled with the one thought: his head ached, his limbs trembled, his hands were icy cold, his eyes burned: see her he must. Five, six, seven times did he make errands to his apartment upon the staircase, which led, as we know, also to the nursery and to Mary Mitcham's room: he saw her not. He would have stricken some chords on his guitar to attract her attention, but that Helen was weeping. Again he paced the passage, and not again in vain: at length he met the object of his search.

"Mary, Mary!" said he, in a tremulous voice, his tongue cleaving to his mouth,—"for Heaven's sake! Mary, one moment!"

Mary shook her head, and, laying her finger on her lip, passed on. He re-entered his room,—affected to look for some book or paper,—sat down as if to write,—*did* write, and the tremulousness of his hand came out afterwards in evidence against him. Again Mary passed his door, or would have done so; but, maddened by the thoughts which occupied his mind, he drew her in, and closed it.

"Hear me, Mary," said he, clasping her to his heart, "I am this day my own master, ready and resolved to redeem my pledge. You love me, and you have owned it: the crisis has arrived. You leave with Helen in an hour. If you go with *her* to London, if you see your mother there, you will consult her upon this attachment of ours; she will give you worldly reasons why you should tell Helen, and take her advice; she will tell Mortimer; Mortimer will tell *my* mother, and we are lost!—and, by Heavens! Mary, unless you wish to have my blood upon your head ——"

"Oh! Mr. Blocksford," said Mary, trembling, "don't speak so loud! I hear Mrs. Mortimer in the passage: let me go, for Heaven's sake!—If you *do* care for me, let me go!"

"Care for you, Mary!" said Francis; "what words

are these? Listen, listen!—now, be calm,—be still! love,—be still! This journey gives us the opportunity of all others to be sought for!—there's nobody coming, love! Hear me: Helen stops to sleep at Oxford to-night; when she is gone to rest, you will be free. I will be there: a chaise will be ready, and we will start thence to Scotland, where you will become mine for ever. Thence we will return, and the knot once tied, my mother will forget and forgive all; and if she do not, dearest, I have, as I have already told you, a fortune adequate to all our wants and wishes; and if she refuse her sanction to our marriage, I am content to possess your love."

Mary, dreadfully agitated, said nothing, but left her hand clasped in that of Francis; at length the word " Impossible!" passed her lips.

" Mary," said Francis, drawing her still closer to his heart, " the moment has arrived: do you hate—do you detest me?"

" No, no!" said Mary, bursting into tears, why should I?"

" Then," said Francis, scarcely able to give the question utterance, " do you love me, Mary?"

Her hand remained clasped in his: the grasp was not relaxed.

" Let me go, Francis,—pray, let me go," said the trembling girl.

" Francis," whispered Blocksford to himself,—" she calls me Francis!"

" Mary," said he, in a hurried yet resolute tone, " I trust you—I rely upon you—at twelve to-night at Oxford! I shall easily find out at which inn you stop. At twelve!—for Heaven's sake, do not deceive me!"

Mary decidedly pressed his hand, and rushed out of the room. Blocksford threw himself upon the sofa, and hid his eyes:—was it a dream?—was it reality? Did he, in truth, possess the treasure he had so ardently sought; or, at least, was it so immediately within his grasp? It seemed like a bright vision; but his delight, even in the moment of triumph, was accompanied with a sensation of dread at his success. The instant he felt himself secure, there arose in his mind a crowd of thoughts which had never before entered it, — cares, responsibilities, and a thousand incidents, involving even the details of the expedition. As far as these were concerned, he resolved, lest he should have no other opportunity of enlightening the fair companion of his intended excursion, to write a note, which he would convey to her as she was starting; and accordingly, with as much composure as he was master of, scrawled these lines : —

"It is natural, dearest, that your feelings should be deeply affected at this moment; and I own that nothing but my conviction that this is an opportunity not to be lost, would have induced me to be so peremptory; but, as you have made me the happiest of happy men, few words may save us much trouble. Whether you stop at 'The Star' or 'The Angel,' of course I shall know; trust to me for the rest, and fear nothing: I, of course, have plenty of *friends* in Oxford, and at either house. I believe, knowing your kind and tender heart, that parting from the dear children will give you the severest pang of all; but you must not let that feeling get the better of those which you own I have inspired. Heaven bless you! Before this time to-morrow we shall be safe from the persecutions of all spies and enemies. Remember — twelve!

"Ever yours,

"F. B."

He might, however, have spared himself this address; for, his door being still ajar, his ears were delighted with a soft, short cough, which he recognised to be that of his Mary, and of a character to which the Faculty have assigned no particular designation. He started up : sure enough Mary was there.

"Go down, — pray, go down!" said she. "Mrs. Mortimer is gone down already : they are just going to luncheon: if you stay away, we shall be discovered. I shall die! Oh! pray, think better of it!—some other time!"

"No, no, no! you have promised. Mind, I shall be there; somebody will give you notice :—it will be all right. rely upon it."

" There, then, go now, for Heaven's sake ! Oh ! what
will become of me !"

" Luncheon is ready, sir," said Mr. Wilkins, who had
taken upon himself a new character upon this special occasion, and fatigued himself to volunteer the announcement,
for what purpose Francis did not exactly understand, but
Mary did. Blocksford said, " Very well," with an extremely ill-acted carelessness ; and Miss Mitcham looked
upon the house-steward as she felt, for the last time, with
a scorn and contempt in which there was no acting at all.

" Upon my word ! my dear Mrs. Mortimer," said Lady
Mary, " you are undertaking a great performance — a
journey of a hundred and twenty miles, alone !"

" Oh ! nothing," said Helen, " when the heart is interested ; besides, in these days of civilisation, a lone lady is
not likely to meet with many perilous adventures, while
protected by the presence of her maid and a man-servant,
and two postillions."

" Upon my honour !" said Lord Harry, " I do think
one of us ought to offer himself as cavalier, for I am quite
sure that our being here prevents Mortimer's going with
you."

" No," said Mortimer ; " Helen knows my reasons for
wishing her to leave me behind. I should, I assure you,
make no ceremony, if that were not the case ; nor need our
both going at all disturb you, so long as Colonel Magnus
and Mr. Blocksford are here : they know the ways of the
house, and are quite capable, either one or the other, to be
my *locum tenens.*"

" Why, what on earth is the matter with *you*, Frank ?"
said Captain Harvie to Francis, as he took his " seat at
the board."

" Matter ! Nothing is the matter with *me !*"

" Did you ever see anybody looking as *he* does, Mrs.
Mortimer ?" said the captain.

" Come," said Francis, " don't worry me ; I want some
luncheon."

" Your hand is not over steady," said Magnus, casting
a significant look at Mortimer ; — " what has flurried
you ?"

" Nothing," said Francis, colouring crimson.

" Umph!" said Mortimer, whose glance at Magnus Helen saw; and too quickly guessing its import — too well knowing the cause of her arch-enemy's hatred — *her* cheek, pale as death before, caught the infection, and fired with rage. This really inconsequential, but unfortunate exhibition, was not lost upon Lady Mary or her friends, who all exchanged looks, none of which were lost upon Mortimer.

The struggle with her contending feelings was too much for poor Helen, who burst into tears, and quitted the table. Mortimer did not follow her; Lady Mary did, — for she knew enough of *all* the history to pity, although her great delight was only to alarm her. The carriage was shortly brought to the door; and then the wretched husband — for what else was he? — proceeded to his still more wretched wife to announce its arrival.

During the incidental preparations for the departure, Magnus watched poor Francis like a lynx: he hoped, in the activity of his *surveillance*, to pick up some of those " trifles light as air," upon which he might give something like a colouring to the suspicions he had endeavoured to awaken in Mortimer's mind; and he was most fortunate; for poor Francis, the very first day after he had legally arrived at years of discretion, having done, perhaps, in a worldly point of view, the most indiscreet thing he possibly could do, was in a state of nervous agitation far beyond the colonel's most sanguine hopes. Full of the anticipation, — not of his future life, for that was by far too remote an object for his young and sanguine mind, — but of his arrangements, and the journey, and the marriage; and of the thought that she who was to be the sharer of his fate and fortunes, was to be, before his eyes, packed up in the rumble of a carriage in a hot day, with a huge plush-wearing footman, who, because the seat was so narrow, would, for mere convenience sake, in all probability carry his arm round the slender waist of his fair companion. What must have passed in his mind? Magnus recommended an extra glass of wine; but Francis refused it, and exhibited signs of irritability when the colonel joked him in *his* way, which had never been previously observable in his manner :—all which convinced the said colonel that he was doing wonders in the way of discovery-making.

The time fast approached for poor Helen's departure. Her parting with her children, whom she loved better than life, and from whom she had never yet been separated, was, indeed, a trial; and Mary Mitcham was so much affected, that Mortimer went the length of taking her hand, and begging her not to agitate herself — that she would see them again in a few days; at which the poor girl burst into a fresh torrent of tears, and Helen wept more than before; and in this fashion the lady of Sadgrove took her leave.

She leant on Mortimer's arm as she passed through the hall, and bowed her *adieux* to the few guests left, for she could not speak; and when seated in the carriage, and the door was about to be closed, motioned with her hand that Mitcham should accompany her inside. This mark of her consideration—not altogether unselfish—threw poor Francis into a new fit of terror. Mary was to be *tête-à-tête* with Mrs. Mortimer for six or seven hours, on the eve of the deciding movement of her life,—and that movement to be made in conjunction with so near a friend of the family :—was it possible that she could play the hypocrite so as to conceal this most important fact from her who had been so unboundedly kind to her? He doubted—he dreaded — and would have almost preferred the rumble and plush to the influence of such a woman as Helen over such a girl as Mary in the way of inducing a confidence; but he might have spared himself all his anxiety. Mary never let fall either remark or observation which could in the remotest degree lead her mistress to suspect anything more than she always had suspected, namely, that Frank thought Mary an extremely pretty girl, as indeed did everybody else; and that he had told her so, as indeed Frank, in his frequent conversations with Helen about her, had confessed. Mary's only remark during the whole journey, at all to the point, was,—" that Mr. Blocksford was a remarkably nice young gentleman, and she wished him all sorts of happiness."

They are, however, gone ; and while they are on their journey, we shall have plenty of occupation in watching the proceedings of other and very different people.

---

## CHAPTER III.

It would be difficult adequately to describe the feelings of the different persons who witnessed Helen's departure from Sadgrove. Mortimer resolved to make use of her absence in endeavouring to satisfy himself by all means, fair and unfair, of the justice or groundlessness of his suspicions. Wilkins determined to avail himself of the same opportunity to confirm those suspicions ; while Magnus, whose disappointed pretensions to Helen's favour had rendered her doubly hateful to him, proposed to discuss the subject with Blocksford only just so far as might strengthen him in the belief of her attachment to *him*, if he found the feeling of affection for her really there,—in order, by the results, to realise the anticipations of Mortimer, the hopes of Wilkins, and the schemes of Mr. Brassey, by breaking up the establishment at Sadgrove, and reducing its master to a state of single blessedness, consequent upon a separation from his wife ; in which position Magnus, with his satellite, the attorney, would have him as completely under their control as he had been when Magnus had, in earlier days, involved him in all the misfortunes, except one, which had debased his character and destroyed his peace.

Magnus knew Mortimer's failing — his ruling passion, it might be called — the morbid sensibility which the consciousness of his own demerits had excited in his mind, and which, as we know, could be roused to something like positive madness by the belief (which more or less continually existed) that he was despised, not only by the world, but by Helen ; and with the knowledge of her character which the reader has, in the course of his perusal of these pages, probably obtained, and which Magnus completely pos-

sessed, neither the one nor the other could be at a loss' to
perceive that the mode of treatment which Mortimer
adopted to uphold his fair fame was precisely that least
calculated to produce the desired effect upon his wife,
devoted as she was to him in the outset, warm and
affectionate as was her heart, and generous as was her
disposition.

Mortimer made no allowance for the innocent gaiety of
a girl—for what else could she be called?—who had
been courted, flattered, followed, and cried-up to the skies
in the best London — society, whom he had suddenly withdrawn from the sphere which she brightened, into a retirement which she was prepared to enjoy, if the seclusion had
been enlivened, as she in the romance of her mind had
hoped it would be, by the affectionate confidence of the
man she loved, and that interchange of feeling to which
she had looked forward as the charm of a married life.

But no: she had been disappointed. The estrangement
of the neighbouring gentry on their first arrival at Sadgrove
struck her forcibly; for it must be confessed, that Helen's
notion of retirement included the presence of an agreeable
society, though, when she found circumstances prevented
the enjoyment of it, in *her* case, she was the first and
readiest to disavow the feeling, and declare her dislike of
country visitings. And from whom did she learn the reason
of this defection, but from the last woman on earth who
ought to have been near her?

Does anybody suppose that Helen, brought up as she
had been in the full glare of worldly knowledge, could long
continue undeceived as to the nature of the influence which
Madame St. Alme asserted at Sadgrove? Even if her own
innocence had blinded her to the character of the intimacy
which at some time or other must have existed between
Mortimer and the Countess, the amiable activity of her
friends was not wanting to enlighten her.

Was it by this association, strenuously insisted upon by
Mortimer, that she was to be taught to respect his morals?
Was it by his almost insane destruction of his once favourite
retreat, the Fishing-Temple, the chief ornament of his
place, because Helen had inadvertently made some remark

upon his earlier attachment to it, which he misconstrued into a reproach, that she was to estimate his mildness and moderation? Was it by his uncourteous violence, upon more than one occasion, to young Blocksford, for whom Helen entertained feelings of genuine friendship, chiefly excited by the kindness which Mortimer himself generally exhibited towards him, that he expected to seal her lips or close her eyes, so that she might neither speak to Francis nor look on him? If so, he was radically wrong in his system and principles. Helen, conscious of her rectitude, would rather increase than diminish her kindness to Francis the moment she found herself insulted by Mortimer's suspicions; — and so in every case where their tempers clashed.

After the birth of her first child, the boy, she felt that she had a new claim upon Mortimer's affection, and, to do him justice, his attachment to his children was enthusiastic; but still the same gloom hung over him : the second, as we know, was a girl, but she never excited so much of his affection as the elder one. The main point he carried, in consequence of these additions to his family, was that of prolonging his stay in Worcestershire; and during one of the three matrimonial years they did not visit London at all.

All this would have suited Helen, because the professing nun at the altar, on the day when her long tresses are shorn from her head, is not more determined to fulfil her vows than Helen was to assimilate herself to Mortimer's tastes; but she required in return that confidence and assurance of regard which she knew she merited. Perhaps — who knows? — if they had at once proceeded to Sadgrove, and the meeting between them and the St. Almes had never taken place, all might have been well: it is, however, now too late to speculate upon possibilities; and truth compels us to say, that after the most implicit devotion to Mortimer through a long and serious illness, when, as the reader already has been told, she watched the life-breath quivering on his lip, his earliest remark, when his returning health gave sufficient vigour to his mind to make it, was, that he was afraid his young friend Francis must have missed her society very much.

That *was* a crisis ; it was from what then occurred that
Mortimer discovered the danger of trifling with his wife's
feelings.    Her anger at that moment knew no bounds.    It
was an awful sight to see one so young, so beautiful, and
so inherently good, torn and tortured by rage which
amounted to frenzy.    Nothing, but the dread of causing
the cruel man who had inflicted the wound a relapse, prevented her at that moment from flying to her father : her
feelings had way, and a torrent of tears relieved her agony
of mind.    Mortimer was alarmed — subdued — and peni-
tent ; and endeavoured to assure his wretched wife that
what he said was meant in perfect good-humour.    Helen
insisted that Francis should never more visit the house ;
but Mortimer persuaded her into the relinquishment of this
condition by again assuring her of the playfulness of his
remark, and by pointing out how injudicious it would be
to exclude him from their society : a circumstance which
would naturally call for explanation, and, though absurd in
itself, give some colour to a story to which, in fact, there
was not the slightest foundation.

So completely did Mortimer live for the world — out of
which he had removed — that the idea of any " history "
with which his name was connected getting abroad, agitated him just as much as did the apprehension of the
occurrence of anything like " a scene " at home.    Peace,
upon the present occasion, was restored ; but it seems probable that one of the conditions of the treaty was, the exclusion of the countess from the Sadgrove circle during the
following season.

Well, — *revenons à nos moutons,* — Helen is gone.    To
all eyes, but especially to those of Mortimer and his friend,
the agitation of Blocksford was evident ; and the looks
which these two personages interchanged during the forenoon were eminently expressive of their thoughts upon the
subjcet.

" I hope," said Lady Mary, " dear Mrs. Mortimer will
meet with no accident or worry on her journey.    I am
used to travelling alone : if I could not muster courage for
*that,* while poor dear Sandy is abroad, I don't know what
I should do."

" In these days," said Mortimer, " as I told Helen, there are not many perils to be apprehended."

" Come, Blocksford," said Magnus, " let you and I take a stroll down to the river. Is the fly up yet?"

" I — I" — stammered Francis, " have some letters to write; one to my mother — and ——"

" Dutiful boy!" said Lady Mary, with one of her most captivating looks. " What a charming thing it must be to have such a son! — don't you think so, Mr. Mortimer?"

" Delightful!" replied the master of Sadgrove, not quite master of himself, inasmuch as he knew enough of Lady Mary to know that she seldom said any thing without a meaning."

" I hope," said Magnus, " that when *his* boy grows to be of the same age as Mr. Blocksford, he will be equally dutiful, and that we shall be all alive to see it."

" Is the countess coming over?" said Lady Mary carelessly to Francis, knowing perfectly well that she was *not*.

" I really don't know," said Francis, convinced at the same moment that she had not the slightest intention of doing any such thing.

It would be a waste of time to linger long over these minor manifestations of worldly feelings, while so much of importance to all parties immediately concerned is impend_ing. The amusements of the day went on as usual, and Helen was not much missed. At the accustomed period the carriages, the horses, and every thing which contributed to make up the amusements of the morning, were at the door, as usual; even while poor Helen was travelling from scenes of gaiety, in which her heart reposed not, to those of grief and sorrow, in which it was so deeply engaged. What then? Lady Mary, seated in her delightful little carriage, with the two fat, long-tailed ponies, which she loved to drive before her, and Lord Harry, whom she loved to lead, by her side, thought no more of, and cared no more for, the weeping Helen, than — let me take of care what I say — for the veteran Captain Sanderstead, with the cocoa-nut head, who was pottering about in the Mediterranean, and whom she had married only because he was next but one in remainder to an earldom.

To anybody else there might have arisen some difficulty, as being the only lady left at Sadgrove; — not so to Lady Mary: she could not go to the Fogburys before a certain day, and she had nowhere else to go to in the intermediate time. In a woman of spirit, there is nothing like independence; and the moment she establishes a character for that truly English quality, she may do what she likes. Having dropped a few "*natural*" tears for Helen's misfortunes, she soon resumed her wonted gaiety, and volunteered the command of the house, which Mortimer, with one of his sweetest smiles, accorded her; and so she was installed accordingly. By the inability of the Fogburys to receive her exactly on the day which she selected, she was compelled to endure the society of Magnus, whose presence was rendered doubly hateful by the consciousness that he was a universal spy — a watchman-general of every thing that was going on; still, as the evil was irremediable, she resolved to fasten herself upon the master of the house during her brief stay, in order, if possible, to divert the attention of the lynx from the *liaison* which had been notorious for many years.

All her ladyship's playfulness, however, went but a little way to divert Mortimer's attention from the marked abstraction of Blocksford. His almost sharp refusal of Magnus's invitation to walk; even his evasive answer about his mother's visit — a new proof of his powers of dissimulation — struck deeply into Mortimer's mind; and every succeeding ten minutes added to the conviction that Helen's departure was the cause of the alteration in his manner.

*N'importe* was the motto — and away went Lady Mary and Lord Harry in the pony phaeton — away cantered Harvie — and away rode together Mortimer and Magnus — Francis having for the first time declined their society. What the surmises of the two friends might have been, far be it from us even to conjecture. All that is necessary for us to know is, that having enjoyed — (what sort of enjoyment it was can best be appreciated by reading in the papers of some respectable gentleman deceased, who for many years had *enjoyed* an exceedingly bad state of health,) — their itinerant *tête-à-tête,* they returned to the house, where matters went on much as usual till dinner-time.

The effects produced by the first tocsin are not evident: but when, upon this special occasion, the second had been rung, and the extra ten minutes' law had been given, and dinner was actually announced, and no Mr. Francis Blocksford appeared, great, indeed, was the consternation of the master of Sadgrove. Nobody knew when or whither the young gentleman had gone : Mortimer was fearfully agitated ; Lady Mary, however, preferring her soup to the suggestions which were made by sundry persons as to his destination, said, with one of the sweetest simpers into which her brightly-vermilioned lips could twist themselves, — " I really don't think it either fair or hospitable to make such very urgent inquiries after a gentleman of Frank's age."

The mystery in which his sudden departure was involved was exceedingly amusing to Lady Mary, to Lord Harry Martingale, and to Captain Harvie ; it was not at all un-pleasing to the magnificent Magnus ; but it was torture to the master of Sadgrove.

Not a sound that could reach the dinner-room fell upon his ears but he hoped it might be connected with the re-turn of Francis. He sat and talked, and even smiled, but the extraordinary disappearance of this hated — yet na-turally loved — rival was an event against which he could not successfully rally ; and Lady Mary being the only lady left, and being not at all anxious to immure herself in the drawing-room alone to wait the "coming men," she lingered longer than usual at the dinner-table, until her stay seemed to Mortimer eternal, so anxious was he to make further inquiries after the missing guest.

At length her ladyship quitted her seat, and Mortimer, excusing himself to the men, hastened to his own room, whither he instantly summoned the trusty Wilkins — as, indeed, Wilkins was perfectly well assured he would. From his evidence, delivered, as the reader may easily imagine, in the manner best calculated to give it point, Mortimer gathered that Blocksford had ordered one of the saddle-horses — Mortimer's horses ! — and having first despatched a boy with his "carpet-bag"—in all probability to Worcester — had told the groom who brought out the horse, that, if he did not return that evening, the boy who had taken the bag could bring the said horse back to Sadgrove.

"The boy with the horse is not returned?"

"No, sir," said Wilkins, "I believe not;—but—I—should think it very improbable that Mr. Blocksford will be back to-night."

"Why?" said Mortimer; "what are your reasons for thinking so?"

"I don't *know*, sir," said Wilkins; "but ———"

Now the villain *did* know; he knew, as certainly as *we* do, that Francis Blocksford's departure from Sadgrove was consequent upon Mary Mitcham's journey towards London; and, although he did *not* know the particulars of the arrangement for carrying Frank's mad scheme into execution, he could in one instant have relieved Mortimer's mind from the growing anxiety with which it was tortured, and, by the mere mention of the girl's name have diverted his thoughts into another channel, and saved that which might have been a happy family from misery. But that was not *his* game: he was playing for the ruin of old Crawley, and the stewardship; and the fellow had the hardihood to thank Providence for having afforded him so speedy an opportunity of gaining his point.

Shakspeare, who has better said than anybody all that can be said of the passion of jealousy, has described its workings so minutely, that it would be as vain as useless to expatiate upon its power over Mortimer. For months — nay years — he had been brooding over the one subject which had so long taken possession of his mind. That he had subdued his feelings — or at least the expression of them — generally speaking, is true; but the feelings were still at work: and now that he connected the disappearance of Francis with the excursion of Helen, so far from being surprised, he seemed to consider it what he might have expected; and, in that mood, scarcely repented that he had not sooner interfered to terminate their intimacy.

"No, no," said Mortimer, "you are right — he will not come back this evening: — no, no; he will never come back to this house!"

' " I don't think," said Wilkins — " I — it would be best to wait — it is not nine yet ; — and ———."

" Oh! I shall wait — what else have I to do? She went at three, and ———."

" Who, sir?" said Wilkins, with a look of honest anxiety.

" My wife!" said Mortimer.

" But, sir," said Wilkins, " you don't think that Mr Frank is — is ———."

" I *do* think so," said Mortimer, pale as death, and· trembling with emotion — " and so do you !"

" I shouldn't have ventured to say a word on the subject, but — it *is* strange."

" Strange !" said Mortimer — " it is certain — sure as we are alive here in this room : — let me but wait to know it. However, I must go to the dinner-room ; they will wonder what keeps me from them. Let me know the moment Francis comes — ha, ha, ha !— he come ! — no, no : — let me know when the boy returns with the horse — for that will be *it :* — but not a word to anybody else !"

Mortimer returned to his guests not much calmed, as we may suppose, by this interview ; and Wilkins, who pretty well anticipated the results, proceeded to his room to arrange the accounts, which were under his special care, in order that if his master should put his threat of breaking up his establishment and flying from England into execution, no impediment in the way of business, as far as his department was concerned, should be interposed.

By ten, as had been anticipated, the boy and horse arrived. Coffee was being served in the drawing-room : Wilkins made his appearance, and crossing over to Magnus, who was expatiating upon the splendour of the view from one of the windows of one of his houses, gave him a letter, and, as he was quitting the room, stopped before his master, and in an under-tone mentioned that the boy was come back.

If he had plunged a dagger into his master's heart, he could scarcely have done him greater injury. The realisation of his own prophecy — of his own anticipations ! — prepared, .as he thought himself, and resolved, as he

believed himself, upon the line of conduct he should adopt,
the news was worse than death. He started from his
chair, and hurried again to his room, bidding Wilkins
follow him.

"There's a letter from Mr. Frank," said Wilkins.

"A letter!" cried Mortimer: — "where there's life
there's hope! — we may be saved yet! God grant it
may be so! What letter? — who has it? — where is it?"

"I delivered it to Colonel Magnus," said Wilkins;
"it was directed to *him*."

The next moment brought the colonel to the door of
the room.

"Is Mr. Mortimer here?" said he, seeing only Wilkins.

"Yes, sir," said the man.

Magnus entered the room, trembling with agitation, and
looking as pale as usual, and even paler than his friend.

"It is so! — I know it all!" cried Mortimer.

Magnus paused — spoke not — but, not aware of the
humiliation of Mortimer, and the consequent importance
of Wilkins, waited as if he expected him to leave them.
Wilkins, however, seemed inclined to stay.

"Leave us!" said Mortimer. Wilkins obeyed, but his
move was not a long one: he went no farther than the
lobby, and his ear was forthwith at the keyhole.

"Frank," said Magnus, you must be firm; — you must
bear up against it."

"Merciful Heaven!" said Mortimer.

"See what the serpent you have cherished says!

"'Dear Colonel—You must have wondered at my refusal
to join you in your ramble this morning: at that moment
my fate was sealed. The step I have taken is ruinous —
but it was irresisible. How I can ever palliate my conduct to Mortimer, or to my mother, I know not. Pursuit
is, however, useless: before this reaches you, I shall be far
on my road to Oxford, whence we start across the country.
London is not our destination. I should not have written,
but that apprehensions might be entertained of her safety.
Our minds are made up to the consequences.

"'Yours, in a state of distraction,
"F. B.'"

Mortimer sat with his eyes fixed on his friend as he read this most unfortunate letter. Magnus had been so short a time in the house, since his last return to it, that he had never noticed either the beauty of Mary Mitcham, whom he had never seen before, or the attentions which Blocksford paid her; and Mortimer, conscious of a somewhat too tender feeling towards the girl himself, had neither mentioned her in his letters to Magnus, nor attracted his notice to her since his arrival at Sadgrove. Possessed, therefore, with the one idea—wholly engrossed by the one doubt— the words of this dreadful note were an unequivocal corrohoration of all his worst suspicions. Magnus, being of course ignorant of any thing connected with Francis and Mary Mitcham tending to throw a doubt upon the real meaning of the communication, felt that it could refer to nothing but that to which he certainly had rather enconraged his friend to look forward. The question is, if Magnus *had* known enough of the family politics to put another construction upon the note, whether he would openly have done so, seeing that it would have instantly cleared up the affair, and produced a satisfactory explanation, which was exactly what he did not desire?

That he did not even think of the possibility of its referring to another person entirely, is most true; therefore, as it is not fair to question the intentions of others, he must be exonerated from the charge of wishing to keep up the misconstruction to which it was liable. But what will be said of that basest of human beings, the listening menial, who, having overheard the letter, and satisfied himself that its construction would further his villanous objects, raised himself from his knees, and, hurrying to his room, filled a brimming glass of port wine, and drank, by himself alone, with fiend-like exultation, a bumper to the success of his odious machinations?

Mortimer heard the letter out; and, when Magnus had concluded, threw himself back in his chair, and covered his face with his hands: Magnus himself, overcome by a thousand contending feelings, no matter what their character, spake not.

" My friend," said Mortimer, starting up, " my heartstrings are bursting!—my brain is on fire! I have lost her!—she is gone for ever!—and with whom? God is just! Now am I taught to feel the tortures I have myself inflicted. When *I* triumphed, and Amelia was the part-ner of my flight, *her* husband felt as I do now. What did I care then? He was my friend!—what of that? Had he *not* been my friend, the opportunities would not have occurred which led to his disgrace. *I* am disgraced!— *I* am dishonoured!—and by him who —— Oh! is this to be borne? Will my mind hold?—will my senses remain?—What am I to do first? I knew it—I knew it all!—saw it—fool that I was to suffer it! But it is now too late?—all *that* is past:—what is to be done is for the future."

There can be no question but that the existing state of affairs was such as to puzzle the wisest counsellor. The relative position of Blocksford and Mortimer, Magnus knew, must prohibit any appeal of that nature to which it is the fashion to resort under similar circumstances; but he knew enough of Mortimer's temper, and saw enough in the convulsive agitation of his features, to assure him that the result would be terrible.

After a pause of a few moments, Mortimer, apparently more collected, said,—

" Magnus, leave me: my course is resolved upon. My heart is broken; but I have deserved all that has happened: it is right it should have happened. I will act for myself; no human being shall be involved in the responsibility. Go back to the drawing-room—say I am unwell—that I am gone to bed—that we shall meet in the morning:—but do not drop a hint—do not whisper—do not even look so as to create a suspicion about Helen. I have not been unprepared for this: my arrangements have been made for some time in anticipation of her defection. But what meanness!—what hypocrisy!—and how unlike her!— the anxiety—the pretended mad anxiety to visit her father!—and now to discover that she has abandoned him, to fly with this wretched boy! Go, Magnus, go; let us part for the night; to-morrow you shall see me: I shall be calmer, more tranquil."

" I really do not like to quit you, my dear Mortimer," said the colonel, " under such circumstances. I ———"

" I entreat as a favour that you will," said Mortimer. " Rely upon it, I am right; I do not think over this matter now for the first time. I shall probably not go to bed early, for I have much to do. No word henceforth shall pass my lips upon this subject; and remember that no allusion is to be made to my disgrace to-morrow. The public news of the event cannot reach this till the next day. Save me from the humiliation of condolence from the hollow friends who are here. To-morrow Lady Mary goes, and, of course, Lord Harry. — Ha, ha, ha! I can see *that* — can join in the world's laugh against the brave and worthy man absent on his country's service ; — and yet ——— Oh! mercy!—mercy! Leave me, my dear friend, but, as you value my existence, keep my secret."

After some ineffectual remonstrances, Magnus acceded to Mortimer's desire, and quitted him; the latter pledging himself to discuss in the morning, with calmness the details of proceedings naturally resulting from the event which had occurred. Magnus accordingly returned to the drawing-room; and before the party separated for the night, every individual composing it knew that Mrs. Mortimer and Frank Blocksford had gone off together. Each one of the guests had his joke against his host, even though the sneer were clothed in sympathy, and the ridicule tempered with pity; but Lady Mary at length broke up the conclave by sagaciously observing, " that if men who had excellent wives did not know how to take care of them, they had nobody to blame but themselves."

## CHAPTER IV.

THOSE who have voyaged on the deep blue waters of the mighty ocean know that, when the tempest rages in its greatest violence, it has the effect at times of keeping down the sea. In the struggle of elements the imperious wind lords it over the rebellious waves, and holds them in sub-

jéction: so with Mortimer's rage and passion. The pangs
he felt were beyond expression. To have looked at him
when Magnus had left him, pale, calm, and collected, one
might have fancied his heart wholly occupied by grief; but
no one would have suspected the real character of his sufferings, or the resolution to which he had come in order to
avenge his wrongs.

Wrongs!— poor, wretched, deluded man! Oh! if the
miserable master of Sadgrove could have been permitted
the privilege we have assumed, of looking into that letter-
box which we have examined, what ruin might have been
averted! But no — the wickedness of man must work its
way, and treachery still triumph over the best of us. To
fancy that, having pre-determined his wife's guilt, he
should, upon the " trifle light as air," (for so it was, inasmuch as a second or third reading of the giddy boy's letter
to Magnus must have somehow explained the fatal mistake,) adopt the course which was eternally to blight his
hopes of happiness, and turn the amiable Helen a solitary
outcast upon the world! Yet so it seemed destined to be.

After Magnus left him, Mortimer proceeded to the
nursery: he found his children sleeping soundly. When
they first met his eyes, his agonised mind was relieved by
a burst of tears, which he in vain endeavoured to conceal
from the nurse who was watching over them. She saw
him weep, but of course said nothing to *him* — only re-
marking to the maid, after he had left the room, that she
really did not, till then, think master cared so much for
missus — attributing this burst of sorrow to the temporary
absence of Helen in London.

From the nursery he proceeded to his wife's boudoir.
The first objects that met his eye were the two drawings
which Francis had made nearly three years since for
Helen; these, not with the violence of rage, but with all
the method of sober sense, he dragged from the ribands
which held their frames to the wall, and tore into atoms.
He next searched for her writing-desk, feeling all the
while like a thief in the night, and dreading lest he should
be interrupted. He found it not, for it had been put into
the carriage with her dressing-case and other personal re-

quisites. This added new fuel to the flame; it was in their writing-desks that wives left the records of their sin: — Amelia's writing-desk rose up in evidence against him on his trial — but no; — Helen was more artful, and had taken the precaution to remove the proofs of her criminality.

Poor Helen! — there was not in her desk a line that might not have been read at the market-cross; she did not even know that Mitcham had been so attentive as to give it to be packed in the carriage: however it was gone.

He passed into their bed-room, and stood and gazed wildly and vacantly around him, his limbs trembling, and the cold dew standing on his forehead; again that agonising pang which all of us have felt when a loved object has been lost to us, and all the scenes of happiness which we have enjoyed together have flashed into the mind, shot through his heart. What! was he never to behold her more? — NEVER? — oh, dreadful word! — And where — where was *she* at the moment he was calling on her name? He flung himself upon the bed, and madly seizing the pillow she had abandoned, clasped it to his breast, and covered it with kisses.

Why, in the name of all that is dreadful, should these people be eternally parted?

All this evil — all this misery, although ripened to perfection by the accidental circumstances with the real nature of which we have been made acquainted, were caused originally by a want of candour and of confidence, which alone were necessary to secure the devotion which Helen sincerely felt when she married her husband. But there was a fate in it, or rather, let us say, a retributive justice, destined to inflict on Mortimer the pangs which it had been his glory to inflict on others. If Mortimer's conscience had permitted him to have taken his bride in the first instance to her future home, the excursion to Paris would have been avoided. From that excursion sprang the renewal of his acquaintance with the countess, and the fatal association with her son.

Had Helen never been subjected to an intimacy with the countess, happiness with Mortimer would in all probability have been her lot; and most assuredly would it have been so, if the prejudices which the countess constantly kept alive in his bosom against his exemplary sister, Mrs. Farnham, had been suffered to subside, and he had consented to her visit to his young and high-spirited wife at the time she volunteered to come to her.

Having quitted the bed-chamber, Mortimer proceeded down the back-stairs to his own room; and, as he passed a door which opened into the hall, he heard the merry laugh still ringing in the drawing-room where his friends were still assembled. The echo of their mirth made him shudder: it would be many a day before those walls resounded with joyousness again; — and how much of retrospect that thought involved may be imagined.

The night that followed was a night of horrors. Mortimer, having wreaked his vengeance upon the memorials of Francis, rang and summoned Wilkins to council.

" Lock the door !" said Mortimer, ashamed and afraid of being detected by Magnus in this confidential association' with this creature.

Wilkins obeyed, delighted to find that he had superseded even the colonel.

" To-morrow I leave this place — for ever !"

The words were music to the miscreant.

" I take my children with me; but this you are to keep secret till the morning. I have found you faithful: — you have my confidence. I had promised that if — and I *did* foresee it — I should be driven to this extremity, you should be left in charge of every thing. I will prepare such a paper as shall insure you this control. Tell me, have you been near the rooms which that — I cannot describe him — occupied ?"

" I have been there, sir," said Wilkins, " and, as you suggested, placed his clothes and papers in order."

" Papers !— were there any letters ? — any ⸻ ?"

" Yes, sir," said Wilkins, with an affected hesitation.

" Go — go," said Mortimer — " fetch me those papers; and, mark me — not to-night, but early in the morning, tell some of the women to pack up my wife's wardrobe."

" Sir !" said Wilkins, with a well-acted start of horror.

"Ay, all," said Mortimer. "Her maid is gone with her, but let any one of them pack up every thing that is hers — jewels and all, if they are left: let Bennett do what Mitcham would have done if she had been here: — I cannot even look upon the records of other days: — have them all packed up, and Mr. Blocksford's things you can arrange. Send them all off; send them — I know not where — best to her father's, whose sickness and illness are all a fiction. I will write to him myself during the night. You will see to all this: get ready whatever accounts are necessary to be settled, and to-morrow I start for the Continent with my two poor babes — but remember, not a word to anybody: you shall have powers left to manage every thing after my departure."

It would be impossible to describe the savage joy which animated the heart of this wretch when he found all his hopes and expectations on the point of being realised. It seemed not only that fate had favoured him, but that Mortimer was actually playing into his hands in a manner almost calculated to make him sceptical as to its reality.

That Mortimer was virtually mad at the moment, there can be little doubt: his placidity of manner, combined with the firmness of purpose which we have noticed, was sbsolutely awful. To have seen him and heard him making arrangements for the morrow, the effect of which would be his eternal separation from his wife, and the utter ruin of all his hopes of tranquillity, in a tone and temper suited to the common-place directions for a short journey, or even an excursion of pleasure, would have startled anybody who was aware of his habitual violence. Wilkins was astounded, and could scarcely bring himself to believe that his deluded master really intended to fulfil all he now projected. It will be seen that this active minister determined to leave no effort untried to bind him to his purpose.

Having sent Wilkins to his manifold duties, and had a few minutes' conversation with Magnus, who came to him, on his way to his room for the night, in which he referred but slightly to the all-engrossing subject, appearing anxious to act entirely for himself, without either seeking advice or involving others in any responsibility, he parted from him with the ordinary phrase of " We shall meet at breakfast;" and, as the door closed upon him, felt relieved from a world of anxiety by finding himself again free to take his own course. That it was a desperate'— a cruel course, no one that knew Mortimer's temper could doubt.

In the midst of his doubts of poor Helen he had, as we have seen, satisfied himself that the illness of her father, if not altogether a fiction, had been greatly exaggerated in order to bring about the journey. The affectionate anxiety of his unhappy wife to see that father — to hear his last sigh — to receive his last blessing — was construed into a haste to put her criminal designs into execution ; and her ready acquiescence in his desires that she should go without him, was perverted into an unquestionable manifestation of her eagerness to be rid of his society.

Convinced of the validity of his reasonings, he resolved, in his uncertainty as to the destination of Helen and her paramour, to write to Batley himself the history of her crime, detailed in all its horrors, and his final renunciation of her, consequent upon its commission. Thus would he wreak his vengeance upon him who, according to the colonel's account, had hunted him down as a husband for his giddy, flirting, portionless daughter; and stab the parent while he spurned the child.

" Nothing," says Lavater, " is so pregnant as cruelty. So multifarious, so rapid, so ever-teeming a mother, is unknown to the animal kingdom : each of her experiments provokes another, and refines upon the last; though always progressive, yet always remote from the end." When Mortimer came to the resolution of writing to Batley, he almost smiled with satisfaction at his own ingenuity in devising misery for his wretched friend—for so he once esteemed him; and, as if no thought of his brain, no action of his life, might be uninfluenced by the fate which hung over him, he was roused from the reverie into which he had fallen by a gentle tap at the door of his room. The usual " Come in " presented to his view ' the miscreant Wilkins, who, according to orders, had brought down the papers which lay on Blocksford's table. They consisted of two or three sonnets, partly original, and partly transcribed from those popular receptacles for nonsense upon stilts, the Albums and Annuals ; but, above and beyond all these, was the hastily written note, which we know he had addressed to Mary Mitcham the evening before, when, at the time, he did not anticipate the opportunity of speaking to her again.

" I have brought the papers, sir."

" Right," said Mortimer — " give them to me : there, go — leave me ! — and do not come again till I ring, or at least till you are going to bed. Bring fresh lights ; I shall stay here till morning : I have much to do."

. Wilkins did as he was bid, and Mortimer, anxious not to betray his weakness before the fellow whom he had raised to the state of a confidential counsellor, waited till the lights were brought, and the man again gone, before he ventured to read the papers which the crafty villain had laid before him.

The first, the second, the third, were harmless verses — all of love, but no more ; the fourth and last which he looked at was the note — *the* note which the reader re-members.

Mortimer shuddered as he read : his eyes traced and re-traced, as if they were written in blood, the concluding words, ," Remember — twelve !" The thought — the notion that the consummation of Helen's ruin and his own disgrace was at that period pending, maddened him ; and, as if to sharpen every pang which his misery involved, at that moment — that very moment the clock on the mantel-shelf struck the hour of midnight ! — Mortimer started at the sound, clasped his hands on his forehead, and fell backwards in his chair.

Truly, indeed, did Mortimer admit the power of retributive justice. Some fourteen years before this night of misery, he had borne from the arms of a confiding husband the wife whose affections he had won from her lord — to the very house now desolated by imaginary crime had he brought this treasure of his heart: there had she lived with him, in all the feverish anxiety of unhallowed love —there had she died;—and now came the avenger. What on earth is so terrible as the black retrospect of an ill-spent life! What made Mortimer's firm heart ache, and his proud spirit quail before the ills which oppressed him, but the hôrrid consciousness of what he *might* have been, and the dreadful recollection of what he *had* been? The combination was tremendous: his former crimes—his still continued acquaintance with the countess — the result of that acquaintance—the flight of Helen—her partner in that flight.

All this flashed into his mind—flashed and burned and raged: his brain was maddened! He started from his seat, and, having fastened the door, proceeded to the table on which lay his pistol-case: he opened it, took out one of the deadly weapons, deliberately loaded it, and then walking towards the glass which was over the fireplace, and looking steadfastly and intently on it, placed the muzzle of the pistol to his throbbing temple.—One instant and all would have been over: a faint sound caught his ear: it was the waking cry of his infant boy. It acted like magic: the hand that held the pistol fell motionless.

"God is just!" said Mortimer—"but he is merciful. I hear the cry of my child—my deserted child: it is a call from Heaven!—humbly, devoutly, gratefully do I respond to it! For my children, abandoned by their mother, will I live—yes—and consent to bear a load of wretchedness, and be a mark for the finger of scorn to point at."

He listened; no further sound was heard:—the poor babe had sunk to sleep again.

With equal calmness and firmness Mortimer drew the charge of the pistol which had been destined to send him from a transitory world of woe to one of eternal punishment; and, replacing it in its case, returned to his chair, and, after a self-communing of some hour or so, commenced with a firm hand the following letter to his father-in-law.

"Sadgrove, One o'clock, A.M., April 11, 18——.

"You may imagine the embarrassment in which the

necessity of writing this letter involves me; it is a task of terror, but it must be performed. Helen has left me. I have for a considerable time doubted, suspected, and believed her guilty : I have even hinted as much to her; but, with an artfulness which I too late discovered to be her characteristic, she appeared to be unconscious of my meaning. It is all over now. Under the pretext of visiting you in an illness which I have good reason to believe never afflicted you to the extent described, she quitted Sadgrove yesterday at three o'clock : at dinner-time Mr. Francis Blocksford was absent : he has not returned; and I have before me proofs that they met at Oxford, and thence took their departure for some other destination.

" Far be it from me to reproach you for the character of the education which you were pleased to give Helen. In the earliest stage of my affection for her, I always felt the difficulty which a man would incur who should try to domesticate so much spirit and pretension, excited as they had been by your own unlimited indulgence, and the flattery of a herd of fops and fools, who set up an idol on a pedestal in society, and worship it, God knows why !

" When you persecuted me back to London, after I had quitted it, disgusted with Helen's conduct with Lord Ellesmere, whom she jilted, I was weak enough to believe my authority sufficiently strong to render her the means of restoring me to happiness : but the delusion was brief ; I soon found that the opinions of some very old friends of mine, that I had miscalculated the results of my marriage, were but too well founded.

" In fact, my life has, for the last three years, been a life of misery — misery created by an anxiety which I can scarcely describe ; she universally betrayed a want of confidence in me ; she always appeared estranged from me — rather afraid of than loving me with the cordiality which her apparent ingenuousness had led me to expect. A marked effort to be obedient, and never to thwart my wishes, and a strained desire to be remarkably careful never to do what she thought I should not like, were not the genuine fruits of a real attachment. In fact, she never could forget that I had been devoted to another ; and, as I know from unquestionable authority, listened with pleasure to histories of my former indiscretions: nay, to such an extent did she carry this, that very soon after our marriage I found, by accident, in her room, a volume containing the trial between Hillingdon and myself about Amelia, selected out of ten thousand other volumes in my library for her special edification. When I charged her with this needless anxiety to detect my faults, she made some pretext that the Countess St. Alme had sent it her for some other purpose, I forget what. This the countess, however, positively denied to me; and, though I did not condescend to mention the matter again, it has remained registered in my mind.

"You may wonder how what may appear to you a trifle can occupy me at a moment like this, when she has worked her own destruction and my disgrace; but, as I dare say we shall hereafter find the lady justifying her crime by something like retaliation, I think it important to mention a circumstance so illustrative of the spirit upon which she has uniformly acted.

"To you, who must be aware of my early intimacy with the Countess St. Alme, the fact that Mr. Francis Blocksford is the partner of Helen's flight will perhaps be particularly shocking: that I have sense enough left to write these lines is my only wonder. I thought that Helen, during the last few months, must have known more of this connection than she previously did, because she made a condition that the countess should not pay her annual visit here this season; now I believe this exclusion to have had its origin only in an apprehension that the countess might have detected the intrigue in progress between her and Francis. If she were to object to an association with the Countess St. Alme on any other score, I have only to observe that you were aware of the intimacy which had long subsisted between us, as well as of the delicacy of the countess's position in society, and that you never objected to her being an inmate in your daughter's house.

"The line I have determined to adopt will have been taken before this reaches you. By noon of this day — for it is past midnight while I write — I shall have quitted Sadgrove with my children, who must be preserved from the contamination, which any further intercourse with their wretched mother would involve. . I shall write by this post to my solicitors to take such steps. as may be considered necessary, and to provide Helen with the income secured to her either as jointure or by that most extraordinary clause in the settlements, inserted, I believe, at *your* suggestion, ' in case of separation.' I really do not know which to compliment the more, your instinctive providence as a parent, or your knowledge of the world as a man, in having made this special condition : in either case it does you infinite credit, and your daughter shall have full benefit of your ' diplomacy.'

" What measures I may subsequently adopt will be matter for consideration : the initiatory proceedings which I have instituted are simply those of sending out of my house every thing that belongs to the. fugitives. As my hand is stayed against vengeance on the partner of her flight by ties of which the world may not. be told — they may be guessed at — it will be of little consequence to. me whether or not I rid myself of a guilty wife by a course of law ; the feeling which must spare the life of Francis Blocksford may extend even to saving him from ruin in, a worldly sense of the word. His fortune is small, for his mother's husband was reduced in circumstances before his death.

" As I have already said, as far as money matters. are concerned, your unfortunate daughter is, *providentially*, at her ease, and therefore my care for her is at an end. She may rest assured I shall never farther interfere with her : the connection she has formed may secure her a happiness on which I shall never intrude, and a tranquillity which I have no disposition to disturb. The only point on which I take my stand is, as regards the children. . Within eight-and-forty hours of the moment in which I. write this, they will be removed beyond her reach, never to be restored to her sight until they are old enough to shun her whom, if her own misconduct had not destroyed the claim, they ought to have loved and obeyed.

" This is the last letter that you will ever receive from me. Ten thousand circumstances had estranged you from

me previously to this disgrace; your brother I never could
endure; and the person whom you have thought proper to
marry appears to be by no means an unlikely confidante in
the scheme, the success of which imperatively separates us
for ever.

" I have left to the servants the immediate removal of
every thing belonging to Helen, with directions to send the
whole to your house, and with it whatever the viper I have
cherished in my bosom may have left behind him. I dismiss them both for ever from my mind:—my deepest,
bitterest, curses be upon their heads! Mark me again, in
conclusion — no supplication with regard to the children,
no remonstrance no palliation, no explanation, nothing
will avail;—I repeat solemnly and finally, they will never
see their unnatural mother until I have taught them to hate
and despise her.

" If I fancied you were an hundredth part so ill as the
deceiver painted you, I would not inflict this letter upon
you; but I discredit the whole story. If you feel yourself
aggrieved, or are romantic enough to espouse your daughter's cause, a line to my solicitors shall afford you the opportunity of vindicating *her* and exposing *yourself* at any
time you may suggest. Whatever reflections your conduct
in the arrangement of our marriage may suggest, I shall
not so far shelter myself under my own opinions as to
refuse you, even now, the consideration of a gentleman.

" F. M."

Mortimer, besides this letter, wrote to his solicitors, ap-
prising them of what had occurred, and directing what
should be done; for, be it understood, that men who have
extensive connections and various concerns to conduct invariably use more than one lawyer. In the management of
his affairs, properly so called, Mortimer naturally consulted
his solicitors, who were men of honour and of reputation;
but in the jugglery of usurious money-raising, compro-
mising dirty actions, and all such business, one of the
grubbers of the profession was retained: hence his association with Mr. Brimmer Brassey. Quick, ready, and
indefatigable, there was scarcely any capacity in which

Mr. Brassey would not act to oblige an aristocratic client; but as to confiding to him the conduct of a case like this, Mortimer would as soon have cut off his right hand as permitted their names to be associated in the public papers, through which, as it seemed probable, the particulars must eventually be given to the world.

But now, could it be believed that Mortimer — mad — absolutely mad, as we have already seen — on the verge of suicide, and reckless of all that might happen, should be able to sit down and write a letter of studied insult to his father-in-law, wherein (but see how that marks his character) he could rake up the smallest circumstances that had occurred years before, and been treasured in his mind, to justify his earlier suspicion of his wife, who, at the moment he was writing this very letter, was on her knees praying for his happiness and that of her beloved children, before she sank into a deep and sweet sleep, induced by the journey and excitement, which so overcame her bodily strength as to give her repose during a night through which, if it had not so happened, her anxiety for her suffering parent would have kept her awake.

Mortimer read over what he had written, and felt a savage pleasure in pointing every word which he knew was best calculated to inflict pain upon his unhappy father-in-law; and when he folded the letter, there was a sort of triumphant satisfaction in his manner of concluding his elaborated cruelty highly characteristic of the man : nay, so far did he carry his solicitude to mark the firmness of his resolution, even in the tempest of his feelings, that he took the trouble to hunt out from a long-neglected drawer a seal upon which *his* arms alone were engraved — the Mortimer bearings without the alloy of the Batleys : — so much method was there in his madness.

Having achieved this measure, of the atrocity of which, to be sure, he was not conscious, Mortimer proceeded to write to his solicitors, to his bankers, and to every body in any degree professionally interested in the great move he was about to make; so he remained until nearly four o'clock in the morning, when, worn out with fatigue of mind and body, he threw himself upon a sofa, and fell into a restless slumber.

It is not permitted us at this moment to know what had been passing at Oxford during the same period; but it *is* permitted us to hate and loathe the wretch who could have saved all the misery which we see in progress, and who, while his wretched master was agonised even to the point of suicide, was sleeping soundly and dreaming of future prosperity.

---

## CHAPTER V.

It may be imagined that Mortimer's slumbers were neither sound nor refreshing. That nature was so far exhausted as to sink under the excitement, and that he actually did sleep for two or three hours, there can be no doubt: — but what a sleep! — and where! We must not indulge in reflections; we shall have enough to do within the short space allowed us, to record events.

As Wilkins was the last person with his master at night, so was he the first called into council in the morning; and the first subject upon which the master consulted him was, the method of getting rid of his visitors without exciting a suspicion of the cause of their sudden dispersion, or letting them know his determination to quit Sadgrove in the course of the day. This trouble he need not have taken, for upon a mere hint of his difficulty, his prime minister informed him that all the carriages, except that of Colonel Magnus, were ordered to be at the door immediately after breakfast, and that two sets of post-horses had already arrived from Worcester, having been sent for as early as six o'clock.

" How is this?" said Mortimer: " Lady Mary did not mean to go for two or three days; — nor Harvie — nor Lord Harry."

" No, sir," said Wilkins, " but, of course, after what has happened, they naturally think their presence would.

not be very desirable; besides, they could not stay after you were gone, and ———"

" Gone !" exclaimed Mortimer — " 'after what has happened'—what do you mean? They know nothing of what has happened ; — or what I propose to do." ·

" Lord bless you! sir," said Wilkins, " they knew all about it last night. The colonel, I believe, told Lady Mary in confidence, that she might go; she mentioned it to Lord Harry, that he might go too: and as they were both making arrangements for going, it was thought best to let Captain Harvie into the secret: and then the horses were to be ordered early in the morning: and then, after Lady Mary's young lady had undressed her, and seen her to bed, *she* knew of it; and so after supper it was generally talked of in my room, and the under servants, of course, could not long remain ignorant of it."

" Then I am proclaimed!" said Mortimer. " I thought I could have trusted Magnus with any secret, but I was deceived."

" Ah! sir," said Wilkins, " there is no relying upon anybody in *this* world. The colonel, to be sure, might as well have kept it snug: as for me, the grave is not more silent than I was, until I found that everybody in the house knew as much as myself."

" That being the case," said Mortimer, " I will see none of them : it will save us all a world of effort. Say that I am too ill to leave my room. Tell Colonel Magnus to come to me as soon as they are gone. Desire the nurse to bring the children here: I will not run the· risk of encountering any of them in my way along the lobby to the nursery : let me see the children directly ; — and take care that I have four horses here at two o'clock. When the colonel leaves me, bring breakfast here, and then let me see your books, and I will settle the current accounts, leaving you a sufficient sum to pay the Worcester bills and bills here."

" This, sir," said Wilkins, endeavouring to hide his exultation under an expression of sorrow, " is a sad and heavy day! — more hearts than yours, sir, will ache at this break-up."

· "I knew too well how surely it must happen," said
Mortimer, "but the blow has fallen, and talking will not
relieve me from its weight; so do all that I have told you,
and let it be understood that I do not join my friends at
breakfast."—"Gracious Heaven!" added he, "what re-
volutions may be effected in one day! This time yesterday, Helen, the admired and flattered mistress of Sadgrove,
was surrounded by companions vying to do her honour;
and now —— I must not think of this: I have much to
do that must be done on the instant. My heart might,
even now, relent, if I hesitated. The children must be
saved, and, to save them, they must be instantly placed
beyond her reach — ay, even beyond her knowledge of
their destination."

"Why, sir," said Wilkins, "it is a hard thing to do,
but if you feel it right to take such a step, why, the sooner
it is done ——"

"Ay, and the more decidedly it is done," interrupted
his master, "the better. When *they* are safe, I shall return to await the call of my father-in-law, if my letter
should have roused his anger. As for the wretched cause
of my misery, he ——"

"Ah! sir, there it is. Of course *you* couldn't think of
raising your hand against *him!*"

"Why, sir?" said Mortimer, doubting the evidence of
his senses when he heard these words.

"Oh! sir," said Wilkins, apparently alarmed at his
master's sudden excitement, "I don't know, sir."

"You *do* know, sir!" said Mortimer — "and how do
you know it?"

"I beg a thousand pardons, sir! I ought not to have
said what I did."

"Said!" exclaimed Mortimer, "you may say what you
please — you have *said* nothing: — but what do you
*mean?* Why should I not raise my arm against Blocksford as against any other violator of my honour?"

"Why," said Wilkins, doubtful whether he should proclaim his knowledge of the whole truth — "he is your
godson, sir — named after you; — and — his mother,
sir ——"

" Well, sir, what of that?" said Mortimer. " You mean more than you say. What have you heard? — what do you know? Why speak of the Countess St. Alme? — what has she to do with her son's criminality?"

" No, sir ; but considering how intimate you have been for so many years, and ——"

" That's not the point," said Mortimer. " Tell me, this instant, what your knowledge — what your suspicions are, to induce you to believe that there exists some ·tie which holds my hand from taking just revenge upon his villany !"

" I wish I had not said a word upon the subject," said Wilkins.

" But you *have* said a word upon the subject," cried his master, " and more words you must say before I part with you. You know I implicitly trust you — in return have I not a right to demand an explanation of an expression which conveys so much ?"

" It was foolish to let the word drop," said Wilkins, whose affected unwillingness to let his master know how perfectly his secrets were in his keeping, produced exactly the effect upon his victim which he intended — " but what I meant, sir, was — and you will not be angry — I spoke without thinking — I did hear, some twelve months since, that Mrs. Woodgate said openly that Mr. Francis was more likely the son than the godson of her master."

" What ! — Woodgate, Helen's former maid?" said Mortimer.

" The same, sir," said Wilkins, " and *I* believe she knew more than she chose to say."

" This makes matters worse than all," said Mortimer. " If Woodgate knew it, Helen knows it — at least," cheeking himself, " whatever there is to know."

" I believe, sir," said Wilkins, " Mrs. Woodgate did not stick at trifles to find out any thing she wanted to get hold of. In fact, I have caught her listening, with her ear to the keyholes of rooms in which parties have been conversing — ay, fifty times, sir."

" Infernal treachery !" exclaimed Mortimer.

" Horrid duplicity !" murmured the man.

" Why did you not tell me of this at the time ? " said Mortimer.

" I did not like to intrude, sir. I always fancy that a master to whom one servant informs against another may fancy it is done to get unfairly into his good graces."

" Ridiculous ! " said Mortimer. " So, then, it is generally thought here that Mr. Blocksford and I are more nearly related than our names would lead the world to suspect."

" No, sir," said Wilkins, " not generally. Miss Nettleship, Lady Bembridge's young lady, said that *her* lady was never comfortable where the Countess St. Alme was ; and she thought it a pity she was so much here ; and she remembered something, and that sort of thing ; and Miss Nettleship said she could not make out what her lady meant, because she never spoke out ; but when she had done talking about it, she laughed, and said she really thought Mr. Francis Blocksford very like you, which, considering your Christian names were the same, was odd enough."

How much farther this dialogue might have been carried, it is impossible to say : it was one of deep interest to Mortimer, inasmuch as it convinced him that Helen herself had been enlightened upon the point of Frank's connection with him, and that her knowledge, or even suspicion, of such a fact, increased her criminality in a tenfold degree. A tap at the door terminated it : it was Magnus who solicited admission.

This unexpected arrival induced Mortimer to change his arrangements, and desire Wilkins to send the children when he rang.

The dialogue which ensued between the friends may easily be imagined. Magnus did not attempt to dissuade him from his resolution of not again seeing his guests ; and when reproached with having let slip the secret which he had promised to keep, he satisfied Mortimer by a justification of his conduct founded on the belief that it would be much better — as he himself admitted — that the party should break up without further discussion, which would have been impossible if an attempt to conceal the truth had been made, inasmuch as during breakfast the conversation would naturally have turned upon Mrs. Mortimer's journey and the absence of Blocksford; after all, there must have been some explanation of the reason for Mortimer's dismissing his guests, and quitting his house so abruptly: — "And so," said the colonel, "eventual publicity being inevitable, I considered it the best way to let so much of the truth be understood last night as would relieve you from the necessity of telling the whole of it this morning."

To the man earnestly anxious to get rid of his visitors, and to put into execution a decisive scheme of cutting at once the ties which held him to Sadgrove, a much less plausible explanation than that of the colonel would have been perfectly satisfactory; Magnus, therefore, was commissioned to convey the best wishes of Mortimer to his friends, who were well pleased with the arrangement, seeing, as Lady Mary observed, "that nothing is so unpleasant as melancholy stories; and as to condolence, it is the greatest possible bore to both parties: and on such occasions it was so difficult to know what to say, and the poor man would, of course, be so wretched: and then they had known Helen so intimately — and it was altogether so exceedingly shocking!" — having said all which, Lord Harry Martingale handed her to her carriage; and finding that by some mistake neither his carriage nor the horses which he had desired his servant to order had arrived, her ladyship was good enough to offer him a seat in her britscha as far as Worcester, if he was not afraid to venture, and if Colonel Magnus would not be censorious.

Thus flirting, giggling, and chattering, the dear friend of the Mrs. Mortimer of yesterday, left her desolated home for ever, not having thought it necessary to take one look at the innocent babes whom she had left behind.

When they had all departed, Magnus returned to his friend, who then left his room, and visited again, and, as he felt, for the last time, the drawing-room, the favourite boudoir of his wife, and all that *suite* which she had so lately cheered by her presence. The song she had last sung still rested on the desk; the flowers she had last gathered still bloomed where she had placed them; and as Mortimer gazed on them in the dead stillness of his de·

serted house, big tears rolled down his cheeks. All her
grace and beauty, all her kindness to him during his long
and painful illness, seemed in array before him. He
thought of her as dead: his conscience accused him of a
thousand faults — a thousand weaknesses — for his heart
was melted; and if his friend at that moment had made
the effort, the probability is, that his departure would have
been delayed, and all might yet have been well. But no:
— the friend was anxious that he should go; and when
he saw how powerfully the recollection of his lost Helen
affected the wretched husband, he led him from the scene
which so excited him, and begged him to bear up against
a misfortune now inevitable, and make those arrangements
which his own honour, and justice to his children, demanded
that he should forthwith conclude.

The clock had not struck three when Mortimer, with
his two children and their nurse within the carriage, and
his valet in the rumble, bade adieu to Sadgrove, having
arranged his domestic affairs, and installed Wilkins in an
office, the nature of which was not precisely defined, but
which, according to the authority which his master had
left in his hands, gave him full control over the domestics,
and by the unguarded terms in which it was couched,
rendered him absolute monarch of Sadgrove, with the
power of dismissing or retaining the subordinate members
of the establishment, his verbal instructions being, to
reduce them to the smallest necessary number. Mr. Fisher
appeared delighted at the intelligence of his principal's
retirement (he did not call him master), as it permitted
his aspiring spirit to take an unencumbered flight to the
regions of taste, where his genius would be far better
appreciated than in the house of a gentleman of a gloomy
temper, who ate roast mutton and salad *par preference*.

Mr. Tapley also received notice that his services would
be dispensed with, with perfect composure. It was, however, wholly out of his power to make up the cellar-books
before Mr. Mortimer's departure, and therefore his vouchers
were necessarily to be rendered to Mr. Wilkins: this took,
as appeared in the sequel, two or three days properly to

arrange, during which period it was observed that a most extraordinary number of *empty* bottles left the Hall in sundry carts for Worcester.

That Mr. Wilkins and Mr. Tapley were *d'accord,* nobody can doubt: they agreed in rejoicing at the advantages of such an occurrence as that which had taken place, and in possessing a master who, however democratic his taste might be as to the *cuisine,* had a soul above the paltry consideration of his cellar.

The reader need not be informed that the unfortunate Crawleys were speedily ejected from their tenement, as the consequence of their father's removal from his stewardship — a measure which Mr. Wilkins represented as the result of an order from Mr. Mortimer. Ten days were allowed the old man to render his accounts and make his retreat; which effected, Mr. Wilkins set the workmen belonging to Messrs. Dabbs, Splash, and Wypum, painters and paper-hangers at Worcester, to fit up in the nicest possible manner the very agreeable house which the ejected steward had for many years occupied, previously to paying their bill for work done at Sadgrove, in which his little " commission" was, of course, included.

Such being the state of affairs at head quarters, we may perhaps be permitted to take a glance at what has been doing elsewhere.

In the outset, it may be as well to inform the reader that Mr. Jacob Batley, having realised as much money as he considered essential to his own comfort, had retired from business and taken a box at Walworth, where he ruralised during the morning, but whence, in order to prevent being forced into any thing like hospitality, he regularly proceeded to town in a low four-wheeled carriage, built to hold only " one inside," and drawn by one horse, in which he dinrnally journeyed to " The Horn," where he dined, varying his habits only inasmuch as that on Sundays he favoured his brother with his company.

In order to place himself completely *a l'abri,* and out of reach of the effects of mercantile speculation, he had disposed of his business, and invested in the funds the net profits which he had realised. He thought that if he bought land, it would entail upon him innumerable cares; bad tenants, appeals to his consideration, legal involvements, and a thousand other inconveniences. By his present arrangement, he had nothing to do but to receive his dividends, and as they amounted to a sum vastly exceeding his annual expenditure, Mr. Brimmer Brassey, who managed all his matters, was directed to continue investing the overplus, though no power could induce old Batley to make a will. In fact, his horror at the mere suggestion of "giving or bequeathing" any thing was such, that his legal adviser felt his tenure of office dependent mainly upon his evitation of that extremely disagreeable subject.

During John Batley's illness, Jacob had called but once, and that was on the Sunday preceding Helen's visit to London. On that occasion having come to dine, and being told that his brother was worse and in bed, he asked the servant whether his master would be able to go down to dinner. The man shook his head, and, with a countenance expressive of a melancholy anticipation that he would never go down down to dinner again, replied in the negative. Jacob answered with a grunt, and then, in a tone of vexation caused rather by the disappointment of his expectations as to his dinner, than by any thing like fraternal solicitude, let down the front glass of his " sulky," and, addressing his coach-boy, said,——

" Well, then, Thomas, I suppose you must just go back to the ' The Horn.' I have no pity for such people. ' I never was ill in my life. Psha ! — there, go on."

As regards Helen's progress from Sadgrove to Oxford, her resting there, and the events which occurred during her stay, the reader is pretty well prepared for the results. True to her faith to Francis, Miss Mitcham, throughout the journey, never permitted herself to be betrayed into an expression calculated to awaken her mistress's suspicions of the step so shortly to be taken by her and her devoted, infatuated lover: actuated by the same spirit of affection for him and submission to his will, she contrived, after having seen Helen safely deposited in bed, to conduct her part of the enterprise with so much dexterity, that it was not until nine o'clock on the following morning, and after

Mrs. Mortimer had rung thrice, that the diffident fair one was] returned " absent without leave." Upon a " reference " to her room, it appeared that her bed had not been slept in ; but on the table was left·an open note, containing these words :—

" When Mrs. Mortimer inquires for me in the morning, tell her my flight is voluntary, and that I am safe and happy : all I regret is, the inconvenience my departure may occasion her. I live in hopes of forgiveness.

" M. M."

Helen, who was really interested in Mary's fate, was entirely relieved from the anxiety she felt on the first announcement of the young lady's elopement. In her present state of solicitude about her father, the trifling discomfort arising from her maid's defection gave her little uneasiness ; one of the chambermaids officiated quite satisfactorily : and when Helen sat down to her hurried breakfast, the footman who was in attendance on her was questioned as to any knowledge of the circumstances connected with Mitcham's unexpected departure ; but he denied all cognisance of her movements; and Helen contented herself by writing a hasty note to Mortimer, informing him of the circumstance, and of the progress she had herself made.

Having finished these matters, Mrs. Mortimer pursued her journey, and reached Grosvenor Street at about four in the afternoon.

When Mortimer quitted Sadgrove, in order effectually to shut out any thing in the shape of explanation from his wife or her father, he left directions with Wilkins to transmit whatever letters might arrive, to his solicitors in London, who received instructions to keep them until they should hear further from him ; nor was even Wilkins trusted with the knowledge of his master's destination, his secrecy on that point being induced by the anxiety that the unfortunate Helen should obtain no clue to the place to which her children were to be removed : all that was known to anybody was, that the horses were ordered to Tewksbury. In consequence of these arrangements, Mortimer did not receive the following answer from his wife until many days after' its date.

" The vile, atrocious letter which you addressed to my father, and which was received this morning, came too late; — he was dead before it arrived : — and if any thing can alleviate the grief which I feel for the loss of the kindest and best of parents, it is the blessed reflection that even in death he escaped the savage insults with which you had proposed to assail him, and a knowledge of the infamous falsehoods with which you have dared to calumniate me.

" I write this at his bed-side : my eyes are fixed upon his calm, placid countenance. The hand which would have avenged his injured child is clasped in mine.; and I thank God that he was taken from me unconscious of the degradation to which I have been subjected, or the fate to which I am doomed.

" What a heart must that be — which I once believed I had gained — in which could rankle, year, after year, feelings such as those which your letter avows, and which could lead you to address such a letter to the father of a devoted wife, while stretched on the bed of sickness and of death !

" If I could humble my proud spirit to answer the odious allegations which that letter contains, I would ask you what grounds I have ever afforded for your suspicions of my honour, or your belief in my duplicity and deception? — I would inquire upon what actions of mine was founded your opinion that the much-censured openness of my mind, and consequent freedom of expression, was assumed ; or why you should imagine that a feeling of jealousy, founded upon a long-past attachment of yours to another — the quiet of whose neglected grave I envy — should have damped my affection for *you*, or have estranged me from the only man on earth I ever loved, and whose happiness it was my object, as it would have been my pride, to secure, or rather restore, regardless of all the bitter insinuations of the perfidious woman with whom you thought it wise and honourable to associate me, and whose criminality you have thought proper to establish, while endeavouring to aggravate the character of the crime of which, in your baseness, you have thought me capable ; by doing which, even if I had been the guilty creature you suppose me, you have drawn down upon your head' the execration of every honest man and honourable woman, by admitting, in your rage, that you have made the partner of your early crimes the inmate of your house, and the constant associate of your wife.

" To that woman — fiend is a better word — are attributable all those acts of mine which have entailed upon me your anger, and excited the belief that I was desirous of keeping alive the memory of your conduct towards the last of your victims. I knew it was useless to endeavour to undeceive you, or gain your confidence; but from the earliest of my errors, the visit to the Fishing-Temple (since sacrificed to your violence), to the last, having reference to the subject which I never wished to touch upon, my counsellor and adviser was the Countess St. Alme.

"You reproach my dead father with not objecting to that person's constant residence in our house. My father, knowing the world so well as he did, and therefore, perhaps, not judging too favourably of its ways, could not have conceived the possibility of such conduct as yours has been to me : on the contrary, having entrusted me and' my honour to your charge, the very fact that the person in question was selected by *you* as a companion for me, decided at once any doubts which might have floated in his mind, and convinced him that the rumours he had heard injurious to her character were unfounded.

" But why do I condescend to argue or explain ? Why should I declare my entire ignorance of Mr. Blocksford's destination, or why should I even write his name, considering who he really is, and why the secret of his origin has been divulged ? I even doubt the truth of the assertion, for I cannot believe that a son can inherit candour, honour, and sweetness of disposition, from a father who possesses no such qualities, but who, base and wicked himself, dares to criminate a wife whose only defection from the path of rectitude was her unfortunate marriage with him.

" I tell you, my father is dead — lies dead here before me ; but I answer your letter as *he* would have answered it,

had he lived to receive it.    Your offers of money and allowances I despise and reject: you may tell your solicitors to
burn the settlements, and cancel whatever documents exist,
by virtue of which I have any claim upon you.    I should
feel myself debased and degraded, even as much as if I
were what your vile imagination has painted me, if I accepted one shilling of your money: all I ask is, in return
for the injuries you have done me — for the insults you have
heaped upon me, the history of which must soon become
universally known, — all I ask — and I will accept it even
gratefully — is the restoration of my children.

"Mortimer, I am innocent! — God knows the truth,
and the world will know it too! Whatever may be the
fate of Francis Blocksford — whatever his objects, his intentions, his destination, they are all alike unknown to me.
A few days must clear up the mystery of his disappearance, and establish my reputation clear and unsullied;
there can, therefore, be no reason why my children, whom
I love better than life, should be kept from me. But mark,
the concession must involve no condition as to a reconciliation with their father: — no, Mortimer — once-loved
Mortimer — the die is cast! If your letter had contained
simply the outpourings of a heart deeply affected, and the
effusions of a mind highly excited by designing persons,
and filled with the belief of my criminality, which the
lapse of a few hours would have disproved, I might, devoted as I have been to you, have made myself believe that
your violence, acting under extraordinary delusion, was the
result of ardent affection. But it is not so: it is the outbreak of a volcano which has been long smouldering in
your breast, and in its fury such horrid truths have been
developed, that our separation must be eternal! Therefore,
when I ask for my children, I ask for the possession of
them as an atonement for the wrongs I have suffered —
for the suspicions under which I have laboured — for the
meannesses to which I have been subjected — for the deceptions to which I have been a victim. Let me have my
children, and I am content to bear all the ills the world
may have in store for me; they shall be always at your
command, whenever you desire to see them, and you may

trust me for teaching them to love you: *their* love may be reciprocated as mine never was: rely upon it, they shall never hear of your faults from *me*.

" As yet, dearest, dearest babes, they are unconscious of the fervour of a mother's affection, and even now scarcely miss me; but ask yourself, even as a matter of policy, whether it would not be wise to confide them to *me*, at least till they arrive at a certain age. I could not condescend to ask a favour where I claim a right, but that the ties of nature are not to be broken — a mother's love is not to be quenched; and if my *claim* is denied, —on my knees, even to the destroyer of my happiness, will *I beg* for my children.

" The struggle is over, and my proud spirit has yielded; even now, I beseech you to let me have them : — upon all other points I am firm, and repeat the words which are registered in my heart — OUR SEPARATION IS ETERNAL !

" Why this decision, on my part, is irrevocable, I need hardly explain: it is not founded entirely upon your groundless repudiation of a fond and faithful wife, which in itself, taken with your reasonings on the subject, would be sufficient to justify it but; I have made it, because no reconciliation, even were I, for the sake of my children, to submit to it, could be permanent after an avowal such as yours — of your suspicions of me — and of facts which supersede all my suspicions of yourself: I repeat, therefore, our separation is eternal !

" It may be right to say that I shall remain here with my father's widow until after the funeral of my beloved parent; that here I shall expect your reply to my claim — my request, if you will—as to the children. As my letter of yesterday, written in the blessed unconsciousness of your real character and disposition towards me, has acquainted you with the disappearance of my maid from Oxford, I need not recur to that event, which appears to *me* unaccountable.—It may be only an additional incident in my history of horror.

" I cannot close this as I began it : I cannot end the last letter I shall probably ever write to a being I have loved as I have loved you, without one prayer, that the

God of Heaven may forgive all the cruelty and injustice
with which you have requited my affection, and that you
may be made sensible in time for a due repentance of those
crimes, the memory of which has destroyed the best attributes of your nature, and irrevocably sealed the misery of
your wretched

" HELEN."

" I despatch this to Sadgrove, whence, I presume,
should you really have left it, your letters will be forwarded."

The reader will see, that as Mortimer quitted Sadgrove
on the afternoon of the 11th, having despatched his letter
to Batley so as to go by that afternoon's post to London,
his wife's first letter of the same day, despatched from
London to Sadgrove, giving a detailed account of Miss
Mitcham's disappearance, did not reach Sadgrove till the
forenoon of the 12th; so that their letters crossed each
other on the road; and Mrs. Mortimer, agitated and over-
whelmed by her anxiety about her father, which rendered
the defection of her maid a matter of almost indifference at
the moment, not having thought it necessary to write from
Oxford (her doing which might have saved the whole of
the misery which ensued), both *her* letters arrived after
her husband's departure, and, having undergone the most
ingenious scrutiny at the hands of Mr. Wilkins, who rolled,
twisted, and peeped into them with indefatigable curiosity,
were, according to the orders which that admirable servant
delighted to obey, returned to his master's solicitor in
London.

With regard to the feelings which existed between poor
Helen and her mother-in-law, the barbarity of Mortimer's
letter, which Mrs. Batley, at Helen's desire opened, decided the question.   Helen, in the hey-day of her youth
and gaiety, thought it either fine or right to set down Mrs.
Catley as vulgar, or a bore, or something to find fault with,
without exactly knowing why; but affliction softens the
heart, and the voice of sympathy in grief is sweet.   Teresa,
in the hour of desolation, was all to Helen; and her un-

affected sorrow for the loss of poor Batley seemed to unite the two in bonds, not only of friendship, but affection.

In the midst of the misery with which they were over-whelmed, Mr. Jacob Batley, who had not been present at his brother's death, nor paid the slightest attention to him during his illness, arrived in Grosvenor Street. He was, of course, admitted, and Mrs. Batley saw him. Of Helen's arrival he probably knew nothing, and certainly cared no more.

"Well," said Jacob, "so it's all over: — poor Jack! I suppose you have killed him with kindness. Well, there's no use in grieving for what can't be recalled. Have you looked for a will? I dare say he never made one: died intestate, most likely; — so much the better for next of kin."

"My dear sir," said Mrs. Batley, "I have never given a thought to any thing of the kind. The few short hours that have passed since my dear husband's death have been devoted to feelings wholly disconnected with any such points."

"Feelings!" said Jacob; — "ay, feeling, I dare say, is a mighty fine thing; but feeling won't settle an intestate's estate; nor will it bury a dead man. What undertaker d'ye mean to employ?"

The widow looked at Jacob, utterly unable to answer — scarcely to comprehend — his question.

"Why, dear me!" said Jacob, "this is nothing new to *you!* Don't you recollect how nicely we buried your first, Kit Catling? What I was thinking is, that you better have the same chap this time as before. Black jobs come fifty per cent. cheaper at our end of the town than at this; and I was saying to myself, as I was coming up here, that it would save trouble and expense to have poor Jack put in the same vault with Kit, at Islington: it will be only to get Chipp, the stonemason, to pop on an epitaph under the other, and leave a space for something about yourself, when your time comes, unless, in due time, you should like to take a third."

"Dear, Mr. Batley," said Teresa, "how you talk! I

c c 3

am sure I shall be too grateful to you to relieve me from
the details of the sad duties to be performed.  I am not
aware that he expressed any particular wish as to the
place of interment" — and here she burst into tears: "and
I ——"

"Well, then — there, that 'll do," said Jacob; "I'll
manage it all.  But you had better hunt about for his
will, or send down to his lawyer's, — it *may* be there;
because he may have had some fancy as to where he should
like to be buried; and it's always as well to know how a
man has disposed of his property before another man en-
gages himself in troublesome business on his account."

Jacob had, unconsciously, hit the point.  The moment
Teresa was made to think it possible that, if there were a
will, it might contain some request or instruction relative
to his funeral, she acceded to his worldly suggestions, and
despatched a note requesting the presence of one of the
partners in the firm of her solicitors; while Jacob, who
never even asked to see Helen, set off in pursuit of his
favourite undertaker.

After Helen had rallied all her energies to write to
Mortimer, she sank into a state of unconsciousness, and
was led from the chamber of death to her own room,
where, overcome by fatigue of mind and body, she sank
into a sleep which lasted nearly four hours, and from
which she awoke calm and refreshed.

As it turned out, Jacob was wrong; there *was* a will,
and Batley had, with the exception of a few legacies, be-
queathed everything to his wife: there were, however, no
injunctions as to the funeral, and the necessary arrangements were therefore left in the hands of his eccentric
brother.

In the midst of her afflictions, Helen, whose anxiety for
the welfare of Miss Mitcham was really sincere, did not forget to write to her mother, acquainting her with her flight,
and her inability to account for it.  The morning after
the death of poor Batley, Helen, however, received a hurried note from the unconscious cause of all the mischief
which was in progress.

" Newark, April 12. 18—.

" Dear Mrs. Mortimer, — You must forgive me: the anger of my poor dear mother, and the vengeance of my father-in-law, I care little for, in comparison with the fear I feel of having put you to some inconvenience. Secure now from all pursuit, I halt for five minutes to apprise you of Mary Mitcham's perfect safety : by to-morrow night she will have ceased to bear that name. I have written to her mother by this post. I never shall repent of the step I have taken ; she is as good as she is lovely. I have written to Mr. Mortimer three times, and also to Wilkins, to desire him to send my moveables to the hotel to which we shall go on our return. I hope and trust Mr. Batley is better — much better.

" We shall go to London on our return from the north. Mary sends her dutiful regards, and joins in imploring pardon for having so abruptly quitted you. I had no alternative. Yours most sincerely,

" FRANCIS BLOCKSFORD."

A double mystery was unravelled for the unhappy Helen by this communication. Francis *had* justified Mortimer's suspicions as to an elopement, though his suspicions as to the companion of his flight were unfounded. Helen could not help feeling mortified that Francis should have taken so indiscreet a step, and almost reproached herself with having permitted him to speak to her so much in Mary's praise. His letter produced another effect upon her heart and mind: it was the first communication she had received from him since she had become acquainted with their relative position as regarded Mortimer : *that* knowledge had, almost unconsciously, changed the character of her feelings towards him, and invested him with an interest, the nature of which she could scarcely characterise, but which, if thoroughly analysed, would, more than any thing, have proved the nobleness of her generosity, and the intensity of her devotion to her husband.

It would pain — perhaps tire — the reader to touch more than lightly on the preparations for the mournful ceremony which awaits us all, and which were, as we know,

placed under the direction of uncle Jacob; but there are
certain circumstances connected with the events of the
week to which we *must* refer.

On the Thursday arrived, without note or notice,
trunks, boxes, &c. addressed — " To Mrs. Mortimer,—
to be left at J. Batley's, Esq., Grosvenor Street ; " — containing all her wearing apparel, jewels, trinkets, &c. —
and all Mr. Francis Blocksford's " moveables," guitar,
painting-boxes, &c. included, which, coming without one
word of communication from anybody, seemed to decide
her fate.   The supposed community of interest between
Francis and herself, so forcibly implied by her husband's
directions, struck the wretched Helen to the heart.   She
could have loved Francis Blocksford more now than she
had ever fancied she might have dared to love him, and
have felt the deepest interest in his welfare; and this —
even *this*—would she have felt for Mortimer's sake.   But
no :—her fate was sealed — her destiny decreed !

In the course of Jacob's visits to Grosvenor Street, he
never expressed the slightest desire to take a last look at his
brother's remains ; on the contrary, he positively declined
to visit them.   He discussed with perfect philosophy the
goodness of the lead, the soundness of the wood, the fine-
ness of the cloth, and the excellence of the nails, of which
the coffins were composed — for those he *had* seen, — but
he could not bear the sight of death.   He did not like to
think of dying: money would be of no use after death ;
and even if it would, he must leave *his* behind him : — and
why should he look at a corpse ? — he could'nt bring it to
life !—could it do any good ?— no — and he would rather
not.

Nevertheless *there* he was every day, and there he dined
every day.

" Helen," said he, " I don't see why I shouldn't pick a
bit.   You eat nothing—no, nor even Teresa — neither
of you: I suppose grief spoils the appetite.   I never
grieve ;—I can always eat.   Now they always serve dinner here every day just as usual ; it is quite as well I
should have my bit here, as that it should be wasted, and
I go and pay for my feed at ' The Horn : ' "—accordingly,

he did "pick his bit," and drink his wine; and as neither of the ladies were very communicative, remained four days in blissful ignorance of what had occurred at Sadgrove, and endeavoured to impress upon Helen his readiness to be reconciled to Mortimer by drinking his health in a bumper, before the disconsolate sufferers sought refuge from his coarseness in flight.

But with all this, and fifty other oppressive inflictions from the same quarter, the poor mourners were compelled to bear—indeed, more—for, under the circumstances in which they were placed, they were necessitated to rely upon this uncouth creature for advice in all the arrangements which were to take place: in the midst of which difficulties came to Helen the letter from Mortimer's solicitors, of which we have heard before, touching the income to be allowed her according to her jointure, during her separation from her husband, in which they assured her, by his direction, that he had no intention to proceed legally in the case, (nor could he have done so under *any* circumstances, considering what had happened to himself,) and that she might draw on them for the amount of her income quarterly.

Proud in the consciousness of innocence — broken down by sorrow for the loss of her parent — mad with disappointment at the failure of all her hopes of happiness with her tyrant, and resolved to let the world judge between them, when the fit season should arrive — conceive what her feelings were, when uncle Jacob presented himself, just at the dinner-hour, in a state of grief such as she had never suspected him capable of feeling.

" Dear Mr. Batley," said Mrs. John Batley, " what has happened to excite you in this extraordinary manner?"

" Oh!" said Batley, " he is gone — gone,—and I never shall see him more!"

And he burst into a flood of tears.

" My, dear uncle," said Helen, distressed to see the old man so agitated, " it is our duty to endeavour to reconcile ourselves to losses like these. Heaven knows how *I* suffer; but we are told to hope."

" Hope !" said Jacob " what hope have I ? — none !
He will never, never come back, Helen !"

" No," said Teresa, " but perhaps we may go to
him !"

" I've thought of that myself," said Jacob ; " but I
doubt the possibility : no chance of our meeting !"

" Why, dear uncle ?" said the subdued niece.

" The world he is gone to is a wide one," said old
Batley ; " but if I thought I could see him once again, I
should be very ready to follow him this very night."

" My dear Mr. Batley," said Mrs. John, " what has
caused this sudden desperation ? It is something new to
see you so excited."

" New !" said Jacob ; " to be sure : I have lost my
all — every thing on earth I cared for ! — I have ——"

" Oh ! calm yourself," said Helen. " I certainly am
little calculated to offer advice or comfort — but *do* reflect.
The laws of Providence are just."

" Ay, ay," said Batley, " I dare say they may be : —
but what are the laws of New York ? Providence and
New York are two different places ; there can be no doubt
he has gone to the latter."

The ladies looked at each other, and made up their
minds that Jacob's grief had turned his brain.

" Where, uncle ? " said Helen.

" Oh !" said Jacob, " I can't tell where ; but he's
gone, that's all we know ; and if I could but find out, I
would be after him in the first ship that starts ——"

" Of whom are you talking ?" said Mrs. John Batley.

" Why, what should I be talking of ?" exclaimed Jacob.
" You all know, I suppose — all are aware of the heavy,
the ruinous loss I have sustained ?"

" Too well, uncle !" said Helen, bursting into tears.

" Well then, if you are," said Jacob, why ask about
it ? I have been every where in the city to-day, to discover where he is gone to; — but no — not a trace !"

" Of whom, uncle ?" said Helen.

" Of the scoundrel who has given me the slip," said
Jacob — " Mr. Brimmer Brassey, my infernal attorney

who has taken French leave, having carried off with him all my funded property, having, for some time past, been kind enough to permit me the use of a certain portion of my dividends."

The mourners, though released from the surprise which Jacob's conversation had excited, were by no means pleased with the truth, which, as far as Mrs. John Batley was implicated, appeared likely to throw her into a difficulty.

"What did you think I was talking of?" said Jacob, seeing that his announcement of the fact had astonished his companions — of Jack? — ha, ha! — not I — he is settled: — no use going to look after *him!* — but as I am still here, and mean to stay as long as I can, it is something to me to look after the fellow who, as it at present appears, has swindled me out of all my property. If the smash is what it looks like, I must come and live with you, Teresa, for your seven hundred and fifty per annum is snug."

Involving, even as it did, Mr. Jacob Batley's ruin, this disclosure, and the mode in which it was made — the tone which the narrator had adopted, coupled with the knowledge which his hearers had of his unqualified selfishness, rendered the *denouément* almost entirely uninteresting. It seemed to them as if meanness and selfishness had met their reward; and the only part of the history which excited the auditors, was that which involved the possibility of his future domestication with the widow.

True it was, however, that Mr. Brimmer Brassey, after having, by dint of wriggling and shirking, and sneaking, in every possible way, contrived to secure Jacob's confidence, and by having obtained for him high and usurious interest for loans and mortgages, and charged low costs for the *legal* arrangements necessary to their *illegal* settlement, become master of all his available funds, and having lost largely on the turf and at the gaming-table, and having been threatened with a strike off the Rolls, not to speak of ulterior proceedings, had taken his departure from this country, his voluntary destination being supposed to be America. If his exile had been longer delayed, it might have become a matter of compulsion, and the fertile shores of Australia have been honoured by his presence.

The astonishment which Jacob's explanation caused was, at all events, not so great as that which the manifestation of that grief had previously excited, when attributed to excess of fraternal feeling. Helen herself felt assured, that as her early suspicions of Mr. Brassey's character had been realised by his flight, it would turn out that her apprehensions as regarded Mortimer's property were not groundless:—but, alas! what, now, was Mortimer to *her*, or *she* to Mortimer!

The funeral of poor Batley took place on the following Saturday; and though Jacob was as little moved by the event as if a dog had died, he attended upon the occasion, and, with the physician, occupied one mourning-coach of the two,—the other containing three equivocal personages somehow connected with the family; and the remains of the once aspiring, gifted member of society were thus conveyed to what his brother*thought proper to call the " family vault," at Islington, where they were deposited side by side with those of his predecessor in Teresa's affections.

The procession moved from Grosvenor Street at one, by Jacob's especial direction, in order that when the ceremony had terminated, the mourning-coach might set him down at " The Horn" in time for his dinner, as near four as possible.

## CHAPTER VI.

LEAVE we the house of mourning to trace the progress of the master of Sadgrove, who, having excluded the possibility of communication with his wife, or her friends, pursued his route to Southampton, where he first announced to his servants his intention of proceeding to the Continent.

Here a difficulty occurred, for which he was not prepared. The nurse, who was exceedingly fond of the children, no sooner heard of her master's scheme of going to France, than she at once announced her determination not to budge one inch from England : — no ; — she would do any thing — every thing, to serve Squire Mortimer, or any body belonging to him ; — but as to going to France, nothing could induce her to do it. Her own brother had been murdered- by the blacks at Bongowbang, and she could not venture abroad on any consideration whatever, especially amongst the French, where, besides the cruelties of the negroes, they lived upon frogs and toads ; not to speak of the dangers of the sea. It was in vain that Mortimer endeavoured to enlighten her ; — she was resolved — go she would not.

Now the wolf who was so exceedingly kind to the Messrs. R. in other days, was not better calculated to travel in a britscha with two "babbies," as Mr. Swing called them, than our hero. A nurse, or some female attendant who might take that brevet rank, was essential. Fortunately, all men's minds are not alike — or women's either ; and it did so happen that a remarkably nice, ladylike-looking person, was actually at that moment waiting for the Havre packet, on her way to an English family resident at Tours, in order to undertake the management of the nursery. Mortimer's valet, who knew the world, soon induced the nice, ladylike-looking person to take charge of the children on the journey, by which undertaking she secured herself, besides the gratuity, the *agrémens* of travelling by easy stages in a comfortable English carriage, and in the society — if she had but known it — of one of the most accomplished and dangerous men that ever existed.

When they departed, the poor old antigallican, who believed in her heart that the " babbies" would be eaten by the natives, even in preference to the frogs, stood on the pier — in no small degree resembling the hen watching the ducklings which she has hatched taking the water : she wept, poor soul ! and her heart ached even at her own timidity, which hindered her from partaking of their peril.

The reader may, perhaps, guess the point to which Mortimer was hurrying. Mrs. Farnham, the sister of whom he stood in such awe, and whom he did not love, was, as we have already heard, living at Beaugency: this nurse was going to Tours; nothing could be more convenient than that she should " tend the children " until they. were deposited at their aunt's, and then be forwarded to the place of her destination: — in fact, the event was one of those lucky coincidences which sometimes happen even in the " worst regulated families."

Yes, the children were to be consigned to Mrs. Farnham. Her rigid morality, her high principles, her various accomplishments, were so many guarantees for their well-doing; and, as she had never personally known Helen Mortimer, however anxious she had been in her inquiries about her, she would naturally accept a trust so reposed with a high sense of the obligations it involved, and a strong feeling in favour of her ill-used brother. It was true she had serious thoughts of returning to England; but still, even if her stay in France were but short, her reception of the infants would shield them from the approaches of their wanton parent, and even leave her in ignorance of their abode.

All this was done as proposed: Mrs. Farnham heard her brother's history, clasped his infants to her bosom, and promised to be a mother to them. He was satisfied, — nay, grateful to his exemplary sister, who implored him to stay with her, at least till his mind had regained some composure. But no: the old, predominant feeling haunted him; she knew his faults, — and, of course, as he fancied, despised him. The tone of her conversation did not suit him; her friend he could not endure. Would that their influence had been greater, and that he could have resolved to remain where he was: — but no. Having reluctantly left his darlings, for his feelings of paternity were strong and ardent, — he took his departure on the seventh day after his arrival, and proceeded to Paris.

It will be, perhaps, recollected that the St. Almes had an estate not very remote from Beaugency: this estate, from which either he derived his title, or had conferred the title upon the estate, the count had sold. The countess, although English born, had grown sufficiently French to disrelish a château: to her, Paris was France: out of it she could not exist. To a mind like hers, what were the beauties of nature, about which she affected to be enthusiastic?—what attractions had a life such as Mrs. Farnham loved to lead, for a woman *of* the world, and always struggling to be *in* the world, and who, having now lost those personal attractions so misused in early life, seemed determined to repel the approach of age by fresh excitement?

To ensure herself the amusements of society, she had made a society of her own:— she *was* visited by persons of consideration; and, as talent and genius are not exclusively aristocratic or prudish, contrived to make her *salon* one of the most agreeable places of resort in Paris. To achieve this great object of her restless life, she had prevailed upon the count to sell his *terres;* and from Christmas to Christmas again, Madame St. Alme was at home, ready to receive anybody and everybody who were willing to be her guests.

To this woman, and to this house, Mortimer proceeded, his mind filled with the horrors which their first interview must produce. In all probability — nay, almost to a certainty — the English papers would have proclaimed the flight of his wife long before he reached Paris. What course the countess would pursue, or what course he was to pursue towards the countess, considering who the partner of that flight actually was, he knew not; still the impulse — infatuation, if you will—was so strong that he could neither remain with his sister nor go any where except to the countess.

The desperation with which Mortimer had put himself beyond the reach of any intelligence connected with what he considered his misfortunes, were perfectly characteristic of the man, who, in order to rid his mind of painful associations, went the length of razing to the ground one of the principal ornaments of his park. From all shocks of that kind he had by his arrangements secured himself, until he should arrive in the French capital, whither he had directed his solicitors to transmit his letters; having written a brief note to the countess, bidding her expect him on a particular day.

That day came, and Mortimer was at the door of her

hotel within an hour of the appointed time. He had driven
thither first, postponing his visit to his banker's, where his
letters were awaiting him, until he should have seen the
lady whose interests appeared to be so intimately connected
with his own.

The reception he met with from her astonished him :
she looked cold, and even angry, but there was nothing of
sympathy or agitation in her manner, such as he had anticipated.

" You know all, I suppose," said Mortimer, trembling
as he spoke.

" Yes, Mortimer," replied the countess, " and nobody is
to blame but your extremely liberal wife."

" Ay," said Mortimer, " that is often the world's cant ;
— it was said in *my* case. Have you heard from Francis ? "

" Yes," replied the young gentleman's mother, whose
style of conversation, it must be confessed, somewhat con-
founded her companion. " He, of course, deprecates my
anger, and urges the truism, that what is done cannot be
undone ; that his happiness was at stake, and however
much the world may blame him, he has made up his mind
to all that."

" This sounds exceedingly philosophical," said Mortimer ;
" and does the lady carry herself with equal calmness ? "

" From her I have not heard," said the countess ; " but
Frank infers, although he does not say so exactly, that
Helen had been long aware of his attachment, and whenever he spoke of it to her, her discouragement was not of a
nature to make him believe her sincere in her opposition."

" By Heavens ! " said Mortimer, " this is the most extraordinary course of proceeding I ever met with ! That
he should write this sort of vindicatory account to *you*, is
in itself strange enough ; but that you should repeat it to
*me*, with a view of calming my resentment, òr healing my
wounded feelings, is marvellous ! What possible advantage
is to be derived from telling me of Helen's faults, when the
result to which they have led proclaims her guilt with
killing clearness ? "

" Would you, then," said the countess, " have me shut
him for ever from my heart for one act of indiscretion ? —

a deciding one, I own — but can I quite forget that discretion has never been a *failing* of my own ?"

"Good Heavens !" cried Mortimer, "how you talk! You speak as if the step he has taken was one of ordinary occurrence, instead of breaking the holiest ties, and tearing from me what might have been the dear companion of my latter days !"

"Mortimer !" exclaimed the countess in her turn, — "what are *you* talking of? Do you mean that I should understand that you were really attached to her yourself ?"

"Attached to her !" said the still wondering husband; "if I had not been attached to her, why should I have plighted my vows to her ?—why——"

"Your vows !" screamed the countess in an agony of despair : — "what ! have you been endeavouring to gain *her* affections ?"

"Have I not?" said Mortimer. "For days, and weeks, and months, my sole object has been to endear myself to her, — to gain her confidence, — in fact, to win her heart; — but I have failed. I always felt that I was never fully trusted, — never really loved ; — and I was right. I have watched her, — seen her looks, and heard her gentle words, when Frank was by : I have shuddered at the thoughts which the sight and hearing conjured up in my brain. I had not courage to speak, — and now the die is cast."

"But, Mortimer, was Frank aware of your extraordinary infatuation ?"

"I conclude he was," said Mortimer—"and infatuation you well may call it. Having such a wife as Helen, my line of conduct should have been more circumspect."

"Why, there," said the countess, "I agree with you ; and the confidence you have now thought proper to make is, considering all things, more astonishing than anything." It struck me as strange that you should be so greatly affected by these circumstances as to quit England — just, too, at a moment when your father-in-law's death was hourly expected."

"Death !" said Mortimer—"why should he die? His illness was all a fiction !"

"But that of his death is not; he has been dead these ten days."

"Dead!" said Mortimer — "is he dead?"

"Most assuredly," said the countess. "But I cannot comprehend how or why you have remained in ignorance of a fact so important to your family."

"Are you certain?" said Mortimer.

"Certain," replied the lady: "not only has his death been announced in the English newspapers, but Frank mentions it in his letter. He had not himself reached London from his hopeful excursion, — but Helen was with her father when he died. — How long is it since you left home?"

The mystification which began now to overwhelm Mr. Mortimer was created, it should be observed, by the extraordinary precautions he had been wise enough to take under the erroneous impression which had been made upon him. In announcing his intended visit to the countess, he, for reasons perfectly satisfactory to himself, abstained from mentioning his previous visit to his sister, or the removal of his children to her care. His motives were, no doubt, equally prudent with all the rest of his conduct; but the effect it produced upon the countess was such as to leave her in a perfect state of ignorance as to the real cause of his sudden emigration, and make her attribute his journey to Paris to his nervous anxiety with regard to Frank's extraordinary indiscretion in carrying off his wife's waiting-woman.

"Helen with her father when he died!" said Mortimer: — "did they separate, then? — how — what do you mean?"

As we are already aware of every thing that has occurred, it is needless to prolong our "report" of the dialogue between Mortimer and his fair friend. The reader can imagine the state of mind to which he was reduced, or rather exalted, by the explanation which the countess gave him. He flew rather than ran to the banker's where his "despatches" were deposited, and there found, amongst his letters, that from Helen which we have read.

His first impulse, as may be naturally anticipated, was to hurry off to England, and throw himself at Helen's feet in all the bitterness of repentance. How did he curse his rashness—how denounce his cruel and ungenerous suspicions—how long to make every atonement for his barbarity, not only to Helen herself, but to her dead father! and acting upon sudden impulses, had he been left to himself, that night would have found him upon his road to England. Unfortunately, he had promised to return to the countess; unfortunately that promise he fulfilled; and in the plenitude of his confidence—or rather in the excess of his delight at finding himself relieved from all his horrors,—he gave her Helen's letter to read.

"And you mean, Mortimer," said the countess, when she had finished its perusal, "to submit yourself to the dominion of the woman who could write this? What! are you indeed so fallen—so lost—that, after insults like those she heaps upon you, you will go, and fawn, and cringe, to regain her favour? Believe me, Mortimer—as I said at first—this marriage of Frank's, which has led to such extraordinary misunderstandings, was made up by her: she was privy to it—accessory to it—in order to inflict a wound on *me*. Why was I excluded from your house?—why was I shut out, and my boy so gladly received? Why does she hate me?—only because I have your best interests at heart, and because I cannot dissemble. If she *is* innocent, it is only because she wants courage to be what the world calls guilty."

"If so," said Mortimer, hesitatingly ——

"*If*," said the countess,—"what *if* all that you suspect is true!—and *if* this hateful match has been contrived to blind you to the truth, while it injures us—what then?"

"But her letter is that of wounded pride—of conscious rectitude—of natural indignation," said Mortimer.

"How easy it is to *write*," said the countess: "there is no blush in ink—no faltering in a pen. She can be bold in her letter. She asks for her children—where are they?—at Sadgrove? If they are, she will get possession of

them, and then you will have no hold over her — no means
of bringing down the tone she has assumed."

" The children are with my sister."

" Your sister!" exclaimed the lady ; — " why, you
never told me this! With your sister, whom you hate ; —
with your sister, who hates *me*. Why not bring them
here ?"

This question will perhaps serve as an answer to the
reader, if he inquires why Mortimer did *not* inform his fair
hostess of their destination. That Mortimer did not love
his sister might be true ; but that be respected and esteemed
her for virtues and qualities which he could not emulate, is
true also : — true, moreover, was it, that the countess hated
her ; and the causes of that hatred were the very qualities
which excited Mortimer's esteem. It is not to be imagined,
considering the terms upon which Mortimer and the countess were, that she had not known the contents of Mrs.
Farnham's letters, in which she implored him not to make
her the associate of his young wife — it was not, therefore,
to be believed that the countess, now that she saw an opportunity of marring the happiness which she was not destined
to share, would feel less inclined to do her worst, when
she found that the children of the man over whom she believed she possessed a commanding interest had been
placed under the care of her bitterest enemy.

" Now," said Mortimer — " now the children must be
restored to their mother — their mother restored to her
home."

" Yes," said the countess, " if she will condescend to
listen to your humble petition ; and then the children will
be brought up to despise their father, who will be, of
course, described to them as a madman and ____"

" Mad I *shall* be," said Mortimer, " if you talk in this
manner! I *have been* mad already : I have injured my
excellent Helen."

" Excellent!" said the countess — " oh! excellent, certainly! I have had opportunities enough of appreciating
her excellence : — it was excellent in her, was it not, to
gloat over the trial in which you were exposed to the public?

It was excellent in her to act her part about the fishing-temple ! — to go and lament over the wretched Lady Hillingdon's monument, and make a show of sorrow before the parson ! Whenever she has had an opportunity of pointing at your faults, has she not done it? Has she not complained of being left in solitude by the neighbours, who, according to her version of the history, shun your society, and shudder at your name? And is this the lady to whom you are to supplicate to be taken back into favour, because, by a mistake so natural, you have misapprehended her conduct !"

" But she *is* innocent !" said Mortimer.

" In this instance, probably," said the countess. " Now, follow my advice : — she is evidently determined to take what she thinks a high line, and you and your barbarity are destined to become the topic of general conversation. Make your conditions. You see she refuses your money ; — she separates herself from you : — let the condition be this — that unless she lowers her tone, and admits the justice of your conduct — which admission will keep her infinitely more circumspect hereafter — she shall neither have possession of, nor even see, her children. A mother's feelings nothing can overcome. She loves — fondly loves those children ; — try her upon that point. Where they are they are safe ; — of *that* you are sure. That you have been wrong, there can be no doubt : put yourself right with the world. If, after your first concession, she remains obdurate, and chooses to destroy at once your happiness and your reputation, punish her ; and you will find that pride and indignation will yield to maternal affection, and that, for the sake of her children, she will sink back into the subdued wife, more especially now that her vain and foolish father, who spoiled her, is in his grave."

Upon this advice — generous, friendly, and sincere — Mr. Mortimer was wise enough to resolve to act — at least to a certain extent. He left Paris the day after it had been given, and started for London, where having arrived, he proceeded to Grosvenor Street, resolved to make a " scene," as he called it, and effect a reconciliation off-hand ; but he was baffled. The house was shut up, and the old woman who opened the door told him that Mrs. Batley had left town immediately after the funeral, and that Mrs. Mortimer had accompanied her ; she did not know where they were gone, nor when they would [be back ; all the servants had been discharged, and the house would be let or sold.

Thence, maddened with anxiety, hating, as he did, Mr. Jacob Batley, the only surviving relation of his wife, he hastened to the counting-house of that worthy personage— or, rather, to that which had once been his counting-house, for, when he reached the place, he found it occupied by some other person in some other trade; and when he inquired after its late owner, he was told that he had retired from business, and was domesticated in his suburban villa.

Thus beaten, Mr. Mortimer resolved upon finding out Mr. Brassey, from whom he felt sure he should obtain some tidings of Jacob ; and ordered a hackney-coachman to drive him to Barnard's Inn, which he had never before visited, at the door of which, looking much like the entrance to a private house, he was deposited.

He managed to find Mr. Brassey's chambers ; but the "oak was sported," and upon the panels some wag, in imitation of the little notices occasionally so exhibited, of "back in half an hour,"—"return at six," or others of similar import, had chalked in large letters, "Gone to America ― call again this day ten years."

For the solution of this mystery, Mr. Mortimer was indebted to the porter of the "aunciente societie," who confirmed his worst suspicions, by informing him that B. B. had really bolted, and that a great number of gentlemen had been to look after him, with no better success. Under these circumstances, which, for many reasons, were by no means of an agreeable nature, Walworth was Mortimer's only resource ; and having procured Jacob's address from his late town place of business, thither he travelled in a similar conveyance to that in which he had visited the inn: but here again was he foiled. A little white-haired girl, with weak eyes, a dark frock, and a pinafore, "answered the bell ;" and, coming from the street door along the paved walk of the little garden in front of the house, with the gate-key in her hand, informed the half-mad wife-hunter, that Mr. Batley, " please, sir, was gone abroad."

" Abroad !"

" Yes, please, sir," said Sally ; " to America, sir."

" America !" exclaimed Mortimer. " Why, everybody is gone to America."

Whereupon Sally stared, and, seeing the road and foot-path still thronged with human beings, opined that the gentleman was mad, and rejoiced exceedingly that she had the key still in her hand. Mortimer muttered some unin-telligible words, and, resuming his place in Number 583, returned to his hotel completely " thrown out," and utterly uncertain as to the course he had best pursue.

His next proceeding was to his solicitors : there he found a second letter from Helen, which had been addressed to Sadgrove, in which she stated, that by his silence with re-gard to the children he had added insult to injury, but that her affection for her infants induced her to humiliate herself to entreat that they might be confided to her. The world, which was to judge between them, would justify such a determination on his part equally with hers — never again to submit herself to his dominion.

This letter, written with more acrimony than the first, occasioned, no doubt, by the imaginary neglect of her former indignant appeal, seemed at once to change the na-ture of Mortimer's feelings. All that the countess had said to him on the subject — all the bitterness with which she had contrived to charge his mind and temper, burst out, and, dashing Helen's letter upon the floor, he stamped upon it, and, clenching his fists in a paroxysm of rage, exclaimed, —

" May curses light upon her ! She shall never see the children more ! Am I to be insulted — degraded — bullied ? — No ! If her proud spirit comes down, and she will accept her income, pay it her ; but as for terms — as for humiliating myself to *her* — it never shall be said that I was so mean — so abject a wretch ! I have borne

much — suffered much — but it is over! — And these, sir,"
added he to the solicitor, " are my final instructions: —
no letter of hers will I open — no communication with her
will I endure: we are separated eternally! Let her take
what legal measures she may, my children are mine, and
never will I part from them. If she applies to you, let
this resolution be made known to her; and though you are
aware where the children are, it is my positive command that
you never let *her* know the place of their residence. This
evening I leave England. I shall, in the first place, return
to Paris, and thence start for Italy: you will know of my
movements, and let me hear what steps this woman takes
— for she is not likely to sit down quietly under what she
may think her wrongs. I am determined not to be her
creature. Our marriage was altogether a mistake: I mistook *her* — she mistook *me*: — but those who knew her
character and disposition better than she ever permitted *me*
to know them, have put me upon my guard. She wants
to establish a grievance. I should have been ready to
make every explanation and atonement for what has happened; — but not now. Her real temper shows itself;
and when she tauntingly says, ' no power of entreaty or
supplication shall induce her to return to me' — I answer,
no power or supplication shall induce me to receive her.
So, sir, you know my decision, and have the goodness to
act upon it."

Here, then, seemed to be the termination of that connection which, to those who really know the world, never
could have promised real happiness. Tempers like those
of Mortimer and Helen never could have been brought
into unison, unless the most perfect confidence had been
established between them. That this never was the case,
we, unfortunately, know; and we also know, that the fault
originally lay with Mortimer himself. Helen's heart —
her entire heart — which she was ready and willing to
give to the man she loved — was worth winning; but —
such is the provoking character of our story, and of the
principal persons concerned in it — his own mistrust

of himself checked the natural impulse of her candid and confiding nature.

It is now, however, useless to reason, or regret, or repent; the outbreak has happened; and, acted upon not less by his own feelings than by the atrocious contrivances of others, Mortimer and his wife are parted — perhaps eternally ! —— Let us hope not.

Mortimer, firm in his decision, returned the next day to France, seeming almost to forget — or perhaps he would have rejoiced if he could have forgotten — that such a place as Sadgrove existed. He returned to the countess. With her and her miserable little husband he remained but a short time; thence he proceeded to Beaugency, and thence to Italy, where he intended to remain for some time, and whither he despatched a letter, inviting his dear *friend* Magnus to join him.

The treacherous countess was delighted to hear of the success which had attended her endeavours to force on the separation of Mortimer and Helen; and the approbation with which she received the account of his proceedings and resolutions, so reconciled him to the infamous injustice he had committed, that he left Paris convinced that he was a persecuted and injured man.

Helen, who had quitted London with her young mother-in-law, had become a topic of general conversation. Her particular friends were, of course, most active in canvassing the affair: Lady Mary Sanderstead shrugged up her shoulders, and said the story of Francis Blocksford and the maid was curious, and she did not quite understand it — but she supposed it was all " as it should be : — Lady Bembridge thought that when a young married woman disappeared from her house exactly at the same period with a young man who was generally supposed to be very much attached to her, it had an odd appearance ; and that the matter was made little better by his choosing to marry the maid afterwards — not that she meant any thing as applying to any particular person." Lord Harry merely shook his head, and praised the good humour of modern husbands; and Colonel Magnus smiled contemptuously, observing that "it did not signify much: Mortimer's loss ought not to break his heart, even if she did ride the high horse, and never came back."

Helen, when she found out — which she did in time — that Mortimer had left England, and had returned, and left it again, and had written no answer to her letter, which ought to have produced a reply, addressed a third to the solicitor, who, obeying the orders he had received, allowed her to understand that Mr. Mortimer, whatever he might feel as to her innocence with regard to *the* case in point, would not submit to the course she had adopted; that her income was at her command, but that he declined all further communication with her; and, as a father, not only positively refused putting his children under her care, but denied her access to them.

And so was Helen left! — proclaimed to the world innocent of the charges publicly made against her by her husband — denounced by *him*, while indignantly refusing again to place herself under his tyrannical command, or accept his proffered munificence. But what of these? Her high spirit, and the consciousness of rectitude, would buoy her up amidst storms of society; — yet, to lose her children — to be deprived of those by whom, by night and by day, she had watched and prayed — whom she had tended — nurtured from her own bosom — for whom she had suffered a mother's pangs, and felt a mother's joy; — those, whom it would have been her pride, her happiness, her honour, to have trained in the ways of truth and goodness — one of whom she had already taught to lisp the word "father," and in whose countenance she saw that father's features likened — to have these darlings torn from her — to be made as much an outcast as he that she had dearly loved could make her: — surely, this was enough to break the stoutest heart!

Helen, after having received the answer to her last communication with the solicitors, almost repented of the warmth of language in which it had been couched. The children were all to her; but it was now too late. Her disdain of the infamous allegations against her character, disproved as they were, had engendered the hatred of her husband, and all hope of reconciliation was destroyed. The liberal members of society looked cold upon Mrs. Mortimer; her husband was pitied; the escape of the children was considered providential; and, without one friend upon earth except her young mother-in-law, she quitted London, and, in one week after, was never missed from the circles of which she had once been the ornament.

It is painful to record the circumstances of a disunion, so trivial in point of cause, and so important in its results; but, nevertheless, two years elapsed after the separation between Mortimer and his wife; and although mutual friends — (they had but few) — had interfered, in the hope of reconciling them, her proud spirit would not bend, nor could his resentment against her be softened; because, let it be remembered, the burst of feeling displayed in her letters was only corroborative of *his* suspicions of *her* suspicions of him. Magnus joined him on the Continent, and there they remained. Jacob, who had followed Brassey to America, returned, having recovered a portion of his property, the volatile attorney having disgorged a part of his embezzled funds. Mr. Brassey subsequently was obliged to leave even America, and whither he went was never exactly ascertained. Jacob, after his return to England, muddled away the rest of his life at his house in Walworth, where he ended his days; and, having inexorably refused to make a will which, with his own knowledge, could possibly benefit anybody, died intestate; and the wreck of his property, amounting to some forty thousand pounds, devolved upon Helen, as next of kin.

The few people who remembered the once charming Helen Batley, now and then gave themselves the trouble of wondering what had gone with her. It was altogether curious, and the marriage of Mr. Blocksford with the maid was curious; but Mr. and Mrs. Blocksford were an extremely happy couple, and the Countess St. Alme had departed (we hope) to a better world! Frank had one son, with every probability of a further increase to his family; so that our register of Births, Deaths, and Marriages has not been ill kept.

Mrs. Farnham, after a year's residence at Beaugency, rather, perhaps, under the influence of a suggestion from Mortimer, who, knowing all he did of French manners and French prejudices, preferred that his children should be "trained" in England, returned after a lengthened absence to her native country; but loving retirement, and being prepossessed in favour of the west of England, not only from its natural claims upon the admirers of calm and quiet rural scenery, but by the connection of her friend with Somersetshire, she selected, after a search of a few weeks, a house well adapted to her wishes, at Minehead, a town beautiful in its simplicity, and charmingly situated on the edge of the Bristol channel, which, bounded by the distant Welsh hills, has, in the fresh clearness of summer, an Italian brightness, delightful to the eye of Mortimer's long-alienated sister.

In this retreat the young Francis Mortimer and his beautiful little sister, Rosa, grew in grace and loveliness; and never did father more anxiously feel for the happiness of his children than Mortimer, who, amidst all his dreadful passions, possessed the affections of paternity in the highest degree. Judge, then, what was his horror at hearing, by express, at Milan, that both his darlings had been attacked by small-pox of the most virulent nature, which was raging in the place. In these days of expeditious journeys the news — which, being bad, proverbially travelled fast enough — was not long in reaching him. Strange, to be sure, are the conformation and construction of the human mind! He whose proud spirit, brought in opposition to the prouder spirit of his wife, would not listen to the proposition of a reconciliation, even if *she* would have listened to it, raved with horror at hearing of the danger of those children which were hers as well as his. Not an instant did he lose: one hour was not suffered to elapse before he started for England; and as fast as horses or steam-boats could bring him home, he came.

To describe the dread, the trepidation, the hope, the fear, which agitated the anxious father, when he found himself at the house which contained his children, would be impossible. His britska stopped before it; — so did the pulsation of his heart.

"Are they alive? — are they safe?" cried Mortimer, as the servant opened the door.

" Both, sir, alive and safe," was the man's answer, who knew to whom he was speaking.

" Thank God!" said the grateful father, and leaped from the carriage.

A thousand things had affected this unhappy man, with which we have little to do: — Magnus had involved him seriously; Brassey had injured him much; and the miscreant Wilkins had committed all sorts of peculations and thefts at Sadgrove; — but these words, — " alive and safe," drove from his mind the memory of all other things.

Mrs. Farnham received him with warmth and kindness, and Mortimer found relief in a flood of tears. It is a triumph to see a sinner weep; and if this Mortimer, who had permitted the best of wives—whatever her own high spirit might have led her to do — had only felt towards her as he ought to have felt, the widowed feeling of paternal love which he now experienced would have been spared him, and all the evils which had been accumulated on his head would have been supplanted by those blessings which never can be bestowed on a husband but by the affectionate love of a virtuous wife, and her tender cares as a devoted mother.

" My beloved sister, the children are safe!"

" Yes, Mortimer," replied Mrs. Farnham. " They have been dreadfully — dangerously ill!"

" Their unhappy mother knew nothing of it," said Mortimer; " at least, I thank God for that! — for, oh! Emily, we have been both wrong! — and when I heard of the illness of these dear babes, I thought of *her* — of the madness which separated us: — she loved them as I loved, them. For mercy's sake, let me see them!"

" Francis is quite recovered," said Mrs. Farnham; "but
Rosa is still, though out of danger, not entirely restored—
safe, remember. But I must tell you something which
must, in a great degree, qualify our happiness:—about
four or five months since, a most respectable person— I
should almost say elegant and graceful—but evidently in
ill health, a Mrs. Miles, applied to me for the place of
nursery-governess; and I was too happy to engage her.
She is a widow, and, having lost a child of her own,
seemed most anxious to devote herself to ours. Indeed, I
never saw such kindness — such care— such fondness!
When the children were taken ill with this fearful complaint, no power could keep her a moment from them, and
night and day has she attended them with incessant watchfulness."

" How shall I ever repay her!" said Mortimer.

" Ah," said Mrs. Farnham, " I fear you will never
have the power. The children are now with her — they
will not quit her; but, during her constant attendance on
them, she has caught the dreadful infection, and the me-
dical men have pronounced her recovery hopeless. In
fact, she is, as I believe, at this moment in the agonies of
death!"

" How dreadful!" said Mortimer. " O! let her live,
that I may breathe my prayers of gratitude for her."

" It must be speedily, then," said Mrs. Farnham; " a
little time, I am afraid, will end the painful scene. Come
— come!"

Mortimer followed her: his children, as it were instinctively, ran to him when he entered the room in
which they were; and, although still disfigured by the
effects of the dreadful disorder, were evidently conva-
lescent: he clasped them to his heart, and covered them
with kisses.

The physician, who stood near the bed in which the
nurse was lying, placed his finger on his lip, to announce
that the lamp of life was flickering in the socket, and that
the spirit was almost on its way to Heaven.

Mortimer anxious at least to proffer his grateful thanks to *her* to whom he owed the salvation of his infants, advanced to the bedside. He spoke. The suffering woman, rallying all her energies at the sound of his voice, raised herself in the bed, and, half stifled with agitation, muttered, —

"Thank God! I see him once again. He knows my innocence—and I have done my duty to my children!"

"What do I hear?" said Mortimer.

"HELEN!" shrieked the sufferer: — her head fell against his shoulder—and she DIED!

THE END.